Confessions of a Serial Masturbator

A novel

Kitty K. Free

First Edition
ISBN: 978-0-615-56807-2

The publisher would like to thank beta readers, J. E. Hilton, M. Roundtree, and D. G. Wright, as well as, 8th Day Music for their permission of the use of lyrics from "Never Gonna Lose" by UGF (United Grind Fam).

K'LaHea Publishing
Cover Illustration copyright© 2011 by K.L.H.
Edited by Autumn Conley, Josef Teti & K.L.H.

Author website KITTYKFREE.COM
Publisher website KLAHEAPUBLISHING.COM

This is dedicated to my mommie. You are my world.

I would also like to dedicate this to every woman in the world with a dream living inside of her that's dying to get out. Live sisters, live.

Prologue

It got to the point where just hearing my phone vibrate made me want to cum. Riding the subway drove me crazy; I had to stand, because if I sat the hum of the train between my legs reminded my body of the slow, steady build up to an explosive orgasm.

Everything was phallic to me. Even the Empire State Building turned me on; all long and wide, shooting into the air, penetrating the sky.

It was pleasurable, and even amusing at first. But it was starting to get out of hand. I wanted to cum all day long.

Kitty K. Free

Chapter 1

I walk these streets,
I ride these trains,
day in and day out,
nothing seems to change.
I drone at my workspace,
another face in the city.
But there's a flutter in my middle;
I'm on the cusp of a new reality.

E ither I liked rushing to work, or I liked running late. It didn't escape me that if I hadn't hit the snooze button at least fifteen times before I decided to get up, I could catch the train earlier and be one of the people that could just walk to work. Instead, I had to do a walk-skip-run through the street, dodging cars first and then people, as I ran down the subway stairs. Metrocard in hand, I whipped through the turnstile, ran down the next flight of stairs, then slid through the closing #6 train doors. *Yes!* Only to get off at 125th Street just in time to see the 5 train across the platform pull off. *Dang it! Bastards could've waited.*

I looked at my watch, then leaned over the edge of the platform trying to see the next train. As if looking down the tracks would make it come faster. This guy, clearly with the biggest head on the IRT that day, decides to lean over too, blocking my view. I huffed. Now I was mad at the 5 train *and* him. And I wasn't too thrilled with the chick standing to my left, popping her gum and chewing like a cow; or the dude behind me with the loud-ass iPod (I was jealous because I'd forgotten mine); or the woman on my right, who was rocking from side to side and kept tapping my knuckle with her purse. Sure, I could move my hand, but I was there first, and I'd rather be pissed at her, since she chose to stand right next to me.

The station was baking. Big Head was covered in so much sweat that if he turned fast enough he'd spray us all.

Finally, the iron horse galloped into the station. Its rush of hot air kicked up debris from the tracks, causing my eyes to water and blink rapidly. I was already standing in *my* spot, right where the train doors would open. A little to the left so I wouldn't be bum-rushed by the people getting off, but close enough to get on quickly.

The screeching of the train braking signaled everyone to prepare to attack. Our collective thought: *I'm getting on this train!* The doors opened, and a herd of passengers scrambled off, rushing like wildebeests across the platform to catch the next downtown 6 train that was pulling in, or running upstairs to change to the uptown trains, or farther upstairs to escape the station altogether.

I put one foot on the train, and this guy comes out of nowhere and pushes me, and everyone else, to get on. *Asshole!*

I followed him into the car and *accidentally* hit him in his face when I reached for the handrail. "Oops, I'm sorry," I lied sweetly.

He huffed.

Moments later, I stepped on his foot with my heel.

"Was that your foot? My bad."

He sucked his teeth.

I adjusted my bag on my shoulder, causing my elbow to hit him in the ribs.

"Ow, lady!"

"Oh, did I get you?" I smiled, then said, "Asshole."

"Excuse me?" he yelled, super loud over the chugging of the train, scrunching up his already mean face and giving me the *up-down* with his eyes.

So I yelled back just as loud, "Asssssss..." I paused for effect, "...holllle!" I said, holding the L a second for emphasis.

"Dumb bitch."

"Your mother," I said, and braced myself for punishment. I felt I could absorb whatever he had to give me that angry morning, and then give it back to him with a strike between his legs.

Instead of giving me the wrath I'd expected, he looked at me hard, shook his head (I imagined him saying to himself, *"Let me move before I kill this bitch!"*), turned his back to me, and pushed his way through the crowded car away from me.

Victory is mine!

I got off at 59th Street and dashed to the N; took that to 49th Street, then ran up the stairs with my fellow mass transients into the thick, noisy Seventh Avenue air.

I tore through the morning crowds, dipped between the exhaust heat from honking cars (I love that smell), and yelled, "Excuse me! Excuse me!" as I zigzagged through any spaces I could find between people, and then glided through the automatic doors of my office building, safely home.

Almost.

Ever since 9/11, we needed a badge to get past security in the lobby. With four minutes to go, I searched my bag, my pockets, and my lunch bag—no badge! So, security had to *detain* (his word) me, until someone came to sign me in. And this guy let me know that his job was not about fun and games. It was serious! The flashlight, sheathed in black pleather, on his state-of-the-art, rent-a-cop, security belt was not for show. He was security for the protection of the country, damn it! Now, this is nothing against security guards, because hey, some of my best friends are security guards, but the overzealous, assholes know who they are. Juicing their security title for all it's worth and giving people a hard time just to get their rocks off. They know who they are.

My short detainment made his day. He rolled his eyes at me, as though my very presence disturbed the air around him.

I popped in a piece of sweet Juicy Fruit while I waited. "Have a stick?" I offered. He looked at me like I'd wiped it along my ass-crack first. "No thanks," he said. The fact that I annoyed him really amused me. And yeah, he really should have taken one because he had the *dragon*.

Sara Weiss emerged from the elevator, clearly agitated. Her graying blonde hair was brushed back into a ponytail that was as tight and narrow as her ass. She signed me in with her skeletal fingers, then I signed in, and *Security Officer Numero Uno of the World* gave me a visitor's badge.

"You're late," Mrs. Weiss said. The tip of her nose moved up and down when she spoke, as if being controlled by her top lip.

"I know. My apologies."

"This is the fourth time, by my record, that I've had to interrupt my work day to come down and get you."

"Yes. I know it's inconvenient. Again, I apologize."

"Maybe you need to work out some kind of badge system for yourself since you can't seem to keep up with it."

"Yes, that sounds like something I should look into."

I could see the subtle amusement behind her disdain. These were phrases we'd been taught to use when our customers were upset: accept responsibility; apologize, but never say, "sorry"; acknowledge their feelings; and let them know you are working on a resolution.

We got off the elevator, and she swiped her badge next to the plain, black, square sign that read, SEARLY & WEISS, in silver letters. There was a quick *buzz*, and the double mahogany wood doors gave way.

The company took up the top eight floors of the twenty-story building. Searly & Weiss was a conglomerate of bill-pay kiosks, prepay lawyers, life insurance, debt consolidation, payday loans, and pawn shops. The company was an absolute mess. The complaints they received were completely avoidable. But the peons—myself and the other employees who had to dissuade customers from lawsuits—had no say. We knew what was wrong, and what needed to be fixed. However, a quick, and steady flow of money outweighed quality. Their attitude in regard to their customers disgusted me, and I hated working for them.

Fortunately, I didn't have to deal with their dissatisfied customers often, but I used to. When I first started there as a temp, I was part of the customer service team. But my job became permanent, and my title changed when one of their accountants stood up from his desk—I'd say it was about three in the afternoon—and started yelling at the top of his lungs, "Fuck it! Fuck it! Fuck all of you, and fuck all of this bullshit! I quit!" He threw a bunch of papers in the air, flipped over his chair, then stormed out.

"Sucks to be in the Finance Department. I'd never want to work there," I said to myself.

But Sara Weiss (whose job on the side of signing me in when I was late, was head of Human Resources), saw "bookkeeper" on my résumé and put me right in his seat the next day. Now, I dealt with numbers as bookkeeper number ten. We did everything the accountants did, but for about $20,000 less in salary, and less respect. *Yay for me!*

I could've stayed in school and earned my CPA, but besides not being in the mood for school, being a CPA was not the direction I wanted my life to take. Even though I was good at it, and actually enjoyed it, it was just not who I wanted to be: Breezy Deigh, CPA. It sounded like a prison sentence to me. Nevertheless, it was who I became anyway, sans the title and salary.

Smart move dropping out of college, huh? Maybe people under twenty-one shouldn't be allowed to make major life decisions. Not all of us are mentally equipped at that age. It made perfect sense to me, at twenty, to drop out and turn the part-time bookkeeping job I had into a full-time gig. After all, why get a degree for something I was already getting paid to do? *Brilliant!*

Since then, I've held every job under the clerical sun: administrative assistant, receptionist, secretary, executive secretary, file clerk, mail clerk, front office clerk, word processor, and the list goes on. If I saw a HELP WANTED ad that read, "clerical" or, "type 50 WPM" or, "10,000 KSPH," I was there. I got jobs on my own, but I was also registered with temp agencies throughout the city. I learned early that in the clerical game it's always good to be registered with agencies in every borough, and northern New Jersey. That way I'd never run out of opportunities to make money.

Being fake was a huge part of being a temp—at least in my case. All I had was my reputation, and I was only as good as my last employer said I was. Bosses needed to recognize my value in a relatively short period of time. So I had to play nice with my phony smile; pretend to enjoy the people I met; stroke their egos acting as though they were teaching me new things. I'd masquerade as a team player for companies I cared nothing about.

I was false and it worked. I'd parlayed a few of the temp jobs into full-time positions, but I'd never stay too long. In the back of my mind I'm sure I was suppressing the fact that I didn't really like being part of corporate America. I wanted to be part of entrepreneurial America, or, live-off-the-land America. Not, I-can't-stand-my-job, America. I kept moving on to elsewhere because none of the companies cared about me. They used me, and I used them. *Quid pro quo*; I gave up forty unrecoverable hours of my life every week, and they gave me money to pay my bills.

After so many years however, maintaining my fake was becoming a real chore. I was tired of pretending. I almost didn't know who I was anymore. For eight hours a day I sat there doing something I couldn't stand. Spent another hour going back and forth to the place I couldn't stand, and the rest of the day either preparing for, or winding down from the thing I couldn't stand.

I found myself counting down the seconds, minutes, and hours of my life. There was the countdown for my first break; then for lunch; then for my second break. Until I counted down to five o'clock. Then finally the big TGIF countdown. I worked all day to keep someone else's dream alive, while they paid me what they thought I deserved for doing their shit work. The thought just no longer sat easily with me, and it was starting to show. I swear, leaving my badge was a subconscious effort to forbid myself access to that soul-draining trap they called an office.

When I got to my desk, my co-worker, Cindy, was already making her way to me. Her stride was anxious; she had gossip. I didn't really like gossiping, but she was trying hard to be my friend for some reason, and she loved to share, so I listened.

"Blair—that chick from upstairs—she just got fired for stealing money from the bill-pay kiosks."

I jerked my head back in shock. "What? How?"

"She had a thing going with one of the guys that collects the money, and they were doctoring receipts, you know, to make it look like the kiosk made less money than it really did, and then skimming the difference off the top."

"Wait—Blair Hardy? The short, blonde, with all those puppy pictures all over her desk?"

"Yes, yes, and yes!"

"How much?"

"I don't know, but from what I hear it was going on for like two years."

"Wow! I wouldn't dare."

9

"Me neither. That's just stupid, 'cause you know you're gonna get caught."

"I would," Joseph chimed in from the cubicle across from me.

"Of course your *sheisty* ass would," Cindy said.

"I'll come up any way I can."

Cindy shook her head, "That's a great attitude to have. You see what happened to them, right?"

"That's because they got greedy and didn't know when to stop. See, if it was *me*, I would've done it maybe three times, max. But what did you say? They'd been doing it for two years? That's just dumb. Those idiots were asking to get caught."

Cindy and Joseph went back and forth about it, and it wasn't long before I'd lost interest.

Cindy's full name was Cinderella Slipah. Her mother named her Cinderella because her last name sounded like "slipper." She called us *name sisters*. Some silliness she made up when I told her my mother named me Breezy because my last name is pronounced "Day." Cindy never grew into hers and said she couldn't stand it. As a kid I hated mine, but I love it now.

Cindy's father was from some tiny country in Europe that I can't begin to try to pronounce, and her mother was Haitian. Her thick, curly hair was a colorful mix of blonde, red, and brown. Her eyes were an ever-changing hazel. Even her skin was colorful. She was brown, with what I would describe as a reddish overlay. She looked like some exotic being from far away. But once she opened her mouth, all that Bronx, Melrose Avenue shot out, and you knew she was just Cindy from the block.

She would send emails with "For Ladies Only" in the subject line, in which she'd ask some very personal questions. I never responded because I didn't want any of that to come back and bite me in the ass later. I'd seen that happen far too often on jobs. That was a firing that was easy to avoid. Not to mention, it's never a good thing to let your co-workers in on your personal life.

The first one I received was after working there for about six months. It asked, "How do you tell your guy he's just not satisfying you?"

"U say 'bad boy' & put his face in it until he learns better."

"Say, 'is this really wrkn for u? Cuz it's not wrkn for me.'"

"tell him his performance needs improvement… but I still luv ya."

"Yeah, that sounds like an all-nite ego fite rite there. U gotta tell him like 'ooh, sweetie, put ur tongue here' and go crazy when he does it so he will do it again."

"i agree….direct him like ur Darnell Martin LOL!"

"LMFAO @ put his face in it."

Laughter is wonderful. It added color to the dark gray carpet and the drab taupe walls, and sped up the seconds of the day. I began to look forward to reading the emails, even if I never responded to them.

Another topic she sent was, "What do you like to call your *vajayjay*?"

"Mandy."

"Princess Slayer. LMAO!"

"i'm not talking to mine rite now. she's such a cunt! LOL"

"na na"

"peaches—that's wut my man calls her."

I didn't have one for mine, but I love saying "my pussy." I love that word. Something about it has so much power. PUSSY. If I would've responded, "PUSSY," would've been my answer.

This one was on a Monday: "What do you prefer: tittie suck, pussy suck, or a fuck?"

"sometimes, I just don't want dick. a good pussy suck is all I need sometimes."

"i mean, i'm good w/a pussy suck, but i gotta have sum dick. WHUT? it's almost like what's the point if i don't get any dick?"

"a tittie suck, followed by a pussy suck, followed by a fuck."

"pussy suck."

I love to have my breasts sucked. That has to be one of the best feelings in the world. If I have kids I could never breastfeed them because I have had entirely too much tittie-sucking in my lifetime. They've been stained by one too many slobbering men. More than I've had sex with.

I couldn't believe how open those women were. They acted like we weren't at work, and their blunt X-rated confessions couldn't be monitored. That truly amazed me.

One day, while I was staring intently into space, thinking hard, figuring out something clever to say on my Facebook status, her email popped up: "How often do you masturbate?"

"Prolly once a month, maybe, if u average it out."

"every time I have sex. LOL!"

"Not often, not since I was a teen."

"BLAH!"

"No comment."

"every once in a while."

"CONSTANTLY!!!!!"

I replied to this one. I'm not sure why. I just had the need to let them all know, "Never."

It was my truth, and for some reason, I was proud of it. Well... it was my semi-truth anyway. When I was about thirteen or so, there were times when I'd hug my teddy bear between my legs and rub vigorously. I didn't know what part I was rubbing; I just knew it felt good, even though nothing happened. I'd put my finger inside of me too, because that's what I thought I was supposed to do. But I just didn't like how it felt in there. The feel of that satin skin against my finger did not appeal to me. It was too soft and wet. All the things a man loves about pussy, I don't: the warmth, the squishiness—no thank you.

In my twenties I tried a vibrator. I didn't like how the rubber felt inside of me. It hurt, no matter how much I lubed it up.

I also tried a bullet with an ex. He put it inside of me, and the vibration just felt awkward. This couldn't be what other females enjoyed. It didn't do anything but annoy me. Screw a bullet.

I even rubbed my clit for about ten minutes straight one time, but I got nothing. So, I'd given up on masturbation. I just didn't see the point.

"I can't orgasm if I don't master my ship," another woman replied.

Cindy immediately sent out another email: "That brings me to my next question. How many of you have actually had an orgasm?"

"I have."

"I may have..."

"meeeee!"

"I'm raising my hand"

"not I."

"BLAH!"

There was that mythical word, "ORGASM." I like— scratch that—I *love* the feel of the right man inside of me, but no matter how great it was, I'd never actually had an orgasm. I couldn't count the many times I'd lied and exclaimed, "I'm cumming! I'm...cumming!" I was even lying to myself. I wanted it so bad that I was giving into the fantasy of it, making believe for my own self as well as for him. I'd wonder each time, *Was that it?* I mean, there was a feeling that came over me, a wonderful feeling. *Was that it? Maybe that was it.* But in my heart I knew it was never it, because there was no finish, no climax. I'd get caught up in yelling and moaning and panting and shaking... but it was all fruitless. After fourteen years of fucking, and at least four years of foreplay before that, I think I would've had at least one. I figured it was just not something I was supposed to experience. So I felt like, I'll just fuck and enjoy the ride (because I do thoroughly enjoy the ride). My partner could get his shit off; I'll pretend I got mine, and keep it moving.

"Orgasm? What is that? A drink?" someone else responded.

I felt comfort in knowing I wasn't the only one missing "the Big O," but I found myself envious of the women who'd said they had experienced it.

Chapter 2

Confession: *I'm lonely, and I hate it, and it's no one's fault but mine.*

It's easy to be lonely amongst the eight million souls crowding my city. To see the same people every day, and not say a word to them. There was an episode of *Seinfeld*, when Elaine became "hello" friendly with a guy in her building. It escalated to very small talk, which is the most you can get from the average New Yorker, as a mere neighbor. Then it got weird and deescalated until they stopped speaking altogether. That happens a lot. I'm not sure of the social dynamic behind it, but it's real. Sometimes you speak, and sometimes you don't. You never know what's going on in another person's mind. I know what *I'm* thinking when I see someone that I see all the time, but who isn't a friend: *I'll speak if she speaks, but if she doesn't speak, I'm not going to play myself and speak, giving her the opportunity to* not *speak back to me or have an attitude. No, no, if she wants to speak, she can speak to me first.* And if we are both thinking that... well, then you have eight million people speaking to just a few outside their circle of family and friends.

My parents reverse migrated to North Carolina when they retired from the post office, and I missed them more than I'd expected. They worked hard and were able to retire young. I thought that was great for them, but I don't see myself doing that—working for the same place for twenty-plus years and then retiring. There's no company I would ever trust enough to work that long for them. What guarantee do I have that they won't swindle my life savings away? Not only did I not trust the companies I worked for, but I also wanted to feel some kind of freedom. I wasn't sure exactly how to get that feeling, but I knew not being stuck at one place for too long made me feel at least a little free.

Monday through Friday, I'd wake up, go to work, then go back home. I'd eat. watch TV, several hours at a time, and I'd fall asleep. The next day I'd wake up and do it all over again. This didn't make me happy, but it was at least a familiar routine. I didn't want too much action. Action in my life was if there was a blackout or cable outage and I'd freak the fuck out because I couldn't live without my television. I loved TV so much that I'd get off the phone with people in mid-sentence just to watch a show. Or ignore them all together, pretending to listen. Or not even answer the phone no matter who it was, because TV needed my attention more.

My own mother called me a prude. "You need to go live your life already. You're young. Go live! Have fun."

Thing was, I'd forgotten how. Years earlier, I used to dress up and go out. Then I got into a relationship that was as wrong as it was long, and my world shrank until it was just me and him. To put it short, I was *dickmatized*. Granted, I never came, but his dick felt so good that I was hypnotized and blind to everything else about him for years. I didn't even realize that I didn't like him.

Whenever we went out, or stayed in, it was uncomfortable. Having conversations with him was like pulling teeth—my own teeth. Stubborn, self-torture. When we did talk, we rarely agreed on anything. Instead of arguing we'd get really sarcastic with each other or simply shut down. We just didn't get along. Our bodies got along, but our minds didn't. We liked fucking so much that we built a relationship around it, and that's no way to create a good relationship. It should be built the same way you would a friendship. Step one: you've got to *like* the other person. In my defense though, he was fine! I mean, goodness, was he fine.

We'd been broken up for over a year, but my world was still small. I had grown used to staying in the house and being alone. Not just alone, but lonely. So much so that when Cindy asked me to go with her and some of our coworkers to Atlantic City, I immediately declined instinctively. *Go somewhere? So I have to find something to wear, do my hair, and be up and about when I could be asleep or watching my shows? Nah. I'll pass.*

Not to mention it was to celebrate our co-worker Gia's birthday and I didn't even like her. There was no real reason; she rolled her eyes at me one day, so I didn't like her because I assumed she didn't like me. Stupid and petty, I know, but it is what it is, and it was what it was.

"Why aren't you going?" Cindy yelled at me as I was leaving for the day.

"Because I don't want to!" I yelled back.

"Please, please, pleeeeeeze come with us? It'll be fun."

"No thank you."

"Why don't you ever do anything with us? You don't like us or something? Does my breath stink? I know Gia has a slight underarm odor, but don't hold that against the rest of us."

I laughed because it was true. "I don't have anything to wear," I said.

"It's just AC. Throw on some jeans and sneakers."

"Is that what you're going to wear?"

"Yup. So come on. No excuses."

She talked me to death until I caved. After reviewing the Friday night TV line up in my head I said, "Okay already. Sheesh!"

I was to meet up with Cindy, Gia, Tamara, and Janice at Penn Station at ten. I wished my friend Charise could go with me, but she was out of the country, as usual.

I threw on a pair of good jeans. I say "good" because the only time I wear jeans is to go to the supermarket or do the laundry or whatever little running around I do, and those jeans were all either too tight, too loose, stained with bleach spots, or fraying at the inner thigh. I had one pair of jeans that were actually presentable.

As for my shirt; since it would be fall soon, and the nights were much cooler than the days, I figured the jean jacket that went with the jeans would be good enough. I threw on a white T-shirt to go under that. I was wary of wearing white normally because of my darkness. I thought the white showed up on me too much and made me way too noticeable. But it was cool under a jacket. I pulled my box braids back into a bun, threw on a pair of dark, blue Keds, and was good to go.

I know jeans and sneakers have greater range than what's in my closet, but I didn't expect to be so outdone. They looked like they were in a music video. They wore tight denim with all types of designs on the pockets, dazzling belts, sparkly shirts, and sneaker boots. I felt so underdressed and stupid. They looked so youthful—not younger than their ages, but they didn't look as old as I did. I was thirty-three the same age as Gia and Cindy. Yet I was wearing the same thing as a bunch of grandma-aged women that were getting off one of the AC shuttles coming back from the casinos.

Already feeling awkward and out of place, I was prepared to *not* have a good time.

My co-workers were loud the entire bus ride. The driver had to tell them to be quiet, like we were kids on a fifth grade, field trip. Then Gia pulled out a flask, and they started drinking, and getting really obnoxious.

We went to Chariots Casino. Most of the patrons were women and gay males. There were no waitresses. Only waiters, dressed in bow ties, biker shorts, and boots. I guess research shows that women and/or gay men like to see men in combat boots.

"Girl, you're not going to drink anything? The drinks are free! What is your fucking problem?" Gia asked. Her brown-liquored, cigarette breath singed my nostrils and eyes.

"Yeah," Cindy yelled over the music. "You know what you are? You're one of those people who hates fun. You're a fun-hater," she said and burped in my face, from deep in her gut. I could've thrown up right on her. I should have.

"Drink, Breezy, drink! Drink, Breezy, drink! Drink, Breezy, drink!" Gia started it, and soon all four girls were chanting.

I wanted to drink. I wanted to have a good time, but I felt like shit.

"Drink, Breezy, drink!"

The whole thing felt like one of those *ABC Afterschool Specials* that came on in the eighties. My peers were really pressuring me.

"Drink, Breezy, drink!"

I sucked my teeth and huffed.

"Drink, Breezy, drink!"

I shouldn't.

"Drink, Breezy, drink!"

"Okay, I'll have *one* drink."

"WOOOOOOOO!" Gia yelled. She'd been yelling like that all night.

"Waiter! Wa-ay-aay-ter-er-er! Vodka and *cran*, and don't water down the vodka," Cindy yelled.

"And an Orgasm please!" Gia said as she slapped the waiter on his ass and giggled.

I stopped counting my drinks after the fourth one. I know at some point I had a Lemon Drop and a Rose. I don't know what's in a Rose—something red, something sweet, and something strong. I felt good and loose. The casino had a party vibe. *How could I not have fun here?* The colorful lights were flashing. Gold and white confetti fell from the ceiling every time someone hit a jackpot, which was once every thirty minutes. People were yelling and singing. Music was blasting and bodies were dancing around, having a ball. Everyone was feeling good as they won and lost (well, probably not the people who lost).

I'd been to casinos before, but never one like this. It had been a very long time since I'd been in an environment created for having fun, and I was starting to really enjoy myself.

Before long, I was yelling "WOOOOOOO!" and slapping waiters on their asses too. Then, for some reason, I yelled in a waiter's ear, I guess because it was weighing on my mind, "I've never had an orgasm!"

He didn't skip a beat. "How unfortunate. We may need to work on that for you."

"You can give me an orgasm?" I yelled back, my eyes wide like an amazed five-year-old.

"It's all in the tongue, baby."

"WOOOOOOO!" I yelled.

I gave him a tip, swallowed my drink, and everything after that was blurry lights and loud movement.

I kind of remember getting on the bus. I kind of remember that I possibly cursed out a cab driver, and I recall trying to time my jump onto my bed.

I didn't wake up until a little after two in the afternoon, and when I did, my head was banging. My stomach was growling, and my limbs and back were sore. I went to use the bathroom and the door was closed. I never close that door. I got ready to attack whoever was in there. I turned the knob, then kicked the door in, screaming bloody murder.

Cindy started screaming back at me.

I screamed again.

She screamed back again.

"What are you doing here?"

"I'm trying to take a shit."

"Huh?" I shook my head. "No. What are you doing in my house?"

"You told us to come over."

"*Us?*"

"Yeah. Gia couldn't go home to her husband all fucked up and my roommate is a bitch, so she couldn't come to my house, so you told us to come home with you."

"What?"

"Uh, no disrespect, but can you close the door? You made my shit stop, and it broke, and—"

I closed the door before she could finish her sentence, and I headed for the living room. Gia was stretched out on the floor. She was awake, albeit not completely coherent. Her dyed blonde curls were pressed against her yellow cheek, as she slobbered on my carpet.

When Cindy came out of the bathroom she said, "I'm heading home now. Thanks for letting us stay."

"Yeah, don't mention it," I answered, rolling my eyes, not at her as much as at the situation.

"Geeeaah! Gia! Get up. You gotta go home." She started pulling Gia up by her arm.

Gia shook her hung-over head like a defiant two-year-old and started running off at the mouth in Spanish.

"Yeah, yeah," Cindy said. "Just get your ass up." She turned to me and said, "Oh yeah. Don't forget the guy is coming to deliver your flat-screen on Monday."

"My what?"

"Remember? You won the dance competition."

"What?"

She sucked her teeth, rolled her eyes, and huffed, "The *Soul Train* line. Remember?"

I stared past her, into my memories. I couldn't find that one.

"You were the shit last night! Everyone loved you. You did *everything*!"

"Everything?"

She started listing on her fingers, "The Robot, Electric Boogie, Pop Locking, the Cabbage Patch, Running Man, the Wop, the Dougie, even the Stanky Leg. Every song they played, you danced to."

"Nooo!"

"Yeah! So you won a fifty-inch flat-screen."

I sat down on the couch in utter disbelief. I didn't remember any of it, and I couldn't fathom me doing the Stanky Leg in front of anybody.

"Yeah, you let it all hang out last night. Proved me wrong about you."

"And how is that exactly?" Yes, I was indignant.

"Can I be honest?"

"Please."

"Well, you know, you're kind of stiff around the office. You don't really talk much. Kind of stuck up, honestly. I thought you thought you were too cute for us."

"Really? Is that how I come across?"

She nodded in quick agreement. "When I sent that email to you the first time, it was by mistake. But then you finally spoke to me after that. Remember that day in the break room? So I kept sending them to you."

She'd caught me at the fridge one day in the break room and started talking. I didn't know what to say, so I mentioned her email and told her it made me laugh. I was just making conversation because she wanted to talk. I wasn't really trying to be friendly.

"I don't talk much because I change jobs a lot and I just don't want to get attached," I lied. I didn't talk much because I just didn't know how. I didn't know how because people generally got on my nerves.

Naturally, I was curious about that too-cute part. *Did she mean physically cute or attitudinal?* "So when you say 'cute', how do you mean?"

She smiled. "We women love a fucking compliment, right? I mean, your nickname is Ms. Universe at the office. You walk around like your shit don't stink. Like 'I'm just too pretty and precious to speak to any of you,'" she said in a dramatic high-pitched voice with her nose in the air.

"No I don't. I just hold my head up. You're supposed to walk with your head up."

"Well, put that with the fact that you don't really speak to anyone, you walk around in those stuffy power suits you wear, and you come across like you think you're too good for us lowly mortals."

"I don't mean to come across that way," I said, realizing for the first time that maybe that was why Gia rolled her eyes at me that day.

"By the way, I love that painting in your bathroom."

"Yeah?"

"Yeah. It looks like the girl's taking one of those period shits. Her face is so strained, and she looks so pissed off. And the bag of pads on the floor, like she'd just ripped the package open." She made a ripping motion with her hands and face. "It has so much detail. The pain killers on the floor, the bottled water, and the book falling from her hand."

"I painted that."

"Stop lying."

"I did. I call it *A Period Piece*."

"You did not paint that!"

"Yeah, I did."

"You are so freaking talented! If I could do that I'd be damned if I would be working for Searly & Weiss."

I really didn't want to have thoughts like that, and her saying that agitated me. It bothered me when anyone said those kinds of things. What was I going to do? Post up on a corner and sell paintings like one of those dudes in the street, waiting for someone to say they wanted to buy one? I had bills to pay, and Con-Ed isn't interested in art.

"You want to go out tonight?" she asked, nodding at me, like she was trying to hypnotize me into saying yes.

"I think I've had enough for the weekend. You know we have to go to work Monday."

"Yeah, but it's only Saturday. You have all day Sunday to sleep and recoup."

"Nah."

"Aw c'mon. Come out! Have a little drink, do a little dancing. What? Are you getting too old to hang? Your ancient body can't handle it?"

Her reverse psychology worked. "I don't really have anything to wear."

"Don't tell me all you have are those boring old suits?"

"Pretty much. I don't have too many casual clothes."

"Do you have any casual money?"

"Maybe."

"Okay. Meet me at H&M downtown in about two hours. My cousin works there and gives me his discount. Gonna hook you up for the *low-low*."

And that's just what she did. Each outfit I modeled she would give me the thumbs up or thumbs down. Sometimes I smiled in an outfit and Cindy shook her head. Sometimes she smiled and I said, "No way!" If you spliced each outfit I tried on together, and our reactions, then added some Pointer Sisters' music, it would look like an eighties movie shopping montage. I hadn't been clothes shopping in so long that I'd forgotten how much I enjoyed it.

We went out, and I had a good time—though it was a much tamer time than the night before. We went to Victory, off of 135th Street in Harlem, a lounge with a bar and a stage that doubled as a dance floor. It was a dance floor that night, so we danced our asses off.

I was glad I went. It had been a long time since I'd had a good full weekend. It awakened something in me, or rather, reawakened. It reminded my body and my mind that there was a time when I was bursting at the seams with fun and spontaneity. I should never have let that go.

Note to self: Never lose being you again.

Chapter 3

It was a great gift
Unlike any other
I could use it when I wanted
Simply for my pleasure
I was born with this heavenly gift
Peaking from my slit of creation;
My path to liberation
(Mistaken as sinful temptation)
Was always within me

Like many paths in life
I just needed someone to show me

Now when I start to describe the guy that came to deliver my flat-screen that following Monday evening, he's going to sound like he should be good looking. He was six feet, I'd say between about 250 and 260 pounds, dark-skinned, and bald, with a goatee. That's what my pussy saw when I opened the door to let him in. My mind, however, saw the bigger picture: the gold tooth on his left fang; the fake diamonds in each ear; the gaudy rings on each finger; his receding hairline. And he wasn't one of those men that could get away with shaving it bald, because his head had too many peaks, valleys and off-putting crevices. It sloped down in the front like an ape, then rose up toward the middle, and dipped down again in the back. His face didn't look like an ape, but his head did. A hat would do him justice.

I let him and his co-worker into my apartment. He seemed to be the one in charge, since he did most of the talking. The guy with him was better looking, but he was pretty much invisible to me once I saw his wedding ring.

They mounted the TV in my living room. Seeing them in motion really worked my *girl* up. Especially, the man-sounds of their grunting, as they heaved and hoed. She hadn't been tended to in so long that everything about a man excited her.

I made small talk with him, very small, which he saw as an opening to ask me out. I went ahead and accepted. I hadn't been on a date in a very long time, and I didn't see the harm in it.

We went to the movies on 42nd Street, then to one of those happy-ass restaurants in the area. Mr. Delivery Man was cool—not relationship material, but okay to hang out with.

My breasts, however, were intrigued by his mouth. They wanted as much attention, if not more, than my girl did. *Now, if I could just get them in his mouth, without looking whorish.* I used to be really good at that before my last relationship. I resisted all of his advances despite my nipples' protest. They didn't understand why we'd wasted time going out to the movies, and to eat in the first place.

When we got back to my house, he asked if he could use my bathroom. He thought he was being slick, not knowing he was falling into my tittie trap.

I listened to make sure he washed his hands in the bathroom. If I didn't hear water running, then I was not going to let him touch me at all. When the water shut off, I quietly quickstepped to the front hallway.

"Alright, you get home safe," I said at my front door.

And he said, right on cue like men do when they want some, "Can I get a hug?"

I hugged him tight, pressing my titties against his chest, testing his aggression.

He hugged me tight, and when I pulled away, he tried to hold me a little longer, but he was a teddy bear about it. He let me go and asked, "Can I get a kiss?"

"What?" I said as though even the thought of kissing on the first date was simply something good girls, like me, would never do.

"Just a short quick one?"

I didn't want to kiss him, but if that was what it would take to get my titties sucked, I would make the sacrifice. "Not on the lips," I said.

"Okay."

I kissed his jawbone because it was closest to me.

"You got some nice lips," he said.

"I know."

"Don't you want to know how my lips feel?"

"Not really."

"Damn. So it's like that?"

"Yup."

He didn't want to leave. He was quiet for a moment, searching his mind for something to say. Something that would convince me to let him stay. I waited patiently for him to use some words that would finesse me, and make it ok to pull my *tatas* out.

"Just one kiss?"

I huffed. Was that all he had? That was *wack*. But I wanted what I wanted, so I gave in and said, "Just one. Not on the lips." He leaned over and kissed my neck.

My nipples became super alert, screaming, *"We're next! We're next!"*

He kissed me twice, testing my resistance; there was none. I just wanted him to make his way down to my breasts so he could leave already.

He moaned when he kissed me the third time, on my collar-bone. Now his hands were on my shoulders, and he started rubbing them. I hate when men do that, but I guess they have to work their way down, because they don't want to get slapped with rejection—or a hand. For that reason only, I appreciated the shoulder rub, but that mess is really annoying.

He kissed under my collar-bone, waited a few seconds for me to stop him, then kissed down the way of my V-neck shirt, to the beginning of the fat of my breasts. Then, he moved his hands down and started caressing my nipples.

I moaned so he would keep going.

He worked his hands down my shirt until he found his way underneath.

We were backing up now, into the living room. I let him pin me up against the wall. He pulled my shirt up. Something about having my breasts out, with my shirt bunched up at my neck, made me feel juvenile. I pulled the shirt off, and he kissed my breasts (*finally*!), slowly releasing them from the cups of my bra until my left nipple was in his mouth and my right nipple was pinched between his fingers. He sucked and licked them. I moaned deeply. I couldn't keep my mouth shut. It felt so good my hips started moving.

I pretended not to notice his hands loosening my belt, and then unbuttoning my jeans. They fell quickly, betraying my timing. There was supposed to be at least a little struggle on my part. *No sex, he has gold teeth,* I told myself. And my pussy woke up slobbering like a drunk and said, *"Fuck you! Don't tell me what to do."*

His hands slipped around my ass. He squeezed my cheeks and moaned, like it felt good in his palms. He lifted my right leg up.

Don't be a whore.

Then he rubbed my soaking panties. We both moaned when he did that.

Do not fuck him!

He kissed a trail down to my belly button, pulled my panties down with his teeth, grabbed both cheeks of my ass, pushed me up and buried his face between my legs like a hungry bear.

This didn't excite me. I wanted him to come back up to my titties, where I knew I would feel pleasure. Getting head never felt as good as having my titties sucked. I rolled my eyes, disappointed.

He pulled me down until I was on the carpet, pushed both of my legs up and ate—scratch that—licked away. Stroking my clit with his tongue, nonstop. Slow sometimes. Sometimes fast, depending on my reaction—but he never stopped.

I felt a new sensation; my clit was tight and throbbing, keeping time with my heartbeat. I'd never felt her do that before. Then suddenly, she started tickling. It was the most agitating, wonderful tickle I'd ever felt. I screwed up my face. Moments later, this devious itch rose from between my lips and surged over my clit, so that now there was a tickle, and an itch blending together, assaulting my pussy in some sick, beautiful rush of agonizing pleasure.

My eyes rolled with desperation. The feeling was thick and thin; big and small. I tried to push his head away, but he wouldn't stop. Instead, he started moaning, and shaking his head, up and down, side to side, and in circles. His tongue never leaving my clit.

The itch was... it was torturous! I went from pushing his head away, to grabbing his head and bucking my hips, grinding my pussy in his face so his tongue could scratch that itch. He moaned and moved faster. I bit my bottom lip. The itch just kept intensifying. I wrapped my legs around his head. My left eye met my right. *"Please,"* I begged somewhere deep inside of me, and everything outside of me. I couldn't take it. Tears welled in my eyes. "Oh Gahd!" I buried my nails into his scalp. My body started shaking and quaking. *What's happening to me?* Something *needed* to happen. I was scared. Something was about to happen. My heart pounded. My body strained. Something was happening! I cried out, "Oh Gaaahd!"

My soul cracked. I was blind for a moment and deaf in both ears. My heart was suspended in mid-beat. There was bright light, followed by complete darkness. I was not on Earth anymore. I was ethereal, floating out in the universe. I was everything and nothing all at once. I saw my soul's name. The meaning of life pricked me. Everything was beautiful.

Euphoria.

Silence.

Then I was back suddenly, and yelled "Oh shit!" I had about three seconds of delirium. I didn't know what to do or how to think. *Oh My Gahd!* My eyes rolled around, lost. There was no mistaking what that was. *That was it! Oh yes!*

I curled up into the fetal position, and started rocking.

He put his hand on my thigh.

"Don't touch me," I said. "Please just leave. You have to go."

"You alright?"

"Just go please!"

I couldn't explain my reaction. I wanted to be alone. Wanted him to just go away. I didn't need anything else from him. I didn't want to hear his voice or see his face. For some reason, I wanted to fight him. And I wanted a shower.

When he left, I was bombarded by thoughts. *The pleasure was too intense. Should I be allowed to feel that way? The sounds I made! Oh my, I was singing! The octave I hit was alien for my vocal range. I was Phillip Bailey and Mariah Carey on steroids. I didn't know I could sound like that. I didn't know I could feel like that. Is this how men feel every time they cum? Those lucky bastards. Uh uh. No way they feel this good every time they get off. There would be no wars if they felt this good.*

I was so in awe of myself. I smiled at my new understanding of me and said aloud, with glee, "So that's what my clit is for!"

After that, I was like a crack addict, chasing Jason. I called him every day, asking him to come over. If he said no, I begged. I needed that! I wanted it all the time, and I wanted everyone to experience it. *Does every woman know about this? How come no one told me?*

He went from being the delivery guy with the gold tooth to, Pumpkin Eater Peter, and what he was delivering to me was far more precious than that flat-screen he'd hung on my wall.

Kitty K. Free

Chapter 4

Confession: *Good head makes me stupid.*

It's amazing what I found out I'd put up with for some good head. I didn't like Peter, but I had to feel those lips on my clit. I had to feel that tongue stroke me until that tickle-itch brought me to my moment of sweet death.

Our conversations pissed me off. His naked body repulsed me. His voice irked the shit out of me. I didn't like the way he carried himself. He was sloppy. He wasn't the sharpest knife in the drawer either. But his head outweighed all of that. It was all about having the orgasm—and then kicking him out immediately afterward.

He would say some of the dumbest shit, and I just wanted him to shut up already. The thoughts that came out of his brain made me lose all respect for him, so I'd just talk to him any way I wanted to.

We were watching reruns of that show where they lure child predators into a house and then bust their nasty asses. We were only watching because he made me suffer through TV with him before he would give me any. As much as I love to watch TV, I didn't want to spend time watching with him. I just wanted him to get me off. So, anyway, we get into this conversation about child molesters and he said being gay—a gay man specifically—is just as bad as being a child molester.

"What?" I squinted my eyes in disbelief. "Where the fuck in your stupid-ass head did you get that, dummy?"

"I'm just saying, being a gay man is as disgusting, if not worse, than being a child molester."

"How? How is that even a thought in your fucking head? You know what? Don't even bother to explain. I don't want to hear shit else you have to say."

When I'd get upset it prompted him to please me. Pissing me off was his sick version of foreplay. I started noticing a pattern: he'd piss me off, then go down on me to make up for it, and then I'd kick him out. It became routine.

He was full of that brand of fool's wisdom. He said, "Fuck lyrics. No one cares about lyrics. That's not what hip hop is about. It's about making money."

Now, I'm a hip hop purist, so that made me want to smack the shit outta him.

Another time he said, "You act real light *skin-ded* for a dark *skin-ded* girl."

"What?" I found myself squinting my eyes in disbelief at him, yet again.

"Yeah, you know, you act like a girly girl. You're not all rough like dark *skin-ded* girls are."

"What?"

"Wait, I'm saying it wrong. Light *skin-ded* girls are like, softer than dark *skin-ded* girls. Like, a lot of dark *skin-ded* girls have scars because they fight a lot, but you don't have any."

"Okay, so let me make sure I'm getting this clearly; I act like a light-skinned woman, because I'm not rough, and scarred up? Is that what you're saying? That because I'm dark skinned, I should what, run around acting wild like an animal?"

"No, but the dark *skin-ded* girls I been around, they been in a lot of fights, and they act like they angry at the world. I mean, I never even dated a dark *skin-ded* girl before you."

"You're not dating one now. That's number one. Number two—I'm a woman, not a girl. And number three, it's not *skin-ded* damn it! It's skinned! It's one fucking syllable!"

The whole conversation made my neck hot and my veins and arteries thump. It got to the point where he'd speak and I wouldn't hear words. He was like an adult talking in a *Peanuts* cartoon.

He was a phone talker too. He'd want to sit on the phone with me and go on, and on, and on. I wouldn't say anything and wouldn't respond to his questions. I'd just give him dead air. But he'd pathetically still be there, occasionally saying, "Hello?" to make sure I was still on the line. He bragged about how much money he was making and how much he was going to make and blah, blah, blah, until I couldn't take it anymore one day, and I said, "I think my bathroom is on fire or something. I gotta go." A man's money does not impress me, and it pissed me off thoroughly that he was running down his stats like that because he assumed it would.

My stupid ass clit though. She made me put up with his *babbage* just so she could feel that eye-crossing, lip-biting, soul-draining, tickle-itch. Eventually, my inner pussy got jealous. Sure, she enjoyed the clitoral orgasm, but she wanted to be penetrated. So I gave in to her and let him go farther—or deeper, as it were, and gave him some.

I'm screwing up my face as I tell you this, and I should've known what I was in for when he referred to his dick as a "penis."

"I can't wait to put my penis inside you," he said.

And that was exactly what it was—a clinical extension of flesh for the purposes of procreation only. Not even remotely about pleasure. His was not a *dick, cock,* or *schlong.* There was no colorful name for that thing, nor for what it did to me. It was just intercourse with *just* a penis. Like something straight out of an eighth-grade health book.

His stomach was soft. Not man soft, but female soft. It felt like I was fucking a goose-down pillow. His sweaty stomach pushed down on my diaphragm until I could hardly breathe. But then—he was doing enough breathing for the both of us. He poked around inside of me without rhythm, without purpose. His hands were on my shoulders, pinning me down, as he breathed his hot air on my face. "You like that penis? Huh?"

I screwed up my face. *How dare you talk to me with that* wack-*ass clinical bullshit! "No! No, I don't like that penis,"* I wanted to yell, but I didn't because I didn't want to prolong the torment.

He started going faster, bearing down on me like a sputtering drill. I thought it meant he was cumming, but then he slowed down, as if he was trying to stay in it for as long as possible.

I changed positions, trying to make it better. Now, his lump of a stomach rested on my ass, as he *intercoursed* with me. He really got into it, grabbing my ass with his clumsy hands, as he forced ugly, inept strokes into my steadily drying opening. This seemed to go on forever.

His *penis* turned my *pussy* into a *vagina*.

It was the longest, most heinous, five minutes of my life.

When he was finally done and I felt the tip of the full condom slowly sliding out of me (UGH!), I scurried away from him and into the bathroom. I couldn't get clean! I felt violated. *How dare he come here with that corny-ass penis!* My feelings were hurt, and my pussy was angry.

We—my pussy, my clit, and myself—were temporarily confused, unable to think clearly through all of our disappointment. I couldn't believe he came out of his house, all the way over to my house, with that terrible-ass, textbook-boring, clinical-trial-error, sex. The head was so good, so amazing. And it wasn't his size because he was packing. Looking at it, I expected it to be good. It was his terribly, tragic technique.

The situation didn't warrant that I teach him. I didn't even want his horrible penis in the first place. That was my pussy's fault. Goodness, it was like he was his own sexual opposite. His own yin-yang. The head was so good, and the penis was equally as bad.

I was willing to overlook a lot for the head, but I couldn't overlook this.

When I came back to my senses, it all made sense: The head was spectacular to make up for the disastrous penis. He knew he had to be good at *something*.

I couldn't stay in the shower long enough. I wished I could've taken my pussy out and bleached her.

He kept calling me after that. My stupid ass clit wanted the head, but just the thought of him, after that sorry fuck, made me nauseous. If men only knew the way a woman is able to really feel about what they think is the best thing on Earth. Don't get me wrong—good dick is a joy to behold. But if they only knew that when their dick is bad, it's dreadful. I've heard bad pussy is like bad pizza: It's still pussy, so how bad can it be? If I were to make a food comparison about bad dick, I'd say it's like when you get a hold of some bad Chinese: It tastes horrible, no amount of duck sauce can make it better, and you've got to just throw it out because you can't even finish it. Then, a few minutes after you have it, you're all sick, grabbing your stomach, swearing you will never go to that Chinese restaurant again. And you warn everybody not to go there either. Yep. Bad dick is like, bad *moo goo gai pan*.

It's physically and emotionally draining because you find yourself, lying there, or bent over, or whatever position you're in, just being jabbed. Feeling your stomach turn, as some man becomes a grunting, heavy breathing, grossly moaning monster inside of you. It's a special torment of the mind, body, and soul. Especially because I put myself in that position, you know? I volunteered for that bullshit.

Within two weeks, I let him come back. I mean, *I* didn't want him. It was my clit who craved his attention. So, it was back to the *wackness*. Yes, I know I'm dumb. Don't you think I know that? But ever since that first nut, my clit has had her own agenda. And I obliged her, you know, to keep the peace between us. I figured I could manage to get some quick head, then get him out of the house without another sorry session of lackluster intercourse. That was when he started getting too familiar with me.

When he got to my house, he asked if he could take a shower since he'd come straight from work.

"Didn't you tell me you had showers at your job? Why would you wait until you got here to take one? Or couldn't you stop at your house first?"

"I just figured I could take one here."

"Why?" I really wanted to know.

"I mean, because... well, I just didn't think it would be a problem."

Cocky male bastard! "Do you normally take showers just anywhere?"

He didn't answer for a moment. He just looked like he couldn't believe my response. "Well, can I at least wash up?"

I sucked my teeth. "Go ahead."

He'd gotten way out of his lane, and I had to remind myself of his purpose. But the fact that he assumed that he could get naked and take a shower in my home pissed me off completely. *Take a shower at my house to wash that corny-ass penis? No, sir.*

I was flipping through the channels when he came back into the living room, wearing nothing but a towel.

"Why are you walking around my house naked?" I interrogated.

"I figured... well, you know... that we were going to end up this way anyway." There he was, figuring, again.

"Please put your clothes back on. Please." *You flabby fuck.* The sight of his body was bad from front to back. His ass was pancake flat. His front looked like he'd been impregnated by an alien. His breasts were larger than mine;

he was at least a D cup. His arms were supple-looking like a female's. I mean really, where was his muscle tone?

I felt like crying. I was so disgusted with myself. *How could I have let that inside of me?*

I stopped on a cartoon channel because cartoons make me happy, and I needed to go on a mini vacation from him. He had the audacity to ask, "Don't you watch anything serious?"

"Life is serious enough. I watch TV for entertainment." *Is it really worth hearing him talk?* My clit said it was.

"I never see you watch the news."

"*Never* is a strong word for someone who's known me for what? About six weeks?"

"It's been longer than six weeks."

My clit and my mind were doing battle now. I tried to tell that dumb, non-thinking bitch that it was not worth it, but she made some valid points. "*What are you going to do? Go out on a search for some good head elsewhere? He's already here, and he can already give us what we want. Just close your ears and open your legs.*"

"No, it hasn't. I've had this flat-screen for exactly six weeks. So using the word 'never' in regard to anything about me is ignorant."

"Damn, my bad. You're so uptight."

"Maybe it's because I'm dark skinned."

There was silence, and my clit said, "*See? Just let him be quiet. Stay focused on our goal.*"

Then he broke the silence with, "Can I use your laptop?"

"Use my laptop?" I said like he'd cursed at me.

"Yeah. I need to look something up."

"No! I don't want your trail of whatever you're looking up to be in my history."

"I just need to check my bank balance."

I rolled my eyes. A long elementary school roll. "Fine. Go ahead."

Stay calm.

I had a flashback of his *wack*-ass penis, and a nasty chill ran through me, and now my pussy joined the battle. After all, she was the one who he'd violated, and she never forgets. She didn't even want the possibility of him entering her again. She yelled at my clit, *"Shut up, you dumb bitch! He has to go. Get him out of here NOW!"*

More silence, and then he asked, "Why don't you cook?"

"Excuse me?" I raised my eyebrows.

"Why don't you cook? You're never gonna get a man if you don't cook. Whoever I'm with has to cook at least a little something."

Yeah, that was it.

"Dude, stop talking to me like you know me. Really. 'Cause you don't. You don't know shit about me, and I don't want to know shit about you, or what you like or don't like. And I don't recall asking you the requirements for being in any relationship with you, or asking anything about anything in regard to you at all. You and your *penis...*" I gave him the up-down with my eyes, "need to get the fuck out of my house!"

As soon as I said it there was a loud thunderclap, as if the heavens were either backing me up or cursing me.

"You want me to go?"

"Mutha fucka, did I st-stutter?"

The sky broke, and waves of water started slapping the streets.

"You better hurry up."

The rain sloshed against my windows like someone was standing outside throwing water at them by the bucketfuls.

My pussy yelled at me again, *"Get that bastard out of here now!"*

He just stood there, looking at me in disbelief, like a stupid dog who couldn't figure out why he was being scolded for pissing on the floor.

"Hello? What are you waiting for?"

"But I drove over here."

"So."

"I can't drive in this weather."

"Take the damn train then. You can get your car tomorrow."

"But I need my car."

I sucked my teeth in sheer agitation. "So take your fucking car!"

"I just said I can't drive in this weather."

"Sounds personal."

"Can I sleep here?"

"No," I said and folded my arms.

"He can sleep in his car," my pussy said.

"Sleep in your car!"

"But it's pouring, and there's lightning."

"Goodness, are you actually.... are you whining?"

"Get him the fuck outta here!"

"Can I just stay until the rain stops?"

I huffed so hard I almost blew snot out of my nostrils. I wish I would've, right on him. "Fine!" I yelled through my teeth.

We sat there, just waiting for the rain to stop. But damn it, it never did. At one in the morning it was still pouring. The thunder rocked the streets. Finally, needing sleep myself, I conceded and let him spend the night.

"Thanks," he said and stood up with me as I was heading to my bedroom.

"Where do you think you're going?"

"To bed."

"You see that couch?"

"Yeah."

"I said you could sleep over, not that you could crawl your whiny ass in bed with me."

"I thought you had an extra bedroom."

"And? You act like I asked you to sleep here. Didn't I tell your ass to go home?"

"Alright, alright. Can I at least get a pillow and a blanket?"

"Nope!"

When I woke up the next morning, I heard the shower going. My alarm clock read 5:58. I threw on my robe with such force that my arm got tangled. I flapped around for a few seconds before I got it on. The shower water stopped, and I banged on the bathroom door like a cop.

He opened it and stood back, exposing himself, full frontal. And worse yet; all wet.

I was fuming (and nauseated). I squinted my eyes at him, wishing I had the power to burn a hole right through his blubber. "You..." I took a deep breath to avoid committing a homicide, "took..." I inhaled deep again through my nose, "a shower?"

"Well, yeah."

My nose flared. "Are you completely daft? Why the FUCK would you think you could do that when I just told you no last night?"

He started smiling.

I could smell his *wack*-ass balls, and I realized he took a freaking shower on purpose to piss me off so he could make it up to me. "Please just get your shit and get out!"

"Let me make it better."

"Get the fuck out, and it will be better."

He got dressed, and as he was leaving he said, "I don't know what I did wrong, but I'm sorry."

My clit screamed, *"See! Don't make him go!"*

"But you're a fool for letting this good penis go!"

I gasped, and slammed the door behind him as hard as I could. I hit the locks so hard I almost hurt my fingers turning them.

He left his toothbrush and his wash cloth in my bathroom. I threw them out and then scrubbed my bathroom like I was scrubbing away demons. I wiped the couch down, disinfected it and coated it with a thick layer of Febreze to remove the vile notion of him ever sleeping there.

Me and my pussy were satisfied, but after a few hours, my clit started going through withdrawals. Having expecting to cum the night before and then not being able to was not good. I had the female equivalent of blue balls, I guess. I needed that feeling. I needed to cum.

I was going to have to take matters into my own hands. But first I wanted to see what she looked like. It had been a very, very, very long time since I'd paid attention to anything down there, other than making sure she was clean. My own clit was a mystery to me.

I took a hand mirror from my nightstand, and opened my legs as wide as I could, then spread my lips open, exposing my pink. I pulled the hood covering my clit back, and marveled at it. She looked like a pink pearl. I would not have pegged her for the ability to cause such Earth-shattering pleasure.

I put the mirror by my side, then ran my finger up and down my clit, making tiny circles. Nothing happened. I wasn't exactly sure of what I was doing. I touched my clit again, *Come on. You can do this*. I put my finger in my mouth to wet it and tried again. That was better. I started getting wet. I continued making gentle circles until suddenly, I felt a little bit of something happening. Enough to make me smile, and bite my lip. I continued to rub her until eventually I felt that sweet tickle, followed by that salty itch. I moved my finger faster. My eyes crossed, and I started peaking. The problem was, as I was cumming, it felt so good that my fingers stopped rubbing because they were caught up in the ecstasy of the moment, frustrating the orgasm and stopping it cold in its tracks.

I punched the bed. I had to cum! Then it dawned on me, a wonderful epiphany: *Bullet! Ah-ha!* It wasn't for *inside* of me. No, ma'am. The bullet is for my clit!

My cousin Sandy throws *fun parties*, so I called her. She told me she wouldn't be having a party for another two weeks, but I could order ahead, though she wouldn't be able to get it to me until she had at least ten orders. But if I waited until the party, I could get it about three to five days after that, or have it overnighted, or blah, blah, blah…. I didn't have that kind of time. It was probably for the best because I didn't want her in my business anyway. I would've looked online, but I didn't want that particular search in the files that I was sure some Internet police organization was keeping. Besides, I didn't have that kind of time either. I needed something immediately. So there was only one thing left for me to do.

Chapter 5

An inanimate threat to men.
An inanimate thing I call a friend.
But men don't fret;
It's just a temporary fix.
Ultimately, it's you that I want in the end.

The dark sun glasses were fashionable and covered my face so no one would recognize me. My black wig was long, not something I would ever wear under normal circumstances. Its bangs covered the top part of my glasses. I wore a black trench coat that I'd bought, because it was only ten dollars during my vintage secondhand store phase. I'd never worn it though, because it made me look like Inspector Gadget; perfect for this occasion.

I chose a shop in the Village, because one; in the Village, no one cares about what you're doing; two, it was far from my home in the Bronx, and I wanted to avoid running into anyone I knew; and three, because I was pretty sure I could ask as many questions as I wanted without being judged.

The shop was a storefront on the ground floor of a townhouse, with a big pink neon sign that read, PUS N DIX. I walked down four steps to the entrance. A bell chimed as I entered. The slender, vibrant being behind the counter was dressed in an all-orange jumpsuit, wearing makeup, donning waist-length blond hair, but sporting a mustache. I wondered why. *Is he really a woman with a mustache? No, it's definitely a man... or, uh, whatever.* Something about the mustached she-male made me feel comfortable.

The counter was at the very front of the store, to the right of the entrance. It was like a stage, and the lady-man was in mid-performance, dancing to the techno music filling the store as she/he arranged some phallic-shaped products under the glass counter.

"Welcome to Pus N Dix! Meow!" lady-man said with a smile. Her/his voice was as cheerfully ambiguous, as her/his face.

I smiled back and nodded with a stupid forced grin on my stunned face.

"If you need anything just holler!"

The entrance was narrow, but once I passed the counter, the room opened up. The aisles were a pink and white maze of toys, and accessories, and videos, oh my! There were butt plugs, gags, whips and handcuffs. Lubricants and gels in every conceivable color and flavor. Sex games, sex books, magazines, and skin flicks, ranging from romance geared toward women, to fetishes like, chicks with dicks. There were toe lickers, big and bigger asses, titties galore. Gang bangs, single bangs and *bukkake* (why Japan? Why?). They had titles like *Ass Lickers 12*, *Biters Millennium*, and *Squirters USA,* which was about chicks that could squirt on command. *That has to be peeing,* I thought. And along the walls were all types of colorful dicks and pussies in a variety of sizes. Then some more display cases with some more dicks. Here a cock; there a cock. Everywhere a cock, cock. Some were realistic, and some were fantastic, like alien genitalia. Some had bumps, and some had spikes. *Spikes*? Some were filled with gel, and some were solid. They lit up and vibrated. Rotated and percolated. While some did any combination of the above.

I walked along the wall, mesmerized and mystified. I knew I was behind in my knowledge, but *cheesus rice*, I hadn't expected so much. I thought it would be easy—just get a bullet and get out. I hadn't expected the variety, and I was confused. Yep, that was me, confused about dick.

I guess the bewilderment and wonderment showed on my face, because a man seemed to appear like mist next to me and asked, "Aren't the options fascinating? Don't you just want to take them all home and try them to see what fits best? You look like a first-timer."

I didn't say anything. I just smiled awkwardly.

"Well, you don't want to start off in this section then. Follow me."

I followed, anticipating whatever I was about to learn from this glittery-eyelid having, see-through shirt, tight-pants-wearing, pink-platform-shoes-rocking, cock assistant.

"Is it external, internal, or simultaneous stimulation that you seek?"

"External."

"Very good."

He spun around like a ballerina. I didn't actually see him grab anything, but when he turned back around, as if by magic, he had something in his hand. He said, "Voila! I think this would be perfect for you!"

It was purple, rubbery, and about eight inches long. The package said it vibrated and rotated. It had four settings, two for each action. Near its base was a bullet covered in the same purple, rubbery material, with what I can only describe as a very mini tongue jutting out from it.

"This is a great starter. It will give you the external attention you need, with the option for internal pleasure if you wish."

I held it in my hands as though I was Luke, being handed my light saber. I may have heard orchestra music.

I went to the counter to pay the $39.99 plus tax. That's when I saw the bulge pushing through Lady-man's orange jumper. This was definitely a *he*. He caught me staring at it, as he dropped a free set of batteries into my bag.

"Hypnotic isn't it?" he asked with a smooth smile, causing me to blush.

"I'm sorry."

"Don't worry sugar. He has that effect on people," he said speaking of his massive protrusion in the third person.

I quickly changed the subject, "Your salesman is really helpful."

"I don't have a salesman."

"The guy that just helped me?" I looked over to point at him, but he wasn't there. I got scared for a moment. *Was he a dildo fairy? Did he vanish into body glitter mist?*

"Oh. That must've been Riddles. He doesn't work here. He's just a very knowledgeable and friendly customer."

"Oh," I said and smirked at myself, feeling silly for thinking there was such thing as a dildo fairy.

The wall behind the counter was full of pictures of all kinds of people, holding different toys. All Polaroids which seemed extra naughty for some reason.

"What is that? The wall of shame?"

"No sweetie. That's the wall of FAAAAME!" he sang.

I couldn't believe people took pictures with their toys. They were smiling, proud. Holding everything from vibrators, to penis vacuums, to magazines. Some of the people were famous (I won't mention their names), but most of them were regular people who were just proud to show off their purchases.

The train ride home was long. I was like a kid with a new toy; heck, it was a new toy, and I couldn't wait to play with it. Ooh wee!

When I got home, I immediately cut the package open and washed it. I loaded the batteries and then just stared at it for a moment. Yes I was really going to do this. But I had to do it the right way. I took a shower and ate, then settled in to watch a little TV.

I only watched for about a minute before going to my bedroom. I laid on top of the covers on my bed, turned on my iPod, and took a trip with the Isley Brothers to Atlantis.

I held my new purple plaything in my hand and pressed the first button; it vibrated. I hit the second button; it really vibrated. I hit the third button; the shaft rotated. I hit the last button; the shaft really rotated. *Humph. I see.*

I only wanted the bullet. I put it back on the first setting, relaxed, spread my legs, and rested it against my clit. It vibrated and didn't feel like much. *I don't think this is going to work. Nah, this is* wack. *Nothing is hap—Oh! Oh sh—Oh my.... What the...? Oh! Ohhhhh!* The feeling came suddenly and was super intense. That unmistakable tickle-itch rose through my clit like mercury in August.

I grunted and made the ugliest face; my left eye was low, and my right eye crossed. The corner of my upper lip curled and quivered, and my eyes started itching. I bit down on my bottom lip and blew hard through my teeth, as I reached my peak. The tickle-itch reached its max. My body could no longer hold on, and I burst like a dam, screaming like I was being violated.

I was lost for a moment. My head was spinning. I may have cum too hard and too fast, and I wasn't prepared for that.

The vibrator fell from my hand, and I lay there motionless. I imagined I looked like I'd been killed, with the purple, murder weapon lying next to me. Then these chills started going through me. *What is this?* I had to touch her, rub her until she was done with nut number two. *Sweet agony.* I yelled, "Oh yes! Oh yes! Get that shit, bitch!"

I smiled when it was over, and then I giggled. Soon I was covered in laughter—a laugh of relief and amusement.

Then I was hit by a revelation: I'd ruined myself for frivolous dick. I had the key to make myself cum. Now that I had that, I would want to cum every time I had sex. But since I could make myself cum, I didn't even *need* to have sex. No more getting backed up and accidentally slipping on some dick belonging to an owner that I didn't like—or worse, some *penis* that just annoyed the living shit out of me.

I also felt like I would really need to be emotionally and mentally involved with the next person I'd have sex with. Being horny wasn't good enough. My mind and body would *both* need to be stimulated. There was a freedom in feeling that. I'm not saying masturbation could ever replace companionship, but it meant true companionship would become a requirement in order for me to give in to having sex.

I felt like I'd been initiated into a secret club. One with millions of female members, with its doors wide open awaiting millions more. All were welcomed, but not everyone knew how to join.

Things seemed to fall into perspective about my place in the world. My job wasn't making me happy, but nothing was stopping me from getting a new one. It's time to stop doing things that didn't fulfill me. I should start taking those art classes I'd been thinking about. *What the fuck am I waiting for?* I needed to keep in touch with my family more. I needed to be all I could be. I needed to make my life happen, because it wasn't going to wait around for me. *I need to live, damn it!*

Yes, masturbation—it was that serious. Like some kind of power-granting genie that allowed me to make a hundred New Year's resolutions all at once.

As a kid, I was never a thumb-sucker. Yet there I was, on my bed, in the fetal position, sucking my thumb and twirling my hair, feeling blissful and thinking about taking on the world, right up until I fell asleep.

In the morning, I rolled over to see my body-less lover waiting for me. I picked it up. I thought maybe I should wash it, but there was no time. I would need to be up for work shortly. I put it on my clit and turned it on the first setting. My heart pounded as my clit vibrated. I pushed it down harder, and started to get frustrated when things didn't seem to be happening as fast as—*Oh shit! Shit! Oh yes!*

My next-door neighbor and I were coming out of our apartment at the same time when I left for work. He looked at me and smiled. He had never smiled at me before. Normally, he'd just give a dry, "Morning," and keep it moving.

I bet he'd heard me. Our bedrooms were adjacent and I'd heard him having sex before. He normally didn't get home until late in the evening, so he hadn't heard when The Pumpkin Eater made me scream, but I knew he'd at least heard that morning's activity. I didn't care that he'd heard. I just didn't want him looking at me like that, as if he knew some deep, dark secret about my private life. He probably figured someone was banging me out and probably wanted to see if they were leaving my apartment with me. *Bastard. Over there judging me. Where the fuck does he get off being all up in my business like that?*

I embraced my paranoia and asked, "Why were you smiling at me?"

"Excuse me?"

We were on the elevator. He was dressed in one of his well-tailored suits, maybe Armani (I say that like I know from Armani).

"Upstairs. You smiled at me."

"Did I?"

"Yeah, you did. Why?" I looked at him suspiciously.

"I don't know, but if it bothers you, I won't do it again."

"You better not," I said, squinting my eyes at him.

"I won't," he said as he got off the elevator.

"Well you better not," I said, stepping off after him.

"I won't," he said. He walked quickly through the lobby, a step ahead of me.

I walked quickly too, until we ended up in a race to the door, yelling back and forth;

"I won't!"

"You better not!"

We pushed each other out the front door, and once outside, we sneered at each other as we parted, walking in opposite directions. He went toward a waiting car, and I was on my way to the subway. That was weird.

When I got to work, I sent an email to Cindy saying, "Guess what I did?"

She rushed over to my desk, which made me wonder what she thought I was talking about because it wasn't that serious. Well, it was to me, but it shouldn't have been to her.

"You did anal? O-M-G! See, that shit was good, right?"

"What? No, you freak!" I lowered my voice. "I touched myself."

"You touched yourself?" she said like she was asking the whole office.

"Lower your voice!" I huffed. I raised my eyebrows for effect and said, "I touched..." I made a circle with my hand over my crotch area, "myself."

"Ohhhh!" She laughed. "So how was it?"

"Cindy, I can't believe I've kept that from myself for so long. Amazing! The fact that I can give that to myself anytime I want, and I don't need anyone but me.... I see why men do it all the time. I mean, I can't say it beats dick, or a tongue, but damn, it's a great substitute."

"Oh, it's the shit. It'll help you weed out a lot of bullshit men too."

"I know exactly what you mean. Just thinking about the things I wouldn't have done...." I was hit hard with a flashback of Pumpkin Eater Peter and his sloppy-ass body smothering me. "Wish I'd known about this sooner. I'm done with dudes." I thought about it for a moment and had to clarify, "Sexually, that is." I thought about that too. "Temporarily."

Cindy chuckled at my wavering.

I said, "I swear, it's like I found myself."

"What are you two cackling about?" Jonathan Brooks, one of the few straight men who worked on our floor, asked. Of those, he was one of the even fewer good-looking men, so naturally he thought he was head cock.

Cindy said, "Jonathan, sweetie, cackling is something done by the type of airhead women you like to date. We are having a conversation."

Jonathan smiled, and said, "Weren't you one of those types only a year ago?"

I raised my eyebrows and smirked. *Oooh!*

"We didn't date, Jonathan," Cindy snapped. "We fucked. We all make mistakes and you were one of my biggest."

"I bet I was the biggest; and the best," he said. He winked, then strolled away like his cock was heavy.

"Ugh. Why did I fuck *him*?"

"I don't know," I said, shrugging my shoulders. "Masturbation didn't stop you from that one."

"Well sometimes a girl just really needs some dick."

"I guess." That wasn't at all how I felt. I already told you how I felt; No need for frivolous dick. But I didn't get into all of that with her.

Chapter 6

I possess sweet wonders
A colossal pleasure world
In the precious folds of my joy
Hidden within a small pink pearl.

About a week into masturbating I'd developed a routine. I'd wake up, rub one out, take a shower, wash Purple, go to work, come home, rub several out, and go to sleep. I didn't ever want the feeling to stop, and I refused to deny myself. If I was in my house, I was masturbating.

The feeling even hit me sometimes when I was watching cartoons. I had to mute the TV because I just couldn't do it while hearing that little yellow optimistic sponge laughing in that way that causes me to laugh too. After a few weeks, though, no cartoon stood in my way.

I was in an orgasmic haze: when I got upset, when I was happy, when I was hungry, when I was full, when the TV was on, when the TV was off, when I was listening to music, or when I was enjoying the silence. Any and all situations were worthy nut-busting occasions.

My clit started tickling on her own, with the slightest provocation. I'd walk down the street, and my panties would graze her just right and get her excited. When I washed her in the shower or even wiping her after using the bathroom, she was *ready*. While sitting at work, if I rolled my chair over the power cord under my desk, it caused my thighs to jump just a little against her, and she was ready to bust. If the right man stared at me, she took it personally. She was ready to get off all the time.

I'd never been happier. If I had a headache, I'd rub one out, and the headache was gone. On the flipside, if I didn't have a headache, sometimes it would cause one.

It was hard to do it drunk. I found this out when I was with Cindy and the girls after work, drinking up a storm. I mean, I was slurping Jell-O shots, and cinnamon schnapps and had a couple of Long Island iced teas. I couldn't remember getting home, but I did remember searching for Purple, finally finding him, and letting him vibrate against my clit, with no result.

When I woke up the next day, the vibrator was still going with a tired *hum*, nearly lifeless. It was a Sunday, and I hadn't planned on leaving the house, but I sure took my ass to the store to get some batteries.

And goodness—batteries were becoming a big problem. I was buying batteries constantly. Even when I bought the big pack, they still weren't enough. Here's the thing; vibrators require a lot of energy, so after about four or five good sessions, they aren't vibrating as quickly. I don't know about anyone else, but for me, as soon as it slowed down just a little bit, it couldn't get me off, so I was constantly in need of fresh batteries. Eventually, I invested in a charger because it was cheaper than buying batteries every week.

The dead batteries were scattered all over my bedroom. I'd be in mid- *'bation* and notice it was taking too long to cum, dump the batteries, and throw them across the room in my fervor to hurry and exchange them with a fresh set.

I'd also purchased a bullet, and it was wonderful. WONDERFUL! It was small and silver, and I could kiss it, it did me so well.

After a month or so, I was able to cum in less than five minutes, with minimal stimulation. If I wanted to nut, I was going to nut.

I wasn't quiet about cumming either. Each time was like the first time. I didn't care about my smiling, know-it-all neighbor either. If he heard me so what? I was happy damn it!

While shopping in Pus N' Dix, I decided to buy a G-spot stimulator. Amazing! A whole different type of orgasm. Why didn't anyone explain these things to me? I don't know who, but *someone* should've told me.

Now of course I'd had my G-spot stimulated before, but never intentionally. The G-spot orgasm, for me, is a smooth explosion. It's gentle, like a feather falling. It made me want to love somebody.

Riddles suggested an adjustable stimulator; a pink, velvety, nine-inch, silicone wonder toy. It was about an inch or so in diameter. The bulb-like head was a little over an inch. Only about five of the nine inches was for the inside, and the rest was a handle. It was straight, but could be adjusted to curve into a question mark so that it could stay exactly on target. I put about three or four inches inside of me and rubbed the tip over the ridges of my G-spot. My feet and toes kept flexing and curling into almost inhuman contortions. My mouth hung open, my back arched, and I felt beautiful.

My clitoral orgasms are angry in their beauty. They made my face ugly and made me want to punch things and curse. But that G-spot... oh my! It was a whole different experience. A long, medium-pitched, "Ahhhhhhhhhh," came from my toes, like the sound I'd make stepping into a tubful of bubbles, after a long day. My insides quaked and pushed the orgasm out. It was precious and absolutely emotional.

I dared to double-orgasm. I wanted to see if I could cum from both at the same time. My heart pounded so hard it seemed to slow down, or maybe I was in some warp of mental slow motion. I didn't actually cum from both at the same time, but that was the first time I squirted. I thought I was peeing, but it didn't have the sensation of pee. I have to push my pee out. This just shot right out of me. Of course I sniffed it to make sure, and it was definitely not urine. It didn't smell like anything. I later asked my gynecologist about it during my annual, and she told me females can ejaculate, and it comes from the urethra just like a man. Isn't that something?

Being a woman is wonderful! The Creator blessed us with not just one, but two beautiful, completely different orgasms. How awesome is that? Think about it: Men have a cock, and they cum so they can make a baby. I mean, that is why they cum, even if that's not always the end result. Pleasure is a side effect for them. But when it comes to us, our orgasms aren't for babies. I've read they can help facilitate making a baby, but they certainly aren't necessary. So our orgasms are for pleasure, just to feel good. Ladies, we are created for bliss!

I started calling in late to work just so I could get a few off. Sometimes I would leave early, saying I had an emergency. Then I just started calling in altogether. I was spending days with myself in the clouds. I'd fall asleep with toys on me, in me, or next to me, then wake up and start all over again.

Time was flying by. Those eight hours seemed so long when I was at work, but at home, with my toys, the minutes and hours flashed by.

By mid-fall, my collection was thick. My new hobby proved to be expensive. I'd do my research online (I no longer cared what was in my search history), and then would buy the toys at Pus N Dix, because I had no patience for shipping and handling. As soon as I saw a new toy, I wanted it right then.

I kept coming across this term "phthalate free," so I looked it up and found that phthalates are used to make plastic more pliable. The thing is, they don't actually bond with the plastic, so if you're using toys on, or inside of you, the phthalates are then on, or in you, and—long story short—in high doses they could lead to some pretty damaging effects to me and my future children. There are studies for and against their use, but I wasn't about to chance it, so I threw all of my jelly toys out and told my dealer that I didn't want any more phthalate-based toys. Lady (that's what I'd come to call lady-man) said, silicone was a really safe material, which I was happy about because I didn't want to get rid of my pink wonder toy. He suggested glass, too, and I discovered that Pyrex makes more than just measuring cups.

Not only are there glass dildos out there, but there are *vibrating* glass dildos—in all colors and sizes. I started with the cheapest: a thirty-dollar solid black ridged beast. He was beautiful, and I named him Gregus.

Gregus stimulated my clit like a champ, but then he could go inside of me and soothe the fire that smoldered within. If loving him was wrong, I didn't ever want to be right. The texture of his shaft was nice, and smooth. Even the ridges at his center were smooth. And glass blowing isn't just for those guys at the festivals upstate. I found that I loved to suck Gregus, getting him ready for me; the heat of my mouth making him warm. When I first purchased him, of course, I had to call into work the next day, because we needed the time to get to know each other.

Gregus' brother's name was William. He was a three-inch wide beast. I'd come across him by accident when I was with Cindy. She wanted to buy a toy (I'd inspired her to expand her collection you see), but she didn't want to go to my dealer. She wanted to buy online to avoid embarrassment. And there he was: eight inches long, and clear, with a perfect mushroom-shaped head and red and blue ridges simulating arteries and veins. I didn't want to betray Lady by getting it online, but when I went to the store, he didn't have it, and he showed me something else. I scratched my forearm. I wanted William; I'd already named him. Lady calmed me down, said he would order it for me, and have it there in a day. He told me that if I saw anything online he'd order it, and discount it for me, his most loyal feign—er, I mean—customer.

I had Carlos, Jorge, Walter, and Lawrence. There was Duck, named simply because he was a vibrator in a ducky, so I could use him in my bath.

The most expensive in my glass collection was Mandingo. And yes, he was a warrior! He was $578.15 after tax. He had twelve vibrating speeds, was four and a half inches wide, nine inches long, and was a monster.

Then my dealer put me on to ceramic, titanium, gold, silver, wood—yes wood!

The massagers were among my favorite. I could pick them up anywhere without shame because they are marketed as "back massagers." I'm sure people do use them for knocking out the kinks in their necks and shoulders, but there are many of us who use them to knock out other kinks. Plus with massagers, no batteries are required. I used mine for clitoral stimulation, but some women shove them right up there. OUCH!

We are all so varied in what feels good and what gets us off. No wonder so many men just don't have a clue. It would take a lot of time and care to find out the exact needs of each woman they're with. Even more so if *she* doesn't even know what she needs.

I'd read about the Hitachi massager online and was almost scared of it from the reviews. Some women found it was too much stimulation. So, like a heroin addict that hears of a stamp that killed someone, and feels they've got to have *that shit*, I had to have the Hitachi. That was another day off work. That thing put me out of commission for a while, and my clitoris had an attitude with me. I was suffering from some type of exhaustion. Clit fatigue.

Then there were those freaking Ben Wa balls. WOW! They are so pretty. I kept buying them just because I loved the way they looked—well, not just because of how they looked—but they were like collectables to me (some people collect stamps....), and I loved the glass balls with all the pretty fillings like, flowers, and butterflies.

I had my mind set on finding pure gold balls, but everything was gold plated. I wanted to feel the weight and texture of real gold. After a lot of research, I found a set of solid gold balls at an Asian import store. They cost a grip but were oh so worth it. When I learned how to work my Kegels right and got those balls swirling around inside of me, OH-MY-GAHD! The feeling spread slow like molasses all over my pussy, down into my thighs, up into my stomach, and made my hands reach for things in the air that weren't there.

There was something for everyone, more than I ever could've imagined, More than could fit in any one store. Maybe a mega-store, like a Dildo-Mart.

Funny thing about vibrators; if you place them on the right spot on your nose, they can clear up your sinuses. Don't worry about how I know.

Kitty K. Free

Chapter 7

Confession: I'm a lackadaisical, lazy, lethargic loser.... But at least my mother loves me.

My mother came up from North Carolina to visit for the weekend. She stayed with my Uncle Henry, my father's brother (my cousin Sandy's father), and his wife Regina. My father didn't join her for the trip. I've always loved their relationship. They were like glue, but sometimes they needed their space apart, and they seemed to each respect that. Still, though, he always called her the whole time they were apart, and she'd talk about him the whole time. They truly loved each other. I want that one day.

My friend Charise Carter was in town too. We'd been friends since preschool—not best friends, but really good friends. We grew up in the same building and shared a lot of life together by circumstance because our best friends were also friends. There were six of us that all hung out together back in the day: Stella Jennessy, Charise's best friend; Syaisa Ferris, who also lived in our building, and was my best friend, who married and changed her name to Reyes; Teoshe Mendoza, who lived in Patterson; and Marisol Morales, from Mitchel's. We were called, "The Get-It Girl Crew," a name Stella came up with because she thought we were so *fly*. Correction: She actually thought *she* was so *fly*, and we were fly by association, because there was no way would she hang out with non-*fly* females.

Charise and my mother always got along. She was the only one of my friends that my mother would let in the kitchen. That was how I knew she liked her.

Growing up, we were both, dark, tall, skinny, and lanky, with bad acne. In junior high, we went behind our mother's backs and gave each other relaxers, and messed up our hair for most of the eighth grade. She'd started wearing braids after that, as part of her hair recovery effort. I foolishly hung on to my relaxed strands for dear life and was one of those girls with the ponytail that looked like the top of a twisty-tied garbage bag.

Then one summer while I was away at camp, Charise just blossomed. I came back home, and she was beautiful. Her face had cleared up, and her dark, chocolate, skin glowed. Her lankiness gave way to a gorgeous, head-turning stature, and her hair had grown back like Rudy Huxtable. She was the first girl I knew to go natural. She was convinced that not using the relaxer helped her skin clear up too. Charise was so fine that when we walked down the street, females would look at her like they wanted to scratch her eyes out.

She modeled for a little while in high school, but said she didn't like the pressure of everything being based on her looks. She makes her living now as a very successful photographer.

I loved Charise to life, and I have always been proud of her, and was so glad she was doing her thing. But her success made me feel like such a failure. I hoped I didn't give that off, and I felt bad for feeling that way. It wasn't jealousy. It was just like... when I saw her using her talent and knew I wasn't really using mine, except to decorate my bathroom, I couldn't help but feel shitty. Especially since the only one stopping me from using my talent was me and my fear.

Since they hadn't seen each other in years, I invited my mother and Charise out for lunch, and over General Tso's chicken, beef with broccoli, and sweet and sour shrimp, we got caught up.

"So, how's your mother, Charise? I know she's so proud of you, big-time photographer."

"Aww, Mrs. Deigh, I'm not big time. My mother's doing fine. Great, actually. She just retired."

"Did she? Good for her. And you work for Stella's father?"

"Yeah, for Jennessy Records."

"What do you do exactly?"

"I do photo shoots for his artists. Most of them are outside of the country, though, so I go overseas a lot."

"That sounds exciting. Doesn't that sound exciting, Breezy?"

I nodded and shoved some rice into my smile.

"It is, Mrs. Deigh. I mean, it gets exhausting sometimes, but honestly, I wouldn't trade it for anything."

I felt uneasy in my seat.

"And you shouldn't. There's nothing like waking up every morning and being able to live your dreams. I try to tell Breezy to use her talent to—"

I shot a look up at my mother, cutting her off before she could say it. *Don't you dare say I should paint for a living!*

"So, where upstate does your mother live?" she asked, and shot her eyes at me for a very hot moment, causing me to cower my head before she looked at Charise.

"She lives up in Peekskill."

"Oh, it's beautiful up there. I thought about moving there, but Mr. Deigh already had his mind set on North Carolina."

"Mommy, you love North Carolina."

"I do, but upstate would've been nice too."

I dug into my rice. *All of a sudden now upstate is sooo beautiful and nice.*

"Did she buy a house?"

"Yeah. She had it built."

"See? That's how you get exactly what you want. You build it from the ground up."

"Thing is, she had some deal worked out with the land owner, so that she was renting the land, instead of flat-out owning it. So I bought the land for her, because that just didn't make any sense to me."

I coughed on a slice of carrot, and my mother hit my back instinctively.

"You okay?" Charise asked.

"Yeah, yeah. Keep going."

She continued, "You know; what sense does it make to own the house, but not the land, when you're living upstate where you can actually own land?"

"That makes perfect sense," my mother said.

"I took over her mortgage payments too because I didn't want her to have to worry about that while she's retired—not with all her other bills and everything."

I stabbed my shrimp with my fork.

"Are you alright, sweetie?" my mother asked.

"I'm just saying, you pay all this money, they could at least give you enough shrimp."

She directed her attention back to Charise and they went back and forth; Charise telling her what was going on in her life, and my mother being supremely impressed. I mean, it's not like she'd cured cancer. Though, I was relatively certain my mother thought she could.

When the bill came, I reached for it, and my mother slapped my hand away.

"I got it, Mommy!"

"No. I'm paying."

"I have the money. It's not like I don't have the money."

"I know you do, but this is my treat."

"But—"

"It's my treat, *sweetie,*" she said, raising her brows.

I sat back and pouted. I couldn't buy her a house upstate. At least she could let me pay for lunch.

Who feels like a loser? I do!

I went home and masturbated until I passed out.

* * *

The next day I went to my uncle's house to see my mother off. I felt bad for the other day. It wasn't that I'd done anything wrong, but the whole get-together just left a bad taste in my mouth. I didn't like the way I'd handled myself.

My Uncle Henry greeted me at the door with a big hug. He still pinched my cheeks like I was four years old. My auntie hugged me like she hadn't seen me in years. The house smelled like collard greens and candied yams. Uncle Henry was always cooking. They tried to feed me, but I declined. I felt bad because I really wanted some greens, and I hate hurting people's feelings by turning down food, but he cooked it with smoked, pork neck bones, and I don't eat pork.

I hadn't had pork since elementary school. Not for any religious or spiritual reasons. It was because of *Charlotte's Web*. I just couldn't bear to eat a pig after Charlotte went all out for Wilbur. After watching the movie fifty or so times, I told my mother, "Mommy, I don't want to eat pigs anymore," and she showed me the courtesy of changing my meals. Whenever they ate *Wilburs*, I had *Chicken Littles*. She wasn't going to make two separate pots of greens or lima beans, though, so she started making them with smoked turkey. Until this day that's the only way I'll eat them.

I went to the bedroom where my mother was staying. The door was open, but I still knocked out of respect.

"You know why I named you Breezy?" was how my mother greeted me.

"Because you're crazy?" I said, smiling.

"I know that's what you'd like to think. I told you before it's because I wanted you to be like a breeze, but maybe I should've elaborated. I wanted you to take life easy, and not stress about things you couldn't control. I was going to name you Feather, because they are so pretty, and colorful, and light. But then I thought, feathers are plucked, and gathered, and glued to hats. Feathers don't necessarily have a happy life. I wanted your life to be happy. But most of all I wanted you to be free, and not let anyone stop you from doing whatever you wanted to do. Not me, not your father, not anyone.

"From the first time you put crayon to paper, I just knew you'd be an artist. But then you got all lazy and complacent about it. I told you to major in art when you went to college, and what did you tell me?" I opened my mouth to answer, but she continued, in a whiny voice, mocking my eighteen-year-old tone, *What am I gonna do with an art degree? I can't get a job with an art degree. I'm gonna major in accounting.* She shook her head.

"I knew you were going to drop out, sitting in classes all day that you didn't want to be in, but I couldn't make you. It was your life. You were always a stubborn little girl," she huffed, and gave me a quick eye roll.

"I love you. You know I do, so I'm telling you this because I love the life out of you; You're lazy, Breezy. You always have been. I never understood that. You breeze right past anything that challenges you or makes you uncomfortable. Maybe I should've named you Windy. I was going to name you that you know, because the wind is forceful, but it sounded too much like Wendy."

Now I was tearing up and pouting.

"I'm proud of you, and I'm not disappointed. I just know you're capable of so much more than what you're doing now. I don't know what needs to click in you, but something does. I don't want you to look back one day and think about what you could've done right now.

"Bad enough you don't have any children. You act like you'll have eggs forever. What are you waiting for? You know you don't need to be married to have just one child. I mean, my goodness! Do you know how old I'm going to be? I should be a grandmother already!"

"You just told me how lazy I am. Now I'm supposed walk around with babies in my stomach? That doesn't sound like something someone lazy should do." I was joking, but she was serious.

"Where are my grandchildren? Huh?"

"I can't just go out and get pregnant."

"Yes! Yes you can. I don't know what it is about that, that you just can't seem to get. I don't want to alarm you or anything, but women who don't have babies have a higher risk of breast cancer because they haven't produced any milk."

"Oh my goodness, Mommy!"

"I read it online."

"You should've had more than one child," I said under my breath.

"What was that?"

"Huh?"

"I heard you, with your little smart mouth."

Her phone rang. It was my father, thank goodness.

"Hey, love." She still blushed when she talked to him. "I'm leaving in a few minutes... I can't wait to see you either... Uh..." She looked at me and said, "Sweetie, get out. I have to talk to Daddy." She said it the way she used to when they wanted me to get out of their bedroom for their "private time." I screwed up my face and ran out of the room.

About two hours later, she was up in the air on her way back to North Carolina.

* * *

A week after my mother left, my neighbor, the one from the elevator episode, knocked on my door. I was fresh out of the shower, all prepped to get it on. I threw on my robe, pissed, wondering who'd dare interrupt me. I was surprised to see his face through the peephole.

"Yes?"

"It's your next-door neighbor."

"Can I help you?"

"I have an extra ticket for a play tonight. Wanted to know if you were available."

I opened the door just half way. His *Aqua Di Gio* gently drifted into my nose, threatening to make me smile.

"And you want *me* to go with you?"

"Well, the person who was supposed to go called me about ten minutes ago and said they can't, and I don't really have anyone else available, but I have to bring someone."

"Gee, what an invitation. You could at least try to butter me up."

"Sorry, I'm just desperate. Does it help if I said I picked you because you would look good on my arm?"

I opened the door a little more and asked, "What's the play about?"

"Honestly, I don't even know. My company is a sponsor, and a friend of mine is starring in it. It's premiering tonight....," his voice trailed off, as if he was pretty bored about the whole thing.

"I don't think I have anything to wear to a premier."

"I'm sure I have something you could wear. What are you, a size ten?"

I suppose my eyes asked the question.

He answered, "I'm a buyer for Vahn Vecks. I get all types of samples. I'm sure I have something you can wear."

"Yes, I am a ten." Now my ears were on alert, trying to detect a gay accent. My eyes were keen, tuning into his mannerisms. My *gaydar* is pretty good, but other than him being in the fashion industry, nothing about him seemed gay. Maybe he was bi. *Yeah, definitely bi.* After all, I'd heard him having sex with females—or at least they sounded like females.

I was about to close the door when he said, "My name is Justin, by the way. Justin Morales." He held out his hand.

I shook it and said, "Breezy Deigh." All those years, and it had never even occurred to me that I didn't know his name. I knew he was Puerto Rican, but he could easily be confused for Middle Eastern. His eyebrows were Tupac thick, and his eyelashes had to be just under an inch long. Now that I think about it, most men I know have pretty eyelashes. Why is that? They don't want them. *We* want them. His lips were full and wide, and his smile spread across his whole face, with dimples that popped in five different places: two in each cheek and one in his chin. Men without facial hair look strange to me, so I thought he needed to put a mustache on that top lip or something, but he was still undeniably attractive.

While he went back to his place to find an outfit for me, I unwrapped my hair and gave it a light bump with my flat-iron. I'd just taken out my braids and had gotten a press, which I loved because I didn't want to put a relaxer in my hair. Plus, the stylist didn't use a straightening comb; she just blew it straight with a super-hot-ass blow dryer. It felt like fire on my scalp, but I loved the result. I put on some lip gloss, and that was pretty much it. I don't like makeup, because it's just too messy. I have to pay too much attention to what I'm doing when I'm wearing it, so I just don't.

He brought three gorgeous dresses over. I modeled each one, and he decided on the last one. It reminded me of the green Versace dress that J-Lo wore. The V didn't drop as low in the front, and the back was a U that dropped about eight inches above my butt. It was winter white and had a matching wool coat and three-inch heels that almost didn't fit. I can't lie—I was stunning in white. Yes, it was bright on me, and made me stand out, but I enjoyed standing out in that dress.

His eyes brightened when I stepped out in the dress. I looked so good that I couldn't wait to get back to rub one out. I looked like ice-cream, good enough to eat. Sure, I was going to freeze my ass off, but I was going to look good doing it.

We turned heads when we stepped out of his company-sponsored, black, stretch Hummer. I felt unreal. I mean, people were staring and there were cameras flashing— *at us*. It was far more than I expected. I thought it was just a random play, but it was, in fact, the Broadway production *¡Cantamos!* Complete with white lights, a red carpet, and paparazzi. It was like I was walking through a fairytale. I literally had to pinch myself.

I was nervous about removing my coat for just a moment, but when I did, everyone stared, and there was more camera flashing. *Is this for real?*

We were seated front row center, great seats. The story was about a dark-skinned Puerto Rican girl, named Mariana, who moved to the States and faced racism and also *colorism* from within her own nationality. I felt every moment of her character, from the teasing on the playground, where they called her "*morena sucia*," to her developing into her own as a woman and loving her skin, and men falling all over her.

They sang in Spanish: "We sing because we have to. We sing so we won't cry. We sing because it feels good. We sing because we're alive."

The dancing, the singing, and the acting were all wonderful. The *merengue* beats made the audience sway, and the bodies onstage moved to the African rhythms of the congas, while Mariana, sang out to the audience, "*Cantaaaaaaaamos!*" and waved her hand, motioning for the audience to repeat after her.

I yelled back, "*Cantaaaaaamos!*" And I was rocking to the rhythm in my seat, and snapping my fingers feeling the beat. She sang out, "*Cantaaaaaaamos! Wepa!*" and did a spin with her partner. And I yelled out, along with more of the audience this time, "*Cantaaaaaamos! WEPA!*"

Then she started motioning with her hands for people to stand up, and dancers started coming down the aisles, pulling people out to dance. Any other time in my life, I would've had so much fear in my heart, hoping and praying that I would not be picked. I would have been sinking into my seat, trying to become invisible. But I found myself, despite my normal instincts, standing up, and dancing. Being pulled into the aisles by the music. The people sitting in my row smiled as I passed them while they clapped to the music. When I reached the last seat, a dancer immediately took my hand, and I followed his lead as we three-stepped in circles. I felt so sexy, so real, so free. I couldn't stop smiling. I wanted to close my eyes, but I didn't want to miss a moment.

That was the last number. Instead of me going back to my seat, they danced me and the other people they'd pulled from the audience backstage. The audience was standing up screaming and cheering. The atmosphere was electric, and I felt like static.

Everything was hectic and noisy backstage. People were jumping up and down, smiling and yelling, ecstatic about their performances. The cast members were being so nice. They showered us with hugs and gift bags, thanking us for our participation.

When I tried to leave, someone grabbed my hand. It was Justin. "There you are. So what did you think?"

"Awesome! Amazing! Fantastic! I can't thank you enough for bringing me tonight." I planted one on his cheek.

"I want you to meet my friend Christmas Ramirez."

My mouth dropped in awe. His friend was the performer who played Mariana.

75

"Ms. Ramirez, you were wonderful! I've never seen anything like this. And your voice! The way you dance! You're just wonderful." I don't praise people because it feels too much like ass-kissing, but my appreciation for her just fell out of my mouth in earnest, and it surprised me.

"Thank you."

"And I love, love, love the story! I mean, it was like someone watched me grow up and put it to music."

She looked in my eyes. "Did you really feel that way?"

"Yes! Growing up in the Bronx with kids making fun of me because of my complexion. When I saw that on stage, I cried."

"*Mami*, have a seat," she said, and suddenly there was a chair under my ass. "I wrote it myself." Her Bronx accent got deeper as she spoke

"Did you?"

"Yes. This was my childhood. I wrote this because I wanted the exact reaction you're giving me now. I wanted other dark-skinned women who used to be those dark-skinned girls with all that pain to see this and love it."

"I do love it, and I can't wait to see it again. I've got to bring my friends. I wish they could see it the way I did, so close to the stage, but you and your cast filled the entire theater, so it doesn't matter where we sit. I just want them to see it."

"Our run has been extended. I can put you on the list for tickets front row center. How many tickets do you need?"

"Well, I don't know that we can afford the front row. I mean—"

"Gratis, of course. I'm inviting you as my guest."

That was it. I was done. It was officially the best night of my life... ever!

The after-party mirrored the production. It was big, colorful, and glamorous. There was festive yellow, white, and red, red, red everywhere: big red balloons, red streamers, and ten big red velvet cakes, each in the shape of a letter to spell out *¡CANTAMOS!,* including the exclamation points.

Justin was on. He was very popular. People kept coming up to him, whispering in his ear, and when they did, he made every one of them blush and laugh. People loved the guy, and I was glad to be there with him.

Music from the musical played, and we danced until two in the morning.

On the chauffeured ride home, I asked—because I just had to know, and he didn't seem like the type I needed to beat around the bush with—"Are you gay?"

"Sometimes."

"Are you gay right now?"

"Somewhat."

"Can you hear me next door?"

"Daily."

"Does it disturb you?"

"Depends."

My clit twitched.

"You were just a chatterbox with everyone back there, so why do I get the one word answers?"

"I'm a complicated man," he said with a smile.

I laughed. "Okay, *Shaft*, so what does it depend on?"

"Whether or not I'm getting any."

"I see. Am I really that loud?"

"Yes!"

"I just want you to know it's just me in there. It's not like there are men coming in and out of my house."

"You don't owe me any explanation."

"Yeah, but I just feel better with you knowing that."

I raised my left eyebrow. "Does it ever... does it excite you?"

He looked at me, raised his left eyebrow, and said, "Yes."

The blood rushed to my clit, filling my lips, and I was so wet that my thighs were slippery. Sans panties, I was destroying his dress. My clit was rubbing against my tightly closed thighs. The vibration of the car, the bumps in the street, and the way he looked at me, was all too much. I was about to cum. "Uh... uh..." I bit my bottom lip in a weak effort to stop it.

"Are you okay?"

I looked at him, my brows knitted together. I grabbed my thigh.

He looked at me with odd amusement. "Are you..." He cocked his head. "Are you having an orgasm?"

I couldn't answer. I covered my mouth.

He leaned over to whisper in my ear, "You are making my dick so hard."

I didn't want to hear him say that, but it was just what my clit needed. I grunted, and rolled my eyes up in my head; it was evil the way I came. When I was done and back to my senses (it's amazing how much I don't give a fuck about anything when I'm cumming), I said, "I'm sorry."

"It's okay. That may have been the most amazing thing I've ever seen."

"I mean, I'm sorry about your dress."

"Oh yeah. That is a $2,000 dress, but I guess it's yours now."

I took a glimpse at the driver, who of course heard everything. I could see his eyes in the rearview mirror. He was smiling, trying to contain whatever he was feeling.

"Made your dick hard, huh? I take it this isn't a gay time right now?

He didn't answer. He just smirked, and adjusted himself in his pants.

We were quiet the rest of the way home.

Knowing he was hearing me masturbate added to the excitement of my daily sessions, and made me cum even faster. There's nothing like mental stimulation to create a most devious nut.

Chapter 8

In regard to family, people say,
Blood is thicker than water.
But an ounce of each
Weighs exactly the same.
To some, one holds no more weight
 than the other

My apartment is incredible. People in Manhattan would be so jealous of my place. That's why their asses keep moving to my borough. When I moved out of my parents' apartment, I went to a square box in the Village because I'd always wanted to live there. So, my stupid self, paid $1,200 a month for a piece of a studio that I shared with three other people, which was considered reasonable. Plus, I had to pay my share of utilities, and the cable bill. Then there were my personal bills to deal with, like my cell and credit cards and so on.

I was struggling, working two jobs to maintain my *fly*, part of which included saying, "Yeah, I live off of Astor Place." I was dicking myself, and didn't have so much as privacy to show for it. Not to mention my roommates and I drove each other up the wall. At first, everything was gravy, but after about six months, we were really starting to work each other's nerves.

There was Josh Wellgood; the apartment was in his name. He was a platinum-blond rich kid, and he had to be one of the whitest people on the planet. He pretended not to be rich, which was why he had roommates in the first place.

He didn't want to live off of his father's success. Yet, we all knew about it because whenever he felt insecure, he would say, "I don't need any of you people! Do you know who my father is? My father is—"

"My father is the more-than-honorable, super-holy Dr. Wellgood, and he has more money than Gahd!" our roommate Joanne Conway, mocked, one time. She tossed her short red hair back just like him, and her whine was right on point. "And you people are all poor and jealous and wah, wah, wah!"

Our laughter really pissed Josh off. Of course, the more upset he got, the funnier it was, until we were buckled over, gasping for air.

Greg Riley, the other roommate, laughed so hard he fell off the sofa (which was also his bed) onto Josh's laptop (which he was using without Josh's permission) and broke it. It was nothing new. Greg had broken something belonging to everyone except himself, because he didn't have anything to break. He only owned a cell phone and his bike, which he left chained up to the banister in the stairwell. He had some T-shirts, hoodies, some jeans, and a few sweats, all of which he kept in a duffle bag. Seems he was just passing through, but he was already there when I moved in and was still there when I left. No one knew what he did for a living, but his rent was always on time. I suspected he was selling weed to NYU students. He looked like he was from California, but none of us knew where he was from. He was long, blond, and skinny, and so very laid back. Made me think of a white Snoop Dog. Out of the blue, he said to me one day that we would have beautiful children, but he never actually made any moves on me. He should have, because I was really curious and probably would've given him some.

Joanne was Korean and Irish. All of her facial features were Korean like her mother, but she had red hair and green eyes like her father. She was three inches taller than me at six feet. She was very funny and loud, and a music junkie. All day, all night, no matter what anyone else was doing, she had to have her music. Everyone else in the apartment had to have it too, because she didn't believe in lowering her headset volume.

But we all had our quirks.

Greg smelled like outside, and he thought simultaneous burps and farts were funny.

Josh jerked off starting at four a.m. on the dot every night. Instead of sleepwalking, he sleep-masturbated.

Joanne would turn her music up when he jerked off; A soundtrack.

I don't know if it was because we were female, but during the three years I was there, Joanne and I were the only two that cared about cleaning. I cleaned the kitchen, and she cleaned the bathroom. Neither of us could stand those areas being dirty.

"Stop peeing on the mother fucking blasted toilet!" Joanne yelled every day. Once, she decided enough was enough, and while Josh was using the bathroom, she set a roll of toilet paper on fire and threw it at him.

Nothing anyone did ever made Josh want to kick them out though. Instead, his revenge was to change the locks and lock her out. He gave me and Greg keys and claimed he thought he gave her a new one too. Then they went to war, going back and forth pranking each other, with me and Greg caught in the middle.

It was kind of fun, but I was getting too old to live that way. I was twenty-seven and over $10,000 in debt. Things were falling apart, and I needed to downsize my spending severely. I had to get out of that studio. That was around the time when I got into my vintage secondhand clothing phase, because second hand was all I could afford.

Charise still lived in the building where we grew up and had already been trying to get me back in. She called me one day, super excited. "Some people just came and took Mrs. Thomas away. I think now is your chance!"

Mrs. Thomas was a tenant that had been in our building since the sixties. She had a four room on the sixth floor. A lot of people were waiting for her to *move on*, if you will, so they could get that good rent-controlled apartment. I hate to say I was one of those people, but I was. I didn't want her to die. I just wanted her to move in with her kids or something.

"Took her away like how?" I asked.

"Like I don't think she's coming back. I'll keep you posted. I'm going to get you in my building!"

Charise didn't want the apartment for herself. She was satisfied with her three-room that she'd taken over from her mother. She was rarely home anyway, so that was all she needed. She was in really good with the landlord, too, so it was pretty much a done deal that she could get me in. She told me after the increase, the rent would be $775 a month. If I'd have known how to cum at that time, I would've nutted on myself.

About a week later, Charise told me Mrs. Thomas had been taken to a hospice, so of course she wouldn't be returning. Within a month, I moved in, and had been living there ever since.

I turned my apartment into an oasis, painted and furnished each room in the colors that made me happiest. The living room is my ocean room: ocean blue-green walls with sky-blue Berber carpet and a dark blue loveseat with two matching recliners. Trust me, the colors blended well. At least *I* thought they did. The flat-screen I won in Atlantic City, was mounted on the wall across from the loveseat, and below that was my booming iPod player, the remote for which I lost far too often. It was simple and easy, with no clutter. I like it open and breezy.

My bedroom walls were white and I'd installed the eggshell Berber carpet myself. The bedding was off white. My friend, Syaisa's husband, Efrain, crafted a beautiful white oak armoire for my TV, and on either side of the armoire were large, matching, standing mirrors. All of my clothes were in the two hall closets.

The second bedroom I'd painted yellow and sponged it with white fluffy cloud-like markings. I called it my sun room, and it's my sanctuary. The sun already fills up the room, but even on a gloomy day, and at night, it still felt sunny in there. The bedding was gold and yellow, the night stand was gold, and the lamp atop the stand was yellow. No TV in that room. Just an iPod player.

I worked hard to maintain my apartment. It was one of the few things in my life I've never been lazy about. I cleaned it constantly. Kept vanilla and tropical scented candles in every room. They were so strong they didn't even need to be lit. My kitchen and bath always had a hint of pine, because I cleaned them every day. I vacuumed every night before I went to bed, and mopped the floors once a week. Normally on Saturdays. Mopped, and then, laundry. I started at five in the morning so I'd be done by nine, and have the rest of the day free. Once every six months I scrub the walls.

I loved nothing better than to come home to my clean apartment, fill it with music whenever I wanted to—not when someone else wanted to—enjoy the scent of the candles, and watch cartoons with some J. Leslie's cheesecake and vanilla soy milk.

I'm telling you all of this so you can understand my relationship with my apartment. How I feel about it, and how it makes me feel. So you can appreciate why it utterly pissed me off when my cousin Autumn asked me if she could move in with me.

She called me when I was in the middle of rubbing one out. I mean, it was a good one too. One of those wonderful build-ups; a perfect storm of clit and G-spot stimulation. Sometimes my G-spot gets involved when I'm only touching my clit. I'm not sure how that happens, and I don't question it, but I wish someone could see me when I cum like that because it's pure art.

So, it was one of those, when my cell rang. I was in the sun room, and I purposely don't take my cell in there and I don't have a house phone in there either. I kept doing my thing, until my lip started curling. The phone rang again, but I continued to ignore it. My eye started to itch, and my hips bucked. Then my home phone rang. That worried me because only family calls that number, and I figured there must be some emergency. Still, it would have to wait until I had my release.

Then my intercom buzzed. *Who the shit is coming over to my house unannounced, damn it? Interrupting my... Uhm... mmmm... mmmm! Oh my Gahd!* I love it when they sneak up on me like that. My toes separated, and I had to shake my head after, like someone had hit me upside it.

Now the intercom was buzzing *and* the phone was ringing. I picked up the phone in the kitchen. The caller ID read AUTUMN DEIGH. *Fuck!* I braced myself for the *babbage*. She was a probation officer and was constantly involved in drama. She'd have sex with the men in her charge, pee for them, blackmail them, and whatever else illegal she did with them. Like, she got one of them to rob a *bodega* for her because she'd lost money playing the numbers there, and she wanted it back. Just all types of mess. She was not a good person, and, though, I loved her (I guess), I'd never liked her, and she knew it. It had been like that since we were little.

She told me it was her at the intercom, and begged me to let her up. She gets up to the apartment and says dramatically, "The shit has hit the fan!" One of her probationers told on her, and she was suspended, pending an investigation.

"I went too far with him," she said, and that was all.

I didn't want to ask her any questions. I didn't want to get sucked into her world. Besides, I knew my cousin Sandy would surely be calling me later with the details.

"Hector kicked me out, so I need a place to stay. You know, Sandy has the kids. I mean, everybody has kids. We're the only childless ones left in New York," She was trying to find commonality with me, and it agitated me that she thought she could play me like she plays everyone else.

"I thought you and Hector's mother were tight. Go to her house."

"We are, but after all this shit, I don't know. Don't you want to know what happened?"

"Not really."

She huffed, looked at me, and shook her head. "You still don't give a fuck about me."

I gave her the blank face.

"Show some concern or something. You're so fucking cold."

"Really? You want *me* to show concern?"

"I tell you my life is falling apart, and you don't even care."

I shook my head in disbelief. "Are you serious?"

Either she was dropping acid again, or she was just straight delusional. She didn't seem to remember all the ways she'd hurt the family; like when she slept with our Aunt Deidre's husband; or had stolen money from me; or when she put a cell phone in her mother's name and ran it up to over $3,000, ruining her mother's credit; or when she told everyone that Sandy had an abortion; or the time she blamed her brother for stealing her sister's car when she lost it gambling; or even the time she pushed me off the swings when we were six and made me bust my lip. I still have a tiny scar in the corner of my mouth.

"Are you really asking me—*me* that you stole money from—to let you stay here? Is that what you're asking me? To let your ass stay in my house?"

"That was like ten years ago. I'm a whole different person now. We all got a past. Your mother's always talking about forgiveness."

"So, now I'm stupid, huh? Are you forgetting the reason you're even asking me to move in is because of some new shit you've gotten yourself into? Whole different person my ass. The only thing different about you, Autumn, is the color of the shit you're in."

"Yeah, but it doesn't have anything to do with family."

I breathed hard through my nose.

"Breezy, I have nowhere to go." She gave me the puppy eyes, but they didn't work.

"Nope. You need to leave. I let you in here, I come home one day, and the apartment is somehow in your name or some shit. You are too slick to stay with me. I'm sorry. Can't do it. Like grandma would say, fool me once, shame on you. Fool me twice, and that's when the grease gets hot, and it's time to fry some pork chops."

She left, and ten minutes later her mother was calling me, begging me to please let her stay. And I know why; put her ass off on me so she didn't go stay with her, and wreck her life again.

Son of a bitch. Daughter of a bitch!

Chapter 9

She thrust herself upon me
Under the auspices of family
Penetrating my privacy
Disrupting my orgasmic harmony

Autumn was like a storm in the wilting, death-bringing season she was named after. She whipped into my apartment on a cold November Saturday, knocking things over and changing the atmosphere, with all of her boxes, baggage and personality, as she made my home, her home.

"I don't have the room for all your shit! I thought you said you put stuff in storage. What's all this then?" I asked as I stared at the back of the moving truck.

"I couldn't put all of it in storage."

"Did you bomb the truck overnight like I said?"

"Yeah."

"Really?" I asked, eyebrows raised.

"Yeah, I bombed it already. Sheesh."

"With all of your stuff in it?"

"Yes!"

I had to be specific with her because I knew she'd use any opening as a loophole to avoid telling the truth. Then later on, she'd inevitably say something like, *"You asked if I bombed the truck, not if my stuff was in it when I bombed it."* I couldn't give her any leeway to lie, or she'd gladly take it.

"Alright now, because I don't have any animals in my apartment, and I don't want any.

I watched her and some cop friend of hers block the sunlight from the windows in my sun room by filling it up with a bunch of ugly brown boxes. I could tell by her interaction with the guy that they were having sex, and it made me wonder what the full story was behind all of this mess that she was in. I was sure I'd never know.

"I promise I'll move more of my shit into storage. I just didn't have time. He wanted me out ASAP."

"This is so much. Too much."

She rolled her eyes in her head.

"You're going to make it hard for me living here, huh?"

"Did I *ask* you to come here? And you're not *living* here. Don't let that come out of your mouth."

I had to check her. She was so used to running people that she needed to understand she wasn't going to be running anything at my house.

That first night she was there, I couldn't get off. I tried, but I just couldn't get into it, and I was pissed. She'd thrown everything off.

The third night she was there she made baked chicken and rice. "I made you some," she said, when I walked into the house. She was sitting on the living room floor, eating and drinking. No tray, no coaster.

"No thanks. I already ate."

The kitchen was a wreck. There was food on the floor, on the table, and on the stove. And a greasy hand print on the fridge.

"Autumn, please clean the kitchen. Please."

"I'm going to clean it. Sheesh! I just finished cooking."

"How about next time you clean *while* you cook!"

"Alright already. It's not the end of the world."

I huffed.

"Hey, you going to the store?"

"I just walked in the house."

"I'm saying, it looks like you are going back out."

"You want something from the store?"

"Yeah, if you're going."

"Okay," I said and went to my room and slammed the door. She had the nerve to think she could sit in the house all day, then ask me to go to the store when I got home. She was trying me, and that really pissed me off.

In an angry huff, I went straight to bed. *Nutless.*

The dishes were still in the sink when I woke up, and I could tell by the smelly haze that she'd been smoking in my bathroom. My body felt ill. I hate the smell of cigarettes, and the stink lingering around my place agitated me on about twenty different levels. And to make matters worse, there was a nasty, scummy gray ring around my tub.

Everything was just wrong. The house was dirty. I had no privacy, and I hadn't had an orgasm since Saturday morning, before she moved in. I needed my release.

I bumped into Justin at the elevator. He stuck his tongue out at me, like we were kids, so I stuck my tongue back out at him and laughed. I needed that laugh.

"See? Don't say I never gave you anything."

"Ah, the gift of laughter! Cheapskate."

"What? That's the gift that keeps on giving. You're going to think about it later."

He was right. While I was at work, I thought about him and laughed.

I also thought about cumming. My clit was restless. I needed a release, and I had to find a place, post haste! So, off to the bathroom I went. There was one in the back that people rarely used. It was the shit bathroom, where people went to shit in private. I opened the door and, of course, someone had handled some serious business in it. I didn't know what they had eaten, but it smelled like struggle, and I knew they were glad to get rid of it.

So I went to the front bathroom, which was fortunately empty. I washed my hands, then used a paper towel to open and lock the handicapped stall door, laced the seat with tissue, and put down a sanitary toilet sheet on top of the tissue.

I sat down and spread my legs. I had to use my finger for this impromptu performance, and it took a little longer than it would with my toys. I really had to concentrate. As soon as I was about to cum, two women came in, both of them laughing and throwing my concentration, but I still came. "Oh Gahd!" I yelled.

"Are you okay in there?" one of the women asked.

"Are you sick?" the other one asked.

I was breathing hard through my nose, as normal, with my heart beating fast, also normal.

"Y—Yeah," I stuttered.

"Are you sure?"

"Yes, I'm fine." I stood up and the toilet flushed. I quickly wiped myself with tissue, then with the feminine wipes I keep in my purse. I waved my hand over the sensor so the toilet would flush again. When I heard both of them peeing I left the stall and quickly washed my hands and jetted out of the bathroom.

That evening, I stopped by my dealer and bought a bullet for work. I love bullets. They're straight to the point, without the cumbersome fake dick in the way.

The next day at work, it was right back to the bathroom. I used the one down on the second floor, where I didn't know anyone and I got busy quickly. As usual, it was a good one. The tickle was meeting the itch, and my left eye started to meet the right. Then someone came in, startling me, and I dropped the bullet. I immediately stood up, which prompted the auto-flush, and I watched helplessly, as my bullet shot down the toilet.

I thought it might be a sign that I should stop masturbating. It was kind of ridiculous how often I did it. No less than seven times a day. I could take a break. Too much of anything makes you an addict, and I didn't want to be addicted to pleasuring myself. But, I guess if I was going to have an addiction, I picked a good one.

So I tried to stop. I didn't masturbate for four days straight. When I woke up that fifth morning, which was a Monday, I knew I wouldn't make it through the day. So, I took one of my bullets from home with me to work. I really didn't want to because I liked to keep my home toys at home, but I had no choice, you see—I had to get off.

I intended to wait until right after work, but by lunch my clit was tickling me and it was unbearable. I had to have relief and I couldn't wait until after work to find some place. I needed to do it ASAP!

I was sure I looked like a feign, as I turned in a circle trying to decide where, oh where, I could go to handle my business. The bathroom was too risky. I wasn't about to go through that again. Then it hit me: *The stairwell! Top floor. No one will be up there.*

I was heading for the stairwell when someone called my name from behind me. "Huh?" I was severely agitated, and I scratched my right outer thigh.

"I said, where are you going for lunch?" my co-worker, Rhonda, repeated.

"Oh. Um, errands," I answered not hiding my agitation about being stopped. She was cutting into my *me* time.

"Are you okay?"

"What? Yeah. I'll see you after lunch."

"What errands are you running? Maybe I can go with you."

What the fuck is up with this chick today? She hardly ever talks to me, and now all of a sudden she wants to run errands with me? "Maybe another time, okay? I gotta go. I'm late."

She said something else, but I was already moving.

The tickle propelled me into the hall, and up the exit stairs, to the twentieth floor with ease. I stopped on the landing right before the roof exit so that I was equidistant between the stairs leading up to the roof and the stairs leading back down to the twentieth-floor landing. Both exit doors were in my view. There was a big window on the landing that was slightly cracked, so the wind whistled through it, as I carefully removed my stockings. I had forty-five minutes to take care of business, eat, and get back to work on time.

I pulled out my pink bullet and went to work. It was super quiet, yet powerful. My body was on fire. The coolness of the whistling wind helped set the mood; I was on a beach somewhere all alone with my bullet. I bit my lips together to hold in my moans. I was flowing like a river.

Then, there he stood. I couldn't make out a face, but I knew he was fine. I could only make out his smile, a wide, warm mega-smile like Don Cheadle, Samuel L. Jackson, Lawrence Fishburne and Ice Cube's smiles all wrapped into one. We didn't speak. He just slipped his head between my legs and slurped my clit until... until... "OH MY GAAAAHD!"

For a moment, there was nothing—not silence, not stillness, nothing. I was gone into nothingness. Then as quickly as I was gone, I was back.

The gray floor below me was wet like I'd spilled water. There was a trail of me, dripping down the insides of my thighs. I took some wipes out of my purse and cleaned up. When I wiped my clit, I started cumming again. It was a baby one compared to the one I'd just had, but it still qualified.

I was blissfully drained. I stood there for a few minutes pondering all things wonderful and free. *Life is so good. Maybe I should sell my art. Maybe it is good enough.* I looked at my watch. I still had enough time to grab a knish.

Every day for the next month, I went to my spot on the twentieth floor. I don't know if it was the thinner air, or the echoes bouncing off the walls when I yelped; the cool breeze from the cracked window, or the fact that I was above the city looking down, pleasuring myself; but something about that spot caused me to have spectacular orgasms. Sure, being in the comfort of my own home where I could make all the noise I wanted was great, but there was nothing like those twentieth-floor orgasms. It was safe and free, and full of spirit. Then one day....

I was getting it in! You don't hear me; the tickle-itch blended so well it almost hurt. My eyes rolled to the back of my head. The skies were opening up to let me in. Then there was this loud, obnoxious buzzing. A fire alarm was going off. The sound stunned me but didn't pause my body for a second. I had to get it out. I couldn't take the torture of not finishing. All I needed was a few more seconds.

Feet shuffled at the exit door.

I bit my bottom lip.

The knob turned.

I pressed the bullet down on my clit.

The door creaked as it opened.

I quietly slobbered.

A blonde woman stepped into the stairwell.

My eyes crossed.

She pushed the door all the way back.

My top lip curled.

She bent to put a stopper at the base of the door.

The tickle-itch permeated my puss.

She stood up and kicked the stopper under the base.

I bent my eyebrows in beautiful agony. Then "SPLAT!" I came, squirting all over the floor, disturbing the silence.

Her head shot up, and she looked me dead in the eyes.

Fuck me!

It was Sara Weiss.

Chapter 10

Surprise, surprise! Go ahead and believe your eyes.

S he stood there with her face twisted, like she was struggling to wrap her mind around what exactly it was she was seeing: me—skirt up, right breast out, legs apart, bullet in my left hand, puddle at my feet, with a Sally Doll expression on my face. She opened her mouth as if to say something, studied me some more, then closed her mouth. Her eyes searched my body, and her own mind for answers.

"Whatever you're doing, just...," she shook her head, disturbed and confused, "just be done with it!"

I didn't have time to wipe myself or put my stockings back on or anything. I dropped my skirt, buttoned my shirt, grabbed my bag, threw my stockings and the bullet in it, did a spin to check my circumference, making sure I wasn't leaving anything, and took off down the stairs.

My heart pounded. Embarrassment gave way to fear as my mind ran through the possible consequences of Sara Weiss—of all people—catching me in that position. Not only was she head of Human Resources, but she was also the wife of owner Edward Weiss, and part of something we office peons called the "Build-a-Bear Wives Club," (because all of them had some type of construction, from their pulled faces, to their fake noses, and altered breast). So, not only would she tell her manager friends, but she would tell all the other wives in the club that worked there, and all the husbands would know and would spread gossip with false details to make the story as juicy as possible (granted, it was already pretty juicy). It would spread like a rash throughout the company and eventually get to the temp world. I assumed I'd be fired, but I was more concerned about that story getting out. I just couldn't take the humiliation of that getting around and the affect it could have on future jobs.

I hoped maybe she didn't recognize me. After all, the light from the window was behind me, and it was dark in front of me, so maybe she couldn't make me out. *No, she knew it was me.* This was not good. I was already on her radar. Now I was right in her crosshairs.

People were lining up to come through the exits when I reached my floor. I just went ahead and ran down to the second floor and dipped into a bathroom while everyone else filled the lobby and the garage on Sublevel One.

My heart was pounding. I washed up and stayed there until the drill was over. I hadn't been in a fire drill since high school, and suddenly they have one in my office building? I later discovered it was not, in fact, a conspiracy for me to get caught masturbating, but rather for them to qualify for their new bomb, fire, and terror insurance.

Autumn was sitting on the living room floor crying when I got home. It was for show, I was sure. She would do things like that for attention. I ignored her and went straight to my bedroom to lie down. My mind was working overtime, wondering if I'd lose my job for my stairwell activity.

I heard her crying as she went into the bathroom, then crying as she left. I needed to relax, and she had my relaxation room on lockdown. I turned off the TV and drifted off into some music.

Finally, after listening to a few songs on *Only Built 4 Cuban Linx II*, I calmed down enough to be hungry. When I got to my kitchen to find something to eat, that drama queen cousin of mine, was in there crying at the table, spreading her germs. Then she got up dramatically and ran past me to the living room.

I gave in, went to the living room and asked, "What's wrong? Did you get fired?"

She looked at me, then up at the TV, so I looked up at it too: at a commercial for dog food. I sucked my teeth and was about to leave the room when the news came on. There she was in her uniform, her name plastered across the screen. The reporter was putting her on blast about a possible sex tape of her and her probationer. It was a local cable news channel, so it was replaying every thirty minutes.

"It's all over." She looked at me. "It's all over! My life is over!"

I didn't know what to say. Meanwhile, her cell was blowing up. She looked at it with disgust before throwing her precious Blackberry across the room. It crashed against the wall, split open, and fell to the floor dead, with its insides splattered across the carpet.

I plopped down on the loveseat, my eyes glued to the screen. When she'd gotten suspended, I knew it was serious, but I didn't think it was newsworthy. *A sex tape? Oh my! Is it on the Internet? How did she let someone tape her? Well I'm pretty sure she didn't let them. Or did she?*

"He set me up," she said, as though she was reading my thoughts. "That bastard set me up! I let him tape us fucking, like a dumb ass."

I still didn't say anything. She'd just thrown her most prized possession across the room, and I didn't want to be next. I just waited to see if she was going to say anything more.

"I fucked him in a room that *he* got. I knew better. I fucking knew better! Stupid! How could I be so stupid? I always get the rooms. If this shit gets online...." She shook her head.

"Was the dick good?" I asked, trying to add some humor. It was very bad timing, but it's what she would've said if I was the one crying.

"What? Was the dick good? My life is over. *Was the dick good?*"

"I'm just wondering how you, of all people, the master of setting people up, could get caught up like this. Shit must've been outstanding."

"You're a real bitch sometimes, Breezy. You know that?"

I took it as a rhetorical question, but she looked at me like she really wanted me to answer. "'Cause, Autumn, you know, if the shoe was on the other foot, and the gloves were on the floor, and the feet were stomping, you wouldn't care about me or anyone else crying."

"That is not true!" she yelled, "You're the one that doesn't care!"

I went back into the kitchen, because being in her presence agitated me and I still wanted something to eat. I hadn't noticed earlier, but the kitchen was spotless. She hadn't eaten anything. My heart sank a little—just a little.

Autumn had done so many things to people that something was bound to come back to get her. She'd blackmailed people, bullied people, and the lies! Oh my goodness, the lies. She would make up elaborate lies to manipulate anyone for anything, which was why I didn't believe the severity of her situation when she first told me. But seeing her on TV really brought it home.

I went back to the living room. "So what's next?"

She wiped her eyes. "They're still investigating. I'm still suspended. Hector wants a divorce." She put her head in her hands. I'd never seen her defeated before. She was tugging my heartstrings. Those damned heartstrings. I thought I'd cut her access to them already.

"You remember that time you called cussing me out because some dude in the street thought you were me and grabbed your ass?"

I nodded. How could I forget? This guy runs up on me, pulls me to him, by way of my ass, and starts trying to tongue me down. I mean, we look alike, but we aren't freaking twins. But people were always confusing us.

"Well, I peed for him a few times, you know, for his drug tests, but it wasn't like with the other dudes. I didn't even charge him. I was falling in love with him. I was ready to leave Hector for him." She shook her head. "I... I just can't believe he would hurt me like this. Betray *me* like this. I thought he loved me. I really thought we were going to be together, just as soon as his probation was over. Fuck! So stupid!"

I could've told her that now she knew how the family felt about her. How she'd broken our collective heart until some of us were just numb to her. Instead I said, "You want some Chinese? I want some Chinese." I went back to the kitchen and got the menu out of my menu box on the counter next to the fridge. I didn't know what to say or how to deal, but I knew I was hungry.

She never answered me, so I ordered a quart of sweet and sour chicken and plain fried rice. When I came back with the food, she didn't eat, but she had cleaned up the remnants of her fallen Blackberry.

I'd unplugged the house phone and silenced my cell, because they were blowing up now, just like her phone was before she'd destroyed it.

She wouldn't stop crying. I didn't want to give in to her, but shit, she was family. I sat down on the floor with her and hugged her. She gripped me like a vise and started crying even harder.

I patted her back and said, "Sweetie, it'll be alright. Things always work out for you. You'll get through this."

She intentionally wiped her nose on my blouse before pulling away—all over my $200 blouse. Of course, I'd only paid fifteen bucks for it secondhand, but still.

"You've been through hard times before."

"Nothing like this, Breezy. Everyone knows. Everyone is speculating. Everyone. I don't want to talk to anyone. I just want to go away."

"So go away."

"I can't just go away."

"Why not?"

"Go where?"

I shrugged my shoulders. "I don't know."

"I can't leave the state anyway."

I was on the loveseat now, and she was now at my feet laying her head on my knees. I wasn't comfortable with her there, but I didn't want to tell her to move. I said, "You want to hear about my day?"

She nodded.

I hadn't planned on telling her (or anyone, for that matter), but what she was going through was worse, so I figured I'd share.

She giggled at first, then chuckled. Then she fell out laughing.

"Okay, chick, it wasn't that funny."

"That's about the funniest shit I've heard in years!"

It was good to see her laughing, albeit at my expense. Yeah, I'd lost a little face and would probably lose my job, but it was good to make her laugh because she was on the verge of losing a lot more.

Chapter 11

Confession: I've enjoyed myself in the following places:

- *Battery Park: leaving a client's home—silver bullet*
- *BAM (Brooklyn Academy of Music): watching an amateur opera—butterfly*
- *South Street Sea Port: during an art fair—clitoral humming bird*
- *Bryant Park: Fashion Week with Justin—traveling lipstick-style vibrator*
- *Yankee Stadium: ninth inning, Yankees won—pink spider clit sucker*
- *Metro North: going to Danbury Fair in Connecticut—butterfly*
- *Cindy's bathroom: she was taking too long to get dressed—mini clitoral pump*

"You put it on like a jock strap, with the butterfly going over your clit," Lady said as I stared at the pink package he handed me. He was wearing one of his orange onesies, and had a glittery, orange bow in his hair. I'd gone there at about nine p.m. to get my mind off of the day's events and told him I needed something discrete that I could use at my desk. You'd think I would maybe stop masturbating at work, but I just needed a change of strategy. He told me about hands-free, strap-on vibrators. Specifically, butterflies. "This one has a remote control. Now this one," he said, handing a blue package to me, "has a wireless remote. Then you have your higher-end model." He handed me a shiny silver package that looked like something out of the Space Age. "This one comes with its own phone number, and when it's called, the butterfly vibrates." My mouth dropped.

"So you're saying I could give someone the number, and whenever they call me, the shit vibrates?"

"Yes! It's wonderful for playing games. It also has a timer, so you can set it to give you a buzz at a specified time, for specified lengths of time."

"Get the fuck outta here!" *The people that make these things! I mean, my goodness. It seems they know what I want before I even know to know that I want it.*

I got the butterfly with the wireless remote and tried it as soon as I got home. It was a winner.

I decided to wear jeans for the first time since I'd been at the job. A dark blue pair that fit like a glove, without being overly tight. I almost couldn't take seeing myself in them without touching some part of me. I strapped on my butterfly, slipped my jeans on, slid my feet into a pair of black, three-inch, block-heeled boots, threw on a winter white turtleneck sweater, and put on a white duffle-style three-quarter coat, with a drawstring-style belt that showed my figure. I was really digging my look at that moment, so I took a picture.

I had the most pleasant ride to work. I kept the remote in my hand. It was only two inches long and about half an inch wide. I kept pressing the pleasure button, turning it off and on, torturing myself.

A guy got on at 86th Street and shoved his way right in front of me. His cinnamon breath was intoxicating, and I just wanted to lick him. Every smell was enhanced; every touch was electric.

We were face to face, and I sniffed him.

He looked at me as if to ask, *"Did you just sniff me?"*

I smirked and winked at him.

He returned the smirk and the wink.

The train rocked us.

I pressed my breast against him, and even through our coats that made my nipples hard. I wondered if he could feel my butterfly vibrating. He was smiling at me now. I bit my lip and raised my left eyebrow, not because of him, but because my clit was threatening to make me burst. I hit the pleasure button, to stop the vibration.

He followed me off the 5 train to the N, and got on the crowded car with me. He combed his black curly hair toward the back with his fingers like he was flustered.

We stood face to face again; we both made sure of it.

And the train rocked us again.

I hit the pleasure button, and my clit instantly started tickling. I had to turn it off immediately because I wasn't ready to cum. Plus from the look on his face, I was sure he could feel the vibration this time.

He looked at me as if to plead, *"Please don't go,"* when I moved away from him toward the doors to get off at my stop.

My ass swayed freely as I walked to my job. Men were staring hard at me. But more importantly, some women were giving me the side eye and a jealous sneer. My full lips formed a *Mona Lisa* smile; Yes, I had a secret.

I walked up to Captain Super Security of the World and said, "You want to know something? I've always wanted to fuck a white boy, and if you weren't such a dick, you could've had some," and I switched away. I could feel him burning a hole in my back, and it was a good kind of burn.

That damned butterfly! I could hardly concentrate. I kept the remote at my desk, and every time I felt the slightest bit of agitation about work, I pressed the pleasure button and took a moment just for me, giving myself a literal *buzz*. But I wouldn't let myself cum. I just teased myself because I wasn't prepared to walk around looking like I peed my pants.

It wasn't just the way the butterfly felt. It was also knowing I had that wonderful feeling right at my fingertips. A power no one knew about. It was my clandestine joy. I felt duplicitous, sitting there feeling bliss, while everyone else complained and wore misery on their faces. It was like I was looking down, watching it all from afar. I was up high on Pleasure Hill, and I was going farther and farther away from it all, climbing up Ecstasy Mountain, until I was alone. I caught myself moaning and slapped my hand across my mouth to cover the sound.

That damned butterfly.

I ran into Justin at the mailbox, and yes, I was still in my zone, but the pleasure button was off and the remote was in my bag because it was getting to be a bit much. Taking myself to the point of orgasm and stopping was starting to hurt.

It seemed I pulled nothing but bills from my mailbox. I was getting agitated, and my clit twitched. There was mail for Autumn too. *No she did not forward her mail to my house!* I made a mental note to make sure to have her mail forwarded to her mother's house before the week was out. She was not going to be able to claim my address as her residence. *Ugh! I need to hurry up and bust a nut soon.*

Justin gave me a raspberry, jolting me from my thoughts.

"You wish," I said.

"Don't *you* wish," he said.

I did wish. When I saw that fat tongue vibrating against his juicy bottom lip, I got a tickle. Remember when giving a raspberry was just being a big meanie? There was nothing mean about it now. Now it made my body blush.

We got on the elevator with two other people. We stood in back, and I pinched his side.

"Ow! Stop assaulting me!" he yelled.

A few seconds later, I pinched him again.

He yelled, "No, I will not have sex with you!"

I started laughing.

One of the stuffy women rolled her eyes at us. She got off on the fourth floor.

The next woman got off on the sixth with us, and went in the opposite direction. I knew her face, but I didn't know her. "Would you do her?" I asked.

"The question is, would you?"

"Uh, that's a *fuck no* on that sir. I rolled my eyes. *Men and their fantasies.*

"Hey, you want to see some of Vahn Veck's new *Stained and Tainted* collection?"

"Do I?" I smiled big.

"Come on."

"Oh, you mean right now? At your place?"

"Yeah."

"Alright. Let me go wash the day off me, and I'll be right over."

"Okay. Just come in. I'll leave the door open."

Is he going to try to fuck me? I mean, I'm open-minded, but not that open.

That shower felt so good. *Take me away. Wash away the stress, the pain, the fear.* Something about water falling all over me made me feel like everything would be okay, and it calmed down my need to nut, which was good because I just couldn't do it with Autumn in the house.

I threw on a pair of gray sweat pants, a white wife beater, and some white skips. I wrapped my hair and put a white scarf on my head.

"Where you going?" Autumn asked.

"Not to the store," I answered, and slammed the door behind me.

His door was open like he'd said, but I still knocked. "Close the door behind you!" he yelled, and I did.

His apartment was the same as mine, but everything that was to the left in my apartment was to the right in his. He took me to the spare bedroom, which he'd converted into a closet. It was wonderful!

"May I?"

"Feel free." He sat in his chair and watched me salivate over the hanging clothes.

I pulled some off the racks and put them back. I put some on the short empty rack he'd placed near the door for me. When the rack was full, I played dress-up. I took off my clothes in front of him. He didn't mind, and I didn't care. I love being naked. If I could, I would walk around the streets with no clothes. Well, except for a bra, because I don't want gravity to completely have her way with me.

"You have a really great body."

"Thank you," I said as I looked at myself in the mirror.

"You know, *Stained and Tainted* is made for women built like you."

"I know. That's why I love them. You know how hard it is to find a pair of jeans with an ass like this? And my height on top of that? Unless you like stretch jeans, which I don't, it's not easy."

"You look really good." He complimented me on everything I tried on.

"So, how are things working out with your cousin?"

I rolled my eyes. "I miss my privacy."

"Yeah, I uh... haven't heard anything from you since she moved in."

"Yeah. Like I said, no privacy."

After several outfits, I finally got tired of playing dress-up. I put my clothes back on and sat down on the floor.

"Here," he said, offering me his chair.

I gladly took it because, though the apartment was warm, the bare wood floor was cold.

He left and came back in with a chair for himself.

"You have the best career," I said, dreamy-eyed.

"Yeah, it has its moments."

"I hate my career. It's not even a career. Just a job—something to pay bills."

"What would you like to do? Like if you could do anything in the world."

I shrugged my shoulders. I didn't want to tell him that I wanted to be an artist with a loft down in SoHo, drinking champagne for breakfast, selling paintings for $10,000 a pop. I'd told my ex that, and he'd said both me and the idea that I could make money that way were stupid. He wasn't the only one, so I was cautious about telling anyone.

"When I first started out nobody believed in me. When I got accepted to Art and Design, people were like, *'What kind of job are you going to get studying art?'* Like art is just some bullshit that can't lead anywhere. But I had a plan. I was going to become a buyer and designer. Then when I studied fashion in college, I had even more doubters. But I think I'm doing pretty well for myself."

"Yeah, you are. So I've got to ask Justin, why do you live in the Bronx? I mean, I love the Bronx personally, but people like *you* normally opt for Manhattan."

"People like *me*?"

"Yeah, people who work where you work and live that glamorous life. The Bronx is not too real for you? You should be living downtown somewhere."

"I'm from the Bronx. I'm not really like the *them* you speak of. The Bronx keeps me grounded. Plus, where else am I gonna find a two-bedroom for what I'm paying here? It was between Brooklyn and the Bronx, so I chose to stay in my borough."

"My bad. I judged you by your cover. I try not to do that."

"Yeah, you sure did. You need a spanking for that young lady."

My clit twitched. I turned around in the chair, so that my knees were in the seat, and my ass was in the air. "You want to spank me?"

"Stop playing with me, 'cause I will."

"I'm not playing. Spank me."

I heard him stand up, and the floor creaked as he walked toward me. "You're serious?"

I didn't say anything.

SLAP!

I moaned.

SLAP!

"Owah!"

SLAP!

"You like that?"

SLAP!

"Uh huh!" I yelped.

He started slapping each cheek in rhythm, like he was playing bongos. He was smacking me so hard that my pussy was shaking. He pulled my sweats down a little with each slap, until they were around my bent knees.

"Yes, YES! Slap that ass Mr. Morales!"

"You gonna judge me again? Huh? Answer me."

"Uh uh. Uh uh! You're gonna make me cum!"

I was filled with excitement. I felt that mercury rising; My clit strained, my insides pulsed and pushed, and my whole body throbbed. I felt it in every pore, every muscle. "I'm cum... I'm... I—"

"Come on then," he encouraged me, smacking my ass even harder.

I came, squirting down my thighs, soaking my sweats.

"Oh shit! You came for real. It got on me! Damn, girl; You cum like a porn flick!"

My legs wobbled. I tried to stand, but I couldn't, so I slid off the chair.

I was about to pull my sweats up when he said, "Sit down and spread your legs. Let me look at you."

I got back up on the wet chair.

He went back to his seat and pulled out his huge, perfect, mushroom-headed cock and starting stroking his thick shaft. He moaned, closing and opening his eyes.

"Damn, you got a pretty dick."

He bit his lip and hissed when I said that.

"That feels good?"

"Fuck, yeah. Whatever you do, don't close your legs."

I spread my legs wider, pulled my tank top off, and started playing with my breasts.

"I like that. Yeah, do that shit right there."

I took my right index finger, dipped it in my pussy, and rubbed the juice on my nipple, then put my nipple in my mouth.

"Oh shit!" He stroked himself faster. "Do that again."

I did. With my other hand I massaged my clit, even though neither my clit, nor G-spot, had anything else to give at that moment. Still, I enjoyed watching him, and the fact that he was getting off by looking at me.

He came loud, hard, and far, just missing me with his seed. When he was done we stared at each other. It wasn't awkward, at least not for me, and I assumed not for him either. He looked as satisfied as I was.

* * *

After work the next day, I went home and saw Autumn lying on the couch like a lump of defeat. Her negative vibe hung around the apartment like a fog.

I took a shower, and waited for Justin to get home. When I heard him in his apartment, I knocked on his door. This time I brought my bullet.

This would go on for months. We'd get it in whenever he got home or before we left for work. It was wonderful. There were even days we both called in sick just to have our sessions. Here I had a pseudo-sex buddy with no worries, no emotions, no diseases, and no drama—just great sessions of mutual masturbation. It was awesome.

* * *

"I just wanted to talk to you about that day in the, uh..." Sara Weiss cleared her throat, "in the stairwell."

I was wondering what had taken her so long to address it. She'd sent me an email asking me to come to her office at my earliest convenience. My heart was thumping. I was hoping she'd let that day go. Surely it was too late to report it since it was January already, and the big event happened two months earlier.

"So, am I correct in assuming you were, uh..." she cleared her throat again, "uh, copulating with yourself?"

"Yes. Yes I was," I said with pride. *Fuck it. Fire me. Fire me over a nut. If that's how I had to go out, damn it I was going to do it with my head up!*

"I see."

"So what now?" I asked. I was nervous, but she was the one that looked anxious. My mind immediately went to the worst: *Oh my Gahd! Are they bringing me up on obscenity charges? Can they do that?*

"This is completely inappropriate, but I'm desperate. I really am. I'm not sure how to even broach the subject with you. It's been on my mind since that day, so I guess I'll just say it. Ms. Deigh, I've never had an orgasm."

If I were drinking, I would've done one of those comedic spits, shooting water from my mouth. *I must've misunderstood. She said something else. Now, what rhymes with orgasm?*

"I'm sorry?" I asked begging for clarity.

"I've never had an orgasm. I don't know how to make it happen, and my husband most certainly doesn't know either." She rolled her eyes, then looked at me like she was pleading. "Teach me."

Chapter 12

A helix of unexpected consequences,
(Stemming from my seriate need for self-pleasure)
Has woven itself into my normalcy,
Altering my destiny.

In other words: I'm experiencing a twist of fate.

H er words weren't registering.
"Huh?"
"Teach me how to have an orgasm. I'll pay you."
That registered.
"Okay. Because I just need to make sure I'm not misconstruing what I'm hearing; You want me to *teach* you how to have an orgasm, and you're willing to *pay* me for it?"
"Yes. That's what I'm saying."
I sat there blinking my eyes, staring at her like she'd asked me to... to teach her how to have an orgasm.
"Well? Can you?"
"I don't know."
"Please?"
"I don't know that I can do that. I mean, that might be kind of like teaching someone how to sneeze."
She turned her thin lips down into an awful frown. Her eyes were soaked with desperation. "Please!"
"I don't know. I mean... I don't know.
Maybe I should introduce her to Pumpkin Eater Peter.
She wanted into the club, and I figured I could at least try to help her. I wished someone had taught me.

"Okay," I sighed. "I'll do it."

Her whole face lit up. "Really? You will?"

"Yeah, but no promises."

"I understand. How much will you charge me?"

I thought for a few moments. "How about $100 an hour?"

"That sounds reasonable."

It does? I was just throwing a number out there, expecting to negotiate down. "Plus materials."

"Okay."

"So when do you want to do it?"

"Are you busy this weekend?" she asked, still smiling.

"Actually I'm not."

She started writing on a notepad. "This is my address. How is ten a.m. this Saturday? My husband will be out all day." She tore the sheet and handed it to me.

I took it, stood up, and held out my hand for a shake, because I felt like I'd just made a business deal. "I'll see you Saturday."

She smiled big and shook my hand emphatically, showing a thousand teeth. I'd never noticed how many teeth she had, but there were loads of them crowding her mouth. Especially on the bottom, where they looked like they were fighting for supremacy. I don't think I'd seen her smile before that meeting.

I figured I should prepare something, like a presentation. I did some research because, though I knew about myself, but I didn't really know about *the* vagina. I knew what I'd learned in biology: Fallopian tubes, uterus, clitoris, labia, etc. But that was pretty much all I recalled. I did remember my biology professor calling the clitoris a mini penis, and saying it has more nerve endings than a penis. At the time I'd never experienced any pleasure from my clitoris. And though his words stuck in my head, they didn't mean much to me, until now.

And now, introducing the Vulva from top to bottom:

Pubic Mounds, aka Mons Pubis, aka Mons Veneris
Anterior Commissure of Labia Majora
Labia Major aka Labium Majus, aka Larger Lips
The Cleft of Venus, aka Pudendal Cleavage, Slit or Cleft
Prepuce of the Clitoris, aka Clitoral Hood
Glans Clitoridis, aka Clitoral Glans
Crus Glandis Clitoridis, aka Frenulum of Clitoris
Labia Minora, aka Labium Minus, aka Nymphae, aka Inner Labia, aka Inner Lips
Vestibule of the Vagina
Urinary Meatus, aka External Urethral Orifice aka "Pee pee hole"
Skene's Glands, aka Periurethral Glands, aka Female Prostate
Hymenal Caruncle
Vaginal Orifice
Bartholin's Glands, aka Greater Vestibular Glands
Fossa Navicularis or Fossa of Vestibule of Vagina
Fourchette aka, Frenulum of the Labia Minora, aka Posterior Commissure of the Labia Minora
Posterior Commissure of Labia Majora
Perineal Raphe
Anus

I put together two pages of some quick information about the ins and outs of the vulva and vagina. And what I'd listed still isn't even all of it—that's just the outside. She truly is a mystery wrapped in an enigma. A living labyrinth. I drew a diagram with the names and definitions of each part and printed it on rose-colored paper.

That Saturday, I went to my boss's home, to teach his wife how to pleasure herself, prepared with my masturbation kit: the *Rose Papers,* candles, a bullet, a G-spot/clitoral stimulator, iPod and speakers, a hand mirror, sanitary wipes, and paper towels.

I held out my hand when she opened the door, but she used it to draw me in for a hug instead of shaking it. She was so excited that it rubbed off on me, and I became excited.

"I'm so glad you came," she said. "I thought you might change your mind."

"Not at all. I just hope I can give you what you're looking for."

As I spoke, she ushered me into her huge, warm apartment. I felt like I'd stepped into a *Better Homes and Gardens* photo shoot.

"Your apartment is beautiful."

"Thank you. I decorated it myself."

"Really? You've missed your calling." I didn't say that just to flatter her; the place was gorgeous.

She led me to her guest bedroom. Everything was chocolate and white. It had two cushy chocolate chairs, a chocolate and white bedspread, and a bed that was high enough that there was a stepping stool on its side, and a soft white lamp.

"When will your husband be back?"

"He'll be gone most of the day. We have plenty of time. And what we can't accomplish today, maybe you wouldn't mind coming back?" she asked with her eyebrows raised.

"We'll see how today goes first."

"Okay. So should I get naked?"

Her openness threw me off. She was nothing like I expected. First the hug, and now so ready to get naked. *Oh my.*

"Wow, um, I actually have a presentation."

"Oh?"

"Well, not like a boardroom kind of presentation or anything, but some info I would like to give you before we start."

"Oh, okay."

"To help you get to know your—what do you call her?"

She raised her eyebrows and said, "How about *Suzie*."

"Okay. To help you get to know *Suzie* a little more."

"Oh, that's good. I think I know her pretty well though."

"Okay, then tell me what you know about her."

"Well, um, let's see..." She rolled her eyes up into her thoughts.

"Do you know the difference between your vulva and vagina?"

She shook her head.

"Do you know what your clit can do?"

She crinkled her eyebrows as if she'd never thought about it. "No."

"I remember when I was little I used to think that's where I peed from," I said with a laugh. She gave an uneasy chuckle, as though she may have thought the very same, right at that moment.

"You know about your G-spot?"

"Yeah."

"Do you know where it is?"

She almost seemed ashamed. "Not exactly."

"It's okay. A lot of women don't. Now you'll be one of the ones that knows."

I handed her the *Rose Papers* and pulled the mirror out of my kit and handed it to her. "Okay, now you may have done this before. I know I used to do it all the time when I was little, but take a grown woman's look at *Suzie*."

"Okay," she said.

"It's nice to know what you're working with. I guess you can get naked now."

She left the room and came back in a peach robe with matching peach slippers. She sat in one of the armless chocolate, chairs and scooched (yes, scooched) to the edge, until her bottom was hanging from the chair with her legs wide open.

"That's your vulva," I said, as she eyed herself through the mirror. "It's like *Suzie's* face. Your vagina is the opening. So your clit, labia minora, labia majora, mons pubis, and all that prettiness makes your vulva."

She smiled. "I never thought of her as pretty."

"You should. In fact, she's beautiful. I love looking at mine.

"Okay. Now, pull the hood back on your clit. See? That's your pearl."

"My pearl," she said with a smile.

"Now, I don't want to build your hopes up. This may take a lot of time. The most important thing is that you relax. Second, you gotta feel sexy. Can you do that?"

"I'm not sure."

"I brought some candles." I pulled them out, placed them on the nightstands on either side of the bed, and lit them. I drew the blinds and closed the curtains.

"You know the Isley Brothers?"

"Of course."

I plugged the speakers into my iPod. I picked the Isley Brothers, because Ron Isley's voice sounds like a wave rushing over every part of me. When his voice came through the speakers, I had to fight my own urge to rub one out. I hadn't thought about that. Teaching her was frustrating the shit outta my own pearl. She already wanted to come out and play. I was confusing her by playing her music, and lighting her candles, while not giving her any attention. She was ready to bust.

"Lie down on the bed. Get comfortable. Enjoy your breath. Let go of everything. Just relax. Close your eyes. You have to really let yourself just be human, just be alive. No one expects anything from you, so just relax."

"Okay. I'm trying."

"Don't say anything about relaxing; just do it. Listen to his voice. Listen to the music."

She sighed, as if trying to relax irritated her.

"Feel yourself. Touch your arms, your thighs, and feel your breasts. Enjoy the way your skin feels under your fingers.

She let out a longer sigh and moaned a little as she caressed herself. She'd taken her arms out of her robe so that she was lying on top of it, naked, like she wanted to be. Her breast sat extra high because they were plastic. They looked weird in contrast to the rest of her ready-to-sag skin.

I felt like an intruder. I didn't want to see her naked, or in her moment, so I looked away. After a few minutes I said, "Now, take your index finger and push it gently inside of you, very gently."

She did and moaned.

"Okay. Now you feel the skin is smooth, right?" I had to look at her because she didn't say anything; she was nodding. "Go a little deeper and push your finger up. Do you feel where the skin changes?"

"Ohhhh!"

"Yes, that's your G-spot."

"Ohhhh!

She started grinding her hips, fucking her finger.

"Ohhhhhh! Ohhhhhhhhh!"

I looked away again. My pussy was jealous. She wanted the Isleys to take her on a voyage too. She was soaking wet and couldn't understand why she wasn't involved in this. "Between the Sheets," was playing now, and I could hear *Suzie's* wetness. I learned at that moment that I didn't like hearing another woman's body talking.

I didn't say anything else. She was in the zone. I guess she just needed a little guidance. I just couldn't get over the fact that she was so willing to take her clothes off in front of me, like she couldn't wait to do it. Meanwhile, my clit was throbbing and threatening to cum with or without me.

I sat still in the chair, listening to her moaning as she learned herself. I positioned myself so I could grind my clit against my panties. I rolled my eyes in my head and bit my bottom lip to hold in the sound. *Oh, goodness—this is a good one.* I put both of my lips into my mouth and made the ugliest no-lip smile in the history of ugly no-lip smiles. It was hard to stay quiet, but I did. Something about staying quiet drove me crazy and caused a double orgasm. It was wonderful!

Almost as if she'd felt my orgasm, she came. She let out a hollow growl from her belly. The sudden deepness of her voice reminded me of the Cowardly Lion. EUREEKA! She started giggling, and then she started crying.

I wanted to comfort her, but I really didn't want to touch her, with her being naked and having just busted a nut.

"That's okay. Let it out. That first one can be really emotional."

"I'm forty-two years old, and this is my first orgasm. All these years. I mean, I've read books, I've watched movies.... I wish I would've met you years ago."

"I know how you feel, but don't think about the years as a loss. Now is your time. Appreciate what you now know, and move forward with it."

"I've felt my G-spot before. I didn't know that's what it was. And I've always been so tense. I've never just relaxed. I've never been able to just let go, you know?"

The dynamic of our relationship had changed. At that moment, we were not quite friends, though we'd shared something very intimate. She was not the woman who put me on the accounting team, or who had an attitude about coming to get me from the lobby. Not right then. We were teacher and student. Two women growing together. I felt awkwardly powerful.

"I'll never be able to share this with my husband. He's not going to listen to me try to direct him."

"Does he love you?"

"Yeah, but he's going to take it the wrong way if I try to tell him what to do."

"Well, I can't tell you what to do about that situation, but at least you know how to do it yourself."

"Yeah," she said, then showed her thousands of teeth, in a happy, knowing grin.

"So do you want to learn how to orgasm from your clitoris, or are you good with the G-spot for now?"

"I want to learn the clit!" she said with wide eyes.

"Alright. Now, for me, the clitoral orgasm is way more elusive than the G-spot, but that might not be the case for you because everybody is different."

"Okay," she said and took a deep breath.

"Lie back and relax."

She lay back, took a deep breath, and exhaled.

"Should I use the toy?"

"I'm not sure. It may be too intense, but it'll get you there faster."

"I'll try with my finger first."

"Okay, that's fine. Take whatever finger is comfortable and start gently rubbing your clitoris."

She gave an agitated sigh.

"Take your time. There's no right or wrong way. You just have to find your own way. You have to coax her."

"I don't feel anything."

"Just stay calm. It's not as obvious as your G-spot. When it happens, it's almost surreal. It seems to come from nowhere. For me, it's a tickle that becomes an itch. It's a slow buildup, and it takes time."

She stopped touching herself and asked, "How did you have your first one?"

"This guy," my stomach felt queasy at the thought of him, "basically licked my clit for a long time. I mean, like fifteen or twenty minutes straight. Maybe longer."

"Really?"

"Yeah. And I wasn't expecting anything, because no one had ever made me cum before. It always felt good—I mean like really good—but, eh, you know? But he concentrated just on my clit, and this little tickle kept coming and going, like it was teasing me. Then the next thing I knew, this feeling took over my entire body. It was the most beautiful feeling," I rolled my eyes up into my memory. "It felt like I touched the Universe."

"Yes. That's what I want! My husband goes down on me, but I guess he just doesn't know how."

The thought of Mr. Weiss going down on anyone made me cringe, but I didn't show it. Instead I said, "None of them know if no one tells them, and if you don't know what to tell them, well...." I shrugged my shoulders.

"Yeah. Makes sense. How old were you?"

"Oh, that was just last year."

"Really?"

"Yeah. So don't feel bad. We all find out when we find out. Some of us just find out way after others."

We both smiled, and she said, "Okay. I'm ready."

She lay back, opened her legs, and started rubbing herself.

"Be patient with her. It'll happen."

After about fifteen minutes she got frustrated again. "I don't think this is working."

"Okay." I got the bullet, and handed it to her.

She opened the package and put the batteries in and wiped it down with the sanitary wipes.

"Place it on your clit, on the lowest setting first."

She did.

I sat back and watched. I couldn't wait for her to experience it.

After about five minutes, she upped the setting. About another ten minutes in, and it still wasn't happening. She huffed.

"Don't get frustrated."

"Maybe everyone can't have one."

"No, I think maybe this is not the way for you to have it."

She started crying again, and it was getting to be too much. A part of me wanted to yell, *"Stop fucking crying!"* It was enough already. Another part of me wanted to comfort her.

"I want it so bad."

"I know. You can do it." I was stuck. She was expecting a lot out of me. How can I get her to cum? I didn't know what to do. All I could do was tell her to be patient.

"Maybe you could show me."

"Excuse me?" I didn't like where I thought she was going with that.

"Like, could you do it on me?"

"You mean, touch you? *There*?" I screwed my face up.

"I'm sorry. I just don't know what to do."

"Well, not that. You just need to give yourself more time."

"This is torture. It's like knowing something is right there, but you just can't touch it. You hear people talk about it, and you know it's something real, but for some reason, *you* can't get to it."

That's how I felt about life all around. It was right there, but I just didn't know how to make it happen.

"I want to cum! I want the Big O!" she declared.

"Maybe you're just not able to have a G-spot orgasm and then a clitoral orgasm so soon after. I mean, not yet, anyway. Maybe we just need to take a break."

"I think you may be right. You want to go to lunch? My treat."

"Sure."

She showered and got dressed, and we went to Katsu's On Fifth, the most expensive restaurant I'd ever been to. It was a sushi/hibachi bar. I'd never had sushi and was very apprehensive, but I figured, what the heck? I was teaching a woman how to masturbate; I might as well make it a full day of new experiences.

"Trust me, you'll love it," she reassured me.

I asked her to order for me, because I had no idea what to get. She asked if I was allergic to shellfish, and when I told her I wasn't, she said, "California rolls would be a good place to start."

She ordered that, and tuna, salmon, crab, and eel rolls. Some were wrapped in seaweed, some in rice. There were different, spicy sauces, for dipping. Everything was so colorful. Like looking at a painting. I enjoyed all of it, and to my surprise, I was stuffed.

As we ate, she told me how she'd met her husband. They had both attended Columbia. He was very poor and was struggling to stay in school. She came from money and had only gone to college because it was expected. "His ambition disturbed me at first, and I couldn't stand him, but he was so damned good looking." She was dreamy-eyed. "Then after a while, his ambition rubbed off on me and made me want to do more. There was no way I could be in his presence, and not want to make myself a better person. I mean, there he was with nothing, turning it into everything. He was working so hard toward his goal, while I complained about everything. I got my shit together just so I could have him. So he could be as proud of me, as I was of him. I fell in love with every part of him, and I still love him—even more so now."

"That's what I want; someone I can believe in, and become a better person with. I don't think I'll ever find that."

"Well, it's kind of like what you said about the clit orgasm versus the G-spot orgasm. Love is not as obvious as lust, nor as easy. I mean, that G-spot orgasm is some kind of awesome, you know? But the clit?" She shook her head. "It's worth so much more, and you know it is because it wouldn't be so hard to get it if it wasn't."

I liked that analogy, even though the reverse is true for some women. For some, the clit is easy, and the G-spot is the hard one.

"Is there anyone you at least like?" she asked.

"Nope. I mean, there are some I would like to smash, but a relationship? Nope."

"Smash?"

I'd used the word to see how she would react, and to test the realm of our relationship. To see if she minded me actually being me. "Have sex with."

"Oh. I like that. I'd like to smash a few myself."

We both laughed.

"Yeah, it's not easy for you young girls now. The pickings are slim, especially with the war going on."

"You know, I never thought about that, but it has taken away a lot of men."

"Yeah. The same thing happened with Vietnam. Took a lot of good young men away."

The fact that her mind went in that direction really surprised me. Here I was thinking this woman was heartless, and had no understanding of people, but she did understand. I hadn't even factored in the war. I figured prison, but not war.

"So I know it's hard," she continued.

"Tell me about it. Finding someone that I know beyond a doubt has *our* best interests at heart, not just theirs. A guy whose decisions I can trust. Someone I can build something with. I'm tired of that shaky-ground mess. I want something built in cement, something solid. I don't think I'll ever find that."

"Don't worry, sweetie. You will."

She huffed and said, "Part of me wants to give up on this clit thing,"

"Oh no! We are definitely finishing. You're going to have a clitoral orgasm!" I banged my right fist against the table.

We went back to her house, and she got back into position on the guest bed.

I sat next to her and put my left hand over her right hand and guided her finger over her clit. "You have got to let go. Don't think about it." I kept my hand over hers and slowly moved it back until she was rubbing her clit on her own in a smooth, steady rhythm.

Her breathing was slow, and then it picked up speed. She looked like she was finally in the zone. Her face had that dazed and amazed look that I get. Suddenly, a terrifying sound rose from her belly, like she was releasing demons, or angels. I slapped my left hand back over her right hand, and held it down, so that she couldn't snatch her hand away—like I had done when I had my first hand stimulated orgasm. She growled and yelped and grunted like a Tasmanian devil. For a moment, she sounded like someone was beating her. Then she sang that uncontrollable clitoral song of sirens. I swear I heard the moment she died, and her soul took flight. The sound was caught in her throat, and she was silent for just a few moments, then continued her song. She let out one final grunt, and then floated back to Earth.

When she finally stopped panting and shivering, she looked at me; peace was all over her. It radiated from her. She was so relieved, and I was truly happy for her. After a few minutes she said, "Thank you."

"You're welcome."

"No, really... thank you," she said, in the most earnest tone I'd ever heard anyone use in regard to me helping them.

Including the cost of the toys, she paid me $420. Plus fed me. The last $100 was a tip. That money would go in my forget-about-it jar, where I put money I didn't want to remember I had.

Helping her achieve something she wanted that much was so satisfying to me. I was really pleased with myself. Especially with the fact that I didn't give up on her, and didn't let her give up on herself. That feeling was priceless.

Chapter 13

A Moment of Personal Observation: I know this is cliché (and that saying something is cliché is in itself cliché), but everything happens for a reason. I really wanted the Big O, and I was given Pumpkin Eater Peter. Sure, I'm disgusted by the thought of him, but what I got from him outweighs that. I needed my disgust for him in order to bring masturbation into my life. I needed Autumn in my life to cause the domino effect that followed. Everything is connected. It doesn't need to make sense to me at the time, or ever. Things that are negative at the moment, can actually be positive in the long run. I just need to play my part.

So... right... as you know, I'd taken quite a few days off from my job, had called in late, and left early several times. I was masturbating at my desk throughout the day, and paying less, and less attention to my work, which was starting to show. I was making mistakes I'd never made before, and I didn't care. It wasn't just because of masturbation. It was that the world was opening itself up to me, while I was stuck sitting at that miserable prison of a desk. Masturbation was the only thing that made the work hours bearable.

I hated that I had to go to that wretched place just to pay bills. Doing something only for money didn't get it for me anymore. I wanted to travel. I wanted to get a RV and just go around the country. Life was going on, while I spent eight hours a day droning along like the copier machine. And I meant just about as much to the company as that copier; I was just a machine to be used as much as possible, until the day I went haywire and had to be replaced with a newer model.

Every day the feeling grew stronger. After helping Sara, my heart, and soul, were extremely restless. I could hardly sit still at work. I had all of this stifled energy, fighting to be released. No part of me wanted to sit at that desk. I started fantasizing about quitting, and the scene I would make; how Gia or Cindy would record it, and how many hits it would get on YouTube.

So, in retrospect, I think maybe I cosmically caused the following to happen:

I knew I was on my last leg. I'd received several warnings about being late, and calling in and about the errors I was making, so I was on my best behavior. I couldn't lose my job. No matter how much I hated it, the fact was, I needed the money. I sucked it up, and for the next few months, I made sure I was on time and left just a little late—I stress *a little*. I'm talking not more than ten minutes. And no more mistakes. I couldn't afford to make any more errors, accounting or otherwise, or I was out.

Winter gave way to spring, and it was a beautiful, sunny, May Monday. I was on a roll with my morning routine: wake up at six, get one or a few in by seven (usually with Justin and if not with him, I'd still do it at his house), then be off to work by 8:15 a.m.

That morning, I made my usual stop at the *bodega* to grab a toasted bagel with butter and a hot chocolate. There were only two people ahead of me. I was making good time, when I got too close to a chips display, and ripped my stockings. I sucked my teeth and got out of line to grab a pair of "one times." That's what I called the two dollar *bodega* stockings, because they were only good for one-time use.

Since I'd already gotten out of the line, I grabbed an apple juice for later, because it was cheaper there than at the vending machine at my job. When I got back up to the counter, there were six people in line. *Where did they come from?*

My phone was ringing. I looked at the caller ID and it was Autumn. I was so agitated about her calling me that I put it on silent. I opened the juice to take a sip; the top flew off, and juice shot all over my blouse. *What the fuck? Really? Is this really what's happening right now?* The line slowed up because the clerk, Miguel, was flirting with this chick that obviously was not on her way to work. I'd grown up watching him flirt with any female that said more than two words to him. Any other time it would've amused me, but not today.

"Can we get this line moving please?" the guy in front of me yelled.

The chick sucked her teeth, but she got her ass on.

I didn't even want the bagel and hot chocolate by then. I only stood in line to pay for the juice I'd just spilled. I had my money and my keys in my hand. I put the keys on the counter for a second, so I could get exact change. As I tried to give him the money he looked at my wet shirt and said, "*Mami*, you know I'm not gonna charge you for that."

"Thank you Miguel, I really appreciate that," I said, and I quickstepped home so I could change my blouse. I could still make it to work on time. Fortunately, someone was coming out of the building as I was going in, so I didn't have to waste time unlocking the lobby door.

I pressed the button for the elevator.

Silence. No elevator *hum.*

I heard someone's heels clacking down the stairs. I pressed the button again, you know, just in case it didn't feel me the first time.

When the clacker got down to the first floor, she said, "Don't bother. It's stuck."

I ran up the stairs. Between the second and third floors, my left shoe heel got caught on the lip of a step, and flew off behind me, twisting my ankle. It wasn't severe, but it was enough to make me limp. I wobbled back down the stairs to get my shoe, and then limped as fast as I could, up to the sixth floor. I reached for my keys. *Where are my keys?* Damn it! I'd left them on the counter at the *bodega.*

I banged on the door for Autumn. When she didn't answer, I started screaming her name, and banging with both of my hands. I called her cell. Now this bitch didn't want to answer, after she'd been calling me. *Damn it!* I limped as fast as I could back down the stairs. When I got to the first floor, I could hear the *hum* of the elevator moving. "You mutha fucka!" I yelled at the elevator, raising my fist at it, so it could see my anger.

"Figured you'd be back," Miguel said as I limped into the *bodega.* He handed my keys to me.

I looked at my watch. There was no time for me to go home to change if I wanted to make it to work on time.

The wind blew my wet blouse against my body with its apple stickiness, as I ran down the block to the train station. The 6 was right there. *Thank goodness.* I almost fell down the stairs trying to get to it, but I caught that bitch!

I was hoping it would be one of those days where the 4, or 5, would be sitting across the platform just waiting for me at 125th Street, but it wasn't. My ankle was feeling a little better. Either that or I was just working through the pain. I limped across the platform and waited over five minutes before the 4 finally came.

The train seemed to be in high speed on the way to 86th Street. Then right before 59th Street, the train stopped. It just stopped! It happens all the time... *but please not today.*

It started back up, and we crawled into the station. I wobbled off as quickly as I could. The stairs were killing me, especially with the people pushing behind me. I made it to the N just in time to watch it pull off. *Damn it!*

I wasn't just late; I was over thirty minutes late. And to ensure I'd brought utter attention to myself at work, I'd left my badge at home.

It wasn't Sara who got me this time. It was Natalie Hill. I really, really did not like her, and the feeling was mutual.

When we got to my floor she said, "Would you come with me to my office?"

I followed her. My mind was racing. *Should I plead my case or just let it go?* Every bill I had flipped like a Rolodex through my mind. I wasn't going to beg. I wasn't going to give them what they wanted. *Fuck that. I have plenty of experience. I'm still registered with temp agencies. I can find another job easily. But times are hard. People are being laid-off every day. Thousands of people are jobless. I should be grateful for this job. Grateful for this job? For having someone on my, back micro-managing me to the point of their own twisted, anal-retentive orgasm? I can find another job. How did I even get trapped here in the first place? I've been with them two years. That's one year too long. Fuck them, and fuck their job.*

There were three execs in the room, including Sara Weiss. She stared at me like she was trying to communicate with her eyes. From what I could gather in our short nonverbal exchange, it was over for me.

"Would you have a seat, Ms. Deigh?"

"I would prefer to stand." *I wish I would give you the satisfaction of the equalization of my being seated. I'm taller than all of you bitches! Look up to me to fire me!*

"We would prefer that you sit."

"Is that really necessary?"

"Are we really going to argue about sitting?"

"Please, just tell me why you've called me into your office? Are you firing me?"

Some throats cleared.

My heart pounded. "Don't bother. I quit." I didn't have anything I wanted from my desk. Not even a thought.

Here I was making this fucking security guard's day once again. This time for the last time. They had him walk me out, like I was going to go all Peter Gibbons and steal a copier and beat it to death.

Cindy stared at me with distressed and confused eyes. She mouthed, "I'll call you later," holding her fingers to her ear to simulate a phone.

As we waited for the elevator, Super Security Guard said, "I'm sorry this happened to you."

"Yeah, right."

"I am."

I rolled my eyes. *What-the-fuck-ever.* I pressed the elevator button again. *How am I going to pay my bills?* Tears were threatening to fall, but I didn't want them to. I fought them. I wouldn't give anyone in that building the gratification of my tears. "What the fuck is taking this elevator so damned long?"

"I'm not a dick by the way."

I looked at him, huffed, and then looked back at the elevator.

"It's just—" he paused dramatically enough for me to turn to look at him again, "people look through me all day long, like a piece of furniture. It gets annoying. After a while it's like, eff everybody."

"Do I look at you like that?"

"You look at me like I disgust you."

I sucked my teeth. "Please. Every time I left my badge, and had to wait for someone to get me, you acted like I was some piece of shit standing there."

"That's because you never said anything to me. You never smiled or anything."

"That's because you looked at me like I was a piece shit I just said. It's not like you smiled at me. If you would've smiled at me, I would've smiled back."

The elevator came, and we stepped on.

"Well, I'm sorry. I just assumed you were like everyone else."

"I'm sorry too. I assumed you were just another asshole white man that looked at me like they wished I'd go back to Africa."

He started laughing—hard. "Wow! Is that what you thought? Why didn't you just think I was an asshole?"

"Because anytime a white man looks at me the way you did, that's what I assume he's thinking."

He pulled out his wallet. "This is my girlfriend." He handed his wallet to me.

She looked like a short Alek Wek, with shoulder-length hair. I looked up at his blond curly hair, blue eyes, and pale skin, and then looked back down at the picture. You really never know what's going on in someone else's world. I'd done it again—judged a book by its cover. I needed to get a hold of doing that. At least try to know a little something about people before I put my prejudgments on them. We stepped off of the elevator, and I handed him his wallet.

"You know, people need to talk more," he said.

"Yeah, you're right. We could've been cool."

"Yeah. It's like when I was in high school and made friends with some kid I'd never talked to, but on the last day, we were running around pranking people and having a good time, and I thought, '*Damn! We could've been doing this all year.*'"

He walked me out the door, into the loud, busy street.

"I get a break in a few minutes. Let me take you to get something to eat."

"Your girlfriend won't mind?"

"Not like that. It's just something to eat."

"Okay."

His lunch was early, so I figured he must get to work at about five or six. He was always still there when I got off work, so that meant he was working a lot of overtime. As a fellow employee in the American work system, I could've given him the courtesy of a smile, because most of us were just doing what we had to, to get by, and he was no different. He was just there to pay his bills, like everyone else. Working people should be nicer to each other.

I waited about ten minutes for him, and then we went to a deli. I ordered an egg sandwich, and he had an egg hero with green, yellow, and red peppers, onions, bacon, ham, pastrami, tomatoes, lettuce, and pickles, plus sweet relish, oil, vinegar, garlic salt, and shredded pepper jack cheese.

"That's some kind of sandwich," I said, as we walked to a table with our trays.

He was funny and polite. In another lifetime, we probably would've been good friends. Lesson: A smile means a lot. If I would've smiled at him, or if he would've smiled at me two years earlier, we could've been cool that whole time.

I really enjoyed talking to him, and if he didn't have a girlfriend, I would've tapped that. My pussy said, *"What the fuck does his girl have to do with us?"* She's such a mischievous little bitch sometimes. But I didn't listen to her. Plus, it would've disappointed me to no end if he would've cheated on his girlfriend after seeing how cool he was. He had ample opportunity to get at me, and he didn't. I respected that.

* * *

I'd forgotten that my phone was on silent. It was full of missed calls and messages when I walked out of the train station. Sara's cell number popped up as I was changing the ring settings.

"Sweetie, I'm so sorry. I was calling you this morning to warn you. Why didn't you answer? What happened to you? Did you get into an accident? Why were you so messy?"

I went ahead and told her about the perfect storm that was my morning.

She told me I could use her as a reference for a job, and she kept apologizing.

"Don't be sorry. You didn't do it. I did. And don't worry about it. I'll find another job, just like I found this one."

The walk home was slow and sad. Autumn was gone when I got there. I was so upset with myself I couldn't even bust a nut. The nut kept teasing me. I would get the tickle, then the itch, then nothing. It would just go away. *Damn.*

Chapter 14

Autumn is beautiful,
But its colors don't fool me.
With its schizophrenic weather,
Its game isn't new to me.
You see, I know better,
Than to wear a thin sweater,
Allowing it the opportunity,
To bite and nip at me.
Right now it's seventy degrees.
Give it a few minutes,
It'll be forty.
Nothing grows in autumn.
Autumn just looks pretty.

Autumn came home while I was on the floor in the living room with a whole J. Leslie's, double-strawberry, cheesecake in front of me, and a carton of vanilla soy milk on tap. I was on my third slice, and was just at the part in *Working Girl* where Sigourney Weaver came back from the hospital. Autumn took the remote, muted the TV, and started rambling about her life, like she just knew I wanted to hear about it, and like it was more important than whatever I was doing.

She told me she'd been at a hearing about her suspension. Turns out, there was no video. The guy was bluffing. Or he thought he had a recording, but it came up missing. I'm not sure of the exact story, because as she was telling me, she was giving me two versions. For all I knew, she found a way to get the video and made it disappear.

I didn't say anything. I just looked at her.

"Aren't you happy for me?"

"Yeah. I'm glad for you."

I wanted to snuff her for taking my remote right before Sigourney asked Harrison if "big Jack" could come out to play. I snatched it back.

She dug her fingers in and grabbed a slice of my cheesecake, plopped down on my couch, and said, "You're glad? I'm glad. Shit, it's time to party. What? I invited some of my co-workers over. You don't mind, do you?"

I looked at her. My skin was getting hot.

"What the fuck are you watching?" she asked, twisting her face.

I rolled my eyes at her and turned the volume way up.

"Do you think I can have the apartment for me and my friends for just a few hours?"

"Are you asking me to leave my apartment?"

"Just for a few hours. I know how you are about people being loud."

This chick was looking dead at me, oblivious to my demeanor. She ignored my puffy, sad face, and watery, red eyes. Nothing had changed about her. She was still utterly selfish. At that moment, I completely understood everything about her, and wondered why it hadn't occurred to me before. She didn't have the ability to see past herself. She lived in her own world where no one else mattered, and she would probably be in that world forever. She was humbled for a minute when she thought her life was over. Now she was back to the Autumn I'd always known. I felt silly for even having the notion that she'd change. After the day I'd had, I didn't have the energy to be mad at her for being exactly who she's always been. It was as though a weight lifted off of me. I no longer felt any responsibility toward her.

I did have the energy, however, to get up, open the front door, go to my yellow room, and start taking her stuff and putting it out in the hallway.

On my third trip out the front door, she started to pay attention.

"What are you doing?"

I didn't answer. I just had to get her shit out of my house.

She jumped up and ran into the room as I was gathering as many of her clothes as possible in my arms.

"What the fuck are you doing?"

I didn't stop my stride. She ran up behind me as I dumped a bunch of her clothes in the hall and said, "When your friends get here, they can help you get the rest of your shit, because you are leaving my house today."

"Breezy—"

"You are leaving my house TODAY!" I yelled.

"You can't just kick me out!"

"It looks like I just did."

"But Breezy, please—I don't have anywhere to go!"

"I really don't care."

She followed me back and forth between the room and the hall.

I didn't know where the strength was coming from; I was moving boxes, her TV, her big-ass wooden chest—it all had to go

That was when I saw him. He was on her bed, peeking out from under her pillow. I had to blink several times to wrap my mind around what I was seeing, because he was just in my bedroom that morning.

I spoke slowly, because the words wouldn't come out quick, "What the fuck is Mandingo doing in your bed?"

"Who?"

I pointed at my glass vibrator—my *favorite,* glass vibrator. Then I screamed so rapidly that my tongue felt like it would pop. "Why the fuck is my vibrator in your fucking bed, you nasty bitch? Why the fuck would you use somebody else's vibrator? You filthy, nasty-ass, two-faced, fucking-everybody, caught-on-tape, lying, thieving-ass, hoe-ass bitch!

I hate your fucking ass! I hate you, Autumn! I fucking hate chew! Get the fuck outta my house! Get the fuck out! Get out, bitch, before I fucking kill you!" My voice was so high pitched it was incoherent, but she knew exactly what I was saying.

I was disgusted. I grabbed Mandingo and threw him at her, just missing her head. He crashed against the corner of the wall behind her. He didn't shatter like I wanted. He split in half, width wise, and fell against the carpet.

She ran. I grabbed the top half of Mandingo and ran after her screaming, "Get the fuck out!"

She ran out the front door and down the stairs. I chased her down the six flights. She managed to dodge me in the lobby and make it out into the foyer, then the courtyard, and down the block.

I chased her to the corner, then got in a pitcher's stance, pulled my left hand back, lifted my right leg, and threw Mandingo's head at her. He caught her in the back of her neck. She stumbled and grabbed her neck, but she kept running. It slammed against the concrete and broke into sad chunks of glass

"You gotta come back, bitch! Get your shit outta my fucking house!"

But she didn't come back. I moved all of her stuff out into the hallway, and she had some people come and get everything, probably the same friends that were supposed to be her company that evening. I didn't know, and I didn't care.

I threw the rest of the cheesecake out because I was mad that she'd touched it. It was okay, though, because I had another one: I always buy two.

I looked at my toy collection and wondered how many of my toys had she touched. I kept Mandingo and his brothers in a glass case so they were on display in my bedroom. I just loved the way they looked, so I didn't keep them in my toy chest with the rest of my goodies. The chest had a lock on it, and it was tricky, so I knew she hadn't gotten in there, because I would have been able to tell. But my glass babies! *How many of them had been tainted by her twat?*

I didn't want to throw them away, but I didn't want to use them anymore either. I filled my bathtub up with water and a half a cup of bleach and gently placed them in a row and let them soak for an hour or so, then washed them with disinfectant soap. Still, they didn't seem clean enough. I was going to have to throw them away and start over. I had no choice. I grabbed a trash bag and with tears in my eyes I dumped them. Just the thought of the possibility of them having been polluted by another woman's pussy was just too much to bear.

I was so disappointed in myself for losing my composure like that. I know I curse a lot, but I'd never cursed anyone out like that before. I was wearing sweatpants and a wife-beater, chasing her down the block with half of a glass dick. People must've thought we were lesbians having a fight. But fuck it. She deserved to be cursed at and kicked out. Just the thought of her touching my toys made my pussy feel all out of whack.

Before the night was over, I'd gotten calls from my cousin Sandy, who was quick to say, "You shouldn't have let that triflin' ass trick in your house in the first place," as if I really needed to hear that.

Autumn's mother, my auntie Babs, called, and apologized, until she was crying, and asked if I would please take her baby back in.

I wanted to say "You raised that evil troll, so you keep her," and slam the phone down. Instead, I politely told her, "I never want to see your daughter again."

My mother said, "You threw a dildo at her?" and laughed uncontrollably. I wonder who'd told her about my season's winning pitch? Auntie Babs of course. Why would I even question that?

I wanted to correct her, but what was I going to say? *"No, Mommy. It wasn't a dildo. It was a glass vibrator."*

I think that opened up a part of our relationship that I didn't necessarily want opened. I really didn't even want to know that my mother knew, the word "dildo," let alone to know that *she knew*, I had one. But it did thoroughly amuse me that she found it funny.

The rest of the calls were from Cindy and Gia still checking on me about being fired. I assured them I was okay, and was going to continue to be okay. I hate it when people feel sorry for me.

Autumn was gone, and it felt like a cloud had been lifted and the sun was shining brighter. The storm was over. I didn't even realize how bad I wanted her gone until she was actually gone. I opened all the windows and aired out the apartment. My apartment was happy too. I could feel it breathe a sigh of relief. I went to sleep with the windows open, feeling blissful.

* * *

That next morning, I jumped out of bed, because just for a second, I thought I was late for work. I laughed, and then got sad. I needed a source of income. More than that, I needed something to do to fill my mind up.

I pulled myself out of bed, and closed all the windows. I went into my yellow room and cleaned it from floor to ceiling. I took a shower, and went back to bed.

I got up around noon, made a grilled cheese sandwich, turned on the TV in the living room, and fell asleep on the couch.

I got up again around three, turned the TV off, dragged my feet to the bedroom, turned the TV on, and went to sleep.

At around five o'clock I started crying as it all started to hit me. I had no health insurance, so there could be no more getting sick for me unless it was in the next thirty days, before my policy expired. I felt pathetic and so disappointed in myself. I'd lost my job. They'd fired me because they didn't think I was worth it anymore. I was disappointed in myself more than anything. I'd gotten myself fired. I was the one calling in late and taking days off work. I did that, no one else.

The next few days were a malaise of masturbation, sleep, TV and cheesecake. Cheesecake is wonderful. *What evil genius created this?* I wondered, as I shoved a sweet, slightly tart, completely delicious, piece into my mouth. Who thought to do such a thing with cream cheese? To put together this fantastic symphony of flavors and textures. Who knew crushed-up graham crackers would make a perfect crust? It crumbles, yet it's solid enough to absorb the thickness of the rich and creamy cake. Each bite is like sinking my teeth into explicit joy.

I was stuck in my cheesecake-masturbation funk until I looked up and it was Friday. I hadn't showered, and I hadn't cleaned. There were batteries and graham cracker crumbs all over my bed and floor. A carton of soy milk was lying on my pillow, and a half-full glass of milk was just sitting haphazardly on my carpet, waiting for me to make the wrong move and knock it over.

I was falling fast into something. A rut? Definitely. Depression? Maybe. It was grabbing and pulling me down by my feet, pushing me down by my shoulders, zapping my energy, and making me feel lost. I didn't want to do anything. I didn't want to talk to or see anyone. I just wanted to evanesce into nothingness. I knew I had to get out of that sad place before it became something I couldn't get out of. I needed to move.

I blasted my iPod player. Kraak Smaaks's "Squeeze Me," always makes me feel good. I played it a few times. The first time I grooved in my bed. I swung my feet onto the floor, and started singing under my breath. On the second play, I got up, started singing loud, and began sinking into the feel of the song. By my third go-round, I was dancing around, singing into my pink brush handle, pointing at myself in the mirror like I was pointing out to an audience of people singing along with me.

I started cleaning up, jamming to Mary J Blige's "Just Fine."

The vacuum was going, and my body was in motion, feeling good. I was singing at the top of my lungs. I put all of my bed clothes, all of my underwear, and some jeans, in my shopping cart to take them to the laundry. I took a shower that felt too good to be real, with my speakers blasting UGF's "Never Gonna Lose." I chanted the chorus:

"I dedicate this to everybody that didn't believe,
you can say whatever you chose,
I ain't never gonna lose.
See me on the grind daily, busy paying my dues.
Try walking in my shoes,
I ain't never gonna lose.
So when your back's against the wall,
keep going, going.,
And when the water runs dry,
keep flowing, flowing.
And when the friends become foes,
and they turning up they nose,
no matter which way they go,
I ain't never gonna lose..."

Fuck Autumn, fuck Searly & Weiss, and fuck me for the times I didn't believe in myself. And fuck my ex and anyone else that didn't believe in me. I'm never gonna lose!

I walked to the Laundromat down the block, instead of hiding myself in the one inside of my building. I needed to get some fresh air, and I was feeling good. It's amazing what music can do.

It was about ten o'clock, and there were quite a few people in there already. I assumed the good machine would've been taken, but it wasn't. The day was starting out well. As I loaded my clothes, a guy walked in. I felt his presence before he even opened the door. I gave him a quick glance, acknowledged that he was fuckable, and kept on about my business. He used the machine next to mine. I had more laundry than he did, so when he was done loading his, I was still filling my second machine. He sat on his washer with a hardcover book. My clit twitched.

"I don't mean to interrupt," I said after I loaded my clothes and started my machines, "but what are you reading?" I asked loud enough for him to hear me over the whirr of the machines and the Spanish music playing from the radio where the washing attendant sat.

"*The Agony.*"

"By Ross Hua?"

"Yeah. You know this book?"

"Know it? I read it like once a year. I love that book."

"This is my second time. Dude is weird, but I get it. Maybe that makes me weird too, huh?"

Yeah, my kind of weird.

"Yeah, he is. I love the way he writes. It's like he's painting pictures with words, but that book isn't even in print anymore."

"I know. I've had mine since high school."

"Me too," I said.

I jumped up on one of my machines, the one farthest from him. I pulled out my iPod, put it on full blast, and started bobbing my head. The machine felt really, *really* good. I felt a tap on my shoulder. I turned, and pulled one ear bud out.

"What are you listening to?"

"Rakim."

"Say word?"

"Yeah. Does that surprise you?"

"Yeah."

"That's my dude."

He bent his eyebrows. "You must be older than I'm thinking."

"How old are you thinking?"

"Until you said Rakim, I was thinking like twenty-one, maybe twenty-two."

"I'm way older than that hon'."

"Word?" He studied me for a moment.

"How old do you think I am now?"

"Well, I'm thirty-four, but you can't be...," he looked into my eyes a little deeper, "I'm gonna guess twenty-nine. I'm not giving you more than thirty."

"Wow! You should see my mom. She looks like she's in her thirties."

"How old is she?"

"She's thirty years older than me."

"You're not going to give up the age, huh?"

"I'm thirty-three, if you must know."

"You know what they say."

"Black don't crack?"

"I wasn't going to say it like that, but yeah."

He held out his hand. "Sean."

I took his big, strong, warm hand. "Breezy."

"Really? What a name."

"We can't all be Kellys or Ambers."

"Nah, I like it. It has character."

"Thanks. You live out here?"

He shook his head. "Nope. Visiting my aunt. I come out here to check on her. She's got me down here doing her laundry."

"Where do you live? Wait... don't tell me; Brooklyn?"

"All day," he said with pride and smiled.

My heart stopped, and I lost my breath, for just a moment; he had that Don Cheadle, Samuel L. Jackson, Lawrence Fishburn, Ice Cube smile. *Impossible.* I regained my composure quickly and managed to say, "I swear I can't get away from you people!"

"We take over. That's what we do."

"Okay. I did not mean to venture into *Brooklynism*. You know, once you get you people talking about that freaking borough, you don't know how to stop."

"Do I detect some hate?" he asked, with another great smile that caused the vibration of the washing machine to become almost unbearable.

I had to get down because between his voice, that machine, and his smile, I was going to bust a very loud, public nut. "I went to high school with a lot of Brooklynites, and all day long, B-K this B-K that." I sucked my teeth.

He laughed. "I bet you've dated dudes from Brooklyn."

"Yeah. And?" I playfully rolled my eyes.

"I'm just sayin'."

"I'm sure you've dated girls from the Bronx."

"I've dated girls from every borough."

"Okay. So you know that chicks from the B-X are the shit! Don't play."

This time he smiled at me, as though he liked the way I smiled at him. He was flirting, and I liked it.

We talked until our machines stopped. He offered to help me load my dryer. I declined, because of my underwear.

He wanted to hit it. *Aww, how cute.* If only he'd known that from the moment I saw him, I wanted him to take it. He could've just walked up on me, pulled my pants down, and had his way with me. I would've protested and said something like, *"Why, good sir, I don't even know you. What type of girl do you think I am?"* While kicking my pants off to the side.

We talked and laughed, and it was just sweet and easy. Even though we were flirting, nothing about our conversation was sexual. So of course, I pictured him holding my legs up, making me say his name. One of my biggest turn-ons is when a man doesn't talk about sex. Some men are so busy fishing, trying to get a catch that they'll say just about any stupid, and/or, nasty thing to see who bites. I don't like thirsty men. Pumpkin Eater Peter was thirsty. I mean, that's cool for a jump-off, but not for someone you want to spend time with. But when men don't act thirsty, even though I know sex is on their minds, it's just so much more attractive.

"I really enjoy talking to you. You're smart and cute and different from the guys I'm used to running into. I would really like to get to know you better. That is, if you don't have a girl. " That was what I wanted to say. Instead, I asked, "Are you on Facebook?"

"Yeah."

"Cool. I'll send you a friend request, so be on the lookout." As soon as the words left my lips, I felt corny having said them.

"Alright," he said with that freaking smile, and then told me his last name was Lightfeather.

"You got Indian in your family?" I asked in my Sheh-nay-nay voice.

He laughed. "Nah. My great-great-great grandfather, Sir Williams, was a runaway slave, and he ended up living with this tribe, and the chief renamed him Sir Lightfeather."

"Really?"

"Yeah. Our families are still close. Like, when we have family reunions in Virginia, they're part of it. But no, there's no Indian in my family. Not that I know of."

"Wow! You're blessed to know that. I don't know anything about my family before my grandparents."

"That's on my father's side. I don't know about my mother's side."

"I don't know much about either side of mine."

"A lot of us don't because it can be so painful that a lot of families don't pass the stories down."

A chapel and a kiss, and three children that looked like us, flashed through my mind. It sent a chill through me.

I told him my last name, and he got a kick out of it.

* * *

I didn't have to send him a friend request, because he'd already sent one to me by the time I got home. *SWEET!*

"Hey Sean:) wassup?" I sent to his inbox.

He responded immediately, "Wassup, Breezy. u miss me already, huh? LOL"

"LOL gotta ? 4 u"

"shoot"

"y dnt u ask 4 my #?"

"wldv, but then u sed FB, so I fgrd u wrnt rdy 4 all tht..."

I wrote in long hand, "I didn't want to overstep any boundaries. You know, things are just so weird now. There's all these ways to communicate with people, and I just don't know where to start. I mean, I still like talking on the phone, but some people prefer to text or chat online, so you don't want to just start off talking with them because it can be weird. I don't know."

"You can call me anytime. Anytime you want to talk," he typed, followed by his phone number.

I giggled and twirled my hair with my fingers like a schoolgirl, and then I called him.

We talked the day away. When the call finally ended, I just couldn't get him off my mind. I was sitting in my living room smiling at nothing.

Then he called back, and we talked from a little after ten at night until a little after three in the morning. I still didn't want to get off the phone, but we had to. We were both slipping into slumber.

The conversation went from me saying, "When I saw the movie *Wanted*, I was like, what the fuck comic is this from?" to him saying, "Basquiat? Yeah, I love his work. Obviously art means different things to different people. What's art to me may be shit on the wall to someone else," I shared, "I like the unsalted kind. Salted peanuts make my mouth feel like my teeth are moving." And he adamantly asserted, "Are you crazy? Darth Vader is the best villain ever, hands down." I passionately argued, "I think we should just get rid of the whole monetary system and go back to the barter system," He said, "I'm just saying that if we could wrangle the ins and outs of quantum physics, we'd all be super human."

When he mentioned, quantum physics, I almost came on myself. That was near the end of our conversation and by that point I was so tired I couldn't even get one in before I went to sleep. Which was kind of a shame, since I was really turned on just by simple, random conversation and all the laughs we'd shared.

Chapter 15

Confession of a Good Time Gone Bad: One time I was giving myself the fondling of a lifetime. I was in my bed, under the covers, all warm and toasty. I was feeling super sexy, looking down at my body, thinking how lucky any man would be to have all this chocolate. Lucky, I say! My skin felt satiny smooth and good, and my pussy felt even better. My clit started tickling and itching, and my eyes rolled around in my head and crossed, as I exploded like Old Faithful. I closed my eyes in peaceful bliss, smiling—that is until I felt my eyes were not readjusting. I opened my eyes, and they were stuck! I started to panic. "Oh my Gahd! Oh my Gahd!" I started fanning my hands and blinking hard, trying to blink them back into position, but nothing was happening. So I jumped up, and ran around the house like a lunatic, tears streaming from my crossed eyes, blinking hard, stomping the floor, trying to shake them back into place, hitting myself in the back of the head, so that now I was cross eyed with a headache. I ran into the bathroom and looked in the mirror at two images of myself, started screaming, and slapping the sides of my face. I ran back into the bedroom, tripped, fell, hit my head on the floor, and they uncrossed.

Why I was up so early on Saturday is beyond me, but there I was with three hours of sleep, running up and down the stairs in my building with my strap-on butterfly vibrator. I figured since that stimulation made my working days better, it would certainly make working out better. I went down the six flights on one side and came back up on the other side. I did it three times, and that was my workout. I was exercising because, I was scared of getting out of shape. Not to mention diabetes, high blood pressure, and all the other health issues that go along with not being active. I had to keep my heart going. Things were changing in my body in my thirties, and I wanted to keep everything in place and working well. Granted, it was my first day, but you gotta start somewhere.

Charise was back home, so I stopped at her house on the fifth floor at the other end of the building.

"Wassup, chick?"

"What's going on?" she said, as she let me in the door.

"Just stopping by to holla atcha."

"You look, uh... different," she said, looking me up and down.

"Do I?"

I followed her into her beige carpeted living room. All the walls were beige except for one: A few years back, she'd asked me to paint a mural of her father, holding her when she was a baby. There was a caption that read, REST IN PEACE at the bottom, along with his birthdate and death date below it. The background was a hallway made of black angels and palm trees. I was surprised she wanted that because she's not one for angels. Even though we were ten when he passed, I cried while I painted as though it had just happened.

"Yeah. You look relaxed or something. What? Did you finally quit that job?"

"Well, *technically* they fired me, but I told them I quit before they had the chance."

"What?" she yelled. "Get the eff outta here!" She was working on not cursing; she actually had a swear jar.

"Yeah, man. I should look stressed. Maybe it's because I was exercising today." *Or maybe it's the butterfly between my legs.*

"Well, you don't look as tense as you did last time I saw you. And you weren't even going to tell me about your job, were you?"

"I just told you, didn't I?"

"Only because I asked. See, there you go with that pride. Remember how pissed off you got with me when I didn't tell you what was going on when went I through my shit?"

She never told me the full story, but about three years earlier, she was flat broke. Her boyfriend went to jail—which I was glad about, because he was not nearly worth her time, and I think he hit her—and she didn't know where she was going to live or even find her next meal. She didn't tell anyone what was happening. She didn't want anyone to help. When we (the Get-It Girl Crew) found out what happened, she was already on her road to recovery. I was so mad at her for not letting us help her. I guess now I know how she felt. I didn't want anyone's help either, which is so stupid. Pride is a bitch best kept on a short leash.

"Yeah, I was pissed 'cause I wanted to help."

"Exactly, but you don't want anybody to help you. You need to get over that. Don't let pride be your downfall. If you need anything, let me know. You know I got your back on anything, and you know I can get whatever you need done as far as the rent."

"I know. I'm good though. Speaking of which, how are things going with you and Kareem?" Kareem was the landlord and he was completely and utterly sprung over her, even though she hadn't so much as kissed him.

"He's still trying to get it. The more I don't give it to him, the more he wants it and the more he's willing to do for me. If it wasn't for his wives, I would give him some."

"His wives?" How many does he have?"

"Two right now."

"Right now? You trying to be number three?" I asked with a chuckle.

153

She chuckled too. "Shit, not at all. There's this young girl he's trying to get at too. He doesn't think I know, but I see him sniffing around her."

"Humph. You sound a little jealous."

"Maybe just a little," she said with a half-smile.

"Why? You don't want him."

"Yeah, but that doesn't mean I don't want him to want me."

We both giggled.

"You know you just cursed right?"

"When?"

"You just said 'shit'."

"Damn it! Oh shit! I just did it again."

I fell out laughing. "You've cursed like three or four times already

She sucked her teeth as she wrote out an IOU and put it in her swear jar. "Anyway, you want to see the pics I took in Venezuela?"

We went to her bedroom, and she showed me the pictures on one of her desktops. She has two and a laptop. This was her home studio, a dream she'd had since high school, live and in living color.

I turned to her and said, "I know I've never said this, because we don't talk to each other like this, but I just want you to know I'm really proud of you. Like really proud. I hope that doesn't sound condescending."

"Not at all, silly. Not coming from you."

I felt like hugging her, but neither of us were huggers. I did see her eyes mist up, and so did mine.

We chatted for a few, and then I headed back to my apartment. I was proud of her, no doubt, but I swear I felt like shit all over again. She was successfully living her dreams, the same as Justin. I felt like such a fucking loser. There I was, thirty-three, almost thirty-four, with no kids and no real prospects for a man to have kids with. I was sure I'd probably never get married, never have a real family. I wanted the dream: a house, a husband, and three or maybe four children. I had never thought I needed that before. I tried to fight it and deny it, but deep downsweet way that's what I wanted. And I wanted to love going to work every day.

I left her house, hit the pleasure button, and did one more run up and down the stairs.

My mind was going nonstop: *How long will I be able to have kids anyway? What am I going to do for money? I need to find a job. I'm thirsty. I need some water. Is it that I'm not worthy? What makes me so special that I should have what I want? What if I never amount to shit? I need to get a job. Gahd, how did I turn out to be such a fucking loser? Everything started out so well. It's me. I have a loser personality. What if my eggs dry up? I'm so thirsty. What if I die without ever having any kids? What if I die without ever showing my paintings? I'm so freaking thirsty!*

My breathing changed, and I was gasping for air. A pain hit my neck like I've never felt before. Then it got stiff. My clit started tickling. I couldn't turn my head left or right. Tears started falling from my eyes uncontrollably. My heart started beating hard and hurting. My clit started itching. I tried to sit down on the steps, but my body didn't want to. I didn't feel right standing either. My mind was so clogged, and tight. My pussy was throbbing. I just wanted to make it to my apartment. I held onto the wall. Everything was hazy with color. My nose was getting stopped up because of my crying. I got to my door, fumbled for my keys, and unlocked the door. I was gasping for the green air in front of me. My breath....

* * *

I woke up in a stark white room with an IV in my arm. I looked to my left, and saw hospital equipment, like the kind they always show in movies. I looked to my right and saw Justin. "What happened? Am I in a hospital? Am I in Killer Lincoln?"

"Complaining already? Yeah you're in Lincoln; it's the closest one to us. You passed out."

"I did?" It took a moment for it to come together. "Oh my Gahd! I did!"

"Calm down. The last thing you need to do is get upset."

"What happened?"

"Your blood pressure was too high."

That immediately made sense. I was pissed, running, and cumming. "Dude!" I yanked the bed sheet up to see my toy, but I only saw my gown. I hadn't worn any underwear that day, and I know I was funky because I'd busted nuts all over myself while I was running.

"Yeah, they took your little buddy," he said with a grin. "I know they see a lot of things, but I know they didn't expect to see that."

I covered my face with both of my hands and shook my head as I imagined medics all around, rushing me into the hospital. Taking my pulse, yelling things like, *"I need oxygen, STAT,"* with bright white lights all around, pushing my gurney through double-doors, and sliding me onto the hospital bed. And amongst all that mayhem, when they cut off my shirt and pulled down my pants, they found a pink, silicone, butterfly, still pulsating against my clit. They looked at each other. The nurse yells, *"No time for judgment,"* and they cut the straps off of me. *"Clear!"* someone yells, before they shocked me with a defibrillator. That's what I imagined anyway.

"Am I on drugs?" I asked as I tried to sit up but couldn't. Justin grabbed my arm to help me. My body apparently wasn't ready for quick movements. I felt like I was falling. "How did I get here?"

"I called 911."

"I thought you were leaving for Hong Kong today."

"I was, but when I came home to get ready, you were passed out in front of your door. I'm not going to even tell you what I thought happened. It looked like a horror movie. And you shat yourself."

"Oh my Gahd, no! Say I didn't!"

"Yeah. So you're lying there, all shitty, with your front door wide open. I felt your pulse and called 911." Justin huffed and shook his head. "Yo, I've never been that scared in my life. I don't have a next-of-kin, or anyone to call, no emergency contact. And with your smart ass, your phone is locked, so I couldn't get any numbers from it. I looked all over your house for a phone book. You have nothing! This freaking computer age. You don't have any paper in your apartment."

"Yes I do. It's just all locked up."

"I need an emergency contact for you."

"Okay."

"I'm serious! You don't know how crazy this was."

Just then, the nurse walked in. She had a beautiful spirit about her, and I immediately liked her. Her skin was dark like mine, and flawless, not a wrinkle or pimple in sight. And her smile was warm and earnest. I could tell she was older than me, but not by much.

"Feeling better I see. They want to keep you overnight for observation." She had a slight West Indian accent.

I looked at the IV in my arm. My eyes started tearing up. "But I don't want to stay overnight," I whined.

"Aww, sweetie, it'll be okay," she said, and then took my blood pressure. "You are back to normal it appears, but we still need to keep you here for observation."

"What was it when I came in?"

"You were 160 over 100."

"What's normal?"

"You want to be below 120 over 80. Right now, you're 115 over 75."

"So why can't I leave?"

"One, because you're medicated, and two, because we want to make sure you maintain before you leave."

I shook my head. "What exactly caused this?" I pretty much knew, but sometimes, you just need someone else to bring it home.

"You were, um, overly excited. You have to be careful about your, uh... activities and overexerting yourself." She was carefully choosing her words. "You can't do *too* many things at one time."

"No jerking off while running?"

"Yes. Exactly." She almost blushed. "Are you under a lot of stress?"

"I don't feel stressed. Maybe though. I did just lose my job—"

Justin gasped.

"Oh, yeah, Justin; I lost my job."

"I'm sorry to hear that," she said like she wanted to cry for me. "That's a very stressful situation. You don't think you feel it, but your body is telling on you. The running and the masturbation are both great stress relievers, but you should probably not do them at the same time."

She added, "Let today be the first day of the rest of your life."

That was random, I thought. But it fit her aura that she would say such a hopeful thing.

The nurse left, and Justin handed my phone to me so I could call my parents, but then I decided against it. I didn't want to upset them. If Justin wasn't already there, I wouldn't have told him I was in the hospital either.

Instead (of course), I went online to update my status. "What a day," was all I wrote. Then I smiled as I saw that Sean had posted Rakim's "Mahogany" on my wall. I was thrilled, cheesing big like he'd just handed me a gift.

He was calling as I was hitting the LIKE button.

"Hey, Sean. What's good?"

"Getting ready to go to the studio. Just wanted to hear your voice before I left."

"Is that right?" There was no way I was about to believe that.

"Yeah, that's right. Your voice is addictive."

"Really?" I looked at Justin and rolled my eyes and shook my head, thinking, *"Here's the bullshit."*

"Yeah. Are you alright?"

"Yeah. Why?"

"You sound a little... I don't know. Something."

"I'm in the hospital."

He gasped. "What? You alright? What's wrong?"

"I passed out. I'm good though."

"Are you supposed to be on your cell?"

"Probably not."

"What hospital are you in?"

"Lincoln."

"You need anything?"

"Nah, I'm good."

"Can you tell me what happened?"

"I was running, and my blood pressure got too high."

His breathing changed, and I could tell he was running himself. "Yo, ma, can I call you back? I gotta catch the train. I just got to the station."

"Okay." As I was saying "Bye," he'd already hung up.

"New boyfriend?" Justin asked.

"Nah. Just some dude I met at the Laundromat."

"The way your face lit up just now didn't seem like it's just *some dude*."

"My face did not light up," I denied, while the light of my giddiness illuminated from my pores. I changed the subject. "Did you happen to bring my bag?"

"Yup. I brought a change of clothes for you too." He handed my bag to me.

159

My bullet was safely tucked in its compartment. I figured I needed to calm it down with the self-pleasure for a little while, before the shit killed me. But my clit started tickling just at the sight of the bullet. I pulled it out and showed it to Justin.

He smiled and said, "Don't even think about it."

"*Trust*, I'm not going to." But feeling it in my hands made my pearl hard. That was when I realized I was wearing a diaper—a freaking diaper, for Heaven's sake! I started crying.

Justin rubbed my hair. "It'll be alright. We all get stressed. It's like the nurse said, you know? Let today be the first day…. Don't worry about yesterday. You can't change it anyway." He looked at his cell and said, "I gotta go catch my flight. I'm gonna call you on my layover in Cali to check on you."

I felt bad knowing he had to rearrange his flight plans because of me.

Where was this stress I was supposed to be feeling? I didn't feel stressed. I felt pissed. Mad at myself for being weak enough to pass out. Yeah, the official reason was jogging and masturbating, but losing my job was the real underlying cause for me fainting. I was sure of it. But I'd only lost my job. It wasn't the end of the world. I caused myself to lose my job. It was all my fault. I hadn't ever been fired—not ever! I was disappointed in myself. I'd failed. That loser feeling overcame me again, and I felt dizzy.

Sleep gripped me after that thought.

* * *

I'm not sure how much time passed, but when I woke up, I thought I was seeing things. *Surely that's not him, standing at the foot of my bed.*

"Sean?"

"I didn't want to wake you."

"Wh-what are you doing here?"

"I just wanted to come by and see how you're doing."

"I'm kind of in shock. You're the last person I expected to see here."

"I know we just met, but I had to come check on you and make sure you're really okay."

I smiled at him suspiciously. *What's his angle? He came all the way from Brooklyn, to the Bronx, to see me? Why?*

"Your smile is killing me," he said, causing me to blush. But things were about to get even more embarrassing. I sat up, and the bullet rolled over and exposed himself to Sean. I hadn't used it, but I'd fallen asleep before I could put it back in my bag.

"Is that... is that a—"

"It's for my wrist. I have Carpal Tunnel."

"Oh. Is that what they are calling it now?"

"What, man? Stop smiling at me," I said, trying to stop the chuckle from building in my throat. "It's serious. It's a syndrome, you know."

That really made him laugh. "Is that why you were asleep? Busted a good one, then busted a slob?"

"No!"

"I would be embarrassed, too, but feel no shame, 'cause I get down with the best of 'em."

"I bet I've got you beat."

"What? Not the kid!"

"How many times a day?"

"I'll say in a week, I do it at least twice a day, if I have time."

"You're lightweight, my dude."

"Really?" His eyebrows went all the way up. "Like how much do you do it?"

"I can't even believe I'm talking to you about this. At least five times a day—more now that I lost my job."

"You lost your job?"

Damn. I didn't mean to say that.

"Yeah. It's okay though."

"Is that why you passed out? Stressing about work?"

"I mean, I'll make it. It's no big deal."

"Yeah, that is a big deal. I lost my job a few months back. Turned out to be a blessing, because it forced me to get into my music full time. I'm telling you, if you have any talent, now is the time to explore it. Work on making your dreams come true."

I huffed. "Dreams don't pay the bills."

"When you make them real they do."

Something in the way he spoke to me, and the look in his eyes, made me feel like he was speaking the ultimate truth. Like it could really happen.

"I want to paint," I said, and I waited for judgment, but there was none.

"Like what kind of painting? What medium?"

I didn't expect that question.

"Mostly acrylic and watercolor. Sometimes oil. But there's so much more I want to learn."

"Are you any good?"

"Yeah, pretty good, I think."

"Maybe I can see your work sometime."

Simply hearing him suggest it made me nervous.

"Yeah, sure," I said, expecting that he never actually would.

"And maybe when you're better, you can come down and see me play."

From our conversation the night before, I'd learned that he could play pretty much any instrument, but his love was the guitar.

He stayed with me in the hospital until visiting time was over, again talking about everything under the sun. His brain made me want to touch myself.

* * *

I hadn't painted in about a year. For lack of inspiration, I suppose. I just hadn't felt like it. But when I got home from the hospital, I did some sketches, and got back into the groove of things. Then I picked up my brush and got to work. It felt so good that I wondered how I'd managed to go without it for so long. Why had I stopped doing something that felt so freaking good?

I found myself looking forward to talking to Sean. We didn't talk every day, not at first, but whenever we did talk, it went on for hours. Then we started calling each other saying things like, "Quick, turn to TV One," or, "Look at what I posted on your wall," until eventually, we *were* communicating every day. If we weren't talking, we were texting, or hitting each other up on Facebook. He let me know when he was about to do a show, and would text, or call me afterwards. He was always doing something. I was kind of jealous, because I wanted to be like that. But, my schedule was pretty much empty. There was nothing at all in my planner.

After being in the hospital, I just didn't want to waste any more time. What if I would've hit my head, and died, or become paralyzed, or something? Just existing wasn't enough. And kids were on my mind even more now. *What if I die without ever having any children?* Missing my childbearing window was something I knew I would never forgive myself for. I didn't know about the husband thing, but I was sure about children. Not immediately, but it was something huge that was steadily rising to the forefront of my mind, and another thing the hospital visit set off alarms about. I no longer felt the immortality I did in my twenties. My clock was loudly ticking, and time was passing. Fast.

Chapter 16

I'll be your Fender Stratocaster
play me as you please
pluck my strings
make a melody of me
slide your fingers across
my waiting body
until I emit pleasurable sounds
that unsettle and sooth
that haunt and woo
fill me completely
with your mystical voodoo
make me vibrate
like only you can
move every part of me
with a simple stroke of your hand
my caramel star
play me until I'm weak
lose control
and fully concede
giving every part of you,
every sweet note of me

I didn't tell Cindy and Gia about my little hospital overnight. Those two worried enough already. But I did decide to tell them about Sean.

I met up with the girls for lunch down the block from the job at *La Lingua's*, which was off of Broadway on 51st Street.

Cindy huffed, "He's a musician?" She started shaking her head and said, "Stay away from them. All they do is fuck everything that breathes. Then you become one of their conquests, or one of their jump-offs, and then when they get tired of you, they just fucking leave. And they do the shit in such a cool, sweet way that you damn near don't even realize he's breaking up with you until he just up and stops returning your calls.   And there you are, finally coming to the realization, crying over mint chocolate chip ice cream with almonds in it—"

"Cindy, come back, girl! That was six years ago," Gia said.

Cindy was rocking back and forth now, like a crazy person, locked up in a rubber room, strapped in a straitjacket.

I said, "Cindy, don't worry. That won't happen to me. I'd never eat mint chocolate chip ice cream—especially not with almonds in it."

"You make fun, but you mark my words; Musicians are demons! Fucking incubuses!"

"Isn't *incubi* the plural?" Gia asked.

"I think both are correct. You can say *incubuses* or *incubi*. It's like when you say—"

"Who the fuck cares?" Cindy yelled, "The point is, they sex the life out of you, and all you can do is crave them, like sugar."

"You can't just generalize like that. Every—"

"All of them!"

I shut up about it because I could see she was in a zone. I turned to Gia and said, "Anyway, I want you guys to come with me to see him play at Terry's Place, downtown."

"Down on Hudson?"

"Yeah."

"Wow. He must really be good. My brother's, best friend's, cousin, has been trying to get a gig there for over a year."

"I hope he's good, because if he's not, and he asks my opinion, I'm gonna tell him what I really think, whether he likes it or not."

"That's a sure way to run him off," Cindy said, rejoining us.

"Whatever. I'm tired of holding my tongue about people. No one holds their tongue about me, so it's whatever."

"I hear that," Gia started, "This chick the other day on the train says to me—like I asked her—'I'm feeling those shoes, but that bag is not cute.' I was like, 'Lemme give you the number to the spa I go to, because those tranny eyebrows are not cute.'"

"Okaaaaay!" Cindy said as we laughed.

* * *

That Friday, Terry's Place was standing room only. Wall-to-wall females vied for the attention of the men sprinkled throughout the crowd. But most of all, they, like me, wanted the attention of the men that would soon occupy the stage. I wondered how many women were there on his invitation.

The opening band was Shelly Keith, a five-woman rock band. They wore bright, neon green fitted T-shirts that read, "SHELLY KEITH ROCKS," in red comic book, superhero, style letters, and matching red cargo pants. Their hair was colorful: The bassist had an asymmetrical cut; the left was shaved and dyed florescent blue, while the right was long, pink, and swept over, so it hung straight down, covering the right half her face, until it hit her shoulder; The drummer wore two big afro-puffs: one green, one red. The lead guitarist donned a ten-inch red Mohawk with platinum buzzed sides; The keyboardist's hair was about an inch long all around, curly, and graduated from platinum to peach; The second guitarist sported a florescent red buzz cut.

Their shirts didn't lie; they tore it down! They did two songs. The first was a dark and twisted version of, "Mary Had a Little Lamb," in which Mary killed her lamb, because he wouldn't give her any space. They had the reluctant audience eventually chanting, "Die, lamb, die!" The second song was actually called, "Second Song," and it was about unrequited love. It sounded like the lamb's answer to Mary not wanting him around.

At the end of their set, they all walked to the front of the stage, bowed, and then turned their backs to the audience. The backs of their shirts showed their heritage. Then one of them yelled, "Sound off!"

The drummer turned around and yelled out, "Nigeria ROCKS!" with all the loud zest of an eighties rock star.

The crowd went crazy!

The lead guitarist yelled with the same fervor, "China ROCKS!"

The crowd continued their enthusiastic response.

The keyboardist yelled, "Puerto Rico ROCKS!" and threw up both of her hands with the international rock sign; index and pinky fingers up.

The crowd went wild.

Gia jumped up and stomped her feet, yelling back "That's right, baby! What? WOOOOOO!"

The bassist and the second guitarist both turned and yelled, enunciating each syllable, "Descendants of Africans enslaved in America ROCK!"

I jumped up and started cheering, because I felt that. That was for those of us who didn't have another country to claim. We had America, and we had the continent of Africa, but we had no idea what country in Africa—and it seemed they, nor anyone else, wanted to claim us anyway. That was for those of us whose ancestors were forced to come straight to America to build it, with no stops in the islands. We weren't West Indian, South American, or from any of the other places that black people represent throughout the world. That was for those of us whose families go back to the south: the Carolinas, Mississippi, Louisiana, Virginia, and so on. I love that they said that with pride, with no shame about who we are, or why we're here. Some people looked at them in disbelief, but I completely got it and apparently a lot of others did too, because people were whistling and cheering and shouting.

"We rock!" The second guitarist yelled out again. The group left the stage to a thunderous, standing ovation.

All I could think was, *Damn, I really hope Sean's band is good. Talk about a tough act to follow.*

The next band also did two songs. They were alright, but nothing like Shelly Keith. I can't even remember their name. They were five dudes that I think were just having an off night. They didn't seem to be in cohesion, and they all looked pissed, like maybe they'd had an argument just before going on stage. Their two songs dampened the crowd's mood.

There was a busy twenty-minute intermission. People grabbed drinks, ordered food, went to the restroom, and bought the band's paraphernalia from a concession table with a banner that read, BAND SHYT. Shelly Keith and the other band were there signing autographs and taking pictures. I just had to buy one of their T-shirts. That *shyt* was twenty-five dollars! I took a group picture with the members. We all stuck our tongues out, and held up the rock sign, and they all autographed the T-shirt. It was turning out to be another great night.

When I got back to my seat, the light on the stage was just bright enough to see the faces of the band. Sean stood, left of center, tuning up his guitar.

"Is that him?" Cindy asked.

"Yup. That's him."

"He *is* sexy," Gia said, in a way that I didn't appreciate.

"Act married," I said.

"I can still look."

"Well, look your ass somewhere else."

She hissed at me like a cat. "You got your claws out tonight, huh?"

"She'd better. You see all these bitches in here? How many of them wanna fuck her man?"

"He's not my man. As a matter of fact, I don't even really know him."

"Oh, so it's okay if I try to holla at him then, right?" Cindy said.

"I didn't say all that."

They both laughed at me.

Sean walked to the center of the stage. Some chick shouted, "Yeah, baby!" He smiled, not necessarily at her, but at the crowd. His smile was hypnotic. His whole face changed when he smiled, and it wooed the audience.

I caught myself moaning.

"Is everyone good tonight?" His voice was deep and smooth.

The audience responded happily. *Bunch of bitches in heat.* He played a little chord, and these bitches lost their minds. Even Gia and Cindy started screaming at the stage.

I looked at Cindy, who looked back at me, raising her eyebrows, and shrugging her shoulders, as if she had no idea why I was looking at her.

"Uh huh, I see you Cindy."

"Whaaat? It seems like it's gonna be a good show," she said flashing an innocent smile.

Sean introduced the band. They were average, good-looking men, but as they played, they became glorious, sexual gods, plucking the strings, beating the drums, and playing the keys to every woman in the audience. They had those women moving like the notes were caressing their skin, and about to make sweet love to them.

And Sean? Ooh wee! He played like the guitar was connected to every organ in his body. His face looked pained, and ecstatic; tortured, and orgasmic. There was so much emotion moving between him and his instrument that I wondered who was playing who. He raised his eyebrows and bit his bottom lip, like the music he created felt good, like sex, to him. *Damn*! His saccharine notes surged from his guitar, and tickled my clit. But still, it was deeper than that. He was speaking to me—to my very soul. I was lost in him.

Then he started singing.

"I'm about to come up out my panties!" Gia yelled. Cindy was hollering like the rest of the bitches in the audience. These two acted like they couldn't control themselves.

His voice was like butter. His range put me in the mind of Maxwell with the cadence of Lenny Kravitz. I couldn't believe that voice was coming from him—the guy I met at the Laundromat. My panties were soaked. His voice made me tingle all over. I squeezed my thighs together, struggling not to explode.

And then it was over.

Well, it wasn't over, but I was done! I jumped out of my seat, and ran to the bathroom to get that nut out. I had to hurry up, because I wanted to hear the rest of their songs. I didn't want to sit on the toilet, so I grabbed a bunch of paper towels before I went into the stall. I pulled my pants down, pulled my bullet out, and had an eye-rolling good time in less than two minutes. When I felt my climax cresting, I shoved the paper towels between my legs to catch my stream. I let out a loud "Uhhhhhh!" Then had the nerve to hope no one heard me. I got myself together and went back to my seat.

"You alright Breezy? Stomach okay?" Cindy asked in her comical way.

"Yeah."

"You look all flustered and shit."

"I'm fine."

The audience knew the words to their songs. They shouted at the stage, chanting the lyrics line for line. I'd never personally known anyone that had people respond to them like that. I was in awe.

They did six more songs, and each one got a crazy applause. After the last song, when the long, hungry, standing ovation was over, they walked to the BAND SHYT table. These bitches went wild! Those that were still sitting, jumped up from their seats, and rushed over to stand in line. I watched as women walked away with stickers, CDs, DVDs, T-shirts, and hats. Some were fanning themselves, and biting their bottom lips. Their reactions were way more than I expected.

Gia, and Cindy went over there, but I refused to groupie out. That was what it felt like I'd be doing if I flocked over there with the rest of those chicks, like I was hoping I'd be picked as that evening's treat. I sipped my soda and thought; *I could never be with him. I couldn't deal with all of the females. Somebody might die!*

After about twenty or so minutes, Gia and Cindy hadn't returned and I was almost ready to go. Then someone tapped my shoulder and said, "Excuse me, Miss., can I buy you a drink?"

I looked up at him, and smiled.

"Why didn't you come over to the table?" Sean asked.

"A little too much activity going on over there."

"So can I?"

"What?"

"Buy you a drink? What are you drinking?"

"7-Up."

He sat down and waved for a waitress. She completely ignored me and cheesed so hard at him I thought her cheeks would burst.

"Two 7-Ups, and two sliced limes and lemons."

Then two females came up to us—or rather, to *him*—like they hadn't had enough of him over at the table. "Excuse me. Can I have your autograph please?" one asked, Sharpie in hand, leaning over indicating that she wanted it on her breast.

He said, "How about I sign your arm?"

She pouted, then looked at me like I'd just materialized out of the thin air, rolled her eyes, then held out her arm. He signed both of their arms.

"You didn't have to do that for me. You could've signed their tits. I wouldn't have minded." I lied with a smile. That's how I wanted to feel, and how I was trying to make myself feel.

"I would never disrespect you like that."

"If I wasn't here would you do it?"

"Yeah, I would. But I wouldn't do that in front of you."

I wanted an honest answer, and there it was. But it wasn't like I was going to marry this guy or anything, so whatever.

"If you were married to someone would you do it?"

"Nope. That's a whole different ball game. I wouldn't do anything to disrupt the sanctity of my marriage."

Damn, that was some kind of answer. He seemed passionate about that too. Humph.

The waitress came back with the drinks. As he squirted the lime and lemon into his soda, more women came up to the table, asking for pictures and autographs. There were at least twenty, and I was invisible to each.

After what felt like forever but was actually not even ten minutes, he said, "Alright, ladies, thank you for all the love, but I'm in the middle of entertaining a very special lady, so…." He clapped his hands once, for emphasis.

They groaned, sucked their teeth—at me—and dispersed.

"So, you're kind of a big deal, huh?"

"It's not real."

"Well, it's happening. Right now, I'm seeing it."

"Yeah, but here's the thing—if I wasn't on that stage, how many females would just come up and throw themselves at me?"

"Is that why I tickle your fancy? Because you met me at the Laundromat?"

"Tickle my fancy?" He laughed, then said, "I think, that if I'd never met you, and I saw you here tonight among all these women, I would still want to get to know you."

I blushed. *He's good.*

Cindy, and Gia, finally came back to the table, *cheesing* at me like we were in high school, and I was sitting at the lunch table with the cutest boy in our class.

"Excuse us," Cindy started, "but we are about to leave, sweetie. Are you coming with us?" She blinked her eyes rapidly, with a grin.

"Yeah, missy, you leaving with us?" Gia asked with her eyebrows raised, and a slick smile.

"I'll make sure she gets home safely," Sean said.

How presumptuous! Like he just knew I wanted to stay there with him.

"If you don't mind keeping me company for a little while longer?"

"I don't mind," I said.

Gia cleared her throat.

"Oh, I'm sorry, Sean. These are my friends, Cindy and Gia."

They shook hands.

"Your band is great. I mean, I'm not even into rock music, but I bought your CD," Gia said, still shaking his hand. I cleared my throat to give her a clue. She smiled at me, and rolled her eyes. "Anyway, you guys enjoy the rest of your night."

"I'm sure we will," he said to her.

They giggled.

As they were turning to leave, Cindy said, "Call me when you get home, no matter what time, okay?"

"Yes, *mother*," I said.

He squirted some more fruit juice into his drink, and said, "You should try it."

So I did. "It really enhances the flavor," I said and immediately felt corny for saying it.

He chuckled. "You sound like a commercial."

"I know, right? Not everyone is so gifted to be as cheesy as I am."

"I can appreciate your *cheeseocity*." He had this way of looking at me that made me want to look away, but wouldn't allow me to.

"So how many women are here on your invitation?"

"Honestly?"

"Nah. Lie to me."

"Every woman in here, damn near."

I raised my eyebrows.

"You said lie to you."

I relaxed my eyebrows, and smiled. "Funny."

"I don't usually invite women to see me play. They just come."

"Well, play on, player."

"Nah, Breezy. I'm not a player. I don't play games with women."

"Is that right?"

"Yeah. Playing with people is dangerous."

"So you're a reformed player?"

"I wouldn't say reformed. I'll say I outgrew it. That lifestyle got old quick for me, especially with all the wild mess I've seen happen behind it."

"Like what?"

"I've been with a few bands, and it's like the same thing over, and over again—dudes trying to handle wifey, and the jump-offs, you know? Cuz they want all the women, just because they're there. Next thing you know, there's busted car windows, baby mama drama, people trying to kill themselves, dudes fighting over the same girl, women fighting over the same man, lawsuits, money lost. It's just not good business to play games with people."

"Do you have any baby mama drama?"

"Not at all. All my babies' mothers' know how to act."

"Oh."

"I'm messing with you. I don't have any kids. What about you? Any baby daddy drama?"

"No, sir. No kids."

"Wow. You made it to thirty-three with no kids? You're rare."

"There're a few of us out there—quite a few. You're the rare one."

"Yeah. All my friends have kids. Most of 'em aren't with the mothers. I'm not trying to be like that."

"Me neither," I agreed, even though I'd already anticipated that's what would happen in my lifetime.

He gave me a look that I couldn't read, so instead of guessing, and assuming, I asked softly, "What's that look?"

"Nah, it's just... I can't believe you're single. That some guy hasn't snatched all of that up yet.

I blushed. And I too, couldn't believe, I was single.

"You wanna go out, like, you know, hang out, sometime this week?"

"Oh, uh," I said, trying to think for a moment. I didn't want to seem too eager. "Yeah, we can do that," my mouth volunteered, while my mind was still trying to think.

"You free Friday?"

"I believe so."

"Alright then. Cool."

We sat, talking, and laughing for an eternity. Each second was heavy. He was so funny, and smart. We had the same views about most topics we discussed, and there was no uneasy tension on the rare occasions when we did disagree.

I didn't even know how much time had passed until I looked up, and saw the staff putting chairs up on tables, and sweeping up, as the last of the patrons were leaving.

"Looks like it's time to go."

"I'll take you home."

"That's alright."

"I'm not gonna let you get on the train, or even get a cab by yourself at three in the morning."

"I'm a big girl. I'm sure I can manage."

"Yeah, but I'd be too worried. For my own peace of mind, let me take you home."

"That's okay."

"Oh, I get it. You just don't want me to know where you live."

I laughed. "No comment."

"I understand. I find out where you live, and BOOM! You've got a stalker."

I laughed. "You want to ride the train with me?"

"That, or I can drive you home."

"Okay."

"Lemme go pack up my equipment, and I'll be right back. Don't go anywhere."

"I won't."

Minutes later, three women dressed in the tightest, skimpiest dresses, with the biggest, fake titties I'd ever seen in real life, came up to me.

"So..." the one with the biggest titties, started as she looked me up and down, "what are you? Like, his chick?"

I wasn't in the mood for any drama, and I had little patience. This chick was about to get knocked out—not for Sean, by any means, but because she was being disrespectful to me, and she needed to be silenced. I decided to silence her another way. "No, I'm his wife. And you are?"

"His wife?" She snapped her head back.

"Yes. We got married yesterday. Happened so suddenly, we didn't even have time to get rings."

"Yesterday?" The one with the smallest of the implants said.

"Yeah, yesterday, like she said." Sean came up behind me, startling me. He caressed my right cheek and said, "Best decision I ever made." Then he leaned over, and kissed me. His lips sent electricity through me. He pulled back, and looked at me, like the kiss shocked him too.

"Married?" Biggest Titties said, more to herself, like she was trying to process the information. Disappointment covered her face, followed by resolve. "Well, congratulations," she said, and they walked away.

"What made you say that to her?" he asked, not hiding his amusement.

"I don't know. Kicks. What made you go along?"

"It sounded good."

This guy was something else. I wanted to tell him he didn't have to say things like that to try to hit it. All he had to do was be real with me. But I had to admit, it did have a nice ring to it.

As we got going, I asked, "So, are those your former conquests?"

"Nah. You know I do have at least *some* standards for myself. No fake tatas."

That made me laugh, but I didn't know if I believed him.

Then he said, "The one in the black..."

"Mega Tits?"

He chuckled and nodded. "She's been trying to get at me for a little over a year now. She's been following us around the city. I went backstage one night, and she followed me back there on some super-groupie tip and thought I was gonna fall for it. I turned her down. It wasn't that I didn't think about tappin' that—who wouldn't? But, just her whole approach bothered the shit outta me. I could already foresee all the drama that would go along with that, and I don't like drama."

I liked his answer.

"And you know what?"

"What?"

"I was right. She smashed our former drummer, and he said she was on her back, in the bathroom with her legs up in the air, trying to push the sperm into herself from the condom."

"Whaaat?"

"Yeah. It's like that. She ran through the band but kept trying to get at me."

"She probably thought she was going to make you jealous by smashing everyone in the band. Like, in her head, they were going to tell you how good her *na na* was, so you'd be like, 'Damn, I need to hit that.'"

"Maybe. That's what I'm saying though. Drama. I don't need that."

He took me home in his silver Altima. I'd tell you the year if I knew, but I don't know anything about cars, and I wasn't going to ask him. If it hadn't said, ALTIMA on it, I wouldn't have even known that much. It was nice, very clean, and smelled like cherries from the scent charm hanging from the mirror.

We pulled up in front of my building. I must've had a good vibe from him, because I rarely let men know where I live. Pumpkin Eater Peter was the exception, because he was thrust upon me by circumstance, but normally, it's a no-no.

"So I'll see you Friday then?"

"Yeah."

"You're not gonna stand me up, are you?"

"Now why would I do that?"

"You know how you beautiful women are."

I worked hard to hide my blush. "That was a good one. "

"A good what?"

"C'mon, dude. You know exactly what to say to make a woman blush. You practice those lines?"

"So you don't think you're beautiful?"

"That's not what I mean."

"So you don't think *I* think you're beautiful?"

"No. That's not what I'm saying."

"Well, it's some kind of insecurity that you must have if you think I'm running lines on you when I'm giving you compliments."

"So you're a psychologist now?"

"No, but you remind me of how I used to be. When people told me how good my music was, and how well I played, I thought they were blowing smoke up my ass, because I wasn't so secure about my skills. But now when they tell me, I just thank them, because I know they're right. So when you really believe you're beautiful or that other people think you're beautiful, you'll just thank them."

"Number one, I know I'm beautiful," I lied. I mean I felt good about myself, but beautiful? "I'm actually kind of stuck on myself right now. Number two; I know when a dude is feeding me lines because he's trying to get some. And you just sit there for a few seconds while I think about number three."

"Breezy," I loved the way he said my name, "I don't mean to sound like an overconfident prick, but you saw what was going on back at the club. I don't have to really say anything. If I just wanted to get some, I can just get some."

"Which leads me to number three, I know when a guy likes a chase, and you, my friend, are a hunter."

"You're just gonna make sure you're right, huh? Alright, you got it. I know better than to go back and forth with a woman who has it in her head to win. You win this battle, but I'm gonna win the war," he said with a juicy-lipped smile that was worthy of a thousand kisses.

"And what war is that?"

"You'll know when I win."

I wanted him to take my left leg, and throw it over his shoulder, and grab my ass like he was pulling me apart, and ram me with everything he had.

* * *

I called Cindy when I got home. Instead of saying *"Hello,"* she asked, "Did you beat?" in her sleepy voice.

"No."

"Good, 'cause that's what they want. They'll fuck you, get you hooked on that good musician dick, and then—"

"Oh, look at the time."

"Alright. I'm just trying to warn you."

I had sweet, sweet dreams about that good musician dick, whether Cindy liked it or not.

Chapter 17

That kiss had color
That kiss was rain
It was soaked with honey
And lip licking faith
As simple as spun sugar
With a Tequila twist
Sopped in cocoa magic
A plush resplendent kiss

We are sitting on my fire escape, just chilling, talking to each other, and laughing. The sun is super bright, but it isn't hot. The phone starts ringing. We both answer our phones, but the phone just keeps ringing. Then he starts fading away.

It was the second day in a row I'd dreamt about Sean. I woke up pissed. *Who the shit is calling me at 6:28 in the morning?* I let it go to voicemail, and tried to get back into my beautiful dream, but I couldn't. That rarely worked for me—trying to get back into a dream. The few times it did work, the dream would get all changed around, and *weirded* out, so it wasn't even really worth it.

I got up, and looked at the phone to see who'd called. It was Sean. I didn't bother to listen to the message. I just called him back.

"Hey, I'm sorry for calling you so early," he said. "I wanted to ask if we could change our date. I'm leaving for Europe today."

"Europe?"

"Yeah. I just found out about an hour ago. We're filling in on a tour that's already going on, because one of the bands pulled out. I'll be leaving at eleven thirty tonight. I want to see you before I leave if possible."

"How long will you be gone?"

"About a month."

"A month? Wow, just like that, huh?"

"Yeah. It's like that sometimes."

"Okay. We can go out today."

"I can take you out to breakfast, or brunch."

"Okay.

"Is nine okay?"

"Yeah."

I jumped up out of my bed and stretched hard and good—one of those bounce-on-your-tippy-toes stretches, that comes with a superb yawn. I hopped in the shower. My ducky was already staring at me. I was still a little spooked about masturbating. I'd only done it once since the hospital, but I figured I'd better, because I didn't want to *accidently* have to fuck Sean. Those, *accidental have-tos,* will get you every time.

I turned Duck on, and his buzz caused my lips to part. I rubbed him over my clit. I slapped the shower wall; it felt so good, especially with the water running over my soapy body. I wished someone could see me because I knew I looked good at that moment—until I came. When I came, it was ugly.

As soon as I stepped out of the shower, the phone rang. "Hello?" I sang.

"Hey, it's Sean. Can I send a cab for you? I'm having some car trouble."

"That's alright. We can just meet up on the train."

"No, I'll send a cab."

"Nah, I like riding the train—especially when it's not on my way to work." The train kept my imagination going. If

I could sit on the train, and paint, I would. *Who says I can't? Maybe I should.* "I'll meet you at Third Avenue station."

"If that's what the lady wants."

The way I figured it, he was trying to get some before he left, and as weak as I was for him, I was determined not to give him any. I wasn't going to be one of his conquests.

However, when I saw him, I wanted to fuck him—not make love, but FUCK him. You ever look at a man, and just want to bend over, like on some real animalistic level? The feeling hit me so severely that my body blushed, and goose pimples swarmed all over me for a few moments then disappeared. He wore a zip-down black hoodie over a black and white Jimi Hendrix T-shirt, blue jeans, and black and white Adidas. That was just my style. He smelled so good when we hugged that I wanted to bite him. His breath smelled like Juicy Fruit. His bald head was shining; I wanted to bite that too. His beard was cut low, and met his goatee, encircling his juicy lips, and I wanted nothing more than to feel them all over me.

"You're beautiful, ma."

I blushed. "Thank you. You look good yourself. Loving the shirt."

He smiled. "Thanks."

"You smell good too," I added.

"Thank you. You too. Really good."

Escada's Sexy Graffiti never fails.

He tried to pay my fare, but I swiped my Metrocard before he had the chance. I didn't want him to think I wanted anything monetary from him.

We rocked on the train, standing face to face, only a few inches away from each other, holding one of the poles for balance. It was Monday, and we'd caught the tail end of the rush-hour traffic. I loved being on the train while everyone else was rushing to work, knowing that I was just going to enjoy the day. Money wasn't on my mind. Not having a job didn't bother me right then. I was genuinely happy standing there, enjoying the minutes of my life.

"I'm not a stalker, just so you know," he said just loud enough for me to hear over the chugging of the train.

"Like you would really tell me if you were," I said, playfully rolling my eyes.

"You could've caught a cab, and I would've paid for it."

"That's okay. I really don't like people paying for things for me."

"Oh, so you're one of *those*?"

"One of those what?"

"*I don't need nobody to do anything for me*," he said, mocking a female voice, rolling his head, and waving his right index finger.

I laughed. "I don't."

"You know, sometimes people just like to do nice things for people, because it makes them feel good to do it."

"So it would've made you feel good to have sent a cab for me?"

"Yes, just like it's going to make me feel good to buy you brunch."

"I don't want you to think I want anything from you, like I'm trying to use you for anything.

"You see, right now, I wish we knew each other better."

"Why is that?"

"So I could kiss the mess outta you."

My *lub dub* sped up. I thought about the electricity of that first kiss—and that was just a tap. I could just imagine what him kissing the *mess* out of me would feel like. I had to fight the urge to tell him to go ahead and do it.

He cocked his head, like he was trying to figure me out, and then straightened it back up, as if he'd answered his own inquiry. He kept looking at me as we rode. I know, because I kept looking at him.

He went for my hand in a protective way when we got off at our stop, and guided me off the train. Then he maneuvered me in front of him, as we took the stairs. I know part of that was to watch my butt bounce up the steps, but part of it was pure gentleman. He walked me on the inside of him in the street and opened all doors for me. He did it all so effortlessly, but I didn't trust his chivalry.

We ate at Wild Child, a raw food restaurant. He told me he thought I'd like it since I blasted myself on Facebook when I declared, after watching *Supersize Me* and *Food, Inc.*, online, "I WILL NEVER EAT FAST FOOD AGAIN!!!!"

It was still officially breakfast time, but we ate from their brunch menu. When we left he asked, nervously, "You want to go to the Museum of Natural History?"

I answered him with wide eyes, "Yeah. I would love to! That's my favorite museum." I couldn't believe that was where he wanted to go. He was pushing too many of the right buttons. I'd fantasized about having a boyfriend that I could go to a museum with. One that actually wanted to go, not just because I wanted to. I wondered where else he wanted to go.

We walked around the museum for a little over two hours, and only cut it short because we didn't have much time to spend together. With each exhibit I fell a little deeper in like with him. He was so intelligent, and so willing to learn. I'd never met a man who could arouse me both mentally, and physically. It had been either one or the other.

At around one o'clock we left. He tried to feed me again, but I wasn't hungry; he had my stomach tied up. So he got a pretzel with mustard, at a frank stand, and I got an apple juice.

We went to the Great Lawn, and sat in the grass talking while people played Frisbee, catch, tag, and flew kites. No matter what day of the week there was always activity there. The sun was bright, almost as bright as in my dream, and the weather was just as perfect.

He insisted I sit on his hoodie.

"I love Central Park," I said.

"Me too."

Like a kid, he picked up a few pebbles, and started throwing them, making them skip on the grass.

"So what is it you want to do when you grow up?" I found myself truly wanting to know.

"I'm already doing what I want to do, but I don't know sometimes. I love the traveling, but I might be ready for a little more stability, you know? Flying out of the country all the time, living on the road, the hotels, and all the drama... it's just really tiring."

"Don't forget the women."

He smiled. "Yeah, the women, but you know, after a while that gets tiring too. I mean, there's no love out there. A bunch of sex, which is cool, but it's not enough. At some point we all need something that makes us full. You know what I'm saying? Like eating some microwaved popcorn, versus, taking the time to prepare, and cook a full meal. I want the meal."

I pretended not to see the look of intent he gave me.

"So what would you do if you didn't tour?"

"Produce. I just want to make music—all kinds of music."

"You already do that. So what's the hold-up?"

"It's me. But I'm working on it. I don't like telling people about the moves I'm making. I got a lot of people telling me I can't."

"You say you can, though, right? That's all that matters."

He took a breath and said, "What I want to do is buy a building—nothing too big, just a few stories—and live on the top two floors, have a studio on one floor, and some kind of store or club or something on the first floor. I'd have some tenants too."

"That sounds doable. People do things like that all the time. So make it happen."

He smiled at me and said, "I'm actually going to miss you when I'm gone, I think."

"I'll miss you too. *I think.*"

He threw a few blades of grass at me. They fell short and landed between us. I ripped some blades, and tossed them at him. They landed on his head. We laughed as he wiped them off. I leaned over to pick a blade from his beard.

"So you like to play, huh?" he asked, and threw a handful of grass directly on my head, then jumped up, and ran.

I took off after him, chasing him around in a circle and side to side. He dodged me, stopping short, causing me to run past him. Then he leaned back too far for me to reach him, like Neo in *The Matrix*, and ran again. I stopped chasing and bent over, holding my knees, catching my breath.

"You had enough?" he asked, laughing.

"No!" I yelled and rushed him, knocking him down. Rather, he let himself fall, and I landed on top of him. Our noses touched. *"Kiss me,"* I wanted to scream. Instead I just smiled, dreamy-eyed, and he returned the look.

I rolled off of him, and we sat up. I felt electricity streaming between us. It was sexual, but there was a little more to it. It felt like I'd sat with him, at that very spot, staring at him the same way, sometime before.

We were silent for a few minutes. I looked around at the people. There were a few couples. One of them was making out, heavily. We stared at them, then looked at each other, and blushed at our own tension.

"You ever get déjà vu?" he asked.

I squinted my eyes. *No way.* "Yeah."

"I don't want you to think I'm feeding you a line, but this whole day—the way we're *vibing*—it just feels... I don't know... very familiar."

"I see."

"Uh oh. What's that look you're giving me? You think I'm full of shit? I'm not."

"Nah. It's just that I was thinking the same thing."

More silence.

"You're different from most of the women I've dealt with."

"Well, you know, I am one of a kind," I joked. Then I thought for a moment, and asked, "What type of women do you usually deal with?"

"Not like you. I don't know many women who can chill like we are right now. They don't enjoy simple things. Everything has to be big. They wanna live like a video, you know what I'm saying? Like, popping bottles every day. They think because of the business I'm in that every night is supposed to be a party. That's cool sometimes, but not every moment of every day, you know?"

I nodded.

"They weren't very smart either. But honestly, that's my fault, because I wasn't necessarily in it for smarts. A lot of them were looking to come up some kind of way, like they want a man to take care of them. Not that I'm opposed to taking care of my woman, but it'll take more than sex to get me to do that. Then I meet you, and, I mean, you are holding it down, ma. You have a good head on your shoulders."

"I'm glad you think so."

"I'm sure you're crazy in there somewhere, but your base is good. I mean, the fact that you are even able to sit here with me like this puts you in a whole different category. The way we were just running around? I can't even remember the last time I played like that. You're not afraid that having fun will take your cuteness away. I like that. I just don't wanna mess anything up."

"Like how do you mean?"

"At this stage in my life I know the difference between a fuck-buddy, and a real friend. I want us to have a strong friendship, because you're cool, and I don't want you to go anywhere."

"Oh." *I knew it was too good to be true. He just wants to be friends. I've never had that happen before. I give the let's-be-friends speech. Who does he think he is? So what, the more time he spends with me, the more he realizes he just wants to be friends? Well, he can keep that. This is our first date, so why do I even care? Like he's all that.*

"I've been with a few women and had a few relationships, but they didn't have any substance. It's like you meet somebody, the sex is good, so you start calling them your girl, but then there's no real bond after that. I don't want that with you. When I tell you I've never talked on the phone with anyone like I do with you, I'm serious. I don't like being on the phone, but I'm on the phone with you for hours." He looked deeper into my eyes and asked, "How do you feel about the situation?"

I couldn't believe he asked me how I felt. He was too good. "Like you have a lot of game."

"There's no game here."

"The things you're saying are too perfect. This is just our first date."

"How long should I take?"

"I don't know."

"When I first saw a guitar I had to touch it. When I touched it, I had to learn how to play it. I love that instrument. I just knew from the first moment I saw it that it would be mine, and I had to learn everything about it. There was no waiting. It was like that with every instrument I play."

"Sounds like you've fallen in love with a lot of instruments."

"I have. I love music."

"Is this your way of telling me you want me to be your main instrument while you still play other instruments?"

"Humph. I was trying to tell you that when I see something I want, I don't see the point in waiting."

"I'm sorry. Did I mess up the moment?" I asked, smiling.

"Yeah, you kind of did. I was trying to get my poetic on with you, and you just made it cheap and dirty." He folded his arms, faking an attitude.

"Awww," I said and laughed.

He looked at me with a seriousness that would've been frightening if it wasn't so sweet, and said, "You're not any one instrument. You're the music."

I was stuck for a moment. Then I said, "That was a good comeback."

"Yeah, I like that one. But understand—I'm serious when I say it."

"Okay."

"My life is kind of crazy. I don't know. Sometimes I feel like time is running out."

"Like you're gonna die?"

"Not necessarily. It's more about getting my life on track and making all the big moves I need to make. I wanna make music forever, but I don't want to *have to* do it, you know? I want to be in a position where money isn't a worry for me—where I'm good—and I wanna be young enough to enjoy it."

"You want the time to enjoy the fruits of your success."

"Exactly, but time is flying by quickly. Time is running out."

I felt him on about twenty different levels. I was feeling like my time was running out, too. Like whatever path I was going to take I needed to get on it now. There was no more time to waste. I needed to seize whatever available opportunities were out there, and turn nothing into something, and a little into a lot.

"I wanna be honest with you about something else."

"Okay," I said, preparing myself for the worst.

"I've had a hard time being faithful in the past."

"Me too."

"You have?" He raised his eyebrows.

"I've had three official *real* relationships, and I cheated on all of them."

"Word?"

"Yeah. The first two I cheated because I was just too young to be committed."

"That's understandable," he said.

"The last was because I was just really unhappy."

"Why?"

"We were just wrong for each other. It's like what you said about building relationships based on sex. That was all we had. But we didn't really like, or support each other."

"So you know what I'm talking about then when I say friendship is important to me."

I do now that I'm letting go of my insecurities to actually hear what you're saying.

I nodded.

"I want you to know that my word is my bond. That's the kind of man I've groomed myself to be. I was unfaithful because I didn't respect the relationships I was in. There was no reason to. I wasn't afraid of losing anything."

I confided in him, "I want someone I can walk through fire with."

"That's what I'm ready for."

I could have curled up in the crease of his smile and listened to him talk all day.

We walked and chatted, and time danced quickly around us, until we were down in the Village at a comic book store. I enjoyed walking through the aisles hearing him get excited when he'd come across comics he liked. I just enjoyed him.

Since we were already in the Village....

"You want to go to my favorite store?"

"Before I say 'yeah', what's your favorite store? Is it full of shoes or tampons?"

I laughed. "No, but you're kind of along the right track. I want to see if you can handle what comes along with me."

We walked a few blocks until we reached Pus N Dix.

"Hey, Breezy!"

"Wassup, Lady?" I yelled back.

"Ooh, I see you brought a friend with you."

"Yup. He wants to get to know me." I looked at him to see his comfort level, because Lady is a lot to take. But I couldn't tell either way; he was poker-faced.

"Well, let me tell you about your sweet little friend here. Can I tell him, girl?"

"Uh huh."

He spoke in the grandiose manner that I'd grown to appreciate, full of arm and finger gestures, and facial expressions. "She is one of my best customers. Adventurous. I wish Riddles was here so he could tell you more about her. Sweet as pie. She was so nervous when she first came in here, but now she helps the other customers."

Sean looked at me, and smirked. "Is that right?"

"Yes. You will be very happy being friends with her," Lady said, with a giggle.

I blushed, and then I took him on a tour of the store. I showed him some of the toys I'd bought.

"Wow," was all he kept saying

"So, how do you feel about me now?"

"I was already intrigued, but you just took it to another level."

"You buying anything, sweetie?" Lady asked as we were leaving.

"Not today. I lost my job, Lady, so I need to chill on the toy-buying for a minute."

"Oh, sweetie, I'm sorry! Well, you can always work here, but I can only pay minimum wage."

"I really appreciate that. I may take you up on that depending on how things go."

We left, and as we were walking down the street he said, "I guess I can share something with you too."

I braced myself again.

"I have a lot of porn."

"Oh, is that all?"

"A lot."

"Like, you collect them?"

"I have a closet full of them."

"You watch barely legal?"

"Nah. I like *grown women*. I don't even really like for my women to shave. I like *it* to look grown."

"Oh so you like it hairy?"

"Not a forest, but a nicely mowed field."

I bursted into laughter.

"I see. Well maybe your porn collection, and my toy collection can go out on a date."

His face lit up like he'd hit the jackpot.

"Okay, so who's going to do our nuptials? Rev. Run or Mase?"

I laughed.

He grabbed my hand.

My heart jumped.

I said, "You shouldn't say things like that. I might take you seriously. Then you'll be stuck."

He didn't say anything. He just hit me with a killer half-smile, and squeezed my hand. He took me back home, and walked me to my door. It was a little after five o'clock.

"You want to come in? I know you have to go soon."

"Yeah, I do, but I can chill for a while."

In my living room he said, "Nice TV. You're ballin', huh?

"No I'm not. I won that in A-C."

"Oh? You gamble?"

"No sir. I lost sixty dollars once at the casino, and that pretty much cured me. I won it in a dance contest."

"A dance contest?"

"Yeah. I can't say I remember winning, or even dancing for that matter, but I hear I was the shit."

"Apparently. We need to go out to a club and see what you can do."

"I mean, if you think you can keep up with me," I joked.

"I think maybe I can."

"Imagine watching porn on that," I said, nodding toward my TV.

"I know, right? It would be like being in the theater."

"Do you go to the theaters?" I tried to ask as non-judgmentally as possible, so he would answer me truthfully.

"Nah. That's not my thing. I just watch at home."

"With your lotion?"

He chuckled, "Yeah—with my lotion."

I asked him if he wanted anything to eat or drink. He said no, so I sat down next to him. It was nice sitting there and talking to him after having spent the day with him.

It's hard to open up, and let the other person know what you want and how you feel. But being cautious does not a love story make. So I opened up and asked, in case he was serious, and in case this could be real, "This foundation you want to build, what makes you think I'm worth the trouble?"

"You just feel right."

I had to get really female with him. "Is it that any woman could have come along at this time in your life and you would want to build something with her?"

"Not at all. I wasn't looking for anyone. I mean, if it happened it happened, but I wasn't looking or expecting. It's *you*. The question is; do you think I'm worth the trouble?"

I smiled. "You're asking me a question that will leave me vulnerable."

"You just asked me the same question."

"I like you, Sean—a lot more than I expected. I thought this would be some regular sex or whatever, nothing serious, you know?"

"Oh, so you just wanted to hit it?"

"I assumed you just wanted to hit it."

"That's not all I want."

"Me neither."

"I want to see where this goes."

"Me too."

"But... I definitely want to hit it."

"Ha ha ha! Me too."

We stared at each other for a moment when he asked, "Can I see your paintings?"

My heart jumped, and my head got hot. I guess it showed.

"You alright?"

"Yeah. I just get really nervous about my work."

"You saw me on stage, sweating, screwing up my face and some more stuff. You can certainly find it in yourself to show me at least one painting."

I took a deep breath. "I'll be right back." I grabbed two of my portfolios from my bedroom and took them back into the living room.

"Most of my work is at my parents' house, so these are pictures of my paintings and a few sketches." I sat on the floor to unzip them.

He got down on the floor with me. His eyes lit up as he stared at my paintings—and I mean stared, like he was studying them. He looked up at me and shook his head, like he just couldn't believe I was the artist. Every page he turned came with a compliment, and I believed him because I knew my paintings were good. He asked me questions about each piece, to the point where I felt like I was being interviewed for an art magazine or something. His interest really affected me, and I fell a little more.

At seven o'clock he sucked his teeth, "It's about that time."

"I know."

"You want to come with me?"

"What?"

"You want to come to Europe with me?"

"Are you serious?"

"As a heart attack. Do you have a passport?"

"Yeah."

"I can buy your ticket."

"You're serious?"

"Yes."

"I wish I could, but I can't. I've got to find a job ASAP."

"Alright. I understand. No, no, don't worry about me and my feelings. I'll be okay." He pretended to hold back tears.

"You're so silly." He was just adorable.

"Seriously, it would've been cool."

I looked into his eyes. *Is he trying to hit it right now? He knows I wouldn't up and go with him. That's the game, yo! He just wants me to think he wants me to go so I'll give him some. Or maybe he's being earnest. Maybe he really does think I'm beautiful, and maybe the way he looks at me is pure.* It almost didn't matter either way, because at that moment I wanted nothing more than to kiss him. I grabbed his hand, and like he knew, he leaned in and kissed me. *Mmmm Hmmm!*

His lips were perfectly soft and firm. The first kiss was a peck, then a longer peck, and then he bit my bottom lip just a little. It was so gentle I couldn't even call it a bite, but it was more than a nibble. And he smiled when he kissed me. That set me on fire.

I started sweating just a little, like the kiss was melting me. I felt weak, physically and mentally. His lips touched something in me that had never been touched before.

Energy on top of energy. There was the beauty of life in his kiss. I actually had to fight tears. I was overwhelmed. This was sugar. *His lips should not feel this sweet against mine.* I couldn't stop kissing him.

He kissed my forehead, and I kissed his nose. He kissed my cheek; I kissed his neck. He grabbed my arms like he couldn't take it and said, "Mmm... trying to keep me here. I gotta go, ma. But when I get back, it's on."

We stood at the elevator, and when it came we both got on. I didn't want to let him go. I walked him through the lobby. We hugged. I was lost in his arms, and I could feel him in my bones. He felt so strong and warm. We mutually released each other. Then he pulled me back to him one last time, and kissed me, like he was claiming me. I was his. I'm not sure exactly when it happened, but I'd already given myself to him.

Chapter 18

"I read somewhere that just over half of all women masturbate vs. nearly 100 percent of all men. If that's so, women have a lot of catching up to do. But really, I'm sure that stat is incorrect. It's more likely that just over half of all women will admit to it." ~ Mallory Marx from the *Masturbators Unanimous* blog.

The next day I called my cousin Sandy—hustler extraordinaire—to see what jobs she had for me. She sold some of everything. She sold Avon. If you didn't like Avon, she also sold Mary Kay. She bought knock-off designer purses and clothes on Canal Street and sent them to her cousin on her mother's side, Cookie Doe (yes Cookie Doe, no relation to me) who lived in Memphis. Either they didn't know from fake, or they just didn't care, but she made a killing selling counterfeits. She threw fun parties, did hair weaves, and made birthday cakes. She was the candy lady, and she made clothes. She was the definition of a hustler. She was really outgoing, and could sell sand to a Nomad in the Sahara. I didn't have that kind of hustle. I'm not really a people person. I told her she was short-changing herself and she should sell real estate, but she liked the various titles she held. She didn't want to sell one product and be dependent on just that. She enjoyed running around doing this, that, and the other, for herself only, with no overhead. She paid taxes on the Avon and Mary Kay sales, but everything else was profit after supplies.

So Sandy came to my house with her kids, Daniel and Evan. She gave them those names so they wouldn't have a problem getting jobs—you know, with the politics of name discrimination. She wanted them to at least be able to get a foot in the door. But their middle names were Raequan and Dontrell, respectively, and that was what everyone called them. That, or Ray Ray and Trell. I referred to them collectively as Ray Don Chong. It just rolled off my tongue one day, and I never stopped, but only when they were together and up to mischief. I'd say, "Ray Don Chong, stop throwing stuff out the window! Ray Don Chong, what are y'all doing back there? Ray Don Chong, I told *yous* about playing with matches," and so on.

We sat in the living room while the kids ran around the house. She expressed her sympathy toward my situation: "Yo, that's fucked up. Fuck them nine-to-five punk mother fuckers! Fuck working for companies! That's why I tell you, there's nothing like having your own shit—nothing like it. Your stupid ass wants to keep working in corporate America. That's what the fuck you get."

I rolled my eyes at her. "Anyway, I need money like now."

"You have any savings?"

"I'm about to roll my 401(k) into an IRA, but honestly, there's not much in there, just enough to roll it over, and I can't touch it without penalty."

"Humph. Buy something and sell it. Go to the Goodwill, buy some jeans, and sell them."

"To who?"

"To people!" She huffed, frustrated. "I don't get you. The shit is not rocket science. People buy shit from people. Put yourself out there. Shit!"

"Why did I call your ass?"

"Because you know I know the real. I do have an easy one for you though. It's quick money, and, yes, it's legal. I've been thinking about this one for a few weeks now, but I don't want to do it myself."

"I'm not having sex with anybody."

"Bitch, really? Come on! Do me better than that. I already said it's legal."

"I'm just saying."

She got up and sat next to me, pulled out her laptop, and pulled up a porn page.

I gave her the up-down with my eyes.

"Calm down. You can do this easy. Just sell memberships to this website. There are three different levels. I've already set everything up. There's a ten-dollar membership, twenty-five-dollar, and fifty-dollar. The profit is 80 percent, and of that I get half and you get half. Plus, you get 60 percent of any porn they actually buy. Everything is real incognito. They don't have to give their names to you. They just need to buy one of these cards from you." She pulled up a picture of the card. "And you can also sell DVDs if you want to."

"And exactly who am I going to sell this to?"

"Who the fu—? Men, dummy! Oh my Gahd! Get a little outfit, put some sunglasses on, get a stripper weave, take your ass to the barbershops, and sell that shit!"

"I don't know about this one."

"It's not like you have to do it on your block. Shit, go to Newark. Go to some part of Connecticut or some shit. Plot out a list of barbershops. Learn how to drive. Rent a car. Go make that money!" She had a way of trying to motivate me by making me feel stupid for not making what she viewed as easy money. This is the first time I felt desperate enough to consider it.

"I'll think about it."

I heard Ray Don Chong in the hallway making *Star Wars* sounds, having a duel with their imaginary light sabers. Imaginary until I heard the buzzing sound. Ray Ray was backing Trell into the living room, each wielding one of my glass vibrators. My mouth dropped.

"Damn Breezy!" Sandy yelled and started laughing.

"She got a bunch of these, Mommy! They're all in a trash bag. Are you throwing them out? Can we have them?"

"Yeah! Can we have them, Breezy?"

"Yeah, can we?"

"Y'all give those to Breezy and go to the bathroom and *thoroughly* wash your hands!"

When they ran out of the room, she turned to me and said, "Why aren't you buying your toys from me?"

"Because your mouth is too big." I thought for a moment, and then added, "And you keep your mouth shut about my toys!"

* * *

On Tuesday, I got a call from Searly & Weiss. *What the shit do they want? Do they want me back? Well, I am not going back to them. Bastards. They probably wanted an apology and then they'd take me back. Where the fuck do they get off thinking I'm desperate enough to tuck my tail and deal with them ever again?* I let it go to voicemail.

After rubbing one out, running up and down the stairs, taking a shower, eating, and getting dressed, I listened to the message. It was from Sara Weiss, telling me about an opportunity she had for me. I called her back.

"I wanted to know if you'd be interested in teaching a couple of friends of mine what you taught me."

"How to masturbate?"

"Yes. I belong to the Carolyn Club, and I told two of the members about my session with you. They wanted to know if you'd give them lessons."

"Really?"

"So, will you? I told them they would need to discuss your fee with you but said the minimum is $300 an hour."

The smile came from deep within me and spread across my face like warm butter on bread. I couldn't even contain my excitement. I started laughing.

"So I guess that's a 'yes'?"

"Yeah, it's a yes. And a thank you."

"Don't mention it. If you do well—which I know you will—it makes me look good."

I was so excited, but the only person I could tell was Justin. I called him and left a message to call me back. I wanted to tell Sean, but I wasn't sure if it was something I should share with him just yet. I was pretty sure he wouldn't have a negative reaction, but I just wasn't ready to say, *"Hey, I'm teaching some women how to masturbate."*

I called Jana Leslie first. She had a mousy voice, but she asserted it, speaking with force, as though she knew she had to. Her voice sounded strained, and I wondered if it hurt when she spoke. She lived upstate in Putnam County. We set up an appointment for Saturday morning.

Next I called Eula Ishimoto. With the name "Eula," I expected someone in her seventies but she was in her forties. She lived in Florida.

"I won't be able to make it up to the city anytime soon, but from what Sara says, you're a miracle worker, and I really, really need you. This is the one thing in my life that's lacking. I'm knocking on fifty and have never, ever had the Big O. It's kind of pathetic."

"It's not pathetic at all. We don't know things until we know them."

"I want to see you as soon as possible. How long do you think it will take?"

"Well, it's not really something I can put a time frame on or even a ballpark figure. It depends on you."

"I see. So how about you come here for a weekend? It's beautiful here. Trust me, you'll love it. We can start working on it Friday evening, after I get home from the office. Oh, I'm so excited."

"You want me to fly to Florida?"

"Yes. Is that a problem?"

"No." *YES!* I was terrified of flying.

"I'll pay for your flight and make lodging arrangements. Do you want to buy the tickets and I'll reimburse you, or do you want me to set everything up?"

Since I avoided planes, I didn't know from setting up a flight, so I told her she could set it up. I also told her I'd send a kit to her so I wouldn't have to have the toys on the plane with me. I'd never flown, but I'd watched enough television to know about airport security, and did not want to be embarrassed by questions about masturbation toys when they rolled through the X-ray scanners.

* * *

On Saturday, I took the Metro North upstate to Brewster. It was a long, boring ride, but boring is good sometimes. There doesn't always have to be something going on. Sometimes a bunch of nothing is good.

She stood about five feet, if that. She reminded me of a mini Jamie Lee Curtis, circa *Trading Places*, dipped in butterscotch. She was so tiny that I just wanted to snatch her up and throw her.

She picked me up from the station in her Escalade; I could hardly see her behind the wheel.

She drove fast and was the only one honking on the quiet Brewster streets.

I hadn't been upstate since I was a kid going to sleep-away camp. All the clean air making its way into my body ironically caused my nose to clog up. My eyes were itchy, and I was sneezing horribly by the time we got to her home, which was beautiful. It looked like a small-scale White House.

We walked in through a side entrance into her kitchen. She was just adorable with her strong baby voice, and baby feet. She was so short it seemed her little feet were running when she walked. Two of her steps were one of mine.

She had a staff, and she bossed them around with her left brow raised and her finger pointed. "This table is not clean. This floor needs to be done again, and the cabinets over the stove are sticky," she said to her maid. Of course, I hadn't felt the cabinets, but the table and floor looked spotless to me.

Her demeaning tone really rubbed me the wrong way, and I didn't want to help her learn to rub the right way. If not for Sara, I would've left. Forget the money. People shouldn't treat people like that.

I raised my eyebrows and shook my head, then let the expression go.

She looked at me, telling me to mind my business with her eyes. She told off another maid, a butler, and an assistant, and then we went to her pool house, which was a mini version of her house.

"Would you like something to drink?" she asked, out of obligation.

"Water please," I said. I didn't want anything; I just wanted to make her have to get it.

She left and came back with two glasses of water.

"No bottled water?"

She looked at me like she wanted to roll her eyes and said, "Most bottled water is municipal water anyway, which is tap water that my taxes are already paying for. The ones that come from other sources aren't even regulated. Tap water is safer. So to answer your question, no, I don't have any bottled water."

"Okay." I hadn't asked for a lesson in *waternomics*. I took a sip then said, "So, what brings us together?"

"I want to learn how to orgasm." She said it like, *"Duh! What the fuck else would I have invited you for?"*

"What have you been doing to try to have one?"

"Well.... I've rubbed myself."

"Where?"

"At home. In my bed."

"No." I was intentionally short. "Did you rub your clitoris, between your lips, or—?"

"Oh. Just the whole thing."

I handed her a copy of the *Rose Papers*.

She said, "Oh my," and grinned at herself a few times as she read. Then she used her finger to read part of it. She really got into it. She asked me questions, and I answered as best as I could. We were both being cordial, but not at all friendly. "So, if I stimulate just my clit alone, or just my G-spot, I can orgasm?"

"We are all so unique, but those are the areas that bring me to orgasm."

She took a gulp of water and read some more. "So, I should be wet first?"

"It helps. You don't have to be, but it can make it feel better." I took a gulp of water and asked, "You like to be in control in most situations?"

She looked at me as though she wanted to slap me and then said, "As a matter of fact, yes I do."

"You'll need to lose control to have an orgasm. You have to let your body go through whatever it needs to in order to have it. You can't control it. You can cause it, but you can't force it. You seem like the type that likes to force things."

She took a deep, agitated breath, because she didn't like what I said, and I didn't care that she didn't like it, because I didn't like the way she talked to her staff. You don't disrespect people and yell at them just because they work for you. They are just trying to make a living. I hate bullies.

"So, you think I'm not capable of achieving an orgasm?"

"Didn't say that, but you have to change your perspective. An orgasm has to be coaxed. You have to be nice to your clit or you G-spot—to your body, period. You can't be mean and yell at it. You have to ask it nicely."

She was quiet for a moment, and then she looked at me with spite.

I didn't care. I just didn't like her. Still, I did want to do my job. I wanted to get her to orgasm. I wanted every woman in the world to be able experience the Big O.

She said, "Can you leave me alone for a moment?"

I made sure she saw me roll my eyes, as I stood up, and went outside. She went from a cute munchkin to a wicked elf.

The air was crisp and felt good. Then I started sneezing again, and my head started clogging up. The crisp air became warmer suddenly, and little bugs started biting my face. I was ready to go.

A few minutes later she came out. "You want me to take you back to the train station?"

"If that's what you want."

"Yeah, I think that's what I want."

I shrugged my shoulders.

"I yelled at Luz because she won't listen any other way."

I didn't respond.

"People..." She took a deep breath. "Because of my size, people think they can get over on me, so I have to be bigger than them."

I turned to look her in the eyes as she spoke.

"People only respond when I bitch. Otherwise, they either think it's cute when I talk, or they just ignore me altogether. I need to be a bitch. It's better for me that way."

I understood; she didn't owe me any explanation. And once again, that was what I got for judging someone without knowing their story. And I was guilty of the very stereotype she was talking about. Thinking of her as a little cute doll. I felt bad about that now. "I'm sorry for having an attitude with you. That wasn't very professional."

"It's quite alright. Now then, will you come back inside?" she asked, as though she hadn't asked me to step out in the first place.

I sat back down on my spot on the zebra-print couch, and we started over. I felt a lot better about the situation and I assumed she did too.

I wasn't sure exactly how to read her or where to start. She wasn't ready to just get naked like Sara. I wasn't sure how to approach this with her, or even really sure what to ask. What do you ask a person who wants you to walk them through an orgasm?

"Do you have any fantasies?"

"Sexual fantasies?"

I nodded.

She blushed.

"It's okay. You can be completely open with me. It's just me and you. You can be as vulnerable as you need to be with me. I know that's a lot to ask since we're strangers, but that should kind of make it easier, because you don't have to care about me judging you."

She let that work around in her mind for a few moments and then said, "When I was in the military and my staff sergeant would yell at me, I would get so excited. I'd want to just take him and throw him on the ground and fuck the shit out of him. So I fantasized about him cursing at me and making me fuck him. Ever since, I've wanted a man to just take control of me."

I didn't expect that. "Wow. That's a good one. So have you been dominated before?"

"No. I haven't really found a man that I can be open enough with or trust enough."

As she spoke I handed the packaged bullet and G-spot stimulator to her. She took them and smiled awkwardly.

"I see," I said. Not easy to trust a man with your fantasies."

"Not at all."

I handed her a pair of scissors, wipes, and batteries. She cut the plastic packaging on both toys then wiped them down, and loaded the batteries.

I said, "If I were a man I'd be scared to even attempt to dominate you."

"Why exactly?" She was eager to know.

"Because nothing about the way you carry yourself says you want to submit to anything."

She rolled her eyes in her head, and I could see the light bulb go on. She had a moment of understanding, and I had an idea.

I stood up. "Take your clothes off."

"What?"

"Take your clothes off!" I yelled. "NOW!"

She started to undress.

"Faster!" I yelled.

She tore her clothes off.

"Grab that bullet and lie down," I demanded.

She dropped down on the plush white rug.

"Put it on the first setting."

She searched it for the power button.

I yelled, "Now, I said!"

She quickly found the button. Hearing the *hum* of the bullet awakened my clit.

"Find your clitoris."

She did.

"Is she hard?"

"Huh?"

"Do not 'huh' me! Is she hard?"

"Ma'am, yes, ma'am!"

"Gen-tilaay rub the bullet on your clit." For some reason I'd adapted a Southern drawl.

"Ma'am, yes, ma'am!" She closed her eyes and rubbed her clit. Her labia looked like they were drooling. I was proud of myself; I'd gotten her wet. I felt so powerful.

My own clit strained against my panties. I was silent as I watched her roll her eyes. I didn't want to disturb her.

Minutes passed. She was in deep concentration. Suddenly, she started whimpering. I recognized that whimper; she was in the zone. She started grunting and pulled the bullet away from herself.

"Do not stop!" I yelled. "Put that damned bullet back on your clitoris!"

"I can't—"

"Put the mutha fuckin' bullet back on your clit now!"

She did and bit down on both of her lips. She turned her head from left to right. This time, she dropped the bullet.

I got on the floor and put the bullet back in its place against her clit.

She hit me.

I didn't stop.

She kicked her legs.

I didn't stop. "Come on!" I yelled. "Gimme that nut! Stop fighting it!"

She started pushing like she was having a baby.

"That's right. Push that nut out! C'mon! Don't be afraid."

She curled her lips and grunted some more.

"I want to hear you cum! Let it out!"

"I think... I... OOOOOOOOH!" she screeched, like she was in trouble. She got really quiet then yelled out, "FUUUUCK! Oh my Gahd!" She grabbed the air with both hands; her mouth opened baring her teeth like she was an angry animal. She rolled her eyes back into normal position, dropped her hands, and relaxed her mouth. She was breathing like she'd just finished sprinting. Then she looked at me with wonderful disgust, like she didn't know if she wanted to thank me or beat my ass.

I wasn't sure that yelling at her would work. I was scared she'd reject it and call me crazy, but something told me to be brave and go for it. I gave myself a gold star for that one.

So, I had been wrong. She could be mean to herself and orgasm. Or at least someone else could be mean to her.

I was truly pleased with myself. Then I was hit with a waterfall of thoughts. *Have I stepped into prostitution? Was that considered sex? No, that wasn't sex. Was it? Was that lesbian sex? Oh my gosh! Did I just have lesbian sex?*

She was still shivering, and looking dazed, and confused.

As she recovered, I went to the bathroom to wash my hands and my arms. I couldn't believe I touched that wet-ass bullet with her femininity all over it. I made a disgusted face as I looked in the mirror. I wanted to take a shower.

Then I thought about the money. *Is this how a prostitute thinks?* I didn't want to think or feel like that. I felt like I'd taken advantage of her somehow. I started feeling dirty and regretful.

When I went back into the main room, she'd come back to Earth. With tears in her eyes, she said, "I don't know how I could ever repay you. Thank you. Thank you so much!"

She shook her head, and closed her eyes with a smirk on her lips. She opened her eyes and said, "I'll be honest with you... I had complete doubt in your abilities. But, Breezy, you are a great teacher, and I'm so glad you stayed."

My eyes watered up; she took all of that dirty feeling away. "It was my pleasure. I'm so glad you came. I was worried that I couldn't produce."

She held her hand against her heart and said, "Really... thank you."

"You're welcome."

She sat on the couch for a moment. I stood there for a moment. We were silent. She was still naked. I broke the silence and asked, "Ready for the other orgasm?"

"The *other* orgasm?"

"Yeah, from your G-spot."

"Oh noooo!" She shook her head and waved her right hand. "I've got to get over this one first. I do want to learn though. Can we set up another appointment for next weekend?" she asked, as she finally started putting on her clothes.

"I'm going out of town next weekend."

"How about this Thursday? I can take off work."

"Okay."

"That's perfect!" She was excited and visibly tired.

After she was dressed, she gave me an extra $100 (I really like $100 tips) and a cheesecake.

I immediately recognized the pastel pink box. "J. Leslie's? This is my favorite cheesecake in the world. I mean, it's expensive, but it's so worth it, because it's all organic, and all the ingredients are from a farm upstate—" I stopped in the middle of my commercial, and squinted my eyes. *Wait... she can't be...* "Jana Leslie. Are you J. Leslie's Cakes?"

"Yeah, that's me," she said with pride.

Wow! I had just taught J. Leslie—the woman that had unknowingly brought so much pleasure into my life—how to have an orgasm. *No freaking way!*

Chapter 19

Confession of an inappropriate session: Sometimes I just can't help myself; I masturbated during a funeral for Gia's dog. It was a dog for goodness sake. I couldn't believe she was having a funeral. But he was a part of her family, so she paid just under $5,000 to send him off. There were about thirty people at the funeral. Her husband and their three teenage kids were there, along with other relatives and friends, some of whom didn't hide the fact that this was not how they wanted to spend their Saturday morning. My clit was tremendously agitated (which as you know by now is not unusual), so I disappeared into an area full of animal coffins with photo portraits of animals on them. I thought it was weird that they had their pictures displayed like that. Some were dressed up in cute outfits, and some were in positions with their owners that bordered on bestiality—or maybe my mind is just twisted. Some wanted me to believe they'd been to the Eifel Tower or the Leaning Tower of Pisa. Anyway, I got one off with my butterfly, next to a Burmese cat in a purple and white clown suit, named Sasha. RIP, Sasha. This nut's for you.

That Wednesday I had a job interview for yet another admin position. My mind wasn't there at all. This was bullshit—running head first toward more unhappiness. Being chained to a desk was not what I wanted to do. I didn't want to stare at a computer all day, keeping someone else's dream alive. Someone that could give a shit about me. *But I need money. But I just made some money, and I'll be making more tomorrow. But I need a steady stream of income. I can't just show females how to masturbate for a living. How come? Because who's going to pay for that? Well, you already have three people so far willing to pay for it. Yeah, but how many women need that type of help?*

Back and forth I went with myself while giving robotic answers to the interviewer, whose name I can't even remember and whose face was a blur amongst my thoughts. I knew I'd messed up that interview. About 80 percent of me didn't give a care.

The hum of the train between my legs on my ride back home was driving me crazy. I might as well have worn the butterfly. I stood up and parted my legs so my clit wouldn't touch my thigh, a weak attempt to quell the mercury's rise. But it was too late. My clit had already been ignited. I bit my bottom lip. The train rocked me like a sensual lullaby. I needed relief right then. It was a little after ten, so the train wasn't that crowded. Only about twelve other people were spread throughout the car. I could cum without anyone seeing me. If I needed to, I could tie my suit jacket around my waist to cover any wetness that might soak through my skirt. *Yes, I can do this right here, on the train.*

My heart started pounding. I was excited. My G-spot became supremely stimulated. I mean, my insides were feeling so good I could hardly be still. Then it dawned on me: *The freaking Ben Wa balls!* I kept falling asleep with them inside of me. *How did I spend the whole morning without noticing them?* I knew then that the orgasm wouldn't be quiet enough for me to do it right there.

I headed for the sliding door, so I could go to the next car. There were three people in that car. I kept going back through the cars, exposing my ears to the screeching of the tracks each time I exited one car for the next. Wobbling against the motion of the train, as I made my way through to the last car.

Instead of entering, my body forced me to stop right there between cars. It was the rattling of the chains; the rhythm of the motor chugging, vibrating through me and flooding my ears. It was the funky electric tar smell of the subway tunnel rushing into my nose; the fact that someone could walk up on me at any moment. And even that I could fall, as I balanced myself on the two moving platforms between the cars—that forced me to stop and do it right there.

I steadied myself, hiked my skirt up and rubbed my clit through my stockings and panties. I contracted my Kegels, grabbing the balls until I felt that warm oceanic bliss of my G-spot overflowing with pleasure. Then that fantastic tickle-itch from my clit spread over every part of me. "Oh shiiiiiit!" My eyes rolled all the way back in my head. I imagined I looked like the comic book character, Storm. "Oh, yes!" I was foaming at the mouth. "Oh [inaudible angelic sounds]!"

My mind fell, and my body went limp. I wanted to collapse, but I managed to hold on.

I picked my mind up from the steel beneath my feet, pulled my soul back down from the air above me, and straightened up my body. I went into the last car. I hadn't seen the passenger when I'd looked through the door initially, but there was a man sitting there. He stared at me intensely for just a few moments, then looked away.

The train pulled into the station seconds later. As I got off, I tied my jacket around my waist. It wasn't my stop, but I didn't want to be on the train anymore with the man that knew my secret. He didn't seem to care, but still, I knew he knew.

I was disgusted with myself. I'd touched doors, strap hangers, poles, and then—with all those germs on my hands—I touched myself. But I had no choice. My clit wanted what she wanted. And it wasn't like I touched my bare skin. It was through stockings *and* panties. So really, I didn't have to be that disgusted—or at least that was what I rationalized. But I was still appalled at myself. *Heavens woman! Have some self-control.*

Part of me, though—an undeniable part of me—loved the thought of the dirtiness; the raw griminess of cumming in between subway cars. The thought thrilled me.

So, I did it again. That evening, I took the 6 train uptown, with no destination in mind. It was a little after eleven. As soon as the train started moving, I started walking the cars. I could've just gotten on in the last car, but I wanted to walk through the cars. It added intensity to the rush I wanted to feel. My heart pounded, and my clit strained. I gripped the Ben Wa balls inside of me.

I stopped walking just before crossing into the last car, hiked my skirt up, and started rubbing my clit. I had my bullet this time. I was lost in my own private world between cars. My excitement grew as the train went outside so I could see the Bronx fly by as I held the bullet against my joy.

The tickle-itch ravished my pearl. My whole body tickled and itched. I grunted as I balanced myself and watched the lights of the city rush by. The feeling was incredible. Someone could really see me. I'd be a blur, just as they were a blur to me, but still.

We pulled into the next station and everything slowed down: the air, time, my thoughts—everything, except my heartbeat. I was dizzy for a few moments, and then I regained myself and smiled. I felt devious. I grabbed my breast and pinched my nipple, letting go when the train took off again.

Each time the train stopped and people got on and off, I wanted so badly for someone to see me—to just catch a glimpse of my autoerotic activity.

I held on to my orgasm. I wasn't ready to let go just yet, so I kept driving myself to peak, and then let it slide back down the mountain. I repeated that, until I simply couldn't take it anymore. I felt sick, mentally and physically, like I'd toyed with myself entirely too much. My clitoris, and G-spot both threatened to not give me what I wanted, as if they were protecting me from myself, because I might've actually died if I came. I fought. I wanted to cum! I didn't care what my body wanted. My heart beat so hard that my breath couldn't keep up. My neck felt tight. I tossed my head, and growled from my *lips*. My foot slipped. I grabbed the door handle, my heart hit a high note, and I exploded as we pulled into Buhre Avenue.

I couldn't even get myself together. My whole body shook as I walked into the last car. Not because of my explosion, or that I'd just come out of the cool night air. It was because I was scared; scared of myself. Scared of what else I may do in the name of masturbation; and afraid my next act may be even more public, and more dangerous. Humans escalate. That's our nature. I wanted to be seen. I wanted to fall. If my heart had stopped, I still would've been satisfied in that weightless moment of pleasure. I wanted to let go of every piece of good sense I had. I ignored the fear of death that tinged my skin with chill bumps when my foot slipped. I just wanted one thing. But I knew better. *I shouldn't allow myself to fall like that. But, damn, it felt so freaking good.*

The next stop was the last stop, Pelham Bay Park. I waited for the train to go back downtown. I was a mess. I started biting my nails, a habit I'd given up in college. My heart finally slowed down. I knew my blood pressure was high. That was why my neck felt tight. It loosened after I forced myself into calm.

My soul started speaking to me, warning me, *"Don't turn this gift into a curse."* Then she showed me all these pretty colors....

I woke up instinctively at Third Avenue station. According to my watch, it was just after midnight. The walk home was quiet, except for the *click-clack* of my heels echoing along Alexander Avenue. The air was approaching cold. I sped up my steps, cursing at myself for being out so late when I should have been in bed; for the wetness between my legs that I was sure had stained my skirt so that it looked like I'd peed on myself; and for letting my desire control me. I needed to get a hold of myself.

* * *

I took another break from masturbation and concentrated on creating sketches for my paintings, but everything I sketched was related to masturbation. I was drawing faces of women enthralled in self-ecstasy; women who looked like me; women with braids, locks, short hair, long hair, and Afro puffs; light women; dark women; short women; tall women; fat ones; and skinny ones. No matter what kind of woman I sketched, their faces were twisted in the extreme delight of loving themselves.

I spread the sketches all over the floor in my bedroom and started pulling them together with my brush on one canvas.

Ironically, the more I drew and painted about masturbation, the less I wanted to do it. I was finding relief and release through my art.

That was until I spoke to Sean. It hadn't even been twenty-four hours since I decided to take a break. He called me with that sexy voice and set my body ablaze. As he spoke to me, telling me about what songs they were playing and about the shitty hotels, my hands steadily slid down my stomach until they were in my panties.

"Uh huh," I answered at nothing.

He asked, "Are you okay?"

"Yeah."

"Are you running or something?"

"No. Keep telling me about the tour."

I muted the phone, as he kept talking, unmuting it when I needed to so I could respond. "Hold on, Sean... just a sec.... Hold it please?" I was trying to make sense, but it was hard speaking with the sirens in my throat. I didn't wait for him to respond. I muted the phone, right before dropping it and came so hard my head started pounding.

"Everything alright?" he asked, when I got back on the line.

"Yeah. Wonderful. I can't wait to see you."

"Did you just jerk off while I was talking?"

I was going to lie, but I decided to tell the truth. This was me. Either he would accept it or not. "Yeah. I'm sorry. I really was listening to you though."

He was quiet for a moment. Then he said, "Did you cum?"

"Yeah, I did."

"Good. So then I don't have to worry about you getting it from someone else. Next time, let me hear it."

He must be made for me.

I had to have some cheesecake after that.

Chapter 20

Confession: *I may be especially addicted the silky pleasures of Ben Wa balls. They are threatening to be my downfall.*

I was completely psyched about my trip to Florida. I needed to get away. The farthest I'd been outside of New York was North Carolina, and that was only by car. I told my friends I was going to Florida only because I wanted them to know, in case anything happened. I didn't tell them exactly why I was going. Just to visit a friend, was all I'd said. Except for Justin. I told him exactly why. It was going to be my first-ever flight, and all types of butterflies were fluttering through my stomach.

I packed light. I didn't want to check anything in, or put anything in the overhead. Besides, it was Florida. I knew it would be in the upper eighties when I got there, so what did I need with clothes?

When I was done packing, I twisted my hair in twenty rows going front to back and tied a scarf around my head. I was going to take them out in the morning so my hair would be in a springy, curly Afro. I was tired after doing my hair, but I still had the strength to get a good one in with my gold Ben Wa balls and my bullet, then lullabied right to sleep.

I woke up with a jump. *Shit*! I looked at my alarm clock. Either it had failed me, or I'd forgotten to set it. *Dumb ass.* I had about ten minutes to leave. According to the website, I needed to be there an hour before my flight. I brushed my teeth while I peed, and there was no time to take a shower. I threw on a pair of jeans and a hooded sweatshirt. I put a wig on, because I didn't have time to untwist my hair, and slapped on a Yankee cap. I grabbed my bags, flew out the house, caught a cab on Willis Avenue, and got to Newark just within an hour of my flight.

I ran from the cab into the airport, breathing hard as if I'd run all the way from the Bronx. There were bodies rushing in every direction. The lines for the airlines were thick with agitated people. Someone let their children loose to run and scream. The smell of coffee and newspapers hit me, but that may have been a psychological whiff, because those two smells go along with busy crowds in my mind. I stood there looking lost, and the butterflies in my tummy were working overtime.

A woman dressed in a blue uniform came up to me smiling and said, "If these are the only bags you have, you can check in at the kiosk."

I smiled back and said, "Thank you."

She really surprised me, giving me help when I didn't ask for it. I mean, I knew it was her job, but I think it was the first time I'd ever come across anyone who'd helped me without being asked. I've looked lost many times in stores, and rarely did any of the associates ever try to assist me without me asking first, and without them having an attitude about it.

It took about five tries before I realized I was sliding my credit card in the wrong way. Finally, I checked in, and then I stood in line to be searched. As I approached the front of the line, it hit me: *Ben Wa balls! Are they still in me? Maybe not.* I contracted my muscles. *Damn.*

Fear heated my body. I was three people from the front of the line, and the line behind me was mega long. I knew if I stepped out of line, I might miss my flight. *Shit!* My heart pounded, and I felt my underarms getting wet. My eyes were darting around looking at security and passengers. I chewed my bottom lip.

When it was my turn, I put my bags in the bins and took off my shoes and hat and put them in separate bins. One of the guards told me to remove my laptop from my bag and put it in a separate bin.

A woman, two people ahead of me, set off the alarm. They had her remove her belt, then step through again.

My heart started beating faster.

Then it was my turn.

I walked through the metal detector and set it off like a four-alarm fire. It seemed way louder than when it went off for that other lady. The entire planet looked at me for a few seconds, and then went on about its business.

"Step over here please," the security officer said. When I did, he asked me to put my arms out and scanned me with the wand. When he got to my crotch, the wand started barking like an excited dog. "Are you in possession of any firearms or explosives?"

"No... um, but I have these balls, and—"

They pulled me over a little farther from the line and scanned me again. The beeping seemed louder the second time. I blinked, and when I opened my eyes, I was surrounded by security.

Someone started searching my bags, another security guy stood with his back toward me on a walkie-talkie, while someone else a little farther away from him looked at me while he talked into his own walkie-talkie. An officer asked me to come with him. I was escorted by him and two other security guards on my second walk of shame for the year.

My heart was in my throat. It wasn't just that I felt I was in danger. It was knowing that I had to explain what I was carrying inside of me.

They took me to a barren, empty room with a window that I was sure was two-way glass. After several minutes, two female security guards entered the room, and the guards who escorted me stepped out.

"Do you have any weapons on you?"

"No."

"Hold your arms out and spread your legs please."

"But it's not—"

"Please hold your arms out, spread your legs."

I held my arms out and parted my legs.

She patted me down in a way that made me want to repeatedly slap the shit out of her.

They wanded me again

"We're going to need you to undress."

I tried to explain, "See, I was in a rush this morning, and—"

"Just remove your clothing please, Miss."

I pulled my pants down first so I could get it over with. I didn't have any panties on, and I smelled like nut. I pushed the balls out of me, and they dropped into my jeans. I kicked my foot just enough so that they bounced out onto the floor, where they rolled around playfully toward the security guards.

One guard looked confused, the shorter of the two. She was about as dark as me and looked like she was from India. The other one smiled, and then she started laughing. She looked like she could be black or Puerto Rican; I couldn't tell.

The confused one stuttered, "Is that.... What are those?"

"Those make your vagina strong, right?" the laughing one asked.

I nodded.

"We'll have to confiscate those,"

"Wait! Those balls are solid gold!"

"Sorry."

"So, let me get this straight. I can bring matches on the plane, but not Ben Wa balls?" I didn't even know why I was exchanging words. I should've just been happy it was over so I could get out of there, but it was a bullshit policy, and I'd paid good money for those solid gold beauties.

"What kind of balls? Ben Wa? Is that what they're called?" The laugher asked, no longer laughing.

I sucked my teeth. "Yeah. Ben Wa balls," I said as I pulled my pants back up.

The confused one radioed to someone else, giving the all-clear.

"Where'd you get them from?" Laugher asked.

I didn't wanna talk about my freaking balls. She acted like I wasn't trying to catch a flight. "I'm sorry, ladies, but I've got a plane to catch."

"Oh you missed that flight," Confused said, like it was nothing.

I sucked my teeth and rolled my eyes so hard it almost hurt.

"So where do you get them from?"

"Are you serious? For real? Right now, this is where your mind is? On these balls?"

Meanwhile the balls were just sitting on the floor, getting cold.

I was pissed. I looked at the two-way mirror and said, "There must not be anyone back there."

"Nah. You were never a real threat. This was just procedure."

"So I missed my flight so you people could *look like* you're protecting the country? This is some bullshit!"

They looked at me like they'd heard it all before.

"Or we could not pull potential threats out of line at all and possibly have someone blow up a plane. Is that what you would rather?" the confused one said.

She appealed to my fear. I would rather they check everyone's orifices than get on a plane with someone that even remotely looked like they may be a terrorist, was how I felt. Is that how white people have felt about blacks and Hispanics all these years? We all look suspect, so treat us all the same. Wow! Paranoia is a powerful tool of mass distraction and manipulation. It surely worked on me, especially after 9/11. All Arabs were suspect. *However*, the reality was, they have taken over a lot of the *bodegas* in New

York, so, if they it was really their goal to kill Americans, they could just poison our food. And if that was something they collectively wanted to do, they could've done that years ago. New Yorkers would've been dropping dead every morning, and every afternoon, after breakfast and lunch. Can't blame an entire people for the actions of a few.

"What about my flight?"

"You can make arrangements to trade in your ticket for the next available flight. But still, where'd you get them from?" There was something needy behind her tone, like she just had to know.

"You can get them anywhere. I go to a place called Pus N Dix in the Village. You know the Village?" I asked like I was talking to someone from Kentucky instead of right across the bridge in Jersey.

"I can get those same balls there? All gold like that?"

"No. I got these somewhere else, and they were the only pair. They are very special to me, and I would really appreciate it if you'd let me keep them."

"Do they work?"

I screwed my face up. *Really*? "Yeah, they work!"

"How?"

I huffed. "You put them in your *vajayjay*, and then you move your Kegel muscles, damn it!"

"But how do you do that?"

"Do what?"

"Move your Kegels?"

"I don't know. You just move them. Contract your coochie muscles, like your forcing out pee. Or better yet, like you're having sex and you're trying to grab your man inside of you.

She squinted in thought, and then smiled. "Oh, I'm doing it!"

Then the confused one farted.

We both shot a look at her.

"Not like you're taking a shit! Like you're peeing," I said, trying to correct her.

After a few seconds she said, "I'm doing it too!"

"Aww, that's lovely. Can I go now?"

"You don't have to have an attitude."

"Yes. Yes, I do have to have an attitude."

"Were you going to do that on the plane?"

"No," I huffed.

"So why were they in you?"

"If you must know—which it seems you feel you must—I fell asleep with them and forgot they were in there."

They both started laughing. I didn't find it funny.

"You can have your balls back," the Laugher said.

"Thank you." I used the sleeve of my sweater to collect them from the floor, and with that, I was on my way.

Fortunately, there was another flight leaving a few hours later, and I got the last available seat. I called Ms. Ishimoto to let her know there was a security issue, and I'd be late.

I kept my face hidden in my hood the whole flight. I thought people were staring at me, even though it was a whole different group of people from the ones who'd seen my crotch wanded. I still imagined that somehow they knew. I calmed myself down and, to my surprise, I enjoyed the flight.

All nervousness was gone as I marveled at human ingenuity. I was in the sky because someone in the past said, *"I know I can fly. There's got to be a way."* I'm sure their friends were like, *"People flying? Yeah, right. You sound stupid,"* and called them crazy. And I know there were several people with the same idea, but some were scared to pursue it, some just didn't have the time, some didn't have the support, and some just didn't think they were big enough to do such a grand thing. But then Orville and Wilbur said fuck it! They were so full of belief that they made it happen. And now, decades later, there I was in the air, making a right at a cumulus cloud, avoiding air pockets, flying above a storm, and looking at lighting below me. *Human ingenuity. We can do anything!*

However, as ingenious as the flight was, when we landed, I wanted to run off the plane, drop to my knees, and kiss the ground.

A man in a blue and white Hawaiian shirt stood in front of the airport with a white sign that had my name on it, something I didn't expect.

"I'm Breezy Deigh," I said with a big smile.

"Hello, Ms. Deigh. I'm Ken Harley," he said and held out his hairy hand. His hairiness made me think of Robin Williams. I wanted to touch him everywhere. Hairy men excite me. Especially arm and chest hair. Back hair—uhm, not so much.

I'd never seen palm trees in real life before. I'd studied pictures of them because they looked like freedom to me, so I loved to draw and paint them. Seeing them in real life was breathtaking. They were more gorgeous than I imagined. So sexy, and fun, and free, swaying in the breeze, all tall and proud, as if they knew they were spectacular.

Key West had such a relaxed vibe. As we drove along, I saw people with joy on their faces—not necessarily smiles, but simply joy. Some rode bikes, some fished, and some rode jet skis. The cab felt constraining. I rolled the windows down. I wanted to get out and walk. No—I wanted to run and jump into the water. The ocean was calling me.

After a while, there were no sidewalks, and the ocean was blocked from view by beautiful trees and bushes. Some of them had leaves so shiny they looked like plastic. Some had leaves that feathered out like a million little fingers turned upward, grabbing the air. There were breaks between groups of shrubs and trees, with trails leading to homes, and docks leading to the clear blue-green Atlantic. It was completely different from the green-brown Atlantic in New York; it was hard to believe it was the same ocean.

There were islands, some small and some larger. Some seemed close, but some were so far into the ocean they looked like they'd float right off the planet.

"Do people live on those islands?" I asked my hairy driver.

"Yeah."

"That must be expensive."

"Yes, very. Factor in utilities and making it habitable and yeah, it gets up there."

We drove from Key West to Marathon. A smell slapped me, infiltrating my nose, bringing tears to my eyes. For a moment, I thought it was him, but it was coming from outside the cab. "Oh my Gahd!" I covered my nose. "Are the trees farting?" I said under my breath.

He heard me and started laughing. "It's the still water. It smells pretty bad."

After a few moments, the smell was gone.

We turned onto a dirt road that led to a dock, and I got nervous. *Is this dude going to try to kill me?*

"This is your stop," he said.

"But this is a dock." I didn't have any pepper spray or any weapons on me for that matter. I decided if it came down to it, I could beat him in his head with my sneaker and dig his eyes out with my nails.

"You're going to that island out there," he said, pointing to an island that was maybe two miles away.

I could see that it had a dock, a white sand beach, and a bunch of palm and other trees and bushes. "*That's* where she lives?"

He nodded his head.

"Like, it's *her* island?"

"Yeah," he said with a chuckle at my amazement. "And this is *her* dock, and that's *her* house and garage right there," he said, pointing to the ocean-blue and white two-story house to our left. It was surrounded by enough trees that I didn't see it until he pointed it out. There was a separate five-car garage that matched the color of the blue sky.

"That's her boat?" I asked about the shiny white speedboat to the left of the dock. Looking at it made my legs feel like Jell-O.

"Yup."

I already knew the woman had money. She'd paid for my flight and was paying for a weekend of my services, but sometimes things don't really hit you until they actually hit you. That was when it hit me.

He put my travel bag into the boat. My other bag was my handbag, even though it was just about as big as the bag with my clothes.

Ms. Ishimoto called me to say she'd be there in ten minutes. The driver waited with me until she came, but he stayed in the car.

I stood on the dock, toying with the idea of going to the edge. Two steps at a time, finally I was at the cusp of eternity. The ocean, the horizon, blue sky, and the clouds were all so brilliant. I hadn't seen blue water since I was a kid, back when Brighten Beach was still somewhat blue. It was dark now, but the water in that heavenly spot where I stood, was so clear I could see the bottom.

Time slowed down. I felt relaxed. I looked down at the water. I wanted to dive in. It beckoned me. I raised my arms, bent my knees, and—

"Sharks!" I heard from behind me. "There are sharks in that water."

I wasn't really going to do it, but I liked that he thought I would.

Eula Ishimoto pulled up in a fuchsia drop-top. I don't know what kind it was, but it looked like expensive candy. She stepped from the car like a movie star wearing big white-rimmed sunglasses, with her white sundress blowing in the wind, and her hair flowing behind her. I thought her hair was braided, but as she got closer, I realized they were dreads.

Her skin was dark, brownish, and reddish, and then brown again. She looked like every ethnicity except white. Her lips were full and flat against her face, and her nose was flat and wide. She took off her sunglasses, and I saw the Ishimoto. I can't lie; the woman was gorgeous. A case of when *Blasian* goes right—because it doesn't always.

Her smile was warm, and her presence was humble, in a way that said, *"We both know I'm an extraordinary woman, but there's no need to dwell on that."* I wanted that presence.

"Breezy?"

"Yes." I smiled. "Nice to finally meet you."

"Believe me, the pleasure is all mine."

We exchanged a few more niceties and then got on her boat. I'd been on the Staten Island Ferry, and I'd been canoeing; Of course, neither prepared me for the ride with her.

She was the master of her boat. It took about a minute to get to her island, but I was so caught up in each second that it felt much longer—quite the opposite of a New York minute. This was a Florida minute. The wind and water whipped across my face, cooling me off, and the salty smell of the ocean filled my nostrils. We were going to ride right off the Earth. I took it all in. I was scared and exhilarated all at once. My heart was pumping. It was incredible!

We pulled up a few feet from the island shore. I felt like I was in a James Bond flick. All I needed was a bathing suit and some spy gear. I already had a near-perfect name for a Bond girl.

The heat crawled around my head and down into my sweater as I exited the boat. The island was sexy and exotic. There were all types of shrubbery and colorful flowers growing wild. The white sand jumped into my sneakers; it wasn't course like I expected. I picked some up with my hand, and it was smooth like fine salt. We walked onto a pebbled trail that cleared onto a concrete path. The trees parted, and civilization started.

She said, "Welcome to *La Isla de Ishimoto.*"

Chapter 21

The fruits of her labor surrounded me,
tossing me about like a tornado.
I was dizzy in her world,
grabbing bits of her reality.
Anything is possible!
Dreams can come true.
Nothing in this world is beyond me.

We walked toward her pink and blue concrete home, which was surrounded by three blue-green guest houses that were approximately twenty by twenty feet each. Each house had a cabana attached, covered by mosquito nets in matching blue-green. Even her satellite dish was blue-green.

I didn't know America even had anything so tropical. Standing there, I knew I was closer to Cuba than to New York, which really fascinated me for some reason. I'd never been any place so beautiful. It was official: Florida had turned me out.

She took me to the guest house closest to hers. I smiled big when I stepped in. The bed was huge and fluffy, with blue, white, green, and blue-green pillows. The comforter matched the pillows, the sheets were white. The floor was ocean blue concrete. The room felt like I was in the ocean, like my living room at home on *XTC*.

About ten steps from the foot of the bed were double-doors leading to the cabana that I had seen when we were walking on the trail. I pulled them open and stepped into utter peace. To my left was a swing with wood so polished it looked slippery. To my right was a white hammock. In the middle was a fire pit, about three feet wide and one foot long.

Beyond that, the protection of the mosquito net, then trees, and then that glorious, blue-green, ocean.

I stepped back into the room. There was a closet with double folding doors. I opened the door to the left of the closet, and my mouth dropped. The title "bathroom" didn't hold enough energy or weight to describe this room. The walls were frosted glass, so I could see the shadows of the island trees swaying outside. The ceiling was clear glass, so the big blue sky was looking down at me. The floor was a mosaic of white on white that reflected the blue of the sky. The toilet was clear, so I could see everything in the tank and in the bowl. It was smaller and higher than normal—not too small nor, too high, just different from what I was accustomed to. The clear glass pedestal sink was across from the toilet, so I'd be able to see myself in the vanity above the sink while sitting on the toilet. The shower was about five feet to the left of the toilet, with a frosted door. I slid the door to the left and could see straight through the clear glass wall into the ocean. Unmistakably, I'd arrived in Paradise.

I showered, awestruck at my view the whole time. It was like bathing outside. I untwisted and picked out my hair, got dressed, and then Eula took me on a quick tour of the property in a golf cart.

There were roosters, little lizards and frogs running, scurrying and hopping around. Lots of dragonflies, and other bugs that had been brushed with nature's colorful paint. Fortunately, there were not as many mosquitoes as I would've expected. Red, purple, green, yellow, and blue flowers, trees and bushes, were everywhere. It was like driving through a rainbow.

We made small talk about my trip. I went ahead and told her what happened, in part to explain to her exactly why I was late and why I was dressed the way I was.

She seemed to be entertained by my story, and added, "I need to get some of those balls."

I asked her if there were really sharks in the water.

She asked, "Did Harley tell you that?"

"Yeah."

"He was bitten by a shark, so he tells everyone that. There are sharks in the ocean, of course, but not here—or at least not the kind you're thinking of. The sharks here are a very small. They're just like any other fish."

Humph. Says the woman that lives like James Bond.

After a few more minutes of talking she asked, "What would you like for dinner?"

She was sophisticated and laid back all at once. She was poised and graceful but didn't seem above having a good time. We were in her home, in the living room, where she handed me a basket of menus. It made me think of my menu box back home.

"How about sushi?" I asked.

"Dine-in or delivery?"

I felt like a little kid, all wide-eyed and in awe. "They deliver *here*?"

"Yeah. Well, they deliver to me," she said with a smile.

Who is this woman?

Within thirty minutes, a speedboat was pulling up with a gorgeous, tanned, almond-eyed, Johnny Depp-looking young man dressed in all white. He got off the boat bearing bags that read KIKU NORI. He came up to me and said, "Hello. I'm Ian," in a voice deeper than I'd expected, and held out his hand.

"Breezy," I said.

"Nice to meet you. You staying on the island?"

"Yeah, just for the weekend, and then it's back home."

"And where is that?"

"New York."

"Aww, so far away? Hopefully I'll get to see you again before you leave," he said and winked. Then he went to Eula, handed her the bags, and kissed her cheek. When he did, I saw the resemblance. Clearly, Ian was a family member. I was leaning toward thinking he was her son.

When he passed me to get back on the boat, he smiled at me so sweetly, I was almost embarrassed.

You couldn't have told me a year ago that I'd ever go near sushi. Now I was addicted to it, and was mastering chopsticks. I had salmon seaweed sushi, tuna rolls, shrimp sushi, and a salad with ginger dressing. Each bite was better than the last. We were on the beach under a green canopy with a white mosquito net around it. We sat cross-legged on big, sky-blue pillows. Being there was like being in some fantasy. I just needed a man there. The wind was perfect, the smell of the ocean was inebriating. I wanted to take all my clothes off and run around and dance.

"How long have you lived here?"

"Just over eleven years."

"This is like your own personal Eden."

"Yeah. It's been a long time coming."

"What do you do, if you don't mind me asking?"

"A little of this, a little of that," she said. "I own the restaurant that delivered the sushi and several others in Florida. I also have a couple of gas stations, a few nail salons, some boutiques, and a temp agency." Her tone was proud but lacked the braggadocio that she'd obviously earned. I knew people with a lot less that talked a lot bigger.

"Wow! How did you get into so many different businesses?"

"Without getting into boring details—"

I cut her off. "Please *do* get into detail. I want to hear everything, right from the beginning—like from childhood." I just had to know how someone would become *her*.

She smiled. I'd flattered her. Then she told me her life story:

"My parents were already in their forties when they had me. My father was Japanese, and when I was three, he moved me and my mother to Japan. Needless to say, his family was less than receptive toward me and my mother, but my father didn't care. He opened a restaurant, and my mother opened a boutique, and they were both very successful. It was a stretch in those times, a black woman opening a boutique in Japan. But she did it anyway." She smiled, showing her pride. "When I was ten, they were both taken from me, and I lived in a foster home because neither family wanted me. I ran away when I was twelve and came back to America."

"Wait... how did you come back to America?" I asked.

"I stowed away on a ship with a friend. She got caught almost as soon as we got on the boat." Her eyes started watering. She reigned in her tears and said, "Anyway, I was all messed up and hungry and weak when I got to California. I didn't even know I was in California. I just knew I was in the States. I was taken into custody, along with some other stowaways I met on the ship. They put us in a paddy wagon. I was an American citizen by birth, but I didn't know to explain that to them, so I slipped out and ran down the dock, trying to make it to a street, any street. I ran smack into this kid named Trixy, and we hitchhiked and walked all the way to Portland.

"We were in the streets with the other runaways and throwaways, begging for change, for food. In his case, it was for heroin. When I wasn't doing that, I was in the library. I'd be there from open to close. You know, the librarians are supposed to tell on truant kids, but she never did. Instead, she suggested books for me to read, and after a while, she put me to work. I knew I didn't want to be a librarian. As much as I loved books, I didn't want to do any kind of job that would have me stuck indoors all day long. I hate being confined."

I related completely.

"Trixy did anything he had to for his habit. I watched him get into so many cars with disgusting, nasty johns. He'd always say, 'I'll be right back,' and he always was, until one day, he wasn't."

She said she wandered the streets looking for him, asking everyone if they'd seen him. She went to the police and told them her brother was missing, but they didn't help her. After a few weeks, she told the librarian everything, and the librarian eventually took her to the morgue. That was where they found Trixy.

Then the librarian told her she was going to call Child Welfare to help her find a home, but from what Trixy'd told her about the system, she didn't want to go, so she walked and hitched her way back to California.

She was thirteen and lied to the owner of a restaurant, telling him she was eighteen so she could get a job as a dishwasher, to be paid under the table. She didn't like it. Not because of the work, but because there was no sun in the kitchen, so she became a hostess, to get out of the back of the restaurant, and then a waitress, because she could make more money. When she made fifteen, she bought a bus ticket to New York.

"Of course, prostitution was right there, but I refused to do that, so I started hustling. First weed, then heroin, then cocaine.

"I was in the drug game for a short time because you can't be a career drug dealer. It'll all catch up with you sooner or later. I saw people going to jail and sentencing time rising, so I only did it for a little over a year. I saved all my money. I didn't buy fancy clothes, a car, or anything like that. I stayed in a room that cost me seventy dollars a week. I ate, and that was pretty much my only expense.

"Then this feeling overcame me one day and said, *'Don't even sell what you have. Don't go to Santos.'* That was the guy I used to cop from. The voice said, *'Just leave.'* The feeling was strong, like some force put it into my head and it was something that needed to be done immediately. I should've listened, but I wanted to give him his product back at least. So a little after six the next morning I went uptown to give it to him. As soon as I stepped out of the train station, I saw something like a SWAT team across the street, in front of his building. I looked up and saw men-in-black coming down the fire escape from the roof. I knew they were coming for Santos, and I couldn't even warn him. I walked up the block looking across the street at all this, and a regular officer came up to me and pulled me back and said something like, 'Sorry, but you can't be here right now, little lady.' My heart stopped because I thought it was all over. I thought he was grabbing me to put cuffs on me.

"Next thing I knew, the team on the ground rushed into the building, and the guys on the roof were going in through his window. I heard all this gunfire. I knew he was shooting at them because he always said they wouldn't take him alive. They didn't. Ambulances and cop cars filled up the block. I was standing back in front of the train station, watching them rush bodies into four different ambulances. As they were leaving, two of the ambulance's lights did just one whirl, *the death whirl*, and I just knew one of the bodies was his.

"I kept thinking, *If I'd just gotten here just a little earlier, maybe I could've warned him at least have called him. Or maybe I would've been killed too.*"

I was wide-eyed as she told me her story. She had a hood element about her that captivated me, because it was so unexpected. I couldn't believe what I was hearing.

She ended up selling the last of her product and focused on getting her GED at sixteen. At seventeen, she moved to Florida and started working at a nail salon. She learned everything about the business from the bottom up, and when she was twenty, she used her drug money, the money she'd saved working, and a student loan—which she had no intention of going to school with—to buy the salon. At twenty-two, she bought her second salon. She made sure to tell me she paid back the student loan.

"That was the same year I decided to go to Georgia to see my mother's family and find out why they didn't want me. I saw my grandmother for the first time since I was three. I'd harbored all this anger toward her for so many years because, I thought she didn't want me, only to find out that she'd been in and out of mental hospitals her whole life. She told me she wanted me, but the courts wouldn't let her have me. She died about a week after we reunited.

"Her daughter, my Aunt Ella, told me they'd all been trying to find me. I told her I kept moving and was using fake names because I didn't really want to be found. The life I was living, up until that point, it was to my advantage to be like a ghost.

"She gave me a large envelope. Inside it were copies of my parents' Wills. The two of them had left just over a million, from an insurance policy, for me to collect when I reached twenty-five."

I was eating the sushi like popcorn, I was so engrossed in her story.

She went on to tell me that she fell in love, told the guy about her money, married him, and got divorced. He took half the money, and half the salons in the settlement. She sold her half to someone else because she didn't want to have anything else to do with him. With the money she had left, she bought a gas station.

She started fishing like her father and sold her catch to a place called the Hideaway, whose owner was going out of business. She took out a business loan, this time, and bought it.

"But in my heart I always wanted a sushi spot like my father's, but I was scared because sushi was still fairly new in America. It was elitist to say the least, but in Japan it was common. I opened the first restaurant as a side project. It took about three years for it to start turning a profit. And now I have five."

She kept buying businesses. Wherever she saw an opportunity, she took it.

Hearing her story lit a fire under my ass. I had to live! I had to get out there and say, *"Fuck it!"* And just get shit done.

"Can I ask you a question?"

"Sure."

"Is it that you *can't* orgasm, or that you don't *want* to?"

"Wow. Uh...."

"I ask because it seems you take your life by the horns and won't let anything stop you. You like to read a lot, so I'm sure you've read about this subject."

"I have."

"So what do you think is blocking you?"

She took a deep breath and was silent for a long time. She took another deep breath and said, "I was raped." She then looked away from me for a moment and said, "I've never said that out loud." She said it again. "I was raped, and I hate sex. I hate my vagina. I feel like it betrayed me, and I if could tear it out of me, I would."

I didn't know if I should hug her, or what to say or do.

"So you've been holding that in for how many years?"

"Since I was ten. That was why I ran away from the orphanage. It started almost as soon as I arrived. The person that did it told me I was dirty and bad and that they would kill me if I told." She took a deep breath. "I'm just now coming to terms with it. It was a missionary from England, and she made me pray after—made me pray for forgiveness for making her do what she did to me."

I couldn't believe what I was hearing. *She?* I didn't know females did this kind of thing. I didn't want to hear any more, but she wouldn't stop. She needed to tell someone, to let it all out, but it was so hard to listen to her. I was infuriated. I wanted to find that so-called missionary and get her back for what she'd done to the poor girl who was now a scarred woman. Who knows how many kids she'd violated?

I went over to Eula and hugged her. She held on to me like it was just what she needed at that moment.

"That's the only part of my life I'm not satisfied with. I don't want to hate that part of me. I don't want to be ashamed. I want to conquer this. I just need some help." She was so vulnerable right then. She almost seemed like a different person.

We stopped hugging, and I asked, "Is this something you want to do tonight?"

She shook her head.

"I'm still going to pay you for today though."

"Huh? I wasn't even thinking about that." Honestly, I wasn't. I was thinking, *how can she get over this in order for me to teach her? What can I do to make this okay for her?*

As we talked, the sun shot west, leaving orange, purple, and blue streaks across the sky, until it was the darkest blue, dazzling with stars. Some twinkled, and some were still. It was the first time since I was a child that I wondered why? Why didn't they all twinkle? What was happening up there? It was like the world was new to me again, and instead of the thought of the finite light of stars in the infinite universe scaring me, and reminding me of death, it thrilled me. Not having the answers to every question in life didn't frighten me. Instead of fear, I felt possibilities.

I had to take another shower, just to be in that bathroom at night with the moon looking at me, and the stars winking as they beheld my nakedness, and the trees swaying in the evening breeze. I dried off, and then walked naked into the cabana. Talk about feeling free!

I stood out there for hours it seemed, but it was only about a half-hour—some more of those Florida minutes. I needed my own personal version of this. I never wanted to leave.

Chapter 22

Joyous moment,
never leave me.
These wretched seconds
insist on pushing you farther away.

The clock read exactly five a.m. when I awoke, but it didn't feel that early. It felt like it was about ten or so. I was well rested and ready to take on the day. I hadn't felt that way in years.

The rising sun was so big it looked alien, bigger than I'd ever seen. The water was calm. The seagulls and roosters were loudly gossiping about the lizards and frogs.

I got dressed in a pair of fitted, cut-off jean shorts, and a white tank top, and then went to the beach. I raised my arms and breathed deeply. The sea air brought even more life into my body and a smile to my face. I wiggled my toes in the clear ocean water. I walked farther until I was waist deep, then I dove in. I swam a few feet, and then lay back, relaxed, and floated. I felt like I *was* nature. We were the same. I was so overwhelmed with this sense of wholeness that tears started falling from my eyes. This was what I'd been chasing. Everything at that moment was right. I stayed in that moment for as long as I could before I started thinking about sharks. I left the salty water and headed back to the beach.

There was Eula sitting in a white beach chair, dressed in another white sundress. She watched me smiling as I walked to her. "You're beautiful," she said.

I had expected only a *"good morning,"* so I blushed. It was like getting a compliment from Iman. "Thank you," I said sheepishly.

I was suddenly conscious about my nipples showing through my shirt, and felt overly exposed.

"Come in the water with me," I said.

"I don't really go out there much."

"For real? I'd be out there every day if I lived here."

"I used to, but I'm fine right here."

"Are you serious? C'mon! I've got something I want to show you." I grabbed her hand, and she followed with a huff. I led her into the water; she didn't bother to take off her dress. Once we were waist deep, I leaned back and floated. "C'mon," I said into the blue air.

I felt the weight of the water change as she lay back.

"Just relax and enjoy the water," I said.

After a few minutes passed, I stood up and watched her float. I wanted her to be as calm as possible.

She looked like she was being baptized, floating in her white dress.

"Don't think," I said as I slipped my left hand beneath her dress, between her legs, catching her off guard.

She flinched.

"Relax. It's just me, you, and the water."

I needed her to let go and not be afraid of what she was feeling. To be without shame. She was scared and I understood. I was going to have to make it happen for her in such a way that she could learn to enjoy it without feeling guilty or hating her own body. Allow her to feel that it was as natural as floating on water.

She breathed deep and let it out.

I felt around for a moment until I found her clit through her panties.

She sighed.

I caressed her gently and said, "Let everything go. Just let go." Seconds later, I felt her clit harden. I rubbed her, gently, slowly, trying to figure out where she most enjoyed being touched. She was different from me. When I touched her pearl directly, she didn't like it, but when I rubbed along the hood, she let out quick breaths of air; she definitely liked that.

"Mmmm.... Can you do that faster?" she asked.

I obliged.

She bit her bottom lip, and then let it go. She was conflicted, a feeling I knew all too well. She didn't know what to do with herself.

I rubbed faster.

Her eyes went wild. I put my right arm under her waist to support her as she bucked her hips. She grabbed my arm, grunted, and made some sounds I can't even describe. She locked my left hand between her thighs and was fucking my finger with her clit, scratching the itch. This went on for several Florida minutes and then finally, there came that familiar song of sirens. Her eyes left me and rolled to the back of her head. Her body buckled. She released my hand and sank into the water.

I went under with her to make sure she was okay, and I wanted to see the satisfaction on her face.

Her hair floated above her head, and so did her dress. She pushed it down. Her face looked so relaxed. After a few moments, she let out bubbles of air.

I could see she was crying, and I smiled at her.

She pushed herself to me to hug me, and we rose out of the water together. She backed away, looked at me, and hugged me again. She nodded her head in my shoulder, saying, "*Yes*" to whatever she was feeling.

My eyes were watering for her happiness.

She started crying hard, as though she was releasing the shame and pain she'd built up for so many years. I could feel her heart pounding. Finally she let me go, still nodding her head, smiling with red eyes. She touched the side of my face with her left hand. She tried to speak, but got choked up.

We walked back to the beach, and she did three cartwheels. She turned to look back at me, still smiling, and ran up the trail toward her house.

I took another shower. I just couldn't get enough of that dang bathroom. I can't quite describe what I was feeling. Yeah, it was pride, but there was something else I couldn't quite put my finger on. I was more than happy about her overcoming. I'd done something bigger than I'd expected—bigger than myself—and I felt holy. Maybe that's too strong of a word, but I felt elevated. Not above anyone necessarily, but I felt like I'd touched some spiritual plane that I couldn't have reached alone—some communal spirituality. Oneness with everything around me. That could've just been the sea air in my lungs.

About an hour after my shower, we worked on her G-spot orgasm, which was easy for her. We were in her bedroom, and I directed her—verbally this time—using the G-spot stimulator I'd sent to her. Her eyes crossed, and she slobbered. Her reaction to it was like my reaction to my clitoral orgasms. Every woman is so different.

She was like a bouncy teenager the rest of the day. We went shopping, and she insisted on buying a gift for me.

"But you're already paying me. I kind of feel bad about that as it is."

"What you have given me is priceless." Then she looked at me sternly, like my mother, which almost scared me, and said, "Never feel guilty about being paid for your services. That's the way life works. You give and you get. There's nothing wrong with that. Being paid for helping someone is not a bad thing. It makes the person paying you feel good that they can pay you back for however you've helped them."

That was a new way to look at it, and I appreciated her saying that to me. It relaxed my shoulders.

She tried to buy a diamond tennis bracelet for me, but I told her I don't wear diamonds, because there's really no way to tell if they are conflict free. She said, "Goodness, woman! Don't make me think about things like that."

"Sorry. It's just I watched some show about how even though diamonds are rare they are more plentiful than perceived, and the African market is cornered so the prices can be driven up, and between seeing that and watching both of my future husbands in *Blood Diamond*, I just can't, in good conscience, own a diamond."

"You're going to worry the shit out of yourself. In life, sometimes you've just got to accept the things that are out of your control. Some things just are the way they are, and you have to just enjoy yourself."

"Okay," I said, simply because I really didn't want to go back and forth about it. Besides, she was covered in diamonds, so I probably should've just kept my mouth shut in the first place. I didn't want to make her feel bad for her decision to wear them.

"Well, I'll just send you a gift in the mail, because I see I really need to think about this one. I've never met a girl who didn't want diamonds." She shook her head.

I watched her spend almost $20,000 in that store like it was nothing, paying by check, and then we went to lunch at one of her restaurants. This one was in Miami, about three hours away. I gotta say, I see why people go to Miami and never leave. I needed to learn Spanish! I'd never been around so many Spanish-speaking people—and I'm from the Bronx. It was as diverse as New York, only with more freedom. Not as much freedom as the Keys, but still looser than NY. I mean, people were really walking around in bathing suits.

She took me on the grand tour of her restaurant. It was three stories of romance. Bronze and cranberry walls, thick mahogany wood tables, and dim, sultry house lights. The setup was simple: Each table was a booth, lined up against the left and right walls, ten on each side. In the back behind a silk screen, there was a hibachi bar that seated twenty. The second floor had the same design, except the middle of the floor was open to see down to the first floor. The third floor was also open in the middle, but there were fewer tables, and the hibachi bar had fewer seats. She didn't call it the VIP area, but that's what it screamed. The booths were draped in burgundy silk. Someone could easily have sex in them, and no one would know. It was lovely.

The fourth floor was where we were seated. It was a full floor, with no opening in the middle. She had an office, a separate area for her guests, and an employee lounge with comfortable chairs and a huge flat screen TV.

The kitchen went from the first floor to the third floor, with its own staircase. The restrooms were on the opposite wall of the kitchen. You might miss that they were merely restrooms, because the thick wooden doors painted with gorgeous red and gold dragons, looked like entrance ways to some special areas set aside for royalty.

The place was filled to capacity, plus there were people sitting, and standing in the waiting area, pagers in hand, waiting for them to light up and buzz when their tables were ready.

As we ate, she told me how important it was to treat her employees well. She didn't charge them for meals. She gave them an hour and a half lunch, plus their two fifteen-minute breaks. She'd hired enough people to make sure she could do that. She paid the bussers very well. "I never want anyone to leave me feeling bad or to hate being at work all day and go home feeling shitty. Life is hard enough." As a result, her staff absolutely loved her, and her turnover rate was low. She had waiters and bussers that had been with her for years. The woman was unreal.

I felt I could trust her, so I told her about my paintings. I showed her some pictures on my cell.

She asked, "Can I commission you to do a painting for me?"

"You sure can!"

"Great. I'll be getting in touch with you about that in the very near future. It's a big project. It's for a new restaurant I'm opening in Fort Lauderdale."

"Just let me know when. It's not like I'm busy with a job or anything," I said and laughed. For the first time, saying I didn't have a job didn't feel like anything to worry about.

I told her I'd always wanted to learn how to drive, so on the way back, when we were just outside of Miami, she pulled over at a shopping plaza and let me take the wheel. She said, "There's no doubt you can do it. You see all of these idiots out here? Just don't be afraid. Be cautious, but not afraid."

I got behind the wheel. I was super nervous. She told me it was an automatic. I didn't know what that meant; I thought all cars were automatic. I put the car in drive, released my foot from the brake, and just tapped the gas and the car took off. I hit the brakes hard, and we jerked forward, as far as our seatbelts would allow, then snapped back. I was scared. I didn't want to wreck us, or her car.

She said, "Remember you told me to relax? That's what you do. Relax. You're going to hit the brakes like that until you're comfortable. Just know you can do this."

After about twenty minutes, I was driving around the parking lot comfortably, so she coaxed me onto the street. My stomach was in knots, but I didn't want to punk out and disappoint her, or myself. She put the hazard lights on, and I eased into traffic, doing twenty miles an hour at first. Cars honked as they passed, and some drivers flipped me off, though it was nothing like the sea of middle fingers the drivers flipped in New York. Eula reached over me to stick her middle finger across my face and out the window, which caused me to jerk the car. Someone else honked, and I jerked back into my lane. My heart was beating fast, but I was okay. I was slowly losing my fear.

I sped up to thirty, then to forty, then fifty, then sixty. It was amazing! I drove all the way back to Marathon.

At a red light, she pushed a button, and by the time the light was green again, the top had dropped, and we were riding like *Thelma and Louise*.

The speed limit dropped to thirty, but she told me to go as fast as I felt comfortable. "Don't worry about getting pulled over. I'll handle it if you do."

Well, alrighty then.

She wanted to teach me how to drive the boat too. I told her to slow down. I wasn't ready for that just yet. But I did tell her I was going to buy a car whenever I got the money up, and could afford insurance, maintenance, parking and gas. After I listed those things, I thought maybe it was more than it would be worth to have a car. At least in NYC.

When we got back to the island, Ian was there, sitting on the beach, looking like sugar. Turned out, I was correct in thinking he was her son.

Eula went into the house, came back out a few minutes later, and said, "I'm going out for a while. Ian, play nice with our guest." For some reason, I just knew she was going to get some.

I went to my bungalow, showered in that awesome, wonderful shower, and changed into my bathing suit. Ian was still on the beach when I went back. I went to the beach chair to his right. I wiped the seat first, but I still felt sand underneath me when I sat.

As fine and flirtatious as Ian was, I could've done him right there, easily. But, my mind kept going back to Sean.

I checked my messages, texts, emails, and Facebook from my phone. I hadn't checked any since I'd been in Florida. I had two messages from Sean. I started cheesing as I read, "wassup, lady? ur on my mind way more than I expected. can't wait 2 get back home 2 c u." The next read, "I really can't get u off my mind."

I sent back, "can't get u off my mind either."

"So someone already got to you, huh?" Ian asked, with his flirtatious smile.

"Already?"

"Yeah, before I could." He couldn't be more than twenty-three, twenty-five tops.

"Why do you say that?"

"The way you're smiling from ear to ear. Somebody has you open."

Was I wearing it on me?

"And here I was thinking I could fall in love."

"That's cute," I said.

"I'm serious. I thought you were feeling me."

"Is that what I'm giving off?"

"Yeah, but I think you're just a flirt."

"I'm not. You're the flirt in this situation."

"Nah. I just like what I see."

I smiled, stood up, put the phone on the chair, wiped the sand from my butt, and then walked into the water. He followed me. I didn't want to be bothered. I just wanted to float and smile at my Sean thoughts.

"You ever skinny-dip?"

"No," I answered.

"You should try it."

"You're right," I said and slipped out of my bathing suit. I whirled it around in my hand to pick up speed and tossed it. It actually landed on my beach chair. "Did you see that? Right on the chair!" I said smiling.

His eyes were wide, and not because of my amazing toss. He took his wife beater off, then his shorts, and finally his boxers.

We played in the water, laughing like kids. It wasn't sexual, at least not for me. It was just pure, sweet fun. We splashed water on each other, slow-chased one another, running against the water, which turned into a spontaneous race. We laughed a lot. I imagined playing like that with Sean. *Maybe one day....*

"So, what's your boyfriend's name?"

"I don't have a boyfriend."

"Really?" He moved closer to me.

"What are you doing?"

"Getting closer to you."

"For what?"

"Because you're in front of me, naked."

My clit started twitching, and my pussy started contracting. I backed out of the water until I was waist deep, while he was still neck deep. "I don't have a boyfriend, but I am involved."

"But it's just me and you here." He moved closer to me until we were both waist deep, and his stiffness was threatening to poke me.

"I can't have sex with you, sweetie."

"Can I have sex with you?"

"That's cute, but no." I looked over at the setting sun. My clit was already in her zone, and I couldn't stop her. She didn't feel weird about the fact that I'd just taught his mother how to masturbate that morning. She didn't care about anything except getting off. I took his hand, put it down between us, and wrapped it around his cock.

"What are you doing?"

"I want to watch you jerk off."

"What?"

"I watch you, you watch me."

"Right here?"

"Yeah. Are you scared?"

"No. I just—I've never done that in front of anyone."

The water undulated, gently moving us together, and pushing us apart in a soothing rhythm.

"Even if you don't do it, I'm still going to do it."

"You start then."

"Baby!" I teased, then reached my hands between my legs and started caressing my clit.

We looked into each other's eyes.

He looked like he couldn't believe it was happening.

I smiled at him, and bit my bottom lip because it was getting good to me.

He started stroking himself.

I looked down to watch him grow, and my, how he grew! My pussy started salivating. I rubbed my left middle between my labia and put my right hand on his left shoulder. I closed my eyes and thought about Sean's lips, picturing them kissing every part of me.

I opened my eyes, and Ian's eyes were on my breasts with his mouth open, and tongue out. That excited me. I wanted to rub my titties all over his tongue. But I restrained myself. I started moaning, then he started moaning. Our sounds dueled. He gritted his teeth and grunted. I started cumming. I grabbed his shoulder tighter, and wailed. Without warning he shot all over my stomach, and managed to get a good final squirt on my left nipple. I let go of his shoulder.

"I'm sorry," he said.

"That's okay."

He cleaned my stomach and my breasts with the salty water. He touched me like I was a feather.

"Are you hungry?" he asked.

"Starving."

"I'll make dinner for you—anything you want."

"You make sushi?"

"Of course I do."

We went straight to the kitchen still naked. We both washed our hands, and then he pulled shrimp and fish, which he'd just caught that day, from the freezer. He started the water for the sticky rice and got some seaweed ready. Watching him cook was an event. He showed off his knife skills, throwing them in the air, catching them, chopping quickly, slicing and dicing. Meanwhile the radio played Gyptian's, "Hold Yuh." Of course I started dancing, swaying my hips to the rhythm. He turned to look at me and started chatting along with the song, surprisingly well.

That made me ask, "Where's your father from?"

"Trinidad. Why?"

"I was just curious."

"Yup, I'm a mutt."

"Don't say that!"

"I'm just kidding. Where's your family from?"

"North Carolina on both sides."

We kept talking like that, listening to the radio and dancing until he was done.

"You have a really good energy about you," he said, motioning at me with his wooden chopsticks. The sun was setting and those gorgeous sun streaks, ripped across the sky.

"You think so?"

"Yeah. I would never have done that with anyone else. That's not something I ever pictured myself doing."

"I find myself doing a lot of things lately that I thought I would never do."

"I would really like to do it again."

My clit has her own ears. *Down, girl!*

Too late. She took over, and after we ate, we were in his bed, in one of the guest houses, masturbating for each other. It turned into a competition at some point, of who could bust the most nuts the fastest. I won. He could only pull out three in a row. I don't think a man can win an orgasm contest against a woman that knows how to cum. It was an unfair competition, but it was fun.

His mother returned the next morning. It was a perfect lazy Sunday, and we all relaxed on the beach—just chilling and enjoying the beautiful ocean, the gorgeous sky, and the humid air. And me enjoying the secret I shared with each of them. We ate breakfast, laughed, and kept it breezy.

Chapter 23

When you give without expecting,
you receive without asking
in ways you couldn't have
anticipated.

The Universe is laughing.

I didn't want to leave Florida. That weekend seemed to slow everything down enough to put things into perspective. *This is it. This is the only life I'm going to get. And it's happening right now. I can take this talent I have—this gift, of getting women to open up to me—and make a living with it. This could be a real thing. This is something special.*

On the plane, I pulled out a pen and paper and started writing down ways for me to turn it into a real business. I had to think like Sandy and have heart like Eula. I'd learned from them that it was all about seizing opportunity and just making it happen.

I was thinking of ways to get my name out there and wrote down, "word-of-mouth." That was, after all, how I'd gotten my last two clients. Then I scribbled, "website, blog, business cards." That was the easy part. But how would I approach woman about this? I couldn't just run up on random strangers in the street and ask them if they wanted to learn how to orgasm. I didn't have the answers, but the thoughts and questions were getting me excited.

The freedom feeling was beginning to leave me as I sat on the crowded bus from Newark. It melted away even more when I took the train back to the Bronx; on the elevator ride up to my floor; on my walk down the hallway; putting my key into my door, which was right next to another door. Right across from two other doors, and right above another apartment. One of forty-eight, apartments in my building. Jumbled among about a million and a half people in the Bronx, one of eight million in NYC.

Don't get me wrong—I love New York. I wouldn't have traded growing up here for anywhere else on this Earth. But Florida just felt so uncluttered. I could stretch out my arms and breathe there.

My apartment felt so restrictive. I looked out the window and saw other buildings. That view excited me before my trip. Looking out at so many people in every direction, but my perspective had changed. Now it was like, *Oh my goodness! So many people everywhere, in every direction!*

As the day went on, I settled back into my New York shoes. I didn't take a shower until about five o'clock. That was also when I turned on the TV. Normally, I don't watch the news, but I figured I'd just check it out to see what had happened in the world while I was off in Paradise, eating sushi, and having masturbation contests with the twenty-something chef. I braced myself for the talk of war, missing children, or the latest killing spree.

"...disturbance at Newark International Airport this weekend took a surprising twist. That story and more, when we come back after these messages."

I heard it, but it didn't register.

I turned the TV up loud enough for me to hear it while I was in the shower, and I listened to the commercials. One did its job and made me hungry for pizza.

When the news came back on, the anchors exchanged their corny banter and then one said, "This weekend at Newark International Airport, the woman seen here caused major security alarm..."

It would be funny if they were talking about me, I said to myself, thinking of the Ben Wa episode.

"... security detained her..."

Wait... are they talking about me? I almost busted my ass trying to pull the shower curtain back to get out. I ran into my bedroom. I gasped so hard that I almost choked. My eyes got so wide they started drying out. The video they were showing was grainy, but I recognized myself, walking through the metal detector at Newark.

"...turned out to be an adult toy," the anchorwoman said, with a slick smile.

"Yes. Apparently the woman planned on joining the Mile High Club for one," the other anchorwoman said, with a snicker.

I started screaming like I'd found a horse's head in my bed. "Ahhh! Oh my Gahd! Ahhhhh!" Every time the thought ran across my mind, another screech came out. "Ahhhh!"

Okay. Okay. What? Okay. What? This can't be real. A dream. Yes. This is some wild, super-realistic dream. I'm not awake. Maybe I'm still on the plane.

But I wasn't on the plane. I was in my bedroom, smack dab in the middle of cruel reality.

They kept replaying the image of me going through the metal detector. It was hard to make me out. *I* knew it was me, but it didn't look like anyone else would know. My wig covered my neck and the side of my face, shielding my identity. I was filled with anxious, fearful energy, so I started pacing.

My cell buzzed, causing my heart to jump. It was a text from Sandy that read, "Just checking 2 B sure u arrived hm safe sum shit hpnd in newark holla bk."

"im here...safe," I sent back.

"sum chick wuz jrkn off @ the airprt. LMAO! wuz that u? LOL"

"YES."

Then the phone rang.

"I was just kidding. That was really you?"

"Yes, damn it!"

"Word?"

"I can't talk right now. I'm thinking."

I hung up while she was still saying something. I couldn't quite wrap my mind around the situation.

Ten minutes later, my mother was calling me. *I swear Sandy has the biggest mouth in the world.* I knew what happened; she told her sister, and then they three-wayed with her mother, then her mother called my mother.

"No, Mommy, they didn't sexually harass me.... No, I wasn't planning on doing it on the plane. It was an accident.... No, I *still* don't have a boyfriend.... What does this have to do with getting pregnant?... I know it doesn't make me a bad person, Mommy.... I know everyone does it.... Okay, Mommy that was a little too much information.... No, I didn't need to know that.... Okay, I'm going to throw up now.... No, I was not trying to join some Mile High Club. I wasn't even doing anything.... Ben Wa balls.... Why are you laughing at me?... I love you too.... No, don't put Grandma on the phone.... Yes, ma'am.... No, of course I like men.... Anal plug?... Yeah, I know who Heather Hunter is. You know who she is?... I love you too."

Thank goodness my father wasn't home.

They actually made me feel a little better. The more I let it sink in, the more I realized they were the people I cared most about finding out, or being affected by the incident.

* * *

I had an interview that Monday morning. When I got on the 5 at 125th Street, I had a moment between my thoughts to hear two girls having a conversation.

One girl with a Jamaican accent said to the other, "She's in the line, jerking off, as if no one's going to see her. They pull her off the line, strip her naked because they think the dildo is a bomb. People are running around all wild, and all the flights get cancelled. The shit was crazy!"

I wanted to yell, *"That is not what happened!"*

The other girl said with a Puerto Rican accent, "You know that was a white chick that did *that*." She twisted up her face when she said, "that."

I heard people on their cells in the lobby and in the elevator where I had my interview. There were only a few people, but that was enough. The stories were so varied and so colorful. I heard, "She was literally in the line fingering herself," and, "So the security guard yanks the vibrator out of her, and...."

Mr. Bennett, the interviewer, scanned me, then scanned my résumé, then scanned me again. "You have a lot of experience. Are there any embellishments here? I mean, when did you start working, when you were twelve?" He didn't say it like he was jokingly giving me a compliment about how young I looked; he said it like he thought I was lying about my work history.

"Mr. Bennett, if I don't qualify, that's fine, but please don't question my integrity by calling me a liar."

"Humph." He rubbed his chin. "You can start next Monday," he said like he was doing me a favor.

Nothing about him made me feel good. The Universe had to be messing with me. The job offered a really good salary, and because of that, I felt stuck. My choices felt limited. My world seemed to be shrinking around my shoulders. I didn't want it, but I needed it. *Steady income, right? Even though I just made thousands of dollars over the weekend. Yup. That was a one-time thing. Like that's gonna happen again. Dreams don't pay bills. This job is real and right here. You better take this good job and be damn grateful. Don't be a fool, Breezy.*

I swallowed all the pride, and anxiety I was feeling. I smiled, and shook his hand. I got a nasty taste in my mouth.

* * *

On my way home, I picked up the paper. There was a picture of me going through the metal detector with a big question mark above my nondescript head. Readers couldn't even necessarily tell my race. The photo only had the back of my head and the hood of my sweater, bunched up at the back of my neck, and my wig, which covered the sides of my face. At that moment, I really missed the 90's. Back in the days, before texting, and social media, when news didn't travel nearly as fast. All things considered, it was actually kind of slow. It happened Friday, and the news didn't break until Sunday, as far as I could tell.

The paper actually got the story right, which I couldn't believe. "The woman was wanded, detained momentarily.... The toy was discovered, and then she was released as a non-security threat." There was a lot of filler and fluff added to make the article longer, but that was pretty much it.

No one else got it right though. Everyone else just speculated. It was just the sex toy, and the airport, and they took off with that and did whatever they wanted to with the story, like that telephone game kindergartners play. By the time the story gets to the last kid it's all twisted and wrong.

Cindy called me to find out about my trip and to ask, "Yo, did you see that white chick on the news jerking off on the plane?"

"No."

"Yeah, she got arrested for playing with herself."

White chick arrested for playing with herself? Wow.

"Did they show her face?" I asked to see if she'd seen something I hadn't seen to make her think the woman was white.

"I don't think so."

"How do you know she was white?"

"Because you know how dirty white women are."

"So you think the chick was dirty?"

"Not *dirt* dirty. The nasty, freaky kind of dirty. Women of color, we don't do shit like that, at least not in public."

"Humph. I guess. So you really think it went down like that?"

"It's all over the news."

"You know, you shouldn't believe everything you see on the news. They don't get everything right. I mean, how likely is it that someone is standing in a line jerking off with a dildo? Doesn't that sound all wrong to you?"

"Please! With all the shit going on in the world that sounds right on point to me."

* * *

On Tuesday, there was a panel discussion on an afternoon talk show about the weekly topics of interest so far. People were dying to know who I was. It seemed they all used the same picture from the paper, with the question mark. I tried to listen objectively, but I couldn't. I was on the inside looking out. Everyone had a strong opinion. Everyone had a joke. *Aren't we at war? Isn't the ocean flooding with oil? How is this even on the radar? How is this newsworthy at all?*

At the same time, a story broke about yet another priest molestation cover-up. Yet my incident in Newark was bigger. *How?* I could see how though. People would rather talk about a non-serious sexed-up story versus dealing with the horrible reality of child molestation, oil leaks, and other human against human, or human against Earth crimes. The Newark incident was an escape from all the real depressing mess going on in the world. That didn't change how I felt about it. I wanted everyone to get out of my business—even if they didn't know it was my business they were in. *Still, get the eff out!*

I tried not to think of it. I put it in the back, left corner of my mind, where I put all things unpleasant, and turn them into fluffy, pink, clouds.

* * *

Even though I'd accepted the job offer, I hadn't completely given up on my dream. I concentrated on a design for my business card and website. With no job to rush to in the morning, I was able to concentrate in a way I hadn't been able to since college. It was almost scary at first. I lost myself in my mind and came up with what I felt was a brilliant design: a blooming pink flower with petals simulating the labia, a finger touching what would be the clitoris, and a drop of water falling from the gaping bloom.

I was so anxious that I free-handed the painting instead of sketching it, like I would normally. I was so proud of myself for actually completing the thought. It was in my head first, and then it was in front of me in vivid, living color. It was a good, fulfilling feeling. One that I have every time I paint, and I was going to make sure I never stopped having.

* * *

Though I knew the time Eula, and I'd spent together was intimate, and life changing, I was just not used to people considering me. Growing up, I was usually left out of things. I was rarely invited to birthday parties, or clubs, or any other events, or outings by other kids. With the exception of the

Get-It Girl Crew, I was somewhat of an outcast. I still carried that with me as an adult, which was why I was always surprised when someone extended a friendship hand to me in the vein of wanting to actually spend time with me, outside of what I assumed was our designated relationship. That was why I didn't get Cindy wanting to be my friend, and that was why I was surprised when FedEx showed up at my door while I was painting, with a package from Eula. I thought she was cocktail-talking me when she said she was going to send something, but I guess she wasn't. Not only did she send it, but she'd paid attention to what I'd said about conflict diamonds.

I tore into the package like I was seven years old and it was midnight on December 25th. I opened the four-by-four shiny black wooden box that read, "SAKHA." Inside was a frosty glass box with the same name embossed clear into the top with a gold lock. There was a small gold key. I used it to unlock the box, and sitting atop a white, satin, cushion was a pair of five-petal, half-inch long, white diamond earrings set in white gold, each with a red diamond in its center. I gasped and my mouth dropped. There was a small glossy black folded card, inside of the white box that read, "Conflict Free, 100 Percent Certified, Russian Diamond." There was a small handwritten white card that read, "Every girl should have diamonds."

I was overcome by tears. Not because they were diamonds, but because she'd taken into consideration what I'd said. This was too much. I didn't even know if I should accept it.

I called her immediately to thank her. I wanted to know how much it cost, but of course I didn't ask her.

"Eula, this is an amazing gift. I've never had anyone give me anything like this before."

"I'm glad to hear you say that because I've never had anyone give me what you've given me. I masturbate every day, and each time it gets better and better. I'm learning all kinds of things about my body, and it's all thanks to you."

"But these earrings! I mean, my goodness. They are so expensive."

"That's not your concern, but if it makes you feel better, I have a friend who has a friend... and I got them at a really good price."

No matter what the good price was, I knew it was still too much. "Looks like I need some friends like yours," I joked.

"Well, you have a friend like me, so you have a foot in the door."

The conversation lasted longer than I'd expected. We talked about the restaurants she wanted to open in California and DC. She wasn't ready for New York, she said. "New York scares me a little."

"I can't picture you being afraid of anything. You're like this fearless all-woman. It seems once you set your mind on something, you do it and excel."

"You know, Breezy, you have that in you too. You just don't see it for whatever reason, and it's really frustrating for me to know you're not doing what you need to do. Between teaching women to pleasure themselves and your art, you should never have to clock in at a job ever again—not ever."

I wasn't ready to hear that from her, and I didn't know how to react. Part of me wanted to say, *"Where do you get off? You don't know me like that,"* while the less indignant, smarter part of me thought, *"Lady, you are so right."*

Truth was, I needed a lot of kicking in the ass. I don't know if it was some kind of genetic malfunction or what, but I needed constant reassurance, constant outside sources of motivation. I wasn't enough. I didn't have the wherewithal to completely motivate myself—at least not at first. But her telling me she was frustrated really did something to me. She sounded like my mother. Though my mother would never have said she was frustrated, even though I knew she was—especially when it came to my art.

"I just really don't know exactly what to do."

"I understand that. Just promise me this; Promise me, and yourself, that you won't be stagnant."

I promised, and we ended the conversation on that very high note.

* * *

I got up that following Monday morning to start my new job. I'd ironed my clothes before eating breakfast, and was trying to get back into my get-to-work groove, but when I sat on the edge of my chair to put on my stockings, I just couldn't. My foot wouldn't go in the stocking. It was the weirdest thing, like my toes just wouldn't cooperate. I put the stockings down. When I picked them back up, my head started hurting. I put them back down, and the pain went away.

I huffed, and sat still for a moment, then got up to put on my white blouse. I looked at myself in the mirror. I'd missed a button. I could only laugh at the reflection of my lopsided shirt. I shook my head and redid the buttons, then went to put on my skirt. I'd just tried it on before I'd ironed it, and it was fine. Now, the zipper was stuck, and I couldn't pull it up. I took it off and started looking for another skirt. I looked in my closet, and all of my work clothes looked heavy. I stood there staring at them. I wanted to take them all and throw them out: every skirt, every matching blazer, and every boring pantsuit.

A million thoughts chased each other around my mind: *Bills. Happiness. Bills. Living dreams. Bills. Death. This is it. This moment is my life. Right now. And right now I have enough money to pay my bills. And even if I didn't, I have people who love me, and if I fall, they won't let me crash. And neither will I. I'm ready. Doesn't matter that you're ready. You have responsibilities. You have good credit, and you have an apartment you love. What's the cost of living dreams? What am I willing to sacrifice? What if I fail? What if I lose everything? What if I win? Not trying would be my failure.*

I unbuttoned my blouse and hung it up. I went to my other closet and got a wife beater and a pair of sweats. I called Mr. Bennett and said, "I'm not going to be able to work for your company." I thought for a moment and added, "Also, you're a condescending asshole, and I hate that I ever shook your hand." I hung up and went back to focusing on growing my masturbation business.

* * *

That same afternoon, Justin came back from Asia with a moral dilemma.

We took a cab to meet up with his sister Jessica for dinner. I told him about the Newark incident. He just kept staring at me like I was a puzzle, saying, "That was you?" He said he pictured a tall butch-looking redhead with a vibrator hanging from her.

"You're special," I said.

"That's what I thought. Not that it doesn't make sense that it was you, but I didn't expect you to sit here, and tell me that."

Jessica was waiting for us at a hole-in-the-wall called, Pasta! Pasta!, off of Bruckner Boulevard. They only had five tables since most orders were to go. There was one waitress, the owner Angelo's mother, who insisted on working there, despite his protests. She was about seventy, so the customers were always helping her instead of the other way around.

The whole time we were together, I could tell something was weighing heavy on his mind, but it didn't seem like he was ready to talk about it yet. When Justin was ready to talk, he'd talk.

Finally he broke. He told us about his trip and said, "First we went to the factory in Hong Kong. That one was cool, not like an American factory, but it wasn't a sweat shop. Then we took a flight somewhere about an hour away. We weren't in China anymore and they wouldn't tell us exactly where we were. We landed at some backwoods airstrip, and I swear they were hiding us, like we were *persona non grata* on some top secret mission in enemy territory. Anyway, the factory there was a whole different story. Of course I already knew about the factories and heard how bad they were. I'd seen the pictures, even videos. But being on a tour, seeing it face to face...." He shook his head. "I can't do this anymore. Every time I design something for this company, I'm condoning some horrible shit. I know they were on their best behavior for us, so I can imagine what it's like on a daily basis. I don't...." He huffed. "I don't know what to do."

As he's talking, I'm thinking, *what the fuck is "persona non grata"?* But I didn't want to mess with the momentum of his moment. Instead I asked, "Have you asked if they can change? Like use American—"

He started shaking his head, cutting me off. "Money talks louder than ethics, Breezy. You know that."

"That's right, and we all need money. You have to make a living just like everyone else. You don't have to change the world, Justin," Jessica said.

"Maybe not, but I can change *my* world."

"What does that mean?" Jessica asked, raising her left eyebrow.

"I don't know yet."

"I'm not gonna sit around thinking about sweatshop kids when I buy my clothes. That's just not happening. What the fuck am I supposed to wear? I like to look good."

"Why are you getting so upset?"

269

"Because... I don't know. It sounds like you're trying to make me feel guilty."

"How? I'm telling you about something *I'm* going through. This has nothing to do with you."

"I know, but it does. You just planted a seed in my head. You're always planting seeds in my head. That's why I'm a freaking vegetarian now."

"Stop following after me then," he said, like they were twelve years old. "You make everything about you." He rolled his eyes at her. "Breezy, what do you think?"

"I'm not getting between you guys, but I will say this; we all have moments where we either need to go left or go right."

"Here you go now. You wanna make me feel guilty too?" Jessica sucked her teeth.

"What I'm saying is that you can't keep going straight, because you can't act like you don't know what you know. You can't act like you haven't been affected, not if you're being real with yourself. So now, you're either going to do what feels right or what feels wrong. No one will blame you if you keep on doing what you're doing, because you feel you have no other choice."

"But I *do* have a choice."

And just like that, "The House of JM" was born.

Chapter 24

A Soapbox Moment by Breezy Deigh

The funniest part of the Newark Incident was everyone's assumption that I was white. It's like when I, and most of the country, immediately assumed the DC sniper was white. There are just certain behaviors we associate with certain races, because everything in this country is based on race. Sexual expression—in this manner anyway—is not typically associated with black women. Our country is already hypocritical in its perception of sexuality. It wants to be puritanical, while having a multi-billion dollar sex industry.

In regard to black American sexuality, America is downright schizophrenic—especially with females. Every culture has its sexual hang-ups. For African-Americans, I believe ours stem from us being viewed as non-human, sexual objects during slavery, when we were bred, used, and raped, as an everyday part of slave and master relations. Between the unwanted pregnancies, and knowing that someone can take what's most precious from us with impunity, it created fear, and shame, and made us prudish about sex. Our natural reaction to counter the idea of the black mistress, has been to repress our sexuality—even with each other. That repression has lasted for generations, and it has become part of black American culture. Not every black American individually, but as a whole, we seem to hold a type of shameful relationship with sex. It goes beyond America's general, puritanical, religious shame. It's our own cultural shame. A lot of us don't speak about sex and look at women who admit to certain sexual appetites as though something is wrong with them. I know black women now who won't fellate, or at least *won't admit to it, and not due to some traumatic experience, but just because they don't want to be viewed as someone who would allow a man to have them in that way.*

So, are viewed as sexually prudish, non-experimental, and in some cases, asexual.

Again, I stress, this is not ALL of us, and might I add, not only us.

On the other hand, we are [still seen as hyper-sexual, and easy. Brainless sex toys to be used for male amusement. Just take a look at the majority of main stream hip hop videos (sorry my beloved hip hop, my love for you is real and strong you, but most of your videos, especially since the start of the new millennium, have exploited female sexuality on Hollywood levels. Not Hollywood meaning glamor and glitz, but Hollywood as in them being original, major media exploiters of women.).

But, here's the thing: All women in this country, and most other countries, are viewed as sexual objects. Men can't help it. Pussy is amazing! Men fear our sexuality so much, because they can't deal with how it makes them feel. It's so amazing, in fact, that they have aimed to suppress our sexuality throughout history, so, they can maintain control of their own faculties. The ones who mean to suppress female sexuality suffer from limited imaginations, when it comes to dealing with problems of their own self-control, so they have to control everyone else. That's my take on it anyway. Men with great imaginations don't seem to suffer from the same inadequacy. They appreciate pussy. They sing about it, draw it, and sculpt it. They write about it, and some want to put their whole damn face in it. But those creative appreciators are rarely in power.

So, it's up to us, ladies. We are in the position now more than ever to claim our sexual identity, and that means every one of us! We shouldn't be afraid. If you love to get head, then let him know! Push his face in it! If you want to dominate or be dominated, don't be afraid to express it. If you like to fellate, doggone it, fellate until you get lock jaw! And if you like to masturbate, then damn it, do it until your fingers cramp, and you can cum no more! All of us are here because of sex. Hopefully, consensual sex, but sex none the less. People are so afraid and ashamed of the very cause of our existence. Let it go! Free yourself!

Okay. I'm stepping down from my soapbox.

The Newark Incident took on its own life. It was one of those times when I closed my eyes really tight and wished with all my might that I could will time to reverse. I could almost feel the quantum physics of it all. But alas, there I was in my present-day living room, online, reading a blog about women who masturbate; the topic was "Newark Annie"—the nickname the blogger had affectionately, and unknowingly, given me.

"Instead of demonizing this woman, we should celebrate her courage! I'm so tired of men still trying to control every aspect of our sexuality," the author wrote, ending her blog.

Then her readers went at it:

"I agree w/u. she is my SHERO & phuck men & what they think about it & phuck the uptite women who just don't get it!"

"you women are disgusting and ungrateful. you want to play with your toys in public and be disrespectful. if this woman is your 'shero,' iWillrocku29, then you are just another example of where this country and this world have gone wrong. your man should be enough for you but i'm sure you're a hardcore lesbo."

"u got this chick playn w/hrslf n public. the otha day, I c a lady feedn a baby w/her tit out n public. gay ppl makin out in the street... I mean, WTF is nxt?"

"@TheAmericanWay1212 – & I'm sure ur dick is very small, u latent homosexual. w/men like u around, I just oughta be a lesbo."

"i'm a female & I dnt like ne of this. she shld b ASHAMED of hrslf"

"oh PULEEEZE!!! now no1 has eva jerked off b4? bunch of HIP-O-CRITS!!!"

"sum men r just so threatened by a woman's sexuality."

"We like to jerk off and fuck just as much as men do, but men don't wanna hear that shit."

"Let's all calm down and bust a nut, shall we LOL"

"where is this funny??? society is breaking down all around us."

"if masturbation signals the breakdown of society then it's been broken down since the dawn of man, baby!"

It went on and on for pages, and this wasn't the only blog. It was being Tweeted and Facebooked, and on other social networks I'd never even heard of. It was just everywhere, and everyone had an opinion.

I kept telling myself to have a thick skin about it. It wasn't like these people knew who I was, and I was sure it would blow over soon.

Then the oddest thing happened: This short, blonde, very loud woman got on television claiming to be Newark Annie. She wore a T-shirt that read, "I MASTURBATE ON PLANES," in big red letters. I was amused, but part of me wanted everyone to know she wasn't the real Newark Annie, even if she did masturbate on planes. *I'm Newark Annie, damn it! And I don't masturbate on planes! I masturbate on trains!*

She wasn't the only one. Women across the country claimed to be me. They were online and calling into radio shows. They were on local television stations everywhere, each laying claim to the Newark Annie name.

I felt ambiguous. I didn't want anyone to know it was me, but I didn't want anyone else to claim it either. Underneath it all, I guess I felt kind of proud of all the talk about me. I mean, I really did want it to stop, *but* I really enjoyed reading and seeing the way women responded to the situation. At least the good responses, anyway. The twisted misrepresentation of a simple incident seemed to empower some women. It was as if they'd just been waiting for something like this to happen so they could release what had been building up inside of them, and finally shout without shame, "I masturbate!"

Someone trademarked the name Newark Annie, and started selling T-shirts. They were selling like hotcakes. That caused a feud with the blogger who coined the name, and she brought a lawsuit against him.

Some men were so offended you would've thought I literally shat on them. It was hard for me to wrap my mind around how angry some of their responses were. Many seemed to take it as a personal assault against their manhood that women masturbate. As if it somehow lessened their role as men, or threatened the need for their manhood.

Other men were completely titillated, and wanted to know exactly what women were doing to masturbate, and how it felt. They wanted all the juicy details.

Some women found strength in it, while others were disgusted by Newark Annie, and all women who masturbated. Some people just have fucking issues!

I decided to contact Mallory Marx, the blogger who'd named me Newark Annie—without letting her know who I was. Her picture looked friendly enough; her hair was full of orange curls, and she wore a big Lauren Hutton smile and red-rimmed glasses. Plus, I liked what she'd said in her blog. I sent an email asking her if she thought her audience would be receptive to someone giving personal self-pleasure lessons. She sold sex toys through her blog, so I figured she'd be the perfect person to ask.

Mallory responded, "I don't see why they wouldn't. I get questions all the time about how to use the toys I sell. Women ask me if I can come and show them. I was thinking of a doing a seminar, but I have a regular nine-to-five like everyone else. It's not something I have time for. Is that what you do? Give self-pleasure lessons? If you do, maybe we can work something out."

Her response surprised me, especially since I didn't expect her to respond at all. I took her willingness to help as a sign that the stars were aligning for me. *No excuses! It's time to make this thing happen.* I damn near wanted to tell her who I was, but instead I just wished her luck with the lawsuit, and told her I would be in touch with her soon.

I set up my website, and Mallory let me link it to her blog. I got a few hits that first week—sixteen, to be exact, and they were just people looking. I considered setting up a blog on my site, but I didn't have much to say. Besides, it was so obviously self-serving, and I didn't want to come across that way. So I put the blog on the back burner for the time being.

But I needed to act soon.

* * *

It had been a little over two weeks since I'd actually spoken to Sean. We'd hit each other up on Facebook but we had no verbal communication.

When we finally did speak, I shouldn't have been so happy to hear from him. I shouldn't have allowed myself to get so caught up in the joy of hearing his voice. But there I was, completely elated. When I saw the foreign number on my caller ID, I cheesed so big and wide my cheeks hurt. I'm sure light was shining from me. "Hello," I said, as nonchalantly as possible.

"What's up, Breezy?" He sounded like he was smiling.

"What's going on?"

"Don't try to act like you're not happy to hear from me. I know you are, because I'm happy to hear you."

"I'm not trying to act like I'm not happy to hear from you."

"Yeah, alright."

I changed the subject before it went any further. I didn't need to let my insecurity show. What I really wanted to say was, *"I understand that you have a life outside of me that doesn't include me at all, and it wasn't necessary for you to actually hear my voice, but I wanted to hear your voice, so I'm mad because you didn't want to hear mine the way I wanted to hear yours, or else you would've called me!"* But I reined that in, and instead asked, "Where are you now?"

"Amsterdam. We're not playing tonight, just relaxing. How are things with you? How's the job search going?"

"I found something, but I turned it down. I just couldn't bring myself to get dressed, get on that train, and start that whole routine all over again."

"You alright with money?"

"Are you offering to help?"

"If you need it."

"I appreciate that, but I'm good."

"I know you got your sugar daddies lined up."

"Please! Not at all."

"I'll be home soon. You gonna be ready when I come back?"

I blushed. "Ready for what?"

"Ready for me?"

"Uh huh."

"I can't wait to get back. I need to see you."

I was on cloud nine. No man should be able to get me that high. It would be too far of a fall if he disappointed me.

"Yo, I hear people are bugging out in the States. Some chick got caught jerking off right in her seat on a plane. You hear about that?"

"Uh... not quite like that."

"You know, I don't believe anything in the news. She probably had a vibrator in her bag or something like that."

"Yeah."

"Believe none of what you hear and half of what you see."

"Hey, my mother says that all the time."

"Wise woman. It's true, especially now with Photoshop and the new *art* of made-up news. You can't believe anything."

I took a deep breath and said, "I have some things to tell you when you get back."

"You're pregnant with another man's baby, but you want me to stand in as the father because I'm such a good guy, and you regret that you ever had sex in your life with anyone outside of me?"

I laughed. "Uh, no. Just some stuff that happened while you were gone."

"Alright."

He didn't press for details, and I liked that.

So, word about me had even reached Europe. *Humph. An internationally known masturbator. My mother's pride and joy.*

* * *

A week later, he was at my house, smelling good and looking better. That month he was gone was a month too long. He gave me a big, warm hug and a juicy kiss and said, "I really missed you."

I loved that kiss! It had every color of the rainbow in it. We sat on the couch, and he told me about his trip. I loved watching him talk about his travels: the imitations of the accents, his gestures, and his expressions. He was so entertaining. By the time he'd finished, I felt like I'd gone to Europe too.

Then his whole face changed. I didn't know him well enough to gage the expression, but I expected he was about to say something he was thoroughly disappointed about.

"That was our last tour though. The band is breaking up."

"What? Why?"

"Leland decided he has another direction he wants to go with his music. It all just got real shitty real quick. Whatever. The group is over."

"What about the album?" They were supposed to do an LP, for everyone to showcase their skills individually, while maintaining the flavor of the group. He'd let me hear what they'd had so far, and I was looking forward to the full album.

"There is no album. It's just over. Everything is dead. We have a few more gigs, but after that it's over." He huffed and shook his head. "I think I'm done with this whole music thing."

"What? Are you serious?"

"Yeah. I mean, every time I take a step forward, I get knocked back five. I'm done."

I didn't want to be too familiar with him, and overstep my boundaries, but I wanted to tell him not to give up on his dream. "We've only known each other for a short time, but from what I know of you, I just can't picture you not doing music."

"I don't really want to get into all of that right now. I need to find a job."

"Like a nine-to-five?"

"Yup."

He couldn't give up, and be regular people. I just couldn't see that. "Can I say something?"

"Of course."

"You not doing music is pretty much impossible. It's who you are. This might be a good thing. Like you told me, this may be the push you need to open the studio you were talking about."

He leaned over, and kissed me on the forehead and asked, "Why do you believe in me like that?"

"I don't know. I just have a feeling about you. I see that you're a go-getter. It's not hard to believe that you'll make it happen." And I meant it. There was not anything about him—at least not so far—that made me think he was not going to do what needed to be done, to make things happen.

He planted another color-filled kiss on my lips. His kisses were energizing, like he could kiss a boo-boo and make it better.

I blinked hard.

He smiled. "Your lips...," he said, and shook like a chill went through his body.

"What's this that you had to tell me?"

"Huh?"

"Don't think I forgot."

I was actually still lost in our kiss. "Oh, yeah." I took his hand. "I'm trying to think of the best way to tell you this."

"Just say it."

"It's not anything like a disease or anything life threatening. Really, I don't even know why I'm telling you, but I just don't know how far we are going to go, and I just really want you to know this because—I mean…. Maybe I shouldn't even tell you."

"You're driving me crazy right now. You know that, right? Just tell me, Breezy."

"Okay. There are two things. First, I've been teaching women how to masturbate."

He gave a gawky smile like a little kid and raised his eyebrows. "Word?"

"Yeah. I've only taught three so far, but I enjoy it and I think I want to do it for a living. So far I've made some pretty decent money."

"Really?" He cocked his head, squinted his eyes and asked, "Are you a lesbian?"

"No."

"Bi?"

"No. I'm not attracted to women. I just like helping them, and I'm really good at it."

"Humph."

I waited while he thought. "Well?"

"Do ya thing, ma. If you've found something that makes you feel good, go for it."

I smiled. "So you have no problem with that?"

"I think I'd find it hard to have a problem with anything you do."

"Are you sure that's how you feel?"

"You're a smart woman. I trust your judgment. Now what else?"

I swallowed hard. I didn't want to disappoint him.

"The second thing is, um..." My voice was shaking.

His eyes grew wide as if to say, *Spit it out already.*

"I'm Newark Annie."

Chapter 25

Anticipating reaction.
This moment has too many breaths.
Say something! Speak!
I'm on edge. Say something to me!

He was quiet for a moment. Then he raised his left brow and said, "For real?"

I nodded.

"Humph." He sat back and asked, "So what really happened?"

I told him.

He was silent for a few seconds, and then burst into laughter, not at all the reaction I expected. "So I'm falling for Newark Annie?"

"Are you disappointed or mad or anything?"

"Nah. I'm not sure what I feel, but it's definitely not mad or disappointed. Why would I be disappointed?"

"Because you just said you trust my judgment."

"I mean, it was a mistake. Shit happens."

"Yeah."

"Who else knows?"

"Some of my family. And now you."

"So you're Newark Annie?" he said, and shook his head as if he still couldn't believe it, smiling.

"You're falling for me, huh?"

"Did I say that?"

"Yes, sir."

"I am." He gave me a look that literally moved me. I had to back away from him. My heart started fluttering, and my stomach got tight. We were going to have sex.

"Are you okay?" he asked.

"Yeah."

"You seem nervous."

"That's because I am."

"I'm making you nervous?"

"Yup."

"You want me to leave?"

"No. It's just that I haven't had sex in a long time."

"Who said anything about sex?"

"Okay. Now I'm embarrassed."

"I'm just kidding. I can't wait to make love to you, Breezy. I don't want it to sound like I'm hitting you with game, but I don't just want to fuck you. I want to go all the way."

"Yeah?" My body was on fire.

"I do. I mean, yeah, I want to fuck the shit outta you, bang your back out and all that."

"Damn that sounds good. I love how you said that." That turned me on to no end. I didn't expect to react like that. It sent the blood rushing from my head to my clit.

"You like when I tell you I wanna fuck the shit outta you?"

"Uh huh."

"Whenever you're ready, I'm going all in."

"Okay." I was ready, but my mind kept telling me to slow down. My pussy was like, *Bitch, why? If he stays, he stays. If he goes, he goes. But I want some dick!"*

I excused myself and went to the bathroom. I brushed my teeth with baking soda, then gargled with bubblegum-flavored mouthwash, and washed my face. I'd already done all that before he arrived, but I just wanted to freshen up. Then I practiced my sex faces—you know, because I wanted to make sure I looked good when we were doing it. If he made me cum, I just couldn't make the ugly, contorted faces I made when I was jerking off, or he might run away.

I stood there biting my bottom lip, curling my top lip, making soft sex sounds, and rolling my eyes up in my head in the cutest way possible.

He was watching an old boxing match when I went back to the living room. I smiled as I sat next to him. He put his arm around my shoulders, and pulled me close to him.

Eventually my head landed in his lap, as he flipped through the channels. He caressed my hair. His big hands made me feel delicate.

"Can I play something for you?"

"Yeah."

He stood up, and put his iPod in my player. The guitar came on like it was talking to me.

"Who is this?"

"Jimi Hendrix. 'Midnight.'"

He sat down, and we went back into our position with my head in his lap. Jimi added to the thickness of our intense air.

"You comfortable?" he asked.

"Uh huh."

Each riff tickled my lips, my spine, and my toes. I closed my eyes and saw a dark blue sky sprinkled with sugary white stars, like midnight.

"Play it again."

He did, using the remote.

I took a deep breath.

"Sean?"

"Yeah?"

"I'm ready."

We broke day with him inside of me. I can still taste every salty, sweet moment of that first time. I still feel his hands holding my head, as I gagged and choked; my nails digging into his scalp, as I stared down at his slippery face; his fingers pulling my cheeks apart until I thought I'd split. I can still feel each sweet thrust and his breath tickling my ear; his lips against my skin; his teeth sinking into my neck. I can still hear him moaning, and see his eyes rolling in his head, like I felt wonderful.

There was nothing cute about what we did. All that practicing I did in the mirror went out the window. We were both very ugly, and so carefree. There was no pretending. We fought to please each other, and relished in being pleased. We gave each other everything we had until we were both spent. It was the realest fuck I ever had.

At some point we passed out.

* * *

When I opened my eyes, the sunlight blinded me. He'd opened the blinds, but he wasn't there. I got up and went to the bathroom for my morning routine. The apartment was empty, and silent, and I was disappointed. It was almost like a dream. But I knew he'd really been there. *Figures. Fuck it. We'd had our moment. What's done is done. No! Not fuck it! How could he just leave like that?* My heart was sinking. *Why would he fill my head like that? I shouldn't have believed shit he said. I know better.*

I cursed myself in the shower. The water couldn't hide my tears. What's worse, I could still feel him inside of me. It sent shivers through me. *Stupid. How could you hope like that?*

I turned the water off, reached out to get my towel, and it was handed to me. I jumped. "Oh my Gahd! You scared the shit outta me!" I yelled, and then stepped out of the shower.

He said, "Who you in there cursing out?"

"Huh?"

"*Huh?*" he mocked.

"You. I thought you left."

"Why would I leave you?"

"Because you got what you wanted."

"Nah," He shook his head. "I didn't get everything I want yet."

He took the towel back from me and started to dry me off. "I love your body," he said, the way every woman wants someone to say it—like I took his breath away. "I wanted to make it back before you woke up so I could make you breakfast. Do you even eat? There's no food in your fridge."

"There're plenty of fruit and veggies in there."

"Yeah, but you don't have any *food*."

I chuckled. "I don't like to cook, so everything in there is quick. You know, just throw a salad together with some chicken breast or salmon, and I'm done."

"Ok, but you don't even have any chicken breast, or salmon. Yeah, I see you need me in your life."

I lifted my arms as he dried me.

The air was quiet. The noise of our content filled the silence.

I felt so right, so free. As he finished drying me, "I want this forever," fell from my lips. I wanted to grab the words, and shove them back into my mouth.

But he said, "Me too," and kissed my shoulder.

I watched him make pancakes, scrambled eggs, and turkey bacon. He made a plate for me and poured a glass of orange juice. He cleaned the pans he used before he sat down to eat. He was going to get fucked for that.

I was trying to wait for him to sit down before I ate, but he insisted, "Go ahead and eat before it gets cold." For some reason, that made my *girl* dribble.

We didn't say much as we ate. I told him how good the food was, and he thanked me. After that, there were just the sounds of forks scraping our plates, the sipping of juice, and closed mouth chewing.

When we were done, he took our plates and washed them. "Wanna spend the rest of the day with me?"

"Of course," I said.

"You want to go somewhere?"

"Nah. I just want to stay in and fuck."
And that was exactly what we did.

Chapter 26

Confession: I'm not nearly as secure as I'd like to be. I'd love to walk around believing I'm the shit all day every day, but most days I just feel like little ol' Breezy. And I wonder why someone like him would want someone like me?

Newark Annie faded after a few weeks, as other sensationalized non-news broke, and took its place. The talk of masturbation died down—on TV anyway. The media had its moment to openly discuss the topic, and then the moment was gone.

I got four new clients through word-of-mouth. As for the site, women who found it online called and emailed me with questions, but a lot of them were apprehensive about actually setting up appointments, and that was really frustrating. I wasn't being aggressive enough. I didn't want to talk them into needing the services. Either they wanted them, or they didn't, was how I felt. I was learning that there's not much money to be made in feeling that way.

Mallory Marx put my services to the test. She didn't need any assistance with getting off; she was a certified pro. So, she set me up with one of her *bloggees,* who agreed to let Mallory sit in on the session. They both endorsed me on Mallory's blog, and on my website. The woman, Gabby Caruthers, thoroughly enjoyed her time with me. The session was only about two hours, and at no charge, of course, since it was for marketing.

I changed my approach to the calls and emails I received. I looked online for information on how to sell.

They talked about people like they were sheep ready to be herded. One of the sites basically said, if people were calling, they were already on the line, and they just needed to be reeled in. I didn't like that, not at all. I'm sure it works, but I really wanted to help women, not feel like I was reeling them in, rubbing my hands together, grinning manically, the way I picture some sleazy car salesman would.

So, I decided to open up a little more about the services; to tell them the benefits and make them feel safe about the situation. I would build a rapport with them, really talk to them, and let them know I was there to help. This may seem like common sense, but common sense isn't common, and that just wasn't my normal mental process. I had to change my thinking in the way I interacted with people. I had to stop being scared of rejection and stop being lazy. (Yeah, yeah, my mother was right. I was lazy). Laziness constricts imagination. I needed to go all in, and when I did that, it worked. The callers were becoming clients.

I started handing out business cards everywhere I went. I thought the card was tasteful enough so that it wouldn't offend most women. It was dark fuchsia, and below the picture of the flower I'd painted earlier, it read, "Ladies, learn the art of loving yourself," with the web address, email address, and phone number below that. I hoped it would be enough to pique women's interest.

I asked Jana if I could put some cards in her bakery, and asked Lady if I could put some up in his store. They both gave me the go-ahead. I didn't really expect Jana to agree, but she said, "Anything for you Breezy."

I made the website as pink and pretty as I could. I wanted it to be frilly, happy, and welcoming so that when women visited, they felt safe. Feeling safe was very important. Masturbation is such a touchy subject (no pun intended), and people can become easily offended when it is broached the wrong way. I wanted to keep the site humorous, and light, but still very informative.

At $300 an hour, I only needed a minimum of five clients a month for me to make a decent living. That's not even counting that most women needed more than an hour of attention. I didn't try to drag the time out with them, but we'd get into conversations about the reasons why they weren't able to orgasm. I found those conversations very necessary for most of them to get past whatever it was that was blocking them.

Some of them had been molested or raped. A lot of them had religious hang-ups. There was a lot of shame involved. For some, it was like they were just waiting for someone to give them permission. Most of them just didn't know what to do.

* * *

Sean, Sean, Sean. Every moment we had available to spend together, we did. One day, we went to Whitestone Multiplex and did a marathon. We went from theater to theater and saw four films before I started getting dizzy and just couldn't take it anymore. Every afternoon for a week straight we went to off, off, off, off, over to the left, off Broadway plays. We went to clubs and parties, had a good time pretending we weren't together, and watched each other flirt, until we couldn't stand it. I'd walk up on him and kiss him, or he'd grab me by the waist to claim me.

We went to Yankee games, the Bronx Zoo, and the Brooklyn Aquarium. We drove to the NY Hall of Science in Flushing Meadows just to take pictures and pretend we were in a Craig Mack video. We hit a few art exhibits and a music festival. We also went to Great Adventures and Dorney Park. He traveled so much I was sure he'd just want to chill when he came home, but he loved being active, and he made me active by association.

It seemed we were filling up our short time together with memories, so when we looked back, we would have a lot of, remember-that-time-we-went-to, stories and a lot of pictures to look at.

I loved his company. We were getting so close that we were speaking the same sentences—not just the same words, but whole sentences. Sometimes we didn't have to speak; we'd just give each other a look. We enjoyed each other's quiet too.

I hated when he had to leave the state, or the country, and wondered if I could really deal with him leaving me as part of his livelihood. Even though the band was breaking up, as a musician, he'd still need to travel.

We were sitting on my couch when I told him, "I'm going to need phone sex while you're gone."

"You're gonna *need* it, huh?"

"Yeah."

"I'll try for you. You know I'm not good at it."

"Just talk to me, and tell me what you want to do, and what you want me to do to you. Just like you always do. Only difference is, it's on the phone."

"With your freaky self."

"I'm sorry. Did I go too far?" I asked, smiling and knowing I hadn't.

"Nah. I love that about you. I'm gonna tell you something, and don't use it against me later."

"What?" I was completely curious.

"Your pussy is the fucking best. I love fucking you."

I jumped on him and started kissing him because I had to. Clothes were ripped off, my hair was pulled, his head was grabbed, furniture was kicked, walls were slapped, and limbs were sprained. There were bite marks, and scratches; cursing, heavy breathing, praising, sweating and panting. Lots of squeezing, kissing, licking, and sucking.

* * *

He was going to be gone for a week to Canada for a music festival that the band was already contractually obligated to do. He asked me if I would do him a big favor and let the cable guy in while he was gone. I had been reluctant about going to his apartment. I know it sounds silly, but I was scared that if I went there, I would get pregnant, because I'd be too weak to use a condom, like we had at my house. But he wouldn't be there, so I'd be safe. I told him I would do it, and he entrusted me with his house keys.

The cable guy was supposed to be there between ten a.m. and noon on Friday. I got there a little before ten. His apartment was extremely clean. I wondered if it was always that way, or if it was just to impress me. The studio was maybe 800 square feet, with lots of sunlight pouring through the windows, and bouncing off the bright, white walls. Along one wall was a wooden, full-sized loft bed with dark blue bedding. Underneath the bed was a matching desk with a desktop computer and a printer/fax/scanner/combo.

Across from the loft bed was a thirty-inch flat screen with an entertainment center below it that housed some kind of PlayStation, an Xbox 360, and a flat, wide, shiny black, manly iPod player.

Lined up along the walls, and under the windows were instruments, most in their covers or cases: a bass (I only know that because the case had "bass" spray-painted, glossy like a surfboard on it, otherwise, I would've thought it was a guitar); a keyboard; several guitars; and a sax. Those were the ones I could identify.

Posters of Jimi Hendrix, Eddie Van Halen, Charlie Byrd, Muddy Waters, Rakim, KRS-One, Nas, and Jay-Z lined one wall, while the wall behind the TV had photos of him, with different bands, and people, who I assumed were his family because they looked like him.

I picked up a photo album. It was lying out, so I figured it was okay for me to go through it. I flipped through pictures of him as a little boy. He was adorable. He had a lot of family pictures and photos of him playing his instruments throughout the years. He'd grown up with instruments in his hands. That turned me on, not in a sexual way, but in an, I-want-to-have-babies-with-him, way (I guess that is a sexual way though, huh?).

I went through another album with pictures of him, and a bunch of famous people. I figured he wasn't a show-off or he'd have put them on the wall instead of keeping them in an album out of the spotlight.

He also a lot of pictures of himself with various females—I mean *a lot*. All of them had big breasts. Every last one of them. *How could he be sexually attracted to them and claim to love my body?* I'm a C cup, and all those chicks were toting double-Ds. They wore a lot of makeup; I don't wear any. They were all weaved up, or looked like they were mixed. *Is he tired of that kind of chick, and wants to settle down with something safer? Did they break his heart, so now he's going for someone he thinks can't hurt him?*

I closed the book, and turned on the TV, forgetting that the reason I was there was because the cable was out, so all I saw was snow.

I looked through his DVDs and then remembered he said he had a closet full of porn. I saw three closets. I wasn't going to search through his stuff though, so I picked one of the movies from his caddy. *Friday After Next* was the winner. Sure, I'd seen it over 100 times, but it never got old.

I decided to get a quick one in about halfway through the movie. I went to his bathroom, which was spotless, pulled out my bullet, and went to work. Something was wrong though, because nothing was happening. My clit wasn't responding, not even so much as a twitch. I sucked my teeth, washed my hands, and went back to watch the rest of the movie. Still wondering what was wrong. It was the first time I'd tried to masturbate since having sex with Sean. *Did he hex me? Had he made it so that it had to be him? That sneaky bastard!*

Finally, there was a knock at the door. I looked through the peephole. Instead of the cable guy, there stood a chesty, pretty, all-around attractive woman. I wouldn't have answered, but curiosity got the best of me, and I just had to know who she was. I opened the door.

Before I could say anything she said, "Um, is Sean home?"

"No he's not."

"Humph." She tried to look into the apartment as if I was lying.

I blocked her view. "He's not here," I said flatly, agitated that she'd tried to look around me.

"He must be at the studio then," she said.

My eyes snarled at her. I was feeling territorial, and jealous. I'd never felt that way before, but I was wrapped up in it.

"You must be Windy."

"Breezy," I corrected her, pissed off because I thought she was trying to be funny.

"My bad," she said with a smile intended to lighten my mood. "I'm Veronica," she said and held out her hand.

As I took it, my mind started to absorb the fact that she knew who I was, even though she'd messed up my name. *He's been talking about me.* The attack mode stress started leaving my body.

"I just came to drop these demos off."

"Oh, okay. I'll give them to him."

She handed me a stack of six CDs. "And give him this too," she said, handing me a letter-sized envelope.

"Okay, I will." I'd softened up a little more.

"I'm his cousin, by the way," she said.

I caught myself. I must've still been looking at her like I was going to rip her apart. "Oh, alright," I said and finally smiled.

She laughed. "Trust me, I understand. I'd be suspicious, too, if a girl showed up at my man's house—well, my girl's house—especially one looking as fine as me," she joked. "I'd be looking at the chick sideways too."

We both giggled.

"If you want to take a look in the envelope, you can. It's just pictures of me and my group, Shelly Keith."

"Shelly Keith? I saw you at Terry's."

I didn't recognize her looking like a normal person, with her hair in black cornrows to the back, instead of all rocked out. As I paid attention, I realized she was the second guitarist, that screamed, "Descendants of American Slaves ROCK!"

"Yeah, I remember you," she said.

"You do?"

"Yeah. We took a pic with you."

"Yeah, you did! I can't believe you remember that."

"I was gonna hit on you, but I couldn't read you, so I decided not to. Plus Sean told me to leave you alone."

My eyebrows shot up. "Oh." I was surprised, but also flattered. And then surprised at myself for being flattered.

She left, and I put the CDs and envelope on top of his desk.

Another knock at the door. Still not the cable guy. It was a man that looked similar to Sean, but about a foot taller and a foot wider.

"Who," I asked through the door.

"Antonio. Sean home?"

"Sorry. He's not."

"Damn," he said to himself. Then he said, "I thought he wasn't leaving till tonight?"

"Nope. You missed him."

"Can I leave some money with you for him?"

I didn't want to be responsible for any money. "You may want to wait until he comes back."

"Aw, c'mon. He's been on my ass about it, and I finally got it. Just take it for me please?"

I sucked my teeth. "Alright," I said and opened the door.

"Thank you," he said and gave the money to me. He turned to leave.

"Hold up!" I stopped him. "You need to sign something showing that you gave me this money and how much."

"Huh?"

"Just hold on a sec." I turned to get a pen and paper from my bag. I handed them to him and said, "Just write down your name, and how much you gave me, and today's date."

He looked at me, his eyes asking if I was for real.

I answered "*Yes*" with my eyes. I counted out the bills. There was $250 in twenties, tens, and fives.

He handed the receipt to me, and he'd put my name on it.

"You know my name?"

"It's not a forgettable one."

"Sean told you about me?"

"Look at you, getting all happy. Now you wanna be my friend."

I grinned and asked, "Have you seen me before? What if I was one of his other chicks?"

"Stop fishing for info," he said, smiling like Sean.

All I could do was blush.

"I'll tell you this. You're the only female he's ever had in his house while he wasn't here. After you just made me sign a receipt, I see why."

I felt tingly.

I tried not to get happy because I know how men lie for each other, but I believed him, and it frightened me. Thinking someone may be *the one* is a scary proposition. People leave. Even worse; people change. They put up all these façades to trap you, then the real them comes out, and you're caught off guard, thinking you had something real, when all along, you didn't have anything, but a good time in bed.

Finally the cable guy came, after twelve. I was going to argue with him about his lateness, but I gave him the benefit of the doubt and figured he got there as soon as he could. For all I knew he had a difficult customer or traffic was backed up. Sometimes things just don't go smoothly. I was tired of getting mad at people for things that neither I, nor they, could control.

* * *

As soon as I got off the train, heading home, I got a call from Gia. "Chica, come out with us. Just because you don't work with us doesn't mean you can just vanish out of our lives forever."

She was right. I'd been neglecting her and Cindy, albeit not on purpose. Between Sean, and my clients and, Sean, there was just a lot going on.

I met up with Cindy and Gia at Pusche in the Village. It was four-dollar drinks all night for ladies, so I had quite a few.

The lights flashed to the beat of the music. It was old school house music night. The heavy *thump-thump* of the bass vibrated my chest. Crystal Waters', "Homeless" came on, and we lost our minds, singing like we'd written the words ourselves, and moving stiff, and controlled, like she did in the video. They played "Nu Nu," by Lindell Townsell, "Good Life," by Inner City, "I'll House You," by The Jungle Brothers, and too many songs for me to even name. I'd forgotten how much I loved house music growing up.

My phone started vibrating in my front jeans pocket. My clit started twitching; she twitched every time my phone vibrated. It was almost annoying. I smiled big when I saw "SEAN" flashing on the caller ID. He was calling me on his cell from an after-party.

Between the music in both of our backgrounds, we could barely hear each other. We yelled back and forth.

"Having fun?" I asked.

"Huh?"

"I said, are you having fun?"

"Yeah. Be better if you were here."

"What?"

"I said, it would be better if you were here!"

I'd heard him the first time; I just wanted to hear it again.

"Where are you?" he asked.

"At this club in the Vil'."

"I know the dudes in there are on your back."

"I know those chicks out there are on *your* back, going crazy over you."

"Well, I'm going crazy over you."

"If I were there, they wouldn't even have a chance, because I'd be on you like glue."

"Word?"

"Of course."

"Can you get to a bathroom?"

I wondered for a moment why he would ask me that, and then it clicked, and I got happy, so to speak. I made my way through the crowd of sloppy dancers to the ladies' room. I could hear him breathing, and women giggling as he made his way through his crowd. I imagined they were clawing at him, trying to rip him out of his clothes, but I was sure that was just my half-drunk, and paranoid imagination. Those jealous thoughts were bothering me, and I knew I needed to check that, because they would drive me crazy if I let them.

His background noise lessened, but I could still hear the music. I was closing the stall door behind me when he said, "Breezy?"

"Yeah?" I was already breathing deep in anticipation.

"I've been thinking about your pussy all day."

"Yeah? I've been thinking about your dick all day."

"Tell me what you were thinking about my dick."

I loved the way he said that. "About when you first pushed inside of me, how good you felt." A chill went through me at the thought.

"Mmmm.... You know what I was thinking?"

"Uh uh."

"Of the look on your face when I had your titties in my mouth."

I moaned and grabbed my left breast.

"Mmmm. Touch your clit for me, baby."

I put the phone down to my pants so he could hear the zipper, and then put the phone back up to my ear. "I'm touching her."

"Remember my tongue on your clit? You feel my tongue right now?"

"Uh huh."

I was getting dizzy. All the blood rushed from my head to my clit. I was making a load of noise, moaning at the mere memory of that skilled tongue of his.

"Damn, you sound good."

"I wanna slide my tongue around the head of your cock."

"Oooh shit, baby. Say that again."

"I wanna slide my tongue around the head of your cock, and I want you to push my head down until you hit the back of my throat and make me choke. Remember how you made me choke?"

"Oh my Gahd, baby! Yes! I wanna rub my face in your pussy and shove my tongue inside you until you cum."

We went back and forth, feeling and tasting each other with our words. His breath quickened, and I knew he was about to cum. I wanted to cum with him, so I made sure I did.

"I'm cumming!" I yelled, not caring who could hear me in that bathroom, as long as he could hear me on the other end of the line.

"Oh shit, baby. Tell me again."

"I'm cumming, Sean. I wanna feel you cum in me so fucking bad. Oh... oh..." My left eye met my right, and my siren wailed.

I wasn't the only one in the bathroom, but I didn't give a care. I was with Sean, sharing a glorious nut. It meant so much to me that he would give that to me—that he would step out of his normal for me.

"Was that good?"

"Yes, baby. You were wonderful. Perfect," I said.

"Yo, when you pulled your zipper down... yooo! I almost came on myself."

"I hoped you'd like that. I miss you so much, Sean."

"Me too. I'll be home soon."

"I'll be waiting."

I cleaned up and went back out to my girls. I guess I was glowing because men really were on my back after that. The dance floor became the Serengeti, and I was a lioness in estrus, with all of them vying for my attention. Every time I tried to step away from the floor, someone pulled me back. At the bar, a guy felt the need to tell me he was buying a house. Another one told me how successful his plumbing company was. It would have been a good night to be single, but I didn't feel single. At that moment, I succumbed to the feeling, and let myself think I was in a relationship.

We went to breakfast at a diner, and I didn't get home until a little after seven a.m. I fell out dead tired... and happy.

It seemed as soon as my head hit the pillow, Sandy was calling me. All I heard was "face... TV... bitch..."

"Where are you? The connection is real bad."

The call dropped, but she called me back about five minutes later.

"Can you hear me now?"

"Yeah. What did you say?"

"Your face is on TV, bitch! Your face is on TV!"

Chapter 27

Some questions that were asked of me, as, Newark Annie:

Q: Do you masturbate because you don't like men?
A: Do men masturbate because they don't like women?

Q: Is masturbation better than being with a man?
A: Depends on the man.

Q: Do you feel masturbation is a sin?
A: I think that question is a sin.

Q: Are you a feminist?
A: Are you asking me that, because I masturbate? That's weird. If masturbation makes me a feminist then yeah, I'm a huge one. Was that the goal of the womanist and feminist movements? To make sure I could masturbate just as well as men? Forget equal pay—we want equal play time. Heck, maybe that was the goal.

Q: Do you masturbate to porn?
A: Not to your knowledge.

Q: Would you recommend masturbation?
A: As much as I'd recommend drinking cold water on a hot day.

I started blinking hard. "What?"

"Someone at the airport had you on camera in the background of one of their pics. I mean, you can't really tell it's you unless you know you, but I recognized you right away. I just saw it online on NY News."

I was quiet.

"Hello? Breezy, you there?"

"Uh..." My head was hot, and I just kept blinking.

"I'm downstairs. I'm on my way up."

"Uh..."

I went online to pull up the news site, and saw the pic. I was stuck. My vulva cringed. The caption read, "Will the Real Newark Annie Please Stand Up?"

Sandy had the keys, and came on in. I could hear her run into the living room, and then run down the hall to my bedroom. "We are going to sue for defamation of character and for—"

"For the truth?"

"So what if it's the truth? It's not anyone's fucking business! And no one cares about the truth. All they want to do is expose you for a headline. Fuck them!"

I shook my head. Just when everything was going right. I was getting clients to pay my bills, and then some bad press comes along, threatening to ruin it all. I felt like I was being pushed around, and there's nothing I hate more than being bullied. I was pissed, but I managed to have a clear thought in my *pisstivity*; "I'm coming out."

"What?"

"Before anyone gets a chance to do whatever they want to do, before they start saying things that I can't fight, I'm going to just come out."

"Are you sure?"

"What else can I do? I mean, it's not like this didn't happen."

"But it didn't happen the way they said. It's only gonna get worse from here."

"Maybe I can stop it from getting worse with the truth."

"So you're just going to give the fucking media what they want? Feed the damn sharks?"

"I've watched enough TV to know that if I don't fess up to what really happened, they'll do whatever they want with me anyway, and make it out to be worse than it was, like they're already doing. I might as well put it all out there. Let the chips fall in the sand, and let the ocean sweep them away."

"I don't know Breezy. What about your parents? What about grandma?"

"Thanks to you they already know what happened.

"Look, it's out there already. What; I should let it just happen to me? No. *I'm* going to happen to *it*. I mean, eventually somebody besides you is going to see the pic, recognize me, and say something foul either to me, or in print, or wherever. I want to catch it before that happens. If I take the power away from the mystery, then there won't be anything for them to work with. It'll have no shock value, and the whole thing will go away faster."

She sat quietly with her eyes closed, rocking like she was deep in thought. "Okay. I get it."

"So you have my back?"

"I've always got your back."

She sat there while I called my parents.

"So my daughter is going to be the most famous masturbator in the world," my mother said. "I always knew you'd be famous for something." She agreed with me that getting to them before they got to me was the best move.

My father only told me that he loved me no matter what, and that nothing I could do would ever make him ashamed of me. He never really said much, but always just enough to make me feel everything would be alright.

I called Justin. He was in Texas having a meeting with a textile company. He was really going ahead with his plans for The House of JM. He couldn't really talk at the time, but he told me to use whatever publicity I could to build my business. "Don't see this as something that will stop you. Work it, girl! Get out there in that limelight and do your thing!"

I conference-called Cindy and Gia so neither of them could say I told one before the other. Cindy was mad because I hadn't told her earlier, but she got over it. Gia just kept saying, "You're Newark Annie?" It was the same reaction Charise had when I called her.

I called a few more friends, mainly the old Get-It Girl Crew. It had been years since most of us had spoken, but no matter what they were still my girls, and I felt the need let them know. They were also shocked, amazed, and amused.

I went to my yellow room to call Sean. I was scared. Things were so syrupy with us. I braced myself for whatever his response would be. I mean, it was one thing for him to know that I was Newark Annie, but it was another thing for everyone around him to also know that.

"Are you calling me about the news?"

"Uh, yeah. So you saw that, huh?"

"Yeah."

"So what do you think?"

"I don't know."

"I'm coming out about it."

"Okay."

"Can you give me some kind of reaction?"

"I don't really have one yet."

Since I couldn't look at him, I pulled the phone away from my face, to look at it in disbelief.

"Uhm...okay."

"I'll talk to you later, okay?"

I wrinkled my brows. "Uh, okay."

We hung up. I figured that was the end of that, and my heart broke. I guess it was more than he wanted to handle.

I went back to my bedroom to Sandy.

"What did he say?"

"I don't think I'll be seeing him again."

"Well, fuck him. That shit was a little too perfect anyway."

It pissed me off that she said that.

"Did he say some smart-ass shit to you?"

"He didn't say anything. Nothing."

"Fuck him. You don't need him."

I didn't feel like *fuck him*. I felt disappointed.

"Anyway, later for him. Who are you coming out to?"

I pushed him into a corner of my mind, to let him sit quietly and not disturb me, so I could deal with what I needed to do. "That's who I'm calling now."

Mallory answered on the first ring. I knew she'd seen the news because she kept up with all news for her blog.

"Mallory, I have something to tell you."

"Are you Newark Annie?"

"Yup. That's me."

"Why didn't you tell me?"

"Because I was trying to make it a non-issue in my life, but the cat's out of the bucket now, and I just need to go into the fire."

"The cat what?"

"I want you to have first dibs on the story. After all, you did name me."

"I can't believe I know Newark Annie personally. My own story, right in front of me."

She told me she'd already had questions ready to ask Newark Annie if she ever had the chance to meet her. I held while she pulled them up on her laptop, and then the interview began.

The blog read:

"A few weeks ago, a woman reached out to me for assistance with a new business. Little did I know that she would turn out to be the woman I'd dubbed Newark Annie. Yes readers, I have the *real* Newark Annie right here on my phone!

MM: So, you're the real NA. Tell us what actually happened that day.

NA: I use Ben Wa balls. I'm a big fan.

MM: For pleasure?

NA: In fact it was, Mallory. They are great for pleasure and for keeping the Kegels tight. But that day, I'd forgotten they were in there. I'd been using them the night before. I'm not ashamed of that. I do masturbate. I woke up the next morning late for a flight, so I was rushing. It wasn't until I was in the line for security check that it dawned on me that they were still inside me, and by then it was too late for me to get out of the line. I was hoping maybe they wouldn't be detected, but as you know, they were. They pulled me out of the line, took me in a room, saw the balls, and let me go. That was pretty much it. It wasn't like I woke up that morning and said, 'Yeah, I'm gonna masturbate on my flight today.'

MM: Wow! Way less drama than the rumors.

NA: Yeah. There was no jerking off in the line naked. I wasn't thrown off the plane with the dildo hanging out of me. It was nothing like that at all. Just an accident—an oversight really.

MM: You know, in some circles, you're viewed as a *shero*.

NA: I find that amazing. I'm just a chick with some Ben Wa balls.

MM: LOL! That's funny! I bet Ben Wa balls sales are going to skyrocket.

NA: Guess I should buy some stock in some sex toy companies. Some people also think I'm some kind of sex demon. That's what this guy on a blog called me.

MM: You know, men can be easily threatened, but that's their problem—not ours.

NA: That's what I said. My biggest concern is just that the people in my family may be embarrassed about this, as well as some close friends. To all of them, I'm sorry if they do feel embarrassed. But I could care less what anyone else thinks.

MM: You're my shero just for coming on here and telling your story. For telling the truth.

NA: It's supposed to set you free.

MM: What made you come forward?

NA: About two hours ago, I saw a pic of me on the news. It was a full-on picture of my face. It was still a little blurry, but anyone who knows me would recognize me, and I didn't want to give someone else the opportunity to give some bogus story with my name attached to it. I thought I might as well expose myself since this story is obviously not going anywhere—not for a little while anyway.

MM: Understood. One of the reasons you reached out to me previously was because you were—or rather are—a self-pleasure consultant.

NA: Yes I am. I teach women how to achieve orgasms. I didn't learn how to have one until last year. Someone asked me if I could teach them, and then she recommended me to someone else, and it just kept going from there.

MM: How can women who need assistance contact you?

NA: They can link to my site from your blog or go to my website.

MM: And now, to completely demystify you. Will you tell us your name?

NA: Breezy Deigh.

MM: What a great name!

NA: Thanks.

MM: Thank you for giving me this interview.

NA: You're welcome, Mallory. Thanks for being so nice to me."

I'd sent her a pic of me, which she put on the blog. After she posted it, I was scared to read the comments, but here are just a few of them:

"I just saw her on the news. Didn't expect that 2 b her."

"This is in the news again? all this war and shit & the best thing 2 talk bout is newark annie? PUHLEEEZE!!!"

"She doesn't strike me as Newark Annie. She should be Newark Keisha. LOL"

"@2sweet2nice -You racist fuck"

"LOL @Newark Keisha"

"@imtheone - how is what I said racist? That shit is funny. And I'm black."

"@2sweet2nice-there are some things you shouldn't say in mixed company because it comes across not as funny but as negative."

"she's still my shero! Luv u Newark Annie!"

"is her last name pronounced 'DAY,' like her name is breezy day?"

"I'd fuck her."

"She's pretty. I thought she wldn't be."

"that bitch is ugly."

"so she's a perv all the way around. Not only does she masturbate on planes, but she teaches other dumb bitches how 2 do it 2 WTF?"

"I love that ur black, Annie! WOOOOO!"

"thanks for setting black women back as we are trying to rise."

"@feelingblessed1 – u set ur black ass back! Nothing about this is hurting black women. DO YA THANG ANNIE!!!"

It went on and on. I stopped reading them after the first two pages. A lot of it was shock about me being black, which I found amusing. I wasn't sure what I'd expected, but the crueler comments did hurt. The ones saying I was ugly really hurt at first. No one wants to hear anyone say that about them.

As if she was psychic, Mallory sent me an email that said, "I know this is a lot for you. Just remember that the only people that matter are those that love you. And, there are a lot of miserable people out there, who want others to be miserable right along with them. Don't give in and don't engage."

I took that to heart and consciously worked on toughening up my skin because I knew there was more to come. *Deflect the negative and soak in the positive,* I told myself, but it was a lot easier said than done. Fortunately, for just about every negative comment, there was a positive one to counter it.

By the end of the day, I couldn't believe how many friend requests I had, and how many times my website had been viewed. It was like I was walking through some dream. Mallory's interview had gone viral, within an hour of her posting it, and I was getting phone calls for radio, magazine, and TV interviews. I didn't want to go on television, but I didn't mind the radio.

With the sudden activity, I had a hard time getting off. I couldn't concentrate. Part of it was because Sean was heavy like bricks on my mind. I just wanted to talk to him. We'd have text conversations, but I wanted to hear his voice. I hated feeling like that, but it was my truth. I had fallen, and I couldn't get up. I just wanted him.

My neighbors were whispering about me. They gave me these odd, sometimes scornful looks, in the elevator, and lobby, but they never had the Ben Wa balls to say anything. They just looked at me, judging me. I wanted to say something to all of them, but I was really working hard on not focusing on anything negative. I couldn't control what people thought. I could only control *my* reactions. No matter what I said, they'd keep on talking, so I chose not to react. *Let it go. Let them talk.* Now, if they actually said something to me that would be a different story.

The whispers seemed to be everywhere I went, though. It could've been my imagination, but I'm sure it wasn't. People would stare at me. Some would even point. Then two days after the interview, it happened; my own version of a miracle on 34th Street.

"Excuse me. I don't mean to bother you, but are you Newark Annie?"

I didn't say anything. I was just shopping and minding my business. I shook my head.

"No, I think you are," she said with this bright smile that scared me. "Oh my Gahd! I can't believe it's you! I love you okay! Really. You are like... O-M-G you are like…. Can I have your autograph?"

"What?"

"Your autograph? Can you sign this?" She searched her bag and pulled out a checkbook, snatched out a check, turned it on its back, and asked again, "Will you sign it?'

I thought it was some kind of scam or someone playing a joke, but the look on her face seemed earnest.

"What do you want me to write?"

"Um, 'To my good friend Stacy, from Newark Annie.'"

So that was what I wrote.

"Can I take a picture with you?"

"Are you serious?" I asked, with my eyebrows raised.

"Yes!" she yelled, and fumbled in her bag until she pulled out her camera phone. She stood next to me and said, "Cheeese!"

I smiled, hoping the picture would come out well because I didn't want to show up on some Facebook account looking crazy.

"Newark Annie! I just can't believe it!"

"Newark Annie?" a woman passing by overheard, and stopped to ask. She looked me up, and down, and said, "Oh my Gahd! Is that really you? I've got to take a pic!" She was already on her phone, so she jumped next to me and took the pic. She didn't even bother asking.

More women stopped. I just wanted to go shopping, and I started feeling really nervous. One of the women actually had on a Newark Annie T-shirt. Of course we took a picture. They were telling me things that I didn't want to hear: "I love to masturbate! I fuck myself three times a day!"

I was bugging out. *This can't be real. This cannot be happening. I'm just trying to shop.* I couldn't think straight. My heart started beating fast, and I had to calm myself down; get a hold of myself and the moment. I had to slow my own time down. I just saw all these faces saying things to me, and phones and cameras pointing at me. It was dizzying. All their smiles started to look like vicious teeth snarling at me. Their voices were garbled like a massive roar. I had to move. I had to get away from them. I had to—Justin's voice entered my head: *"Get in that limelight and do your thing, girl! Work the moment."*

I regained my composure and embraced what was happening. This was opportunity. I kept a smile on my face and started signing autographs on the backs of my business cards, talking and laughing. I told them to go to my website and email me. "And if you know anyone who needs help, send them to me!" I said.

I don't know how long I was out there, but a cop came and broke it up because we were blocking the street. I felt like I was high. The attention went to my head, and I had to talk myself down. Still, I floated through Macy's. I didn't buy anything though. I couldn't get out of my head enough to even see clothes.

* * *

The next day, I walked out of my building and someone yelled my name. I turned and saw some guy with a camera behind me. I started walking faster, and I heard his footsteps quicken, so I started running.

Then a car screeched to a stop in the street. The driver jumps out. It's Sean. He yells, "Get in the car!" with this domineering look in his eyes. He runs over to the guy with the camera, snuffs him, "BLAAOW!" The guy drops like a rag doll.

Meanwhile, I ran and got into the car.

Sean takes his camera and throws it up against my building smashing it to smithereens. The guy was out, and he wasn't getting up.

Sean slaps the shit outta him and the guy comes to.

"Stay the fuck away from her!" he yells, with his finger in the dudes face, and then sorts through the camera pieces and snatches up the memory card.

My mouth was in a big O, as I gawked through the windshield at the action.

He got in and slammed the door. He took a few breaths to calm himself down.

I just stared at him, mesmerized.

"You alright?" he asked.

I nodded.

"Sorry. I didn't mean to yell at you."

Every part of me was excited. I leaned over and kissed him.

He kissed me back.

We smothered each other.

Then he pulled off. "I was coming to surprise you."

"Well, you did that."

"Fucking paparazzi?"

"Do you think that was paparazzi? For me? Couldn't be."

"Don't underestimate the media. You're a hot story. It's not important to you, but people want what's new. Papers and magazines are willing to pay a lot of money to be the ones with exclusive pics."

I rolled my eyes. I told him what happened the day before on 34th Street. "How long is this going to go on?" I asked the air.

Sean patted my knee and said, "Welcome to your fifteen minutes."

How did Mr. Warhol foresee all of this about our culture? He was a fucking genius!

"You want me to take you somewhere?"

"I was just on my way to the supermarket."

"I'll take you, if you don't mind."

"No, I don't mind."

My hero. But of course, if that was paparazzi, he couldn't fight them all—not to mention his actions could land his knight-in-shining-armor ass in jail. There I was thinking he was done with me, and he popped up out of nowhere, like my own personal Gotham superhero.

"Thank you," I said and kissed his cheek.

"Damn, your lips feel good."

I kissed him again.

We stared into each other's eyes.

Sugar, sugar. This might be real.

Being in the supermarket with him felt like playing house. We were both pulling items from shelves and throwing them in the shopping cart; him asking me what I wanted for dinner; running with the cart and being silly. Wow—even food shopping with him was fun.

He paid for my groceries. I protested, but he insisted.

Of course I scanned the area as we pulled up to my building to see if the guy was anywhere around. The coast was clear.

When we got upstairs, he started cooking.

"So what's your next move?" he asked, after the water for the spaghetti started boiling.

"I don't know. Maybe this wasn't the best thing to do, coming out. Maybe it would've just blown over."

"No it wouldn't have. It needs to play itself out."

I huffed. "I don't even want to talk about it. What's going on with the group? Is everything officially over?"

He broke the spaghetti in half and placed it in the pot. "We have two more gigs to do, but then it's a wrap."

"Put any more thought into that studio?"

"Yeah, a lot actually. I found a building for sale. Four stories, near Red Hook. It would be feasible for me to buy it, but that's a lot of responsibility."

"Yeah. I would imagine so."

"I've already been approved for a loan."

"Say word? Congratulations!"

He smiled humbly.

"I saw a house too."

"Yeah? Where?"

"Still in Brooklyn. That's the only place I checked."

"Maybe you should look somewhere else."

"Nah, that's alright."

"Alright fine. Stay your ass in that borough, and I'm going to stay my ass in mine."

"Nah, I don't think so."

"You don't think so?"

"When I buy that building, you're living there."

I chuckled. "How do you figure?"

"'Cause you're moving in with me."

"Is that right?"

"Mos def."

"I am not giving up my apartment, hon'. Sorry."

He didn't say anything. He smirked, removed the Italian turkey sausage from the Foreman, and started slicing it.

Finally, I got the gall up to ask, "Why didn't you call me?" It hadn't even been a full three days since our last conversation, but those days were torture.

"I'm sorry. There's been a lot going on with me. I had to take some time to think, do some soul-searching. Remember what you said about walking through fire with someone?" He looked at me to see my reaction. I wanted to scream, and yell, *"What the fuck soul searching did you have to do that you couldn't pick up the fucking phone and call me, bastard?"* But, I simply nodded.

"I just needed time alone to get my mind right. I've been thinking about all this stuff that's going on with you, and my music. About the moves I want to make—about who I want to be and who I want to be with. Wondering where your head is about me. I mean, what do you think about us?" He washed his hands before draining the ground turkey.

"Us what?"

There was just a hint of nervousness in his manner.

"Like, where we stand."

"Where do we stand? That's a good question."

"You don't know?"

"No. Not really."

"Who do you tell people I am to you?"

I blushed. "My friend."

"Word?"

"What do you tell people?"

"That you're my future wife"

"Yeah, okay."

"Are you ready to put a label on us?"

Now I was stuck. Why would he ask me that? I wasn't going to be the one to say "Let's be in a relationship."

"A label? You mean like boyfriend and girlfriend?"

"More like I'm your man and you're my woman."

I watched as he mixed the sausage with the ground turkey in the frying pan, then poured the sauce over it and stirred.

317

"If that's what you want that is. You might not be ready yet," he said.

"What makes you say that?"

"There's a big world out there. You might want to see more of it before you settle down."

"Or we can see it together," I said.

He gave me a half-smile and said, "Eventually I'll need more though. You do understand that right?"

I raised my eyebrows.

After a few moments he asked, "Cat got your tongue?"

"I don't know what to say."

"When I ask you, just say 'yes'."

Chapter 28

A letter from Judy, a fan of Newark Annie:

Dear Nastiness,

That's right, I'm calling you nastiness, you heathen! What you are doing is sinful. Do you really believe going around playing with yourself is what HE wants? Spreading lies about so called "self-love." It's nasty, and women like you are the reason STDs exist and why women are raped. It makes my skin crawl to think about the things you do. That is not what our bodies are for.

I teach classes in real self-love through our Lord and Savior. So if you really want to learn how to love yourself, go through the Lord, not through your vagina.

Truly, Judy

Dear Judy,

Go fuck yourself. Literally. Or go get fucked. Find some way to bust a nut so you can loosen up. I try not to assume, but I'm pretty sure I'm correct when I say you've never had an orgasm or even good sex period. Your ignorance is HILARIOUS! I'd really like for you to explain how masturbation leads to STDs. It would seem in the sane mind that it would stop the spread of STDs. I'm also trying to put together in my mind how masturbation causes rape.

Here's what I'd like you to do: take my number and give me a call so we can discuss the best way for you to achieve your first orgasm. That way, you can lose the bitterness and let some sweet energy flow into your world. Take care.

N.A.

She actually called me, and after a long phone battle, she decided to try my services for "research," to prove her point. She came so hard she passed out afterwards. Literally! She was snoring for a few seconds. When she woke up, she recommended me to her sister.

The *Michael Watts Show* called on Tuesday morning. One of their guests cancelled, and they needed a quick replacement. I was in their studio Wednesday afternoon.

They played Tweet's "Oops" as my intro. I love that song, but it made me really nervous. I just knew they were going to slaughter me.

"We have with us today the woman formerly known as Newark Annie, Breezy Deigh." There was a *TADAAH* type sound effect. "Welcome to the show."

"Thank you for having me."

"And might I say you are a beautiful woman. Those pictures don't do you any justice."

I blushed. "Thank you."

"As you know, we were all surprised to find out you are a *sista*."

"I know. That has been expressed to me several times."

"So tell us the story."

I told the story, they interjected with some funny jokes and radio sounds like applauses, bells, whistles, sirens, and so on.

"So you're still a freak, just not the freak we thought you were?"

"Not exactly."

"Exactly what kind of nasty, freak-nasty, are you?" his costar, Ken asked.

"The same kind as your mother," I said.

"Ohhh! She got in that ass, Ken! You just gonna take that?" Karl, the other costar, instigated.

"Nah, I just think she got my moms mixed up with your moms."

Everyone laughed.

Michael took a call: "Yeah, I just don't like knowing that the person I'm sitting next to on the plane could possibly be getting off. That's all I'm saying."

Michael said, "That's what you're worried about on the plane now? Not a terrorist, but someone getting off?"

"And have you even been listening to the show?" Ken said, "She didn't even masturbate on the plane."

"Ya know? NEXT!" Karl yelled.

"Hey, everyone. Good afternoon. I just want to say I was glad to find out she's black. White women don't have a monopoly on sexuality."

"Now she makes a good point," Michael said, "White women are viewed as way more sexually expressive than black women."

"Yeah, and it sucks. We need to get over that," I said.

"Caller, you're on the air."

"You should be ashamed of yourself! As a black woman, you represent all of us with everything you do. Why would you get on the radio talking about masturbation? That's disgusting, and you're disgusting."

"Lady, you're an idiot," Michael said.

"Really, it sounds like you need to jerk off," I said. I was heated! Not about her calling me "disgusting," but about her saying that I represent black woman in everything I do. I'm just me—just Breezy.

"Can I say something? Yes, I am a black woman, and I may share traits with other black women, but when I was born, it was just me, and when I'm gone, I'll be leaving by myself. I only represent me. Society says I have to represent this and act like that, solely because I'm black. I have a question: Why is that when black women are in music videos, they make *all* black women look bad, but *Girls Gone Wild* doesn't make *all* white women look bad?"

Michael hit a button, and there was a crescendo of bells and whistles, like I'd hit the jackpot. "You are so on point with that! Whites can do anything, and it's just that person doing it, but anytime any black person does something, it represents the whole race."

"Exactly! People act like we're not human. We are individuals. Some of our own people hold us up to all these standards, and for what? Trying to look like who? Like we aren't as freaky as white people? The perceptions of black sexuality are so bogus, and it's sad that as a nation, we still think in such antiquated terms. And I'll tell you another thing; Black men eat pussy, and black women suck dick. There! Boogety boogety boo! Oh, and here's some more: Not all white women give spectacular head, and not all white men eat pussy; All of their dicks are not little, and not every black man is packing. *And* there are white woman who are bitchy and attitudinal too, and they gold-dig with the best of them! Now what?"

Michael hit the jackpot button twice for that one and said, "Teach the children!"

"You're on to something there, because I dated this white chick thinking I was going to get rocked, but she was not giving up any type of head," Karl said.

"Maybe she wasn't giving it up for you, partner," Ken said.

"Your mother has no problem giving it up."

"Oooh Oooh!" Michael instigated.

Ken and Karl went at it for a minute before Michael said, "Back to our lovely guest. Now, I understand you have helped some women learn how to—and I quote—'pleasure themselves'?"

"Yes, I have."

"Hands on?"

"You are something else, Michael. For the most part, I just walk them through it. We talk and try to find out what's blocking the orgasm. Sometimes it's fear. Sometimes shame or whatever the case may be."

"What kind of women come to you?"

"All kinds, from every walk of life."

"Is this a free service?"

"No. There is a fee."

"Charging for the orgasm? I hear that!"

"Don't say it like that. You make it sound like prostitution."

"It's not?"

"No. There's no sex. It's masturbation. I just educate."

We took a few more calls, and then my thirty minutes was up.

Before I left, Michael pulled me to the side and said, "You really riled the people up, and you went head to head with the guys without breaking a sweat. You ever think about doing radio?"

I looked at him, confused.

"Being on radio as part of, say, an afternoon show?"

"Like your show?"

"Yeah. We could bring you on once a week to do a segment for the ladies."

"That sounds cool actually."

"Cool. I'll have my people call your people."

"Looks like I'll need to get some people then."

He laughed.

Excited? What? I was thrilled.

* * *

That appearance was what I needed, because not only did I max out my Facebook friends by the end of that week, but I got thousands of hits on my website and was swamped with loads of requests from women who wanted me to help them. Before the show, I was considering lowering the cost of the sessions, thinking maybe that would help get more business. Eula told me about perceived value, and that my price was very reasonable for a life-changing experience, but still, I was scared that not enough women would pay that much. I'm glad I didn't change, because women were willing to pay, and they wanted to use credit cards.

Everything started moving fast. That Thursday, I took the morning to apply for a business license, open a business account with my bank, and got a PayPal account so I could accept plastic.

Later that day, I got a call and an email from *The Michael Watts Show*. I would start doing a segment not once a week, but once a month, on the last Friday for thirty minutes at four thirty p.m. by phone.

I was overwhelmed with calls. I bought a Blackberry, but I couldn't use it to keep track of the appointments. I guess I just wasn't there yet. I still had to write everything down on paper. I took on two clients a day. I tried more, but I found myself rushing people, and I didn't want to do that. Not only was it not fair to them, but it could ruin my reputation, and I couldn't afford that. I would do one in the morning at nine a.m. sharp and the last at six p.m. Some women booked more than one session, which was good too, and each, and every one was satisfied.

I set down some rules for myself, regarding the way I handled my clients. I would never touch another of them again. I could guide their hand, but I wouldn't do what I'd done for Jana or Eula. Actually, that was the only rule I'd set.

The Lindsey W. Radio Show asked me to do a ten-minute, bi-weekly segment, about sex toys. It was simple enough. They'd give me a toy to review, I'd do my *research*, and then I'd give a short report with a yay or nay. It was called "The Review," and it was done by phone.

324

The Juice, a women's alternative health magazine, asked for a monthly column also on my opinion about their toy of the month. I agreed.

It was weird for me because I know me, and I'm not the way people perceived me. They looked at me and saw a masturbator. Yeah, I embraced it, but that's not who I am in total. It was like people added, subtracted, multiplied and divided me, and the answer was *masturbator*. People didn't see a human with emotions and thoughts. I was the masturbator, and that's all anyone saw.

People wanted things from me. Mainly, they just wanted me to say *"Yes"*: "Yes, I'll review your toy.... Yes, I'll speak at your meeting.... Yes, you can ask me any question you want about my sexuality."

I was quickly learning to take the good with the bad and letting many things roll off of me, instead of letting them fester. When you look for positive, it's easier to ignore the negative. Not easy, but *easier*.

I was traveling all day except for Mondays and Tuesdays. Those were my off days. If someone lived out of state or too far upstate, I would only do them on the weekends, and they had to pay for the flight and/or hotel if they were necessary. My weekends were booked through the end of the year. I didn't mind; I loved being busy. It was something I'd never known about myself until up to that point. All those years of doing the same thing, day in and day out, without any change—not meeting any new people and just being super normal—I'd stored up enough energy for a lifetime of being busy.

* * *

About two months after the Michael Watts appearance, I decided to do one television appearance, and that was on *The Michi Rodriguez Show*. She was local, and I liked the way she handled her guests. National shows were calling me, but I wasn't ready for that. I just needed that appearance to go viral, so I could keep spreading the real story and getting clients. Unless I would've received an unlikely invitation to *Oprah*. I would have busted my ass to get on *Oprah*! (Let's have a moment of silence for the *Oprah Winfrey Show*).

"Justin, can you make something for me to wear on *Michi*?"

His eyes lit up. "Really?"

"Yeah. You act like I know another designer."

"I already have something in mind."

I don't remember what they said when they introduced me. I just know the Divinyls' "I Touch Myself," played as a young woman with a headset rushed me to the stage. Through the glare of the lights I slowly made out the people in the audience, as they stood up and cheered for me. They hooted, hollered, and whistled. Their response completely surprised me. I expected courtesy clapping, but not a standing ovation. And some of them were wearing "I MASTURBATE ON PLANES," and "Newark Annie," T-shirts.

"Girl, first let me say that you are working that outfit, Ms. Thang," she said of my form fitting, crispy white, Justin creation. He'd wrapped a red scarf around my waist, as a belt, and I wore red, three inch heel sandals. Eula's diamond gift worked perfectly with the outfit.

"Thank you. It's from Justin Morales, for The House of JM."

"Justin Morales," she repeated like she was putting it into her memory bank.

"Yeah. One of the things I love about him is that all his clothes are made here in the U.S., from fabric to construction. Check him out on Facebook under, The House of JM. Also, I brought something for you," I said, and handed a bag to her with a J. Leslie's cheesecake.

The interview was quick. I went through the happenings of that day, fast, so I wouldn't bore anyone, mainly myself. I managed to mention that Pus N Dix is a great store to get toys; Mallory Marx was is a great source for toys and tips; *¡Cantamos!* is the best theater experience in the world; and, "If you're in Florida, you just have to go to Kiku Nori." Just call me *Ms. Plug-alicious*.

She asked questions, and I answered. I made dry jokes, and she laughed, so as not to embarrass me. The audience laughed, because she laughed—or maybe the shit was really funny. I couldn't tell anymore.

I felt this fakeness in the air whenever I was talking to anyone interested in me solely for the Newark Annie story. I didn't like it, and it made me very uncomfortable, and wary of my surroundings in a new way. I've always been wary about my physical safety. Now it was my mind's safety. Always wondering who was trying to get what from me.

* * *

"Sweetie! Look at my FB page!"

Justin had over 10,000 likes by the time I met up with him for dinner.

"Wow, Justin! My website crashed," I added happily.

"Yo, you are like a freaking masturbation super-hero! People keep asking me about you and telling me they love you. This shit is crazy!

"My cousin told me that she's getting stopped in the street and all her friends are asking about me. People who never talk to me are smiling all in my face now."

"You're like a cultural icon right now."

"Noooo. You think so?"

"You should do a comic book: The Adventures of Masturbation Girl!"

"Wouldn't that be something? A comic for all the masturbators of the world," I said laughing. And you're her trusty comrade, *Choke the Chicken Boy*."

"We'll go around the world teaching women how to get off." Then he added, like he was announcing Superman, "She travels the world bringing ecstatic bliss, saving the *orgasmically* challenged with her magic wand and a twist of her wrist."

"Ok, you must've been thinking about that one for a minute," I said laughing, then thought for a moment and asked, "Wait, she has a wand? Is masturbation girl a superhero or a witch?"

"She's both. A witch-super-bitch. And they'll do a movie based on the book."

"A straight to DVD classic."

"Yeah, like 'Orgasmo.'"

I was cracking up. But then I really started thinking about it. "You might be on to something Justin."

"I know. Aww man! We are blowing up!" he yelled. He was cheesing big, staring at the comments on his wall.

"Can you believe it?"

"Yeah. We make a good team."

"Yup, we sure do," I agreed.

"Remember how all eyes were on us that night at the theater?"

"Yeah. We were the shit that night."

"That was because we look good together." He gave me the dopey crush eyes.

Oh boy. "Justin, I'm not going to be your beard."

"I don't need a beard. I think I'm really into you."

"You like dick. You love dick, according to you. We can't both love dick."

"But I love pussy too. You know that. You know how you make me feel."

"But that's all fantasy. We just jerk off together. We've never fucked. We've never even kissed."

"So you never thought about anything more with us?"

"Justin, even if I did, I'm in love with someone now."

That was the first time I'd said it out loud.

"Who? The Laundromat dude?"

"You know his name is Sean."

"So that's why we haven't been having our sessions? Because you're in love."

Until he'd said that I hadn't even realized that we hadn't *been together* in a while.

"Does he love you?"

"I think so. I hope so. Look, Justin, you're a really good friend, and I don't want any weirdness between us okay?"

"Don't worry about it. It was just a thought. I mean, you're right. I do love dick. I mean, I'm sure your pussy is good—"

"I agree."

He chuckled. "I did want to tap that and see if it's as good as you make it look. You can't blame a man for trying."

"We're good, though, right? You promise?"

"I promise."

"I'm serious, Justin. You're one of the few friends I have, and I need you."

"I said I promise. Shit." He was silent for a moment then said, "So no more sessions then?"

"You freaking male. No!" I laughed.

.

Chapter 29

It's a scary proposition,
the possibility of love,
without reciprocation.

S o, Sean said all that stuff to me, getting my hopes up about us, just to stop being in tune with me. I didn't get it. I knew we were both busy, but he couldn't even give me ten minutes of conversation?

It had been about a month. He would send me texts at like three in the morning saying he was sleepy. I knew what it was. It had to be another girl. And that was cool with me, you know? He wanted to date other people. Whatever. He can do whatever he wants. *You know what? Fuck him. Fuck him for building up my hopes. I'm not buying that BS anymore.* I was done with him. No more calling. No more texting. If he called, I wasn't answering.

The phone rang, and his name flashed on the caller ID. I picked up on the first ring.

"How you doing?" he asked, all happy and shit.

"Good. Yourself?"

"I'm great. You alright?"

"I just told you I'm good." *Motherfucker!*

"Can you do me a favor?"

"Oh, so now you want a favor?"

"Breezy, don't be like that. I told you I would be busy for a minute."

"It doesn't seem like you even missed me. All I got were *pokes* and these freaking LOL smiley face responses to my texts. I mean, what did you expect me to think? All these fucking females commenting on every freaking thing you say on Facebook and LOLing and shit, like you're just so damn funny. You're not that freaking funny. I know these chicks hit you with invitations and naked pics and shit, and I know you're not saying no, because it's not like you have to. I mean, technically you're single so if you want to see other people, then just be real about it." The dam broke, and I let all of my feelings rush out in a flood of insecure babble that had been building up for months.

"Hush all that fussing," he said. And I did, thrown off by his choice of words.

"You know I've been busy. You know the things I'm trying to do. I thought you were just as busy. You never said anything. When we did talk, you acted like everything was cool. You've let all that build up, and now you're bugging out on me. Now Breezy, is that fair?"

I *was* busy, but I wanted him to sweat me! There, I said it. I wanted him to be all up my ass like he couldn't live without me. "No. I guess not."

"Okay then. Next time you have an issue with the way I'm handling things, just tell me. Honest communication. Didn't we both agree that was part of our foundation?" He knew how to work me.

"Yeah," I said, feeling just a little foolish and so loving the way he'd just admonished me. *Popi chulo.*

"And I told you already about Facebook. You get *and make* a lot of suggestive comments, and do I flip out? No. You know why? Because I know it's just talk. Until you actually prove to me that it's not, I'm going to trust that it's just talk. You need to give me the same benefit of the doubt."

"Okay."

"Now, if you turn on the radio, you can hear the tail end of one of the beats I was working on for Tay."

I jumped up and ran to the radio, no time to search for the remote. I heard the DJ talking over the song as it went off, saying it was the new Tay Prince song. I started screaming. "Oh my gosh! You're on the radio!

"I didn't want to say anything to you until it was actually on the air."

I was so proud.

"I have five joints on his LP and some more for some other dudes. You know, just doing my thing," he said, pretending to brag. "That's why I haven't been in contact with you as much. I was not lying to you when I said I was going hard with this. I've been doing meetings, networking, making beats, getting my name out there, working on buying this building, buying equipment...," he took a breath, and continued, "I wanted everything to be in place before I told you anything so you could see the progress. I didn't want you to think I was all talk. I didn't wanna disappoint you."

"Dude, you just told me about communication. That's for you too. I want to know what's going on in your life. You don't have to worry about disappointing me. Do I need to worry about disappointing you?"

"Nah."

"Alright then. I feel the same way about you."

He was silent, a thoughtful kind of silence.

I asked a question I don't normally ask anyone because a lot of times I just don't want to know. "What are you thinking?"

"Right now, I'm thinking about that day in the Laundromat. What if I'd never gone there that day, because I almost didn't."

"I'm glad you did," I said.

"And I was thinking about what kind of mother you will be."

I cleared my throat to swallow his words.

"You don't think about it?" he asked.

"I do, but I didn't think you were."

"I've been thinking about that since the first time we met."

"Don't play with me, Sean."

"Why would I play about that? Yeah, I wanted to smash when I first saw you. I can't lie about that. But your reaction to the book I was reading, and then you were listening to Rakim. I knew I had to get to know you and hoped you would be exactly who you turned out to be."

I flashed back to the day in the Laundromat. It was a chance meeting. If I'd never been fired, I wouldn't have been in the Laundromat on a Friday. If I wouldn't have been obsessed with masturbating, I wouldn't have gotten fired.

"Damn, boy, you almost made me say something to you."

"Say what you feel."

"Nuh uh. Still too soon."

"You and these limits. I'll say it then. I love you. That's what you were going to say, right?"

My heart thumped, full of honey. "Uh huh."

"So?"

"Do you mean that?"

"I wouldn't say it if I didn't mean it."

"I love you too. I've been in love since that day in Central Park."

"I know."

"You know, huh? Whatever, dude," I laughed.

"I do know, because we fell in love with each other at the very same time."

"So what now?" I asked, because at that moment I wanted 100 kids from him.

"Yo, I gotta call you back."

"Oh, okay." I shook my head. This freaking guy had me going up and down like a yo-yo.

I started cleaning. There really wasn't much to clean, but I needed to occupy my time, so I didn't feel like I was just waiting for him to call me back. I felt like I played myself. I almost didn't want him to call me back.

The phone rang about an hour later.

"Baby, I just did a phone interview with *Weight*."

"Get outta here!"

"Yeah. It's going to be on their online show tomorrow. You gonna listen to it?

"Of course I am."

"You know what would be a good idea?" he asked.

"What?"

"You should really move in with me when I get the building. The way things are going, that could be anytime now."

"I already told you I'm not giving up my apartment."

He ignored what I'd said. "You know what would be an even better idea?"

"What?"

"You should be my wife."

My mouth opened to say something, but nothing came out.

Seconds later, the intercom buzzed. It was him. Then he was at my door. I opened it and he was on one knee, with an engagement ring in his left hand. His hand was shaking.

"Will you be my wife?"

"Yes! Yes! Yes!"

Waiting for stars to align
I sat aging like fine wine
Finally popping my cork
Hoping I didn't waste too much time
We must jump at chance
To make our lives happen
The Universe isn't designed to wait
It doesn't move without the energy of action

I sat on the iron horse, relaxed, in no rush. It was about noon, and I was early for my appointment with a realtor. I flipped through a catalog of toys for my clients, but I was really thinking about where my life had taken me, and the people in my circle.

Sandy stopped all of her hustles, took my advice, and got into real estate. She bought her first house upstate, a foreclosure, and a fixer-upper at that. She fixed it, and flipped it. After that first one, she was hooked! Now she lives upstate in a house that she fixed and just couldn't bear the thought of selling. She said she felt slave spirits in the house. I told her as long as she didn't feel the slave masters too, then she was good money. She still gets to do her running around. Between searching for new properties, dealing with her existing properties, and bringing the kids down most weekends, so they could keep in touch with their friends, and family, she's just as busy as she wants to be.

Autumn lives in North Carolina and became—get ready for this—a pastor! I thought you needed some special schooling, a doctorate or something, but her church is real and her congregation is growing. Is she hustling them? I guess that's between her and her Lord, but she seems to really have her heart in it. But then she always *seems* something.

Pus N Dix blew up after my appearance on *Michi*. Lady thanked me by providing me with toys at wholesale for all of my seminars.

Mallory was able to parlay her blog into a local talk show that's being picked up by cable soon. She constantly promotes my services. She won her lawsuit, and thanks to her huge sales of T-shirt, mouse pad, coffee mug, puzzle, and other novelties, the name "Newark Annie," will live for a very long time. One of the shirts had a picture of a black woman, with a cape behind her. Her face was covered by huge, blue, superhero letters that read "Newark Annie." I was told I could sue her for the name since it's about me, but why would I do that? I just looked at it as two women making the most of a situation. No harm, no foul. But if I wasn't doing so well, would I feel differently? I really don't know.

J. Leslie's Cakes was already big way before me, but she told me every time I'd mentioned her name, her sales went up, and when the appearance on *Michi* went viral, sales really boomed. She gets orders from all over the country now. She wanted to pay me back. I told her I needed desserts for my seminars, and I expected a discount. Instead, she supplies me with free cake samples to give to my clients— good for both of our businesses. Women love to eat the samples while we chat, and then they get hooked on the cakes, and become her customers.

That appearance also affected Eula's restaurants. She opened one in New York. Ian runs it. Cindy took one look at him and couldn't believe I didn't have sex with him. They're dating now, and are scared of each other. It's the cutest thing. They keep asking me what I think the other thinks. Of course, I don't tell them what the other is saying. Neither of them wants to get hurt, which I so completely understand. It's hard to really let go and let someone all the way in. So I told them both, "Sometimes you've just got to jump out the window and see what happens." I hope they don't take it literally.

Gia was able to quit Searly & Weiss. She and her husband invested in their own kiosks. They have four bill-pay and three movie rentals and are planning to buy more. She said she'd been plotting the day she'd quit for months. Her husband called her at work and told her they'd reached their financial goal for that year. It was three months before schedule.

She told me, "I hung up from him, stood up on a table and said, 'Attention, everyone,' and screamed at the top of my lungs, 'I quit, bitches! You stupid, cheap, evil bastards! I quit! You hear me? I quit! Kiss my Puerto Rican black ass! I quit!'" I only wish I could've seen it.

I finally introduced Justin to Charise. I don't know why I hadn't thought to do that before. The fashion designer and the photographer. It was perfect, and they clicked immediately. She's his preferred photographer whenever she's available. The majority of my clothes, and accessories, come from The House of JM. We knew he'd arrived when he was able to afford his own billboard on Broadway.

As time went on, Newark Annie became just another forgotten part of pop culture. Maybe one day I'll be on one of those VH1 *I Love the...* specials. Other way more important topics dominated the airwaves. I was grateful. Honestly, it was all very tiring. I hated the fifteen minutes I got, but when it was over I was thankful I'd had it. It helped me build a brand, but good riddance to it. I still get people coming up to me, telling me they love me (which is weird), and asking for autographs, and pictures, which still amazes me. *Wow! You want my autograph because of masturbation? I'm not worthy.* Not to toot my own horn, but in some circles, I'm kind of a big deal. A college in Connecticut used my story as part of their women's study course. I went out there to speak to the students, and they asked me a million and one personal questions, and were wide eyed waiting for my answers.

Some of my answers made them clap which surprised me each time, but I did enjoy it.

I took a summer off to create and paint five murals for Eula's restaurants in Ft. Lauderdale and New York. My mind was so tired when I was done that I could hardly think straight, like I may have been a little mentally slow after that. She loved the result. So did I, but it will be a very long time before I'd take on something that ambitious again. But it was worth every second. Artist for life!

I was also selling my paintings. Being the most famous masturbator in the world (so far) definitely helped. One of my paintings sold at an auction for what was more than one year's salary at Searly & Weiss. No way would that have happened without Newark Annie.

I started giving lectures around the country to women who needed my help. Women's groups, book clubs, and such were calling *me*, willing to pay me to talk to them. And not about the Newark Incident, but about being a woman, and teaching women how to love themselves, regardless of their circumstances. I love helping them. With the seminars, we'd get into deep conversations, and the women would develop real friendships with me, and each other. I couldn't believe the number of women I met who had been sexually abused by family members, close friends, and people of authority that we are supposed to trust.

So much pain needed to be released. So much shame that had to be dealt with and eliminated. I didn't want to come off like I thought I was a psychiatrist, but those women used me in that way. They vented and screamed and punched pillows, and we hugged. So much hugging! All this time I thought I wasn't a touchy-feely person, but as it turns out, I am quite the hugger.

Now I was looking for a place to hold seminars a few nights a week. I needed a spot in New York because the traveling was wearing on me. With the baby on the way, I didn't really want to run around as much anymore.

No one told me how horny being pregnant would make me. I was on Sean like he had the antidote. When he wasn't there, I had to do it myself. *I had to.* I felt bad at first, thinking, *how could I do this with my child inside of me?* But pleasure was how the child got there in the first place. I spoke to my OB-GYN about it, and she said it's completely fine. Once I allowed myself to masturbate, and had my first self-induced pregnancy orgasm, all of my worries melted away. It became my secondary stress reliever. Sean was my primary. Goodness, I'm so sprung!

Sean bought that four-story building in Brooklyn. Yeah, I gave in and moved to that freaking borough. Bronxites, don't be mad. I did it for love. It took a year to get it up to code. He topped it off by turning the roof into an outdoor living area. The surface is made of recycled tire rubber, dyed blue-green like the ocean. As you know, that's my favorite vibe. He had a four-foot wall put up and a six-foot iron fence along the perimeter. There are benches and a swing long enough to lie down and take a good nap. It's a good spot for our family cookouts, which we have a lot of.

We rent the four apartments on the first floor to college students. That way we can stop whenever we're ready. His studio is in the basement, and we live on the top three floors. I would have the seminars there, but I wanted to do them in Harlem, because that is an easier place for anyone to get to, *and* I don't want to have a bunch of horny, ready-to-orgasm women sizing up my husband.

I'm so proud to call him my husband. It still feels weird to say it. He's done what he said he would do. Living his dream. He does all types of music in all different languages, sometimes using instruments I've never seen before.

His work was keeping him away, at first. He was driving, and flying out constantly, to build his brand. He's built up his reputation, and now people fly to him. Because of that, he lets a few artists stay with us while doing their albums, but he said once our daughter is born, that will be the end of that. I told him it was fine with me; it's not like they would have access to our part of the building. But he's already being super protective. We may stop renting the apartments, too, because of her. Maybe we'll rent to family. We'll see.

We both worked hard to stay together. There were times when it seemed like we wouldn't make it, or like there was no point, because we had to spend so much time apart. We would meet up at hotels if we were in the same city, or have quick meetings in restaurants or diners. We'd try to get quality time in, but it wasn't easy. I'd already miss him before I would even see him, because I knew our time would be brief.

We had a LOT of phone sex. He named us "The Bathroom Bandits" because we were constantly in bathrooms masturbating—public or private, it didn't matter. We'd get on the phone and do our thing. Skype is the best!

In the middle of all the chaos of our separate newfound fames, we had a serious discussion about our future, making sure we were on the same page, and that it was worth us being together.

I said, "It won't be easy being branded as the husband of an infamous masturbator."

He said, "It's not easy being the husband of any woman."

"But people talk."

"People will always talk. That's what people do."

"So when someone says, 'Hey, isn't your wife that masturbator?' what are you going to say?"

"Fucking A, that's my wife!" he said, holding his head up defiantly. "And if they have an issue with it, they can come see me." He kept me laughing.

He said, "Look baby, people are gonna have things to say about both of us. We're gonna hear all types of things about each other from other people. But I've got you, and you have me. You're everything I need. Fuck everybody else. We just need to believe in us."

We married in June. It was a small wedding—just very close friends and family. No *Bridezilla* here! It only took a few phone calls for me to coordinate the whole thing. Justin made the dress—a simple, off-white, white-beaded, goddess bodice, satin dress. Sandy, Cindy, Gia, and Charise were my bridesmaids; they dressed in cute white pantsuits, because I wanted them to wear something they could also wear for other occasions. Of course, Jana made the cakes. Even if I didn't know her, I still would've gotten the cakes from her. She brought her fiancé with her (she'd found the one man not afraid to dominate her). Plus I got a discount on catering from another one of my clients. I was going to use Eula, but everyone isn't into sushi, and I wanted everyone to eat. But, of course, she came to the wedding. Ian came with Cindy. The Get-It Girl Crew came too. Shelly Keith was our wedding band, and they rocked!

My mother cried during the whole wedding. From the depths of her soul. I thought she was going to throw up. I've never seen someone so happy, and so full of relief. At one point when we were alone, before the ceremony, she got on her knees, clasped her hands together and shouted, "Thank you Lord! *Finally*! Thank you!" Which was completely out of character for her. Every time she looked at me she fell out crying again. I wanted to say, *"Really mommy... really? All this? Like you just never thought it was going to happen, huh?*

The ceremony was on our roof. The reception was at a hall two blocks away, and had more guests than the wedding. After everyone was fed, the reception turned into a big bash, with the feel of a New Year's Eve party; full of loud music, noise makers, streamers, confetti, finger foods and champagne. Lots of dancing and silliness. We just wanted everyone to enjoy life that day and be easy with no worries.

I loved having everyone there, but we could've married at City Hall with just the two of us, and I would've been just as happy. As long as when it was all done, I was Mrs. Lightfeather.

Sean bought a car for me on my birthday, and though I love to drive it, I still love all the life on the subway. The city is my muse, and driving around, pissed off in traffic just doesn't inspire me the same as, being pissed off on the train.

I got off at 125th and walked to a brownstone off of Lexington Avenue. Cinderella met me there. She'd told me a few months before how stressed she was at Searly & Weiss, to the point where she found herself hoping to get into an accident on her way to work, just so she didn't have to be there. So, I asked her if she'd be my Client Liaison. I didn't want to call her an assistant, because she was much more than that. She jumped at it. Her salary is not quite as much as Searly & Weiss, but she said she doesn't care because she loves coming to work, and the peace of mind is worth it. She's also subleasing my apartment. I just couldn't give it up.

The spot on Lexington was perfect. It was bright, and spacious, with a loft feel to it. I could already picture the cushioned, black, upholstered folding chairs, two multi-colored couches, and beanbag chairs, all in a circle, full of women exploring themselves, emotionally, and physically. Laughing, and crying; hugging each other, and punching pillows. It was my dream in living color.

So, if you're ever in New York, and you need some assistance with getting to know yourself, look me up! I'd love to be of service.

Yours truly,
Breezy Deigh-Lightfeather, Serial Masturbator.

Did you enjoy this novel? I hope you did. If so, please, feel free to leave a review on Amazon.com. You can also email your thoughts and comments to me at kittykfree@kittykfree.com, and please visit me at KittyKFree.com.

Also, should you opt to throw this book away, please recycle it, give it to someone else, or pass it on to a used bookstore. Thank you!

www.ingramcontent.com/pod-product-compliance
Lightning Source LLC
Chambersburg PA
CBHW020328180626
46812CB00001B/106